BOOK EIGHT

The Kings of Clonmel

THE RANGER'S APPRENTICE SERIES

Book One: The Ruins of Gorlan

Children's Book Council of Australia Notable Book 2005

Finalist for the 2004 Aurealis Award – Children's Novel

Book Two: The Burning Bridge

Children's Book Council of Australia Notable Book 2006

Book Three: The Icebound Land

Highly commended in the 2005 Aurealis Awards for Children's Novel

Book Four: Oakleaf Bearers

Finalist for the 2006 Aurealis Award – Children's Novel

Book Five: The Sorcerer in the North

Children's Book Council of Australia Notable Book 2007

Book Six: The Siege of Macindaw

Children's Book Council of Australia Notable Book 2008

Book Seven: Erak's Ransom

Children's Book Council of Australia Notable Book 2008

Winner of the Australian Book Industry Award – Book of the Year for Older Children 2008

RANGER'S APPRENTICE

BOOK EIGHT

The Kings of Clonmel

John Flanagan

RANDOM HOUSE AUSTRALIA

A Random House book
Published by Random House Australia Pty Ltd
Level 3, 100 Pacific Highway, North Sydney NSW 2060
www.randomhouse.com.au

First published by Random House Australia in 2008

Addresses for companies within the Random House Group can be found at
www.randomhouse.com.au/offices.

National Library of Australia
Cataloguing-in-Publication Entry

    Author: Flanagan, John, 1944–
    Title: The kings of Clonmel / John Flanagan
    ISBN: 978 174166 301 3 (pbk.)
    Series: Flanagan, John, 1944–. Ranger's apprentice; 8
    Target audience: For primary school age
    Dewey number: A823.4

Cover photographs by Quentin Jones and Getty Images
Cover and internal design by Mathematics
Typeset in 12/15pt Caslon Classico by Midland Typesetters, Australia
Printed and bound by Griffin Press, South Australia

Random House Australia uses papers that are natural, renewable and recyclable
products and made from wood grown in sustainable forests. The logging and
manufacturing processes are expected to conform to the environmental regulations
of the country of origin.

10 9 8 7 6 5 4 3 2 1

To Catherine and Tyler:
thanks for everything.

Araluen, Picta and Celtica

YEAR 643 COMMON ERA

One

It was Tug, of course, who first sensed the presence of the other horse and rider.

His ears twitched upwards and Will felt, rather than heard, the low rumble that vibrated through the little horse's barrel-like body. It was not an alarm signal, so Will knew that whoever Tug had sensed, it was someone known to him. He leaned forward and patted the shaggy mane.

'Good boy,' he said softly. 'Now where are they?'

He already had a fair idea who it would be. And even as he spoke, his guess was confirmed as a bay horse and a tall rider trotted out of the trees some hundred metres ahead of him to wait at the crossroads there. Tug snorted again, tossing his head.

'All right. I can see them.'

He touched Tug lightly with his heels and the horse responded instantly, moving to a canter to close the distance to the horse and rider. The bay whinnied a greeting, to which Tug responded.

'Gilan!' Will shouted cheerfully as they came within easy earshot. The tall Ranger waved a hand in reply, grinning as Will and Tug clattered to a stop beside him.

The two Rangers leaned over in their saddles to clasp right hands.

'It's good to see you,' Gilan said.

'You too. I thought it would be you. Tug let me know there were friends nearby a few minutes ago.'

'Not much gets by that shaggy little beast of yours, does it?' Gilan said easily. 'I suppose that's what's kept you alive these past years.'

'Little?' Will replied. 'I don't notice that Blaze is exactly a battlehorse.'

In truth, Blaze was a little longer in the leg than the average Ranger horse, and had slightly finer lines. But like all of the breed, Gilan's bay mare was still considerably smaller than the massive battlehorses that carried the Kingdom's knights into battle.

While the two young Rangers chaffed each other, the horses seemed to be carrying on a similar conversation, with a lot of snorting and head tossing to punctuate the good-natured horsey insults they were undoubtedly swapping. Ranger horses definitely seemed to communicate with each other and Gilan regarded the two of them curiously.

'Wonder what the devil they're saying?' he mused.

'I think Tug just commented on how uncomfortable Blaze must be, carrying a spindle-shanked bag of bones like yourself,' Will told him. Gilan opened his mouth to reply in kind but oddly, at that very moment, Tug nodded his head violently several times, and both horses turned their heads to study Gilan. It was a coincidence, the tall Ranger told himself. And yet it was uncanny how they chose that very moment to do it.

'You know,' he said, 'I have a strange feeling that you might be right.'

Will looked back along the road he had just travelled, then down the crossroad, in the opposite direction to the one from which Gilan had emerged.

'Any sign of Halt so far?'

Gilan shook his head. 'I've been waiting for the best part of two hours, and I haven't seen him yet. Odd, because he has the shortest distance to travel.'

It was the time of the annual Ranger Gathering and it had become the custom for the three friends to meet at these crossroads, a few kilometres short of the Gathering Ground, and ride the remaining distance together. When Will had been apprenticed to Halt, he had grown used to meeting Gilan here. That was after Will's first Gathering, when Gilan had attempted to ambush his old teacher and Will had spoiled the attempt. Since Will had taken over Seacliff Fief and Gilan had been posted to Norgate, they had continued the practice whenever possible.

'Should we wait?' Will said.

Gilan shrugged. 'If he's not here yet, something must have held him up. We might as well ride in and set up camp.' He urged his horse forward with the lightest touch of his heel. Will did likewise and they rode on side by side.

Sometime later, they arrived at the Gathering Ground. It was a relatively open forest area where the undergrowth had been cleared away. The tall trees had been left, to provide sheltered spots where the Rangers could pitch their low, one-man tents.

They rode towards their usual spot, calling greetings to other Rangers as they passed. The Corps was a close-knit unit and most Rangers knew one another by name. Arriving at their spot, the two dismounted and unsaddled their horses, rubbing them down after their long ride. Will took two folding leather buckets and fetched water from the small stream that wandered through the Gathering Ground while Gilan measured out oats for Blaze and Tug. For the next few days, the horses could graze on the lush grass that grew underfoot, but they deserved a treat after their hard work.

And Rangers never begrudged giving their horses a treat.

They pitched tents and swept the area clear of fallen branches and leaves. The fireplace stones had been disturbed, possibly by some wandering animal, and Will quickly replaced them.

'I'm beginning to wonder where Halt's got to,' Gilan said, glancing to the west, where the lowering sun's light filtered through the trunks of the trees. 'He's certainly taking his time getting here.'

'Maybe he's not coming,' Will suggested.

Gilan pursed his lips. 'Halt miss a Gathering?' he said, disbelief in his tone. 'He loves coming to the Gathering each year. And he wouldn't miss a chance to catch up with you.'

Like Will, Gilan was a former apprentice of Halt's. But he knew that there was a very special relationship between the grizzled senior Ranger and his young friend — one that went way past the master and apprentice relationship that he shared with Halt. Will was more of a son to Halt, he knew.

'No,' he continued, 'I can't think of anything that would keep him away.'

'Well, apparently something has,' a familiar voice behind them interrupted.

Will and Gilan turned quickly to find Crowley standing behind them. The Ranger Commandant was a master of silent movement.

'Crowley!' Gilan said. 'Where did you spring from? And how is it I never hear you coming?'

Crowley grinned. The skill was one he was proud of.

'Oh, being able to sneak up on people has its advantages in the political world of Castle Araluen,' he said. 'People are always discussing secrets and you'd be surprised how many snippets I pick up before they realise I'm there.'

The two younger Rangers stood and shook hands with their Commandant. While Gilan brewed a pot of coffee, Will asked the question that had been on his mind since Crowley's sudden appearance.

'What's this about Halt not coming to the Gathering?' he asked. 'Are you sure?'

Crowley shrugged. 'I received a message from him the day before yesterday. He's off on the West Coast, chasing down rumours about some new religious cult that's cropped up. Said he wouldn't have time to make it back here.'

'A religious cult?' Will asked. 'What sort of religious cult?'

The corners of Crowley's mouth turned down in an expression of distaste. 'The usual sort, I'm afraid.' He glanced at Gilan for confirmation. 'You know the type of thing, don't you, Gil?'

Gilan nodded. 'Only too well. "Come join our new religion,"' he mock quoted. '"Our god is the only true god and he will protect you from the doom that is coming to the world. You will be safe and secure with us. Oh . . . and by the way, would you mind giving us all your valuables for the privilege of being kept safe?" Is that the sort of thing?' he asked.

Crowley sighed heavily. 'That's pretty much it in a nutshell. They warn people about impending disaster, and all the time, they're the ones who are planning to cause it.'

Gilan poured three steaming cups of coffee and passed them around.

Crowley watched as the two younger Rangers spooned generous helpings of wild honey into theirs. He shook his head. 'Never could get used to the taste of honey in my coffee. Halt and I used to argue over that in our younger days.'

Will grinned. 'If you're Halt's apprentice, you don't have a choice. You learn to shoot a bow, throw a knife, move silently and put honey in your coffee.'

'He's a fine teacher,' Gilan said, sipping his coffee appreciatively. 'So did Halt say what this new cult are calling themselves? They usually come up with some portentous-sounding name,' he added, in an aside to Will.

'He didn't say,' Crowley said. He seemed to be hesitating over whether to voice his next statement. Then he came to a decision. 'He's worried this might be a new outbreak of the Outsiders.'

The name meant nothing to Will but he saw Gilan's head come up.

'The Outsiders?' Gilan said. 'I remember that name. It must have been in the second year of my apprenticeship. Didn't you and Halt go off together to see them on their way?'

Crowley nodded. 'Along with Berrigan and several other Rangers.'

'That must have been quite a cult,' Will said, surprise in his voice. There was an old Araluan saying about 'One riot, one Ranger'. It meant that it rarely took more than a single Ranger to solve the biggest problems.

'It was,' Crowley agreed. 'They were a very unpleasant bunch of people and their poison had gone deep into the heart of the countryside. It took us some time to get the better of them. That's why Halt is so intent on finding out more about this new group. If they're a recurrence of the Outsiders, we'll have to act quickly.'

He tossed the dregs of his coffee into the fire and set his cup down.

'But let's not worry about what might be a problem until we know that it is. In the meantime, we have a Gathering to organise. Gil, I was wondering if you'd give our two final-year apprentices some extra tuition in unseen movement?'

'Of course,' Gilan said. If Crowley was an expert at moving without being heard, Gilan was the Corps' past master at moving without being seen. To a large degree, his skill was dependent upon instinct, but there were always practical tips he could pass on to others.

'And as for you, Will,' Crowley said, 'we have three

first-years this season. Would you be interested in assessing their progress?'

He saw Will's attention snap back to the present. He could tell that the young man was still nursing his disappointment over the fact that his former teacher would not be coming. Just as well to give him something to take his mind off it, the older Ranger thought.

'Oh, sorry, Crowley! What was that you said?' Will said, a little guiltily.

'Would you care to help out assessing our three first-years?' Crowley repeated and Will nodded hastily.

'Yes, by all means! Sorry about that. I was just thinking about Halt. I've been looking forward to seeing him,' he explained.

'We all have,' Crowley said. 'His grumpy face brings a special light to our day. But there'll be time enough for that later.' He hesitated briefly. 'As a matter of fact . . . no, never mind. That'll keep.'

'What will keep?' Will's curiosity was aroused now and Crowley smiled to himself. Curiosity was the sign of a good Ranger. But so was discipline.

'Never mind. It's something I'll tell you about when the time is right. For now, I'd appreciate it if you'll coach the boys in archery and oversee a tactical exercise with them.'

'Consider it done.' Will thought for a few seconds then added, 'Do I need to set the tactical exercise?'

Crowley shook his head. 'No. We've done that. Just see them through solving it. It should amuse you,' he added cryptically. He rose and dusted off the seat of his trousers. 'Thanks for the coffee,' he said. 'See you at the feast tonight.'

Two

'All right,' Will told the three boys, 'let's see you shoot. Ten arrows each at those targets.'

He indicated three large, standard bullseye design targets set up seventy-five metres down range. The three stepped forward to the firing line. A little further down the line, two senior Rangers were practising, shooting at targets no bigger than a large dinner platter, set at the one-hundred-and-fifty-metre mark. For a few moments, the three first-year apprentices watched in awe as the two marksmen slammed arrow after arrow into the almost invisible targets.

'Any time before sunset would be fine,' Will drawled. He had no idea that he was mimicking the dry, mock-weary tone of voice that Halt had used with him when he was first learning the skills of a Ranger.

'Yes, sir. Sorry, sir,' said the nearest of the three boys. They all looked at him, wide eyed. He sighed.

'Stuart?' he said to the boy who had spoken.

'Yes, sir?'

'You don't call me sir. We're both Rangers.'

'But . . .' began one of the other boys. He was stockily built and had a mass of red hair that flopped untidily over his forehead. Will searched his memory for the boy's name: Liam, he remembered.

'Yes, Liam?'

The boy shuffled awkwardly. 'But we're apprentices and you're . . .' He stopped. He wasn't sure what he was going to say. It was probably something ridiculous like, 'But we're apprentices and you're *you*.'

Because although Will didn't know it, he was a subject of awe for these boys. He was the legendary Will Treaty, the Ranger who had rescued the King's daughter from Morgarath's Wargal army, then protected her when they were kidnapped by raiding Skandians. Then he had trained and led a company of archers in the battle against the Temujai riders. And only the previous year, he had repelled a Scotti invasion on the northern frontier of the Kingdom.

These three would look up to any graduate Ranger. But Will Treaty was only a few years older than they were, and so was a subject for hero worship of the highest degree. As a result, they had been somewhat surprised when they met him. They had expected a larger-than-life figure – a hero in classical terms. Instead, they were introduced to a fresh-faced, youthful person, with a ready smile and a slim build, who stood a little less than average height. Had Will realised it, he would have been amused and more than a little embarrassed. It was exactly the sort of reaction he was used to seeing in people who met Halt for the first time. Unknown to him, his own reputation was beginning to rival that of his former teacher.

Will may not have comprehended the hero worship these boys felt for him personally. But he did understand the gulf they felt existed between a Ranger and an apprentice. He had felt the same way, he remembered.

'You're apprentice Rangers,' he said. 'And the important word there is "Rangers".' He tapped the silver oakleaf amulet that hung around his neck. 'As a wearer of the Silver Oakleaf, I might expect obedience and some level of deference from you. But I do *not* expect you to call me sir. My name is Will and that's what you call me. You'd call my friend Gilan and my former master Halt, if he were here. That's the Rangers' way.'

It was a small point, he knew, but an important one. Rangers were a unique breed and on occasions they needed to assert authority over people who were nominally far senior to them in rank. It was important that these boys knew that they might one day need to call upon the power and trust that the King conferred upon his Rangers. All of them – apprentices and graduates alike. The self-confidence they would need to do so was built initially by their sense of equality with their peers in the Ranger Corps.

The three apprentices exchanged glances as they took in what Will had said. He saw their shoulders straighten a little, their chins come up fractionally.

'Yes . . . Will,' said Liam. He nodded to himself, as if trying the word out and liking what he heard. The others echoed the sentiment, nodding in their turn. Will gave them a few moments to savour the sense of confidence, then glanced meaningfully at the sun.

'Well, sunset's getting closer all the time,' he said to himself. He hid a smile as three arrows slid out of their quivers. A few seconds later, three bows twanged and he heard the familiar scrape-slither as the shots were on their way to the target.

'Ten shots,' he said. 'Then we'll see how you're doing.'

He strolled to a nearby tree and sat beneath it, his back leaning comfortably against the trunk. With his cowl pulled up, and his face in shadow, he seemed to be dozing.

But his eyes were moving ceaselessly, missing nothing as he studied every aspect of the three boys' shooting technique.

For the next two days, Will assessed their skills with the bow, correcting small faults in technique as he did so. Liam had developed a habit of measuring his full draw by touching his right thumb to the corner of his mouth.

'Touch your mouth with your forefinger, not the thumb,' Will told him. 'If you use the thumb, your hand tends to twist to the right, and that will throw the arrow off line when you release.'

Liam nodded and made the slight adjustment. Immediately, his accuracy improved — particularly on the longer shots, where the slight change in angle had a greater effect.

Nick, the quietest of the three, was gripping his bow too tightly. He was an intense young man and eager to succeed. Will sensed that was where the vice-like grip came from. Nick was allowing his determination to affect the relaxed grip that the bow needed. A tight grip meant the bow often skewed to the left at the moment of release, resulting in a wild, inaccurate shot. Again, Will corrected the fault and set the young man to practise.

Stuart's technique was sound, without any minor faults at this stage. But like the others, his skill would only reach the required Ranger level with hours of practice.

'Practice and more practice,' Will told them. 'Remember the old saying: "An ordinary archer practises until he gets it right. A Ranger practises . . .?"' He let the phrase hang in the air, waiting for them to finish it off.

'Until he never gets it wrong,' they chorused. He nodded, smiling approval.

'Remember it,' he said.

On the third day, however, there was a respite from the hours of practice with the bow. The previous evening, the boys had received the written outline of the tactical exercise that had been set for them. They had spent the hours between dinner and lights out going over the problem and forming their first ideas for a solution.

Will had received the details of their assignment at the same time. He shook his head when he read the outline.

'Crowley and his sense of humour,' he said, closing the folder in mild exasperation. Gilan looked up from where he was sewing up a rent in his cloak. He'd chosen to demonstrate unseen movement through a thorntree clump that afternoon, resulting in minor damage to his clothing.

'What's he done?' he asked.

Will smacked the folder with the back of his hand. 'This tactical assignment. The one he said would amuse me? The boys have to devise a way to besiege and capture a castle garrisoned by invaders and set in a northern fief. They have to recruit a suitable attacking force and take the castle. Sound familiar?'

Gilan grinned. 'I've heard of someone having a similar problem,' he admitted. It was almost identical to the situation that had faced Will the previous winter, at Castle Macindaw.

'Seems like my life's become a walking tactical exercise,' Will grumbled.

He was closer to the truth than he realised. Crowley had circulated a detailed account of the siege to the entire Corps. Will's fellow Rangers had studied his tactics and were highly impressed by them. Those with apprentices had begun using the siege as an example of initiative and imagination in dealing with the problem of having a much smaller force than common tactical wisdom would deem suitable.

Gilan knew all this, but he didn't think it would be a good idea to tell Will. He sensed that his friend might be embarrassed at the thought of such notoriety. Naturally, Will had been the only Ranger in the Corps who had not received Crowley's summary.

'What resources do they have available?' Gilan asked.

Will frowned as he opened the folder again, turning to the Assets and Resources list. Having been set the problem, the boys were given certain resources they could draw on to help them devise a solution.

'A travelling jongleur,' he read. That had been his own disguise at Macindaw. 'Very funny. He won't be much help. One mounted knight — hello, Horace. The former garrison of the castle — forty of them, scattered all over the countryside, of course. A troop of acrobats, tumblers and players . . . hmmm, they could be handy. And the people of the local village.'

'No shipwrecked Skandians or reformed sorcerers?' Gilan teased him gently.

Will snorted in derision. 'No. At least he's spared me that.'

He trailed off, chewing on a fingernail as he mulled over the problem. Acrobats. They could be handy in getting to the top of the wall. He riffled through a few pages to find the diagram of the castle. Wall height was between three and four metres. A formidable barrier for a normal man. But a trained acrobat might . . .

He snapped himself out of it, slamming the pages shut once more. It wasn't his problem. The three boys had to find a way to solve it. All he had to do was assess the practicality of their solution.

'Sounds like fun,' Gilan murmured.

Will shook his head. 'I can't wait to see what they come up with.'

Three

Halt lay unmoving in the gorse above the village of Selsey, his cloak concealing him from sight, his eyes moving constantly as he surveyed the scene below him. He had been observing the village for several days, unseen by any of its inhabitants, or by the new arrivals who had taken up residence on the shore.

Selsey was a small and apparently unprepossessing fishing village. A dozen or so cottages were clustered at the northern end of the beach, at the foot of the steep hill. The beach itself was narrow — barely a hundred metres wide. It lay at the end of a shallow cove, where a roughly triangular bite was taken out of the rocky coastline.

The hills on three sides slanted steeply down to the water and the narrow beach. They were high enough to protect the village and the bay from the wind and storms that could sweep along this coastline. The fourth side was open to the sea but even on that side, Halt's keen eyes could make out the swirl of water that marked a bar just inside the mouth of the cove – a jumble of rocks below the water's surface that would break up the big waves as they tried to come pounding in, driven by a westerly wind.

On the southern side of the cove, he could see a narrow section of calm, undisturbed water – deeper water that marked a passage through the bar. That would be the point where the handful of fishing boats pulled up on the beach would gain access to the open sea.

He took in the condition of the cottages. They were small but they were far from hovels. They were well built, freshly painted and comfortable looking.

The boats were in similar condition. The masts and booms were recently varnished to protect them from the depredations of the salt air and water. The sails were neatly furled along their booms. The rigging was taut and well maintained and the hulls were all in good condition, and had obviously been painted not too long ago.

So while the village might appear small and unimportant at first glance, a closer scrutiny told a different story. This was a well-ordered little community. And in a section of coast where there were few other sheltered spots like this, the fishermen would find ready markets for their catch in the neighbouring villages. That meant it was a prosperous community – and probably had been for years on end.

And that, of course, explained the presence of the Outsiders here. His eyes narrowed as the thought struck him. He'd been right to forego the Gathering this year and track down the source of the vague rumours that had been coming in from the West Coast of Araluen.

They were vague because this wild stretch of coastline was one of the few areas in the country that was under the jurisdiction of none of the fifty fiefs. It was a patch of land that had slipped through the cracks when the fief boundaries had been drawn up, many years ago. Possession of the area had been disputed, with a group of displaced Hibernians claiming it for their own. The Araluan king at the time took a quick look at the rugged, inhospitable coastal area and decided they were welcome to it. He had bigger problems on his mind as he tried to weld fifty recalcitrant, bickering barons into a cohesive governing structure for the country as a whole.

So this twenty-kilometre section of coastline was left to its own devices. Of course, had the king realised that he was ceding control of one of the best natural harbours within a hundred kilometres, he might have acted differently. But the existence of this little cove was a well-kept secret. So the little fishing settlement had prospered quietly over the years, beholden to no one and answerable to no king.

Yet it lay close to the extreme western border of Redmont Fief, so in recent years Halt had taken to keeping an occasional eye on the area — unnoticed by the local inhabitants.

In the past few months he had heard rumours about a religious cult whose behaviour sounded disturbingly familiar. People spoke of newcomers who would arrive in a village or hamlet with a simple message of friendship. They would bring toys for the children and small gifts for the leaders of the community.

In return, they asked for nothing but a place to worship

their benevolent and all-loving deity, the Golden God Alseiass. They made no attempt to convert the locals to their religion. Alseiass was a tolerant god who respected the rights of other gods to attract and hold their own adherents.

So the Outsiders, the name adopted by the followers of Alseiass, would live in harmony with the locals for several weeks.

Then things would start to go wrong. Cattle would die mysteriously. Sheep and household animals would be found crippled. Crops and homes would be burnt; wells and streams were contaminated. Armed brigands and bandits would appear in the area, attacking and robbing travellers and farmers in remote farms. As days passed, their attacks would become bolder and more vicious. A reign of terror would begin and the villagers would go in fear of their lives. The village would become a village under siege, with nobody knowing where the next attack might fall.

Then the Outsiders would come forward with a solution. The outlaws surrounding the village were followers of the evil god Balsennis — a dark god who hated Alseiass and all he stood for. The Outsiders had seen this before, they would claim. Balsennis in his jealousy would try to bring ruin to any community where Alseiass and his followers found happiness. But Alseiass was the stronger of the two, they said, and he could help them. Alseiass could cast out the followers of his dark brother and make the village safe once more.

Of course, there was a price. To cast out Balsennis, special prayers and invocations would be required. Alseiass could do it, but they would need to construct a special shrine and altar for the casting-out ceremonies. It would need to be of the purest materials: white marble; perfectly formed cedar, without knots or kinks . . . and gold.

Alseiass was the Golden God. He would draw strength from the precious metal; gold would give him the power he needed to win this contest against Balsennis.

Sooner or later, the villagers would agree. In the face of increasingly fierce attacks and disasters, they would delve into their savings and hidden assets to provide the gold that was needed. The longer they hesitated, the worse the attacks would become. Where originally animals had been slaughtered, now people would become the targets. Leaders of the community would be found murdered in their beds. Once that happened, the villagers would hand over their treasures. The shrine would be built. The Outsiders would pray and chant and fast.

And the attacks would begin to lessen. The 'accidents' would cease to happen. The outlaws would be seen less and less and life would begin to return to normal.

Until one day, when they had stripped the village bare and there was nothing more to plunder, the Outsiders would disappear. The villagers would awake to find them gone — taking with them the gold and treasure that had been accumulated and saved over the years.

The Outsiders would move on to another village, another community. And the same cycle would begin again.

Halt had arrived in the latter part of the cycle, where the Outsiders were praying desperately to protect the village from the onslaught of Balsennis. He had watched the chanting and mock fasting that was going on. He had also seen the secret supplies of food that the Outsiders kept hidden. The 'fasting' was as false as their religion, he thought grimly.

And he had reconnoitred into the surrounding countryside and discovered the base where the Outsiders' accomplices were camped. These were the ones who carried out the dirty work — burning barns, mutilating animals, kidnapping and murdering local officials. The cult couldn't work without them but they remained unseen by the villagers.

It was a well-organised operation. He had seen it all many years before. Now it was back.

He frowned as a figure emerged from the large marquee that served as a headquarters for the cultists. It was pitched on the edge of the beach, close to where the fishing boats were drawn up beyond the tide.

The man was tall and heavily built. His grey hair was long and parted in the middle to fall either side of his face. From this distance, Halt couldn't make out his features but he knew from previous observation that the man's face was heavily pockmarked. Apparently Alseiass hadn't protected him from that problem, Halt thought grimly.

He carried a staff that marked him as the leader of the group. It was a plain, untrimmed branch topped with a stone plaque that bore the Outsiders' symbol — a rune-inscribed ring with an embossed orb at its centre, joined by a thin shaft of stone to another, smaller hemisphere outside the ring. As Halt watched, the elder strode purposefully towards the largest of the houses that comprised the village.

'Off to ask for more gold, are you?' Halt muttered. 'We'll see what we can do about that.'

The leader of the Outsiders met with a group of the villagers — obviously the senior members of the community — and they began an animated conversation. Halt had seen it all before. The Outsiders' leader would be reluctantly informing them that more valuables would be required. Alseiass needed extra strength to defeat his old enemy and only extra supplies of gold and jewellery would give it to him. It was a cunning ploy, Halt thought. By appearing reluctant to ask for more gold, and by not insisting when the village refused, the Outsiders deflected any charge that they were seeking the gold for themselves.

Halt watched as the elder shrugged his shoulders theatrically, seeming to be convinced that no more wealth was forthcoming. He spread his hands in a gesture of friendship and understanding and turned sadly away from the villagers' delegation. If he held true to well-established Outsider methods, he was promising that he and his people would continue to do their utmost to help, fasting and praying unselfishly to protect the village and its inhabitants.

'And tonight,' Halt muttered to himself, 'one of those houses will go up in flames.'

Four

The three apprentices sat in a quiet glade, their assignment folders and pages of notes on their knees, watching Will expectantly.

'Very well,' he began. He was a little disconcerted by the three unwavering gazes that were trained on him. He realised the boys probably assumed that he had already come up with the perfect solution to the problem they'd been set. But that wasn't his role.

'You've all read the assignment?'

Three heads nodded.

'You understand it fully?'

Again, three heads, three nods.

'So who wants to have first crack at it?'

There was a moment's hesitation, then Nick's hand shot up. Will nodded to himself. He'd known Nick would be first.

'Very well, Nick, let's hear your thoughts,' he said, motioning for the young apprentice to proceed.

Nick cleared his throat several times. He shuffled his pages of notes and then, head down, he began to read in a breakneck gabble of words.

'Verywelltheproblemfacingusisthatwedon'thavesufficientnumbersatourdisposaltoeffectivelymountastandardsiegeoperationsowehaveto —'

'Whoa!' Will interrupted and Nick looked up nervously, sensing that he'd done something wrong.

'Slow down!' Will told him. 'Try to bring it down to a gallop, all right?'

He saw the boy's crestfallen face, realised that he was worried he'd be marked down for the mistake. Nick was an achiever, Will thought to himself. His gabbled words reflected the same intensity that had caused him to hold the bow in such a vice-like grip.

'Just relax, Nick,' he said in a more encouraging tone. 'Let's say you were called upon to submit a plan like this to King Duncan . . .' He paused and saw the boy's eyes widen at the enormity of the thought. He added, gently, 'It's not impossible, you know. That's what Rangers do from time to time. But you'd hardly want to go dashing into Castle Araluen's throne room and gabble out, "HulloKingDuncanletmerunthroughafewideasforyouhereandyoucantellmewhatyouthinkofthemallright?"' He managed a pretty good impersonation of Nick's breathless, rattling delivery and the other two boys laughed. Nick, after an uncertain moment, joined in as well.

'No, you wouldn't,' Will answered his own question. 'When you outline a plan you need to speak clearly and precisely, to make sure the people you're talking to have the full picture. You have to have your own thoughts organised and present them in a logical sequence. Now, take a deep breath . . .'

Nick did so.

'And start again. Slowly.'

'Very well,' said Nick, 'the problem facing us is that we don't have sufficient numbers at our disposal to effectively mount a standard siege operation. So we have to find a way to (a) recruit troops and (b) offset the inferiority in numbers, compared to the garrison.'

He looked up expectantly. Will nodded.

'So far so good. And your solution?'

'I propose to recruit a ship's crew of thirty-five Skandian sea wolves to act as an attacking army, under the command of the mounted knight already at my disposal. The Skandians' prowess in battle would more than compensate for —'

But once again, Will had his hands up in the air, waving them in an effort to stem the flow of words.

'Whoa! Whoa! Whoa!' he cried. 'Back up the ox cart a little! Skandians? Where did these Skandians come from?'

Nick looked at him, a little puzzled by the question.

'Well . . . Skandia, presumably,' he replied. Will noticed that the other two boys were nodding agreement, frowning slightly at Will's interruption.

'No, no, no,' he began, then a thought struck him and he frowned at the other two boys.

'Did you all decide that you'd recruit a force of Skandians?' he asked and Liam and Stuart nodded wordlessly.

'Well, what made you think you could do that?' he asked. The boys looked at one another, then Liam answered.

'That's what you did.' His tone said that the answer seemed self-evident.

Will made a helpless gesture with his hands.

'But I knew the Skandians,' he said. 'They were friends of mine.'

Liam shrugged. 'Well, yes. But I could get to know them too. I'm told I'm quite a personable type of fellow. I'm sure I could make them my friends.'

Stuart and Nick nodded their support. Will pointed to the Assets and Resources list.

'But there aren't any Skandians here!' he said. 'They don't exist! So what made you think you could just . . . produce them out of thin air?'

Again, the boys exchanged glances. This time it was Stuart who spoke.

'The exercise says we're to use our initiative and imagination . . .'

Will made a gesture for him to continue.

'So we used our initiative to imagine that there were Skandians in the area.'

'And that we were their friends,' Liam put in.

Will stood abruptly. For the first time, he had an inkling of what Halt might have gone through in the first year of Will's own apprenticeship. To the young boys, it seemed so logical.

'But you can't *do* that!' he exclaimed. Then, seeing their worried faces, he calmed down a little, forcing himself to explain. 'The Assets and Resources list tells you what people you can use. You can't just invent others to suit your purposes.'

He looked around the semicircle of crestfallen faces.

'I mean, if you could do that, why not just imagine a

dozen or so gigantic trolls who could go galumphing in and smash the walls down for you?'

Nick, Liam and Stuart all nodded dutifully and for one awful moment he thought they might be taking him seriously.

'I'm joking,' he said and they nodded again. He sighed and sat down. They knew they were going to have to go back to the beginning and he could see their disappointment. While he didn't intend to do the assignment for them, he decided there was no harm in pointing them in the right direction.

'All right, first of all, let's look at what you've got. Go through the Resources for me.'

'We've got an acrobat troop,' said Liam.

Will looked quickly at him. 'Can you think of anything they could be used for?'

Liam pursed his lips.

'They could entertain the troops and raise morale,' said Nick.

'If we had any troops,' Stuart put in.

'When we've got troops!' Liam interrupted with more than a hint of anger at Stuart's pedantic tone.

Will thought it was best to intervene before they started squabbling. He threw them a broad hint.

'What's stopping you getting into the castle? What's a castle's principal line of defence?' he asked. The boys considered the question, then Stuart answered, in a tone that indicated the answer was an obvious one.

'The walls, of course.'

'That's right. High walls. Four metres high.' Will paused, looking from one face to another. 'Can you see any connection between high walls and acrobats?'

Suddenly light dawned in the three faces, in Nick's a fraction of a second before the other two.

'They could scale the walls,' he said.

Will pointed a forefinger at him. 'Exactly. But you'll still need troops. Where have the original garrison gone?'

'They're scattered all over the fief, back to their farms and hamlets.' It was Liam this time. He frowned, taking it one step further. 'We'll need someone to move around from place to place, recruiting them . . .'

'But you don't want the enemy to notice,' Will put in quickly, hoping one of them would get the message.

'The jongleur!' Stuart exclaimed triumphantly. 'Nobody will take any notice of him moving around the countryside!'

Will sat back, smiling at them. 'Now you're beginning to think!' he said. 'Work together on this and come back this afternoon with your ideas.'

The three boys exchanged grins. They were eager now to progress the plan to its next stage. They stood up as Will motioned for them to go, but he stopped them with one more thought.

'Another thing: the village. How many people in it?'

Nick answered immediately, without needing to refer to his notes.

'Two hundred,' he said, wondering what Will was getting at. 'But there are only a few soldiers among them. Most are farmers and field workers.'

'I know that,' Will said. 'But think about what the law says about any village with more than one hundred residents.'

The law required that any village with a population of

more than one hundred had the responsibility of training its young men as archers. That was how Araluen maintained a large force of trained archers, ready to be called up into the army if needed. He could see the boys hadn't made that step so far. But he decided he'd given them enough help for one day.

'Think about it,' he said, making a shooing motion for them to leave. He listened to their excited, chattering voices as they faded away and leaned back against the trunk of a large tree behind him. He was exhausted, he realised.

'Nice work,' said Crowley, from a few metres behind him. Will, startled, sat up suddenly.

'Don't *do* that, Crowley!' he said. 'You frightened the wits out of me!'

The Commandant chuckled as he stepped into the glade and sat on a large log beside Will.

'You handled that well. Teaching isn't easy. You've got to know how much to prod them in the right direction and when to leave them to their own devices. You'll be a good teacher when you get your own apprentice.'

Will looked at him, slightly horrified by the prospect. There was the responsibility, not to mention the constant distraction of having a young person at his heels, asking questions, interrupting, racing off at tangents before thinking through a problem . . .

He stopped as he realised he was describing his own behaviour as an apprentice. Once more, he felt a sudden twinge of sympathy for Halt.

'Let's not do that for a while yet,' he said and Crowley smiled.

'No. Not just yet. I have other plans for you.'

But when Will pushed him to explain further, the Commandant merely smiled. 'We'll get to that in due time.'

And for the time being, that was all Will could get out of him.

Five

It was after midnight. Selsey was dark and silent as its inhabitants slept. There was no watchman. In this remote, little-known village there had never been a need for one.

But there was a need tonight, just as Halt had expected.

He was crouched behind one of the fishing boats drawn up on the sand, clear of the high water mark. His first thought had been that the Outsiders would strike at one of the houses. Then he'd realised there was a much better target for them. The fishing boats. The source of the village's wealth. If a house were burnt, the inhabitants could live under canvas while they rebuilt. Not the most comfortable situation, but life could continue.

If the boats were destroyed, there would be no fishing, no income, while new boats were built.

It would be in keeping with the Outsiders' ruthlessness to attack the boats, he had decided, and now his theory was proving correct. Half a dozen shadowy figures stole from the trees fringing the beach and moved furtively across the sand towards the fishing boats. As he watched them, Halt wondered vaguely why they automatically fell into a crouch as they came. It did nothing to conceal them from view. It simply made them look more suspicious. Yet most people under similar circumstances would do the same thing.

Four of the men stopped by a pile of fishing nets and equipment ten metres away. The other two continued, heading for the boat next to the one Halt was crouched behind. He peered around the stern as they knelt in the sand, only a few metres away – close enough for him to hear their whispered conversation.

'How many will we do?' asked one.

'Farrell says two should be enough to teach them a lesson.' Farrell was the grey-haired man Halt had observed earlier in the day, the leader of this small band of Outsiders. 'I'll do this one. You take care of the one behind me.' The speaker jerked his head towards the boat where Halt was concealed. His companion nodded and began to crawl on hands and knees towards the bow of the boat, staying low to remain out of sight.

Quickly Halt drew back and moved away from the stern, angling out towards the third boat in line so that he would be behind the saboteur when he turned his attention to his task. The beach was littered with large patches of seaweed and driftwood, tossed onto the shore by the wind and tide. As he heard the man rounding the bow, Halt dropped motionless to the sand, covered by his cloak. If the man noticed anything, he would have taken the motionless Ranger for yet another clump of debris. As the old Ranger adage went, *If a person doesn't expect to see someone, odds are he won't.*

Halt heard the scrape of flint on steel and raised his eyes a fraction. The man was hunkered behind the boat, his back to Halt. As the Ranger watched, he heard another scrape and saw the brief blue flash of light from the flint.

On elbows and knees, he slithered forward like a giant, silent snake, rising to a crouch as he reached the unsuspecting man.

The first moment the raider knew he wasn't alone was when an iron bar of an arm clamped across his throat, while a powerful hand forced his head forward to complete the choke hold. He managed one small gasp of surprise before his air supply was cut off.

'What's wrong?' the whispered call came from the other boat. Halt, continuing to apply the choke hold on the rapidly weakening man, replied in a similar whisper.

'Nothing. Dropped the flint.'

He saw the reflection of another flint striking steel from the other boat as he heard the angry whispered reply.

'Well, shut up and get on with it.'

The choke hold had taken full effect now and the man he had surprised slumped unconscious. Halt laid him down in the sand. There had been no further sound of flint striking steel from the far side of the boat, which meant the first raider had succeeded in getting a flame lit. There wasn't any time to waste. The sun-dried timbers of the boat, coated with varnish and paint, and the heavily tarred rigging, would burn quickly. The quickest way to reach the man was over the boat between them. Halt swarmed over the bulwark, crossed to the far side and rolled over onto the sand.

As he came to his feet, he saw the tiny glow of a flame in the tinder held by the man. The raider was looking at the flame as he heard a slight noise behind him. He glanced up, his eyes dazzled by the tiny patch of flame, and saw only a dark figure a few metres away. Logically enough, he assumed it was his companion.

'What are you doing? Have you finished?'

The time for concealment was over, Halt thought. In his normal voice, he replied, 'Not quite.'

Too late, the other man realised this was a stranger. He rose from his crouch. But as he did, Halt slapped the burning pile of tinder out of his hand, scattering it onto the sand. Then he followed through with his other hand, his left, in a hooking palm strike that had all the power of his twisting body and shoulder behind it.

The heel of his hand slammed into the man's chin, snapping his head back and sending him crashing into the hull of the boat with a cry of pain. As the man slid to the sand, half-conscious, Halt yelled at the top of his lungs.

'Fire! Fire in the boats! Fire!'

He heard a chorus of startled exclamations from the other four raiders as they tried to figure out what had happened. There was no plan to start yelling once the fires were lit. Yet as far as they knew, only their two companions were at the boats.

'Fire!' Halt yelled again. 'Get to the boats! Fire!'

His voice was startlingly loud in the peaceful night and already there were lights showing in the houses of the village. The four men realised now that things had gone seriously wrong and they rose, running towards the boats. Halt broke from cover, angling up the beach and away from them. Instinctively, they turned to pursue him, which was what he'd intended. He didn't want them trying to finish the job of setting fire to the boats.

'Get him!' he heard someone yelling, and the soft thud of feet in the sand was close behind him.

But now there were other voices shouting in the distance, as the villagers awoke and raised the alarm, and he heard the running feet behind him hesitate.

'Let him go! Get Morris and Scarr and let's get out of here!' he heard the same voice yell. Morris and Scarr would be the two who had tried to burn the boats and the raiders wouldn't want to leave them for the villagers to question. The running feet behind him turned away, heading back to the boats. He risked a quick glance over his shoulder and saw the four men heading back to drag their companions clear. Several hundred metres further down the beach, lanterns indicated the villagers heading for the boats, although their initial sense of urgency was gone as they could see no sign of fire at the boats.

The raiding party would have time to get away, he thought. But there was little he could do about that now. The large marquee where the Outsiders were camped was slowly coming to life as well. Doubtless they'd been awake all along, watching for their accomplices to carry out their plan. Now, of course, they could hardly pretend to have slept through the racket.

Halt slowed his pace to a jog as he reached the trees at the edge of the beach. He stopped inside the shadows they cast and took several deep breaths. Like all Rangers, he was in excellent physical condition. But it never hurt to rest when you had the chance and he could feel the adrenaline surging through his system, making his breath come faster and his heart beat more rapidly.

Calm down, he told his racing body, and he felt his pulse begin to slow to a more normal rate.

All in all, it had been a successful night, he thought. He would have preferred it if one or two of the raiders had been left behind for the villagers to question. But at least he'd thwarted their plan to burn the boats.

And he would have thrown a large doubt into their minds as they tried to work out what had gone wrong with their plan and who had interfered.

He smiled grimly to himself. He liked the idea that the Outsiders might have something to worry about. Perhaps it was that small satisfaction that took the edge off his natural sense of caution. As he turned to head for the spot where he had left Abelard, he blundered into a man who stepped from behind a tree.

'Who the blazes are you?' the man demanded. He had a heavy spiked club in his hand and he swung it up now, preparing for a crushing blow onto this stranger's head.

The immediate act of aggression told Halt that this was another of the Outsiders' gang. Recovering quickly from his shock, he flat-kicked sideways at the inside of the man's left knee. The leg buckled and the man collapsed with a cry of pain, holding his injured knee and yelling.

'Help! Help! Over here!'

Halt heard answering cries and the sound of bodies running through the trees and bushes. Moving like a wraith, he sped away. He had to reach Abelard before the pursuers caught up with him.

Six

The Gathering was coming to a close.

The two final-year apprentices were being given the usual initiation into the ranks. Will grinned ruefully as he watched, feeling Gilan's elbow dig into his ribs. Not too long ago, he had been in a similar position, feeling dumbfounded as Crowley bumbled and mumbled and hurled bits of paper around, making light of the whole process.

He watched the two new Rangers as they mirrored his own total bemusement. After five years' hard work and faithful application, a graduating apprentice expected some kind of ceremony. Something to mark what was undoubtedly the most important day of his life to date. And so the Ranger Corps, in its own unique style, went out of its way to avoid any such thing. Because, as Will realised now, graduation wasn't an end. It was the beginning of a much larger and more important phase of life.

Ostensibly, only Crowley, the two apprentices and their mentors were present. But in fact, they were surrounded by a group of silent, unseen spectators as the rest of the Rangers stood concealed among the trees, ready to leap out with their cries of congratulation and welcome, just as they did at every induction.

The boys' parents and several family members had been admitted to the area to see their sons graduate, travelling the last ten kilometres of the trip blindfolded, as the location of the Gathering Ground was a closely guarded secret. They too watched with anticipation and amusement from the shadow of the trees.

Only the younger apprentices were absent. It was a strict rule that nobody would ever tell an apprentice what lay in store for him at his graduation and so three of the Corps' older Rangers had taken the first- and third-year apprentices (there were no second- or fourth-year trainees this Gathering) to a site well away from the Gathering Ground for a final series of lectures. They would return in time for the feast that followed the inductions.

Crowley was coming to the end of his usual, masterful performance.

'So,' he said, eyes down and reading at breakneck pace as if he wanted to get through the entire matter as quickly as possible, 'you, Clarke of Caraway Fief, and you, Skinner of wherever it is you come from . . . yes . . . hang on a minute, where is it . . . Martinsyde Fief, of course . . . have completed all aspects of your training and are ready to be inducted as full members of the Ranger Corps. So I hereby induct you, by the authority granted to me as Commandant of the Ranger Corps and blah blah blah and so on and so on and why don't you both shake hands and that should just about do it.'

He stood quickly, gathering his papers, and shook hands perfunctorily with the two startled graduates.

'Bit like a wedding, really, isn't it?'

The two boys looked at one another, then at Crowley. He seemed to notice their bewilderment for the first time and hesitated, looking at them with a puzzled expression. 'Was there something else? Did I miss something?' He scratched his head and did a quick review of events. Will couldn't help grinning as enlightenment seemed to dawn on the Ranger Commandant.

'Oh, of course! You'll want your silver geegaws, won't you?' Crowley beckoned to Skinner and Clarke's two mentors, who stepped forward with the tiny, glittering objects that every Ranger held dear. 'Well, might as well hand 'em over!' he said casually.

Then, as the two Rangers went to hang the Silver Oakleaf amulets round the necks of their former apprentices, the other Rangers stepped out into the clearing, throwing back the cloaks that had concealed them and surrounding the little group.

'Congratulations!'

The massive roar went up through the trees, waking the birds who were roosting among the branches, frightening them into a chorus that echoed the roar of approval. As the Rangers surged forward to congratulate their newest members, pounding their backs, laughing and shaking their hands, Will saw the two surprised faces transformed as Clarke and Skinner realised they had been the victims of a giant practical joke. He also saw the quick tears of pleasure and pride that sprang to their eyes as they realised that now they were fully fledged members of this elite group. He felt his own eyes sting slightly in memory of his moment of realisation, then he stepped forward to take his turn at welcoming the new members.

'Congratulations. It's been a long five years, hasn't it?'

Skinner was currently being hugged by his tearful mother, a rather massively built woman who dwarfed her slim, dark-haired son.

'I'm so proud of you! So proud! If only your father could be here!' she was saying. Skinner managed to extricate himself from her bear hug long enough to shake Will's hand.

'There, there, Mother,' he said. 'It's all right.' Then to Will, he admitted, 'Sometimes I thought I'd never make it.'

Will nodded. 'Particularly over the last few months?' he asked and Skinner's eyes widened in surprise.

'How did you know that?'

'We all feel that way at the end,' Will told him. 'You realise what a big task lies in front of you.'

'You mean . . . you felt that way too?' Skinner said in disbelief. Skinner found it difficult to believe that a legend like Will Treaty could ever feel self-doubt.

Will grinned easily. 'I was terrified,' he admitted. 'But trust your training. When you get your assignment, you'll find you know a lot more than you think.'

He left Skinner engulfed by a further explosion of motherly pride and moved on to Clarke, who was surrounded by a small group consisting of his parents, his brother and his mentor. After offering his congratulations, Will asked, 'Any idea where you'll be assigned yet?'

Clarke shook his head. Will could see the sudden uncertainty in his eyes as he registered the fact that he would be moving away from the protective wings of his mentor, and striking out in his own fief.

'It'll be somewhere nice and peaceful, I'm sure,' Andross, his mentor, said reassuringly. 'We don't usually throw new Rangers in at the deep end.'

'You'll be fine,' Will told him.

Clarke grinned. 'Anywhere would be peaceful without Andross's snoring,' he said.

Andross raised his eyebrows and looked sidelong at the younger man. 'Is that so? Well, just pray that you're not in the fief next to mine or you might still hear me.'

Will joined in the general chorus of laughter that went round the group. Then Clarke's younger brother, looking admiringly at his newly elevated sibling, asked, 'Will you be allowed to come home and visit for a few days before you go?'

Clarke looked to Andross, who nodded. 'New Rangers get a week's leave with their families before taking up their posts.'

As he looked around the circle of happy faces, Will felt a small twinge of regret. There had been no happy, admiring family to wish him well when he graduated, he thought. Then he shook the small moment of melancholy away. There'd been Halt, he thought. And Halt was family enough for anyone.

Crowley was shoving his way through the crowd now to put an arm around the shoulders of each of the new apprentices.

'Why are we all standing here talking?' he cried. 'Let's eat!'

The meal was a simple one, but none the less delicious for that. A venison haunch had been turning on a spit over a bed of glowing coals for some hours, the juices and fat spluttering into the fire and raising sudden bursts of flame, filling the clearing with the succulent smell of roasting meat. Two of the Rangers now carved it expertly, placing slices of the juice-laden meat on platters with a fresh green salad tossed with a tangy vinegar and oil dressing. Mounds of fresh fruit were placed along the long table for dessert.

After the meal, the Rangers sat back as jugs of steaming hot coffee were set out. Will grinned at Gilan across the table as the tall Ranger reached for a honey pot a few spaces down the table.

'Don't take it all,' he warned. A couple of the older Rangers sitting near them shook their heads in mock condemnation.

'I see Halt's still passing on his bad habits,' said one.

Crowley announced that the entertainment was about to begin and Berrigan, a former Ranger who had lost a leg in battle and now travelled the country as a minstrel (and an undercover agent for the Corps) stepped forward with his *gitarra*. He sang three songs to increasingly boisterous applause, then beckoned to Will.

'Come and join me, Will Treaty!' he called. 'Let's see if you remember what I taught you.' The former Ranger had coached Will in his role as a jongleur when he had gone on his mission to Norgate Fief.

Will flushed with pleasure as he rose from his seat to a chorus of friendly catcalls. He made his way to the cleared space at the head of the table where Berrigan was perform-ing. One of the junior apprentices had been sent to fetch

Will's mandola from his tent — he rarely travelled anywhere without it — and he passed the instrument to him now. Will strummed a chord experimentally.

'I tuned it,' Berrigan told him and Will frowned as he adjusted the top string.

'So I see,' he replied, straight-faced, and a ripple of amusement went through the audience. Berrigan nodded appreciation of the gibe.

'What shall we start with?' he demanded. But Will was ready for that. It was the first trick of the trade Berrigan had taught him. *A professional entertainer is always ready with a song*, he had told him. *Hesitation marks you as an amateur.*

'*Jenny on the Mountain*,' he said promptly.

Berrigan smiled at him. 'I see you've remembered some things then.'

They performed together for three songs. Will had a pleasant voice and Berrigan slipped effortlessly into a harmony as the younger man sang the melody. Will had to admit that they sounded pretty good together. But after the third song, he laid the mandola down.

'You also taught me not to overstay my welcome,' he said and he took his seat to a round of appreciative applause, content to watch the master performer for the rest of the evening.

He rejoined Berrigan for the final song. It was the unofficial Ranger anthem, a haunting ballad called *Cabin in the Trees*, and those assembled all joined in, singing softly along to the chorus.

Going back to the cabin in the trees
Going back to the creek beneath the hill.

There's a girl used to live there when I left
But I doubt she'll be waiting for me still.'

The gentle, simple song of lost love and country living was a marked contrast to the harsh and dangerous life that Rangers led. Maybe that's why they loved it as much as they did, Will thought. As he and Berrigan strummed the final soft chord, there was an audible sigh from the audience, then silence fell over them. Will glanced down the table and saw that the faces of his comrades, so often set in stern, harsh lines, had softened as they thought of old friends and times gone by.

'Right, everyone! Attention please!' Crowley let the moment of reflection extend for a decent interval, then brought everyone back to the present. 'Last official piece of business for this Gathering. Assignments and reassignments for the coming year.'

As Crowley took his place at the head of the table, Will resumed his seat opposite Gilan. There was a tightness in his stomach as he waited for Crowley's next words. He'd been assigned to the sleepy backwater of Seacliff Fief for long enough, he felt.

Perhaps it was time for something more challenging.

'As some of you know already,' Crowley began, 'Alun has decided to retire.'

Alun was the Ranger of Whitby Fief. Now he would move to Castle Araluen, as was the custom for retired Rangers, where he would assist with administrative tasks, taking some of the paperwork burden from Crowley's shoulders.

He was a popular figure and there was a round of warm applause as he stepped forward to receive his Gold Oakleaf — symbol of a retired Ranger — from Crowley.

There was also a scroll of commendation from King Duncan, thanking Alun for his many years of loyal service to the crown.

'I'll think of you all,' Alun said, smiling around the circle of familiar faces. 'I'll think of you when I'm tucked up in a warm bed at Castle Araluen and you're all out sleeping in muddy ditches and draughty barns.'

A chorus of cheerful abuse met this sally and his smile widened. Yet Will could see a hint of wistfulness behind the smile. Alun would miss the freedom of the hills and forests and the excitement of facing the unknown with every sunrise.

But his retirement meant there was a vacancy for one of the graduating Rangers to fill. Not Whitby, of course — it was one of the more important fiefs in the Kingdom, set almost exactly in the geographic centre of the country, where all the major highways intersected and several important trading routes met.

Briefly, Will entertained the hope that he might be appointed to Whitby. He had proven himself over the past two years, he thought, and he knew that Crowley respected his abilities.

'Which leaves a place for us to fill at Whitby,' Crowley was saying. 'And the new Ranger for Whitby Fief will be . . .'

Crowley couldn't help himself. He paused dramatically to ensure he had the attention of all those present.

'Gilan.'

Will felt an instant shaft of disappointment, followed almost immediately by a sense of happiness and pride for his friend. Gilan was rising from his seat, his face flushed with pleasure, as he moved forward to accept the written commission from Crowley and shake the Commandant's hand. Gilan deserved the recognition, Will realised, and he felt guilty about that moment of jealousy that had gripped him when Gilan's name was announced.

'Well done, Gilan. You deserve this,' Crowley was saying.

There was a murmur of agreement from the audience. Gilan was highly skilled, responsible and very intelligent. He was generally regarded as one of the brightest of the younger Rangers. In addition, his family connections would stand him in good stead at Whitby. His father was the Kingdom's supreme army commander.

As Gilan moved to resume his seat, Will rose and embraced his friend.

'Congratulations. Couldn't have gone to a better man,' he said. He was pleased to realise that he meant it. And he knew that he had been unrealistic in hoping for the appointment himself. He was definitely too young. Gilan smiled at him, still a little overcome with this unexpected promotion.

'Well, at least we'll be a lot closer to each other now,' he said. 'That's good news.'

His words raised a nagging doubt in Will's mind. Whitby and Seacliff were almost neighbours, with only one other fief separating them. But now that Gilan was moving from Norgate, someone would have to replace him. Will faced that prospect with some misgivings. After all, with his knowledge of the fief and its people, he was the logical choice.

Yet, eager as he was for a greater challenge, the prospect of moving to Norgate was one that filled Will with dismay.

At Seacliff, he was only a few days' ride from Redmont — and Alyss. In the past months, he had been able to make regular trips to visit the tall, beautiful girl. And she had found several occasions to bring messages to Seacliff — doubtless engineered by her benevolent mentor, Lady Pauline, who thoroughly approved of the growing relationship between her protégée and the young Ranger.

But Norgate! Norgate was several weeks away from Redmont. And the roads were often difficult and dangerous. To visit Alyss for one day would mean taking a leave of absence of almost a month from his post. And Norgate wasn't the sort of fief that a Ranger could leave to its own devices for long periods like that. He might manage it once a year, certainly no more than that.

His heart was in his mouth as he watched Crowley pick up the next commission from the table.

'Norgate Fief will be the new posting for one of our most respected Rangers . . .' Again he paused for dramatic effect. Will could have cheerfully leapt up and throttled him. Get on with it, he wanted to yell. But he forced himself to continue to breathe deeply, to relax.

'Harrison,' Crowley announced and Will felt an enormous tide of relief sweep over him.

Harrison was in his late thirties. Dependable and trustworthy rather than brilliant, he had been badly injured in a battle with Iberian pirates some years previously and appointed to the small, sleepy fief of Coledale while he recuperated. Now fully recovered, he was an ideal choice for Norgate.

'Time we put you back to work, Harrison,' Crowley said.

'I'll be glad of the chance, Crowley,' the short, powerfully built Ranger replied.

Will nodded to himself. Norgate could use a steady, dependable hand on the reins. And Harrison would cope well with the baron and his battlemaster — both of whom were inclined to be a little pompous at times.

The final appointment was to replace Harrison at Coledale and that commission went to the new graduate, Skinner. He flushed with pride as he received his commission scroll from Crowley. The Commandant then turned to the other graduate, Clarke.

'Clarke, I'm afraid there are no other vacancies at the moment. It was a tough choice between you and Skinner but his Assessment marks shaded yours just a little. I'm sure that one of the old fogies out there —' he swept his arm around the assembled Rangers and there was a ripple of laughter '— will be retiring within the next six months or so . . . once Alun tells them about the advantages of a warm bed. Then you'll have your appointment. In the meantime, you'll move to Castle Araluen and work as my personal assistant. How's that?'

Clarke nodded his thanks. Crowley's duties as Commandant sometimes conflicted with his work as Ranger of Araluen Fief. Clarke could fill in for him as acting Ranger in his absences. It was a good solution to the problem. The boy would gain experience in the field and Crowley could shed some of his workload.

Crowley folded up the sheet of notes he had been using for reference.

'And that just about winds us up. There are no other assignments to discuss. It's been a good Gathering and I thank you all for your efforts. So now let's have a glass of wine and call it a night.'

As the assembled Rangers broke up and moved off, forming smaller groups, Will sat quietly for a few moments. He was relieved that he hadn't been sent to Norgate. But he couldn't help feeling a little disappointed at being overlooked. He knew Crowley didn't move people around merely for the sake of it — a Ranger formed a special bond with the fief he was assigned to. But still, very little happened in Seacliff these days.

He shook himself irritably. You worry they'll send you to Norgate and then when they don't you feel slighted, he thought to himself. And he was honest enough to grin at his contrariness. He felt a hand on his arm and turned to find Crowley beside him.

'Give me a minute, please, Will?' Crowley said. 'There's something we need to discuss.'

Seven

Halt was trapped. He cursed himself for taking the enemy so lightly.

Once he'd reached Abelard, he had easily outstripped his pursuers. Gradually, their shouts died away to silence and, confident that he had shaken them off, he eased Abelard down to a trot. He had no idea that another group of enemies were on horseback, and had been riding to flank him and cut him off from the main highway that led back to Redmont Fief.

Worse still, this second party had dogs. Abelard sensed them long before Halt did. He saw the little horse's ears prick up and heard the nervous, warning whinny. A tremor ran through the sturdy horse's body. Halt could feel it and knew something was wrong. He urged Abelard into a canter once more as the sun showed itself above the rim of the trees.

Then he heard the baying and realised that his pursuers had managed to get between him and the highway. He angled Abelard back, hoping to outdistance them and loop around the end of their picket line.

That was when the first of the dogs burst from the trees.

This was no tracking dog. It ran silently, wasting none of its energy on the baying and howling of the others. This dog was a killer. A war dog, trained to chase silently, then attack without warning and without pity.

It was huge, its short coat mottled grey and black and its eyes blazing red with hate. It saw its quarry now and leapt at Abelard, aiming for the horse's throat with its massive fangs.

Any normal horse might have frozen in terror or shied violently at the sudden attack. But Abelard was a Ranger horse, well trained, intelligent and courageous. He spun on his rear legs and skipped sideways, avoiding the head-long rush of the monster. Yet he did it with a minimum of panic and with just the amount of movement necessary. Abelard's instinct, borne of long years of experience, told him that his best defence lay with the figure seated astride him. And a violent, sudden reaction could unseat his rider.

The dog's jaws snapped shut on empty air, missing the horse's throat by centimetres.

It hit the ground, spun and tensed, ready to spring again. Now, for the first time, it uttered a sound . . . a deep rumbling snarl.

Which was cut off almost instantly by Halt's first arrow.

Faced with a head-on target, the Ranger waited until the dog had lifted its head to sound that snarling challenge. Abelard stood rock steady, giving Halt a stable platform. Then Halt shot for the throat, the impact of the heavy arrow, with the eighty pounds of draw weight from his bow behind it, sending the dog staggering backwards and sideways.

The second arrow, coming within seconds of the first, struck the snarling killer in the heart, dropping it stone dead.

Halt patted his horse's neck. He knew the strength of will it had taken for Abelard to stand steadily, allowing him to shoot. He understood the depth of trust the little horse had just placed in him and was glad he hadn't let his old friend down.

'Good boy,' he said quietly. 'Now let's get out of here.'

They wheeled, running at a tangent to the way they had come. The country was unfamiliar to Halt and for the moment all he could do was try to put distance between himself and the baying hounds — as well as any other war dogs that might be loping silently through the woods after them.

The baying was still close behind them as they broke clear of the heavy tree cover and began moving up a slope. The ground was covered in waist-high gorse and shrubs, dotted with rocky outcrops and occasional groves of trees. But as he neared the top Halt saw, too late, that he had made a fatal mistake. What he had taken to be a hill was a bluff — a sloping piece of ground that gradually narrowed and led to a sheer cliff overlooking a deep, wide river.

He wheeled Abelard and began to race back down the slope. But they hadn't gone far before he saw mounted figures moving in the fringes of the trees at the base of the hill. It was too late to head back down. They were trapped halfway up. As he watched, another massive grey and black shape detached itself from the group and came arrowing up the slope after them, belly close to the ground, huge fangs bared in a murderous snarl.

Abelard rumbled a warning.

'I see him,' Halt said quietly and the horse relaxed, its faith in Halt absolute.

Ordinarily, Halt was fond of dogs. But he would kill these beasts without a qualm. This was no dog. This was a pitiless killing machine, perverted by its cruel training so that it sought only to kill and kill again.

The dog was fifty metres away when Halt slid from the saddle, nocking an arrow as he did so. He let the ravening animal draw closer. Thirty metres. Twenty-five.

Abelard whinnied in mild consternation. *What are you waiting for?*

'Settle down,' Halt told him, and released.

It was an instant killing shot. The running dog simply collapsed in mid-stride, its legs buckling under it, its head dropping, so that it rolled several times, its momentum carrying it forward, before it came to a stop. A dead stop, Halt thought grimly.

Abelard whinnied again. Halt thought he could detect a note of satisfaction in the sound but he may have imagined it.

'I told you I know what I'm doing,' he said. But then he frowned. Because he wasn't sure what he was going to do next. He could see men emerging from the trees, gesturing upwards as they saw him and Abelard halfway up the slope. Several of them were carrying bows and one of them began to raise his, an arrow on the string.

He'd barely begun to draw when a black-shafted arrow

hissed downhill and sent him tumbling back into the trees. His companions looked at his lifeless body, looked again at the indistinct figure above them and saw he was nocking another arrow.

As one, they broke back for the cover of the trees, stumbling over the excited hounds as they beat them out of the way. The second arrow slammed, quivering, into the trunk of a tree at chest height. The message was clear. Don't show yourself if you wish to remain healthy.

In the confusion, none of them saw the grey-cloaked figure lead his horse into a jumble of rocks. When they looked back up the slope, there was no sign of man or horse.

The day wore on. The sun rose to its zenith and began to descend towards the western horizon. But still the Outsiders could see no sign of the figure up the hill. They knew he was there — somewhere. But exactly where they had no idea — there were at least half a dozen piles of tumbled rock that could be sheltering the stranger and his horse. And they knew if they tried to rush blindly up the hill, they would pay for it with their lives.

In the midafternoon, they released another war dog to see if it might flush the Ranger out. The dog swung back and forth, sniffing the air for some trace of the man and horse. Then, catching a faint scent on the breeze, it began to run — the remorseless, belly-to-the-ground lope of its kind.

All eyes were on the dog as it settled into its stride. That was a mistake, for no one saw where the arrow came from as it struck the dog down and sent it rolling back down the slope, eyes glazed, tongue lolling.

Up the slope, behind a tumble of large boulders, Halt glanced to where Abelard lay, legs folded underneath him so that he was completely concealed from view.

'In Gallic,' Ranger said conversationally, 'this might be called an *impasse*. But you should know that. You speak Gallic, after all.'

He expected no answer from the horse, of course. But Abelard tilted his head at Halt, liking the sound of his voice.

'The question is, what do we do next?'

Again, Abelard had no answer. And for once, neither did Halt. He knew that when darkness came, he could make his way down the bluff and slip through the line of watchers. Even the dogs would pose no real problem for him. The wind had shifted so that it was blowing from them to him. They wouldn't pick up his scent until he was past them.

But the problem was Abelard. He couldn't hope to take the horse with him and avoid detection. Even if the men didn't see him, the dogs would certainly hear some slight noise from the horse's hooves on the ground. Ranger horses were trained to move quietly. But even they couldn't move as silently as a Ranger.

And Halt wasn't going to leave Abelard behind. That was unthinkable. He had no idea whether there were any more of the killer dogs waiting down there in the treeline. If there were, Abelard on his own wouldn't stand a chance.

He considered moving back up the slope to the cliff. He'd seen the river winding below the bluff, some ten to twelve metres below. If the water were deep enough, he could survive a jump into it. But Abelard wouldn't. He was much heavier than Halt. They would fall at the same speed, but the horse's extra mass meant he would hit the water with far greater force than Halt would. And unlike his master, Abelard couldn't streamline his body to reduce the impact when he hit the surface of the water. He would land on his belly.

'So we can't go up and we can't go down,' Halt said.

Abelard snorted. *You'll think of something.*

Halt raised an eyebrow in his direction. 'Don't be too sure of it,' he said. 'If you get any ideas, I'd like to hear them.'

The sun was well below the treetops in the west now. The light on the slope was becoming uncertain. Halt peered through a small gap in the rocks. There was no sign of movement below.

'Not yet,' he muttered. 'We'll see what happens when it's full dark.'

Sometimes, he thought, all you can do is wait. This looked like being one of those times.

As night fell, he unpacked a folding canvas bucket from his saddle bag and half filled it with water from one of his canteens so that Abelard could drink. He was a little thirsty himself but he felt he could wait a while longer.

He listened carefully to the night sounds that began to fill the still air. Frogs, and a persistent cricket somewhere. The occasional cry of a hunting owl. From time to time, small animals scuttled through the gorse and the long grass. Each time he heard such a sound, he'd look inquiringly at Abelard. But the horse showed no sign of interest, so Halt knew they were all naturally made.

He fully expected the Outsiders to make some sort of

probe during the night. That was one reason why he listened so carefully to the sounds of animals and birds. He was attuning himself to the spectrum of natural sounds around him, absorbing the pattern so that anything foreign or different would stand out like a splash of paint on a blank canvas.

There was another reason. He wanted to find a sound that wasn't there so that he could use it as a signal for Abelard. He listened carefully for some minutes, then decided.

'A kingfisher,' he said softly. Strictly speaking, they weren't nocturnal birds. But occasionally they would take advantage of the fact that mice and small animals felt free to scurry around in the darkness. If his enemies heard the sound, they might be suspicious. But they couldn't be sure that it wasn't a real kingfisher stirring.

He moved towards Abelard and gestured with his palm upwards. The bent-kneed reclining position wasn't the most comfortable for the horse and it responded gratefully, coming to its feet. In the dark, there was little chance of its being seen above the rocks.

Abelard stood still as Halt moved towards him. The Ranger reached out and smoothed the soft texture of the horse's nose, stroking him three times. Then he placed both hands on either side of the muzzle and looked into the horse's eyes. He squeezed his hands together twice and saw Abelard's ears prick. It was a long-established training routine, one of many shared by Rangers and their horses. Abelard knew that Halt was about to teach him a sound. And the next time Abelard heard that sound repeated, he would be expected to respond to it.

Softly, Halt emitted the low, gurgling chuckle of a kingfisher. It was a good approximation of the real thing, but not perfect. If there happened to be a real kingfisher in the area, Halt didn't want Abelard becoming confused. The horse's acute hearing would pick the difference between the real thing and Halt's impersonation. A man might not.

Abelard's ears flicked forward and back twice in quick succession — his signal to Halt that he had registered the sound. Halt patted his muzzle again.

'Good boy,' he said quietly. 'Now relax.'

He moved back to his vantage point among the rocks. There was a cleft between two of the larger boulders where he could sit, his head and face concealed by the cowl of his cloak, and survey the darkened expanse of the hillside below him. The moon wasn't due to rise for at least four hours. He assumed that the enemy, if they were going to try anything, would do so before the slope was bathed in moonlight.

From time to time he heard the muted yelping and snarling of the dogs as they fought among themselves, then the cries of their trainers as they silenced them. They'd be the trackers, he knew. The massive, iron-jawed war dogs wouldn't make noise. They were trained not to.

He considered the possibility that the enemy might unleash another war dog under cover of darkness but decided that it was unlikely. They had already lost three of the monsters to his arrows and dogs like that were not to be squandered lightly. They took years to breed and train. No, he thought, if an attack came, it would be men who launched it. And before they did that, they'd have to scout his position.

At least, that was what Halt was hoping for. He was beginning to see the first glimmer of a way out of this predicament. Carefully, he set his bow and quiver down beside the rocks. He wouldn't be needing them. Any confrontation during the night would be at close quarters. He reached now into his saddle bag and found his two strikers.

These were unique Ranger weapons. They were brass cylinders, as long as the breadth of his hand with a lead-weighted knob at either end. When held in a closed fist, the strikers turned the fist into a solid, unyielding weapon, with the weight lending extra force and authority to a punch. They could also be clipped together, forming a throwing club that had the same balance as a Ranger's saxe knife.

He slipped the two heavy cylinders into the side pocket of his jerkin.

'Stay here,' he told Abelard, although there was no need to do so. Then, belly to the ground, using his knees and elbows to propel himself, he slipped out of the cover of the rocks and moved downhill. Thirty metres below the spot where he'd taken cover, he stopped, slumping prone in the undergrowth, his cloak rendering him virtually invisible as soon as he stopped moving.

Now all he had to do was wait. He thought wryly that he'd spent a great part of his life waiting in situations like this.

So you should be used to it by now, he told himself.

Eight

Will and Crowley slipped quietly away from the other Rangers, the sandy-haired Commandant leading the way through the trees to a small, quiet glade. When he was sure there was nobody else within earshot, Crowley stopped and sat on a tree stump, looking up quizzically at Will.

'Disappointed that I left you in Seacliff?' he asked.

'No! Not at all!' Will answered hurriedly. Then, as Crowley continued to look at him, he smiled ruefully. 'Well, perhaps a little, Crowley. It's awfully quiet there, you know.'

'Some people might not think that's a bad thing. We are supposed to keep peace in the Kingdom, after all,' Crowley said.

Will shifted his feet awkwardly. 'I know. It's just that . . .'

He hesitated and Crowley nodded his understanding. Will had crammed a lot of excitement into his relatively short life. The fight with the Kalkara, the destruction of

Morgarath's secret bridge and his subsequent kidnapping by Skandian pirates. Then he'd escaped from captivity, played a pivotal role in the Battle for Skandia and returned home in triumph. Since then, he'd helped rescue the Skandian oberjarl from desert bandits and staved off a Scotti invasion at Norgate.

With a history like that, it was small wonder that he'd developed a taste for adventure — and that he found the uneventful life at Seacliff more than a little restricting.

'I understand,' Crowley told him. 'You don't need to explain. But I have to admit that I haven't been totally forthcoming with you.'

He paused and Will looked at him curiously.

'Forthcoming?'

Crowley made an awkward gesture with one hand. 'There's something I've been meaning to discuss with you,' he said. 'I think it's important and I think it's a big opportunity for you. But you may not agree. As a matter of fact,' he added as an afterthought, 'it's partly the reason why Halt didn't come to this Gathering.'

Will frowned, puzzled by the news. 'But I thought he —'

'Oh, he's off chasing down rumours about the Outsiders, all right. But that could possibly have waited. He used that as an excuse because he didn't want to influence your decision one way or the other.'

'My decision? Crowley, you're talking in riddles. What decision? What is it that Halt didn't want to influence me about?'

Crowley indicated for Will to take a seat beside him and waited till the younger man was comfortable.

'It's an idea I've been tossing around for some time,' he

said. 'Since you all went racing off to Arrida to fetch Erak back, as a matter of fact. Our world, or rather our sphere of influence in the world, is growing larger every day, Will. It extends past fief boundaries, past our own national boundaries at times.

'The Skandian operation was one example. So was your assignment in Norgate. We were lucky that we had someone as accomplished and capable as you to take that on, and that your own post at Seacliff was relatively quiet.'

Will felt his cheeks flushing at Crowley's praise but he said nothing. Crowley continued.

'Ordinarily, I couldn't drag a Ranger out of his fief and send him somewhere else for weeks on end. But more and more, we're facing that sort of necessity. Some day soon, for example, someone's going to have to go to Skandia to see how the treaty arrangement is working – how our archers are faring over there. Who do I send? You? Halt? You're the two logical choices because the Skandians know you and trust you. But what happens to your two fiefs in the meantime?'

Will frowned. He could see the problem. But he had no idea where Crowley was going.

'That's why I want to form a Special Task Group,' the Commandant said. 'And I want Halt and you to run it.'

Will leaned forward, thinking over Crowley's words. Already, he was interested in the idea and wanted to know more.

'Special Task Group,' he repeated, liking the sound of the words. 'What would we be doing?'

Crowley shrugged. 'Any situation, either within Araluen or overseas, that requires more than a routine response.

Now that the threat of Morgarath has been removed, and with our northern border secured, Araluen is a powerful and influential player on the international stage. We have treaties in place with half a dozen other countries — including Arrida and Skandia, thanks to your own efforts.

'I'd like to think, and the King agrees with me, that we could have a small team ready to respond to any emergency that might crop up. Incidentally, I'd see Horace as part of that team as well. In the past, the three of you have pulled off some amazing successes. He'd remain based at Araluen until such time as he was needed. Then he'd be detached to work with you and Halt. And you'd be able to recruit other people as you needed them.'

'And I'd be based . . . where exactly?' Will asked. Crowley's face showed a hint of concern. He hesitated before he answered.

'That's the problem. We can detach one knight from the Royal Guard without too much trouble. But we can't have two fiefs, yours and Halt's, left without their Rangers for extended periods of time. You'd have to give up Seacliff.'

'Oh,' Will said. Seacliff might be an unexciting little fief but it was his. He represented the King's authority on the sleepy little island and, much as he had been anxious for change earlier in the evening, the thought of simply giving it up came as a wrench to him.

'Exactly,' Crowley said, reading his thoughts. 'That's why Halt didn't want to be here when you decided. He knows that having your own fief is a big thing for a Ranger. It means independence and authority and he didn't want you to be influenced by his presence when I put this to you. He said he'd love to have you back at Redmont, but it had to be your decision to —'

'Back at Redmont!' Will said eagerly. 'You didn't mention that!'

Crowley frowned, then nodded. 'No. I suppose I didn't. Well, that was the plan. You'd take over Halt's cabin — he and Pauline are very comfortable in the castle these days — and you'd oversee one half of Redmont Fief while Halt looked after the other. It's a big fief, after all. There'd be plenty to do for both of you.'

A huge grin was spreading over Will's face at the thought of it. To go back to Redmont, where he'd grown up. To be with Halt and Baron Arald and Sir Rodney.

And Alyss, he thought. The grin, already wide, grew immense. Crowley noticed it. It was hard not to.

'I assume from the ridiculously happy look on your face that the idea meets with a certain amount of approval?' he said.

'Well . . . yes, actually. It certainly does. But . . .' A thought struck him and he frowned at it. Crowley gestured for him to continue.

'Problem?' he prompted.

'Redmont is an important fief,' Will began. 'You can hardly leave that without a Ranger in place if Halt and I have to attend to matters somewhere else.'

Crowley beamed at him. 'I was hoping you'd raise that. Now I get a chance to show what an administrative genius I am. Gilan's new fief adjoins the north-eastern border of Redmont. In fact, Castle Whitby is less than ten kilometres from the border.' He raised a hand to still Will's instant question. 'Yes, yes. I know, Whitby is an important fief too. So that's why, if you agree to all this, Alun will base himself at Whitby rather than Castle Araluen. He can still attend to paperwork and administration for me and he'll be on hand if you and Halt are called away. In such a case, Gilan moves into Redmont Fief —'

'Which he is familiar with anyway,' Will interrupted.

'Exactly. He served his apprenticeship there, after all. Then Alun can resume temporary duty as Ranger of Whitby. And, of course, young Clarke will take your place at Seacliff. Didn't I say I'm a genius?' He spread his hands, as if looking for praise.

Will nodded acknowledgement. 'I have to agree.'

Crowley instantly became serious. 'Of course, we're lucky that at the moment we're blessed with a wealth of talented people. It all dovetails quite nicely. Mind you, you're yet to tell me if you accept.'

'Of course I accept,' Will told him. 'I couldn't think of a better plan.'

They shook hands on it, smiling. Then Crowley said cheerfully, 'Now all we have to do is tell Halt when he comes back from his little holiday by the seaside.'

Nine

alt had been waiting in the darkness for over an hour when he heard the sound of someone moving through the low shrubs close to him.

Anyone else might have turned his head to look, trying to see where the newcomer might be. Halt knew that any movement could lead to his discovery so he stayed still as the rock he looked like. Instead his ears, attuned to judge movement and direction by years of training and practice, told him that there was one man, moving up the hill and slightly to the right of where Halt lay prone, merging into the long grass.

The stalker was good. He made only slight noises as he progressed up the hill. But slight noises were enough to alert a Ranger, and Halt lay, unmoving, as he judged that the other man had moved level with him, then past him.

Now he stopped moving and Halt realised that he was taking stock of the situation. There were four rocky outcrops within the next thirty metres. Any one of them could conceal Halt and Abelard.

After a few minutes, the man was on the move again, angling away to the furthest outcrop on the right. That made sense, Halt thought. If he was going to check them all out, his best course would be to work from one end of the line to the other.

As the noise of his movement faded, Halt raised his head slightly, moving only a millimetre at a time.

He let out the low, gurgling chuckle that he had rehearsed with Abelard. Instantly, the noise of the Outsider's movement stopped as he tried to ascertain whether the sound was natural or not. Then, after thirty seconds — a sufficiently long gap so that it didn't sound like a response to the bird call — the low, snuffling snort of a horse came clearly from the rocks above Halt's position. Then, for good measure, Abelard shook his mane.

Good boy, thought Halt. Chin on hand, he watched a dark shape sliding across the hillside, angling towards the clump of rocks where Abelard was concealed. He was aiming to skirt the rocks, Halt saw, and approach from uphill. It was time to spoil his plans a little. Stealthily, the Ranger began crawling after the other man.

He moved with remarkable speed, making no sound and seeming to glide snake-like over the ground on his belly. He could see the other man still — a dark crouching shape in the night — and hear the slight sounds that he made. Halt, even moving on his belly, was gaining ground on him, approaching him from directly behind and downhill.

Once, his quarry stopped moving and glanced quickly around him. He was obviously no novice at this game. But Rangers weren't novices either. In fact, they were past masters at this form of unseen movement. As the crouching man stopped, Halt froze instantly. His face was up but he knew it was shadowed by his cowl. He also knew that if he dropped his head to hide his face, the movement would catch the other man's eye.

Trust the cloak. He'd dinned that lesson into Will's brain hundreds of times. Now he took note of it himself. The man's gaze passed over him, seeing nothing to alarm him. Then he faced back up the hill and began moving again. After a few seconds to make sure it wasn't a feint, that the man hadn't seen anything he felt was suspicious, Halt followed.

He was only a few metres behind his quarry now. He realised he could actually hear the man breathing. He's tense, Halt thought. With his veins charged with adrenaline, the stalker's breath was coming more heavily — probably without his realising the fact.

If he looked around now, cloak or no cloak, he was bound to see Halt right behind him. It was time to act. Halt rose slowly from the ground and crept forward in a low crouch, one of the strikers clenched in his right fist.

Perhaps Halt made some infinitesimal noise, or perhaps the other man just sensed a presence behind him, but he started to turn, a few seconds too late. Halt swung an overhand blow and brought the striker knob down hard onto the man's skull, just behind the left ear. He felt the shock up his arm as the man emitted a strangled grunt and collapsed, limp as a rag, onto the ground.

Still in a crouch, Halt grabbed him under the arms and quickly dragged him into the shelter of the rocks. Abelard looked at him curiously, but made no sound.

'Good boy,' Halt said briefly. The horse responded by raising then lowering his head.

'Let's see what we have here,' Halt said and rolled the unconscious man onto his back. The would-be stalker was armed with a small arsenal of weapons. There was a short sword slung across his back. In addition, he had a long stabbing dagger in a belt sheath, another smaller knife in a scabbard strapped to his left forearm, and a third tucked into the cuff of his boot. Halt examined them briefly. Cheap weapons, but kept well sharpened. He tossed them to one side. There was a length of cord looped around the man's left shoulder. It was just over a metre in length and had a weighted ball at either end. A bolo, Halt recognised, a hunting weapon designed to be whirled around the head and thrown at a target's legs. When the rope snagged the target, the weighted ends would whip around, tripping the victim and binding its feet together. Drawing his saxe knife, Halt cut the weights off the end and tossed them into the gorse.

The man was wearing a soft hat, folded up to form a narrow brim, and a thigh-length jacket of rough wool, belted at the waist. Halt fastened the stalker's thumbs together with a pair of wood and rawhide thumb cuffs. Slipping the man's patched and shabby boots off, he fastened his big toes with another pair of cuffs, wrinkling his nose at the rank smell of the man's feet. When his prisoner was secured, he slipped his hands under the man's arms and dragged him to a large rock, leaning his shoulders against it. Then Halt sat down to wait for him to regain consciousness.

After several minutes, he moved away from the downwind position he had taken, his nose twitching again.

'Those feet of yours smell like something crawled into your boots and died there,' he said softly. There was no reply.

It was some fifteen minutes later that the man emitted a shuddering sigh. His eyelids flickered open and he shook his head to clear it.

Involuntarily, he tried to reach up to rub his eyes, then discovered that his hands were fastened securely behind his back. He struggled briefly against the restraint, then winced and uttered a cry of pain as the leather thong of the thumb cuffs cut into the soft skin at the base of his thumbs.

'Stay still and you won't hurt yourself,' Halt told him quietly.

The man looked up in alarm, registering Halt's presence for the first time. The Ranger had been sitting, quiet and unmoving, only a few metres away. Halt now saw a bewildered look pass over the unshaven face as the man tried to recall what had happened, how he had arrived in this predicament. From the expression on his face, he had no idea. Then bewilderment gave way to anger.

'Who are you?' he demanded roughly. His aggressive tone left no doubt that he was used to berating people to get his own way.

Halt smiled thinly. Had the man known anything about the grey-bearded figure sitting opposite him, that alone would have been enough to set alarm bells ringing. Halt rarely smiled, and even more rarely was it a sign of good humour.

'No,' he said calmly, 'I think that's my question. Who are you? What's your name?'

'Why should I tell you?' the Outsider demanded. His tone was still blustering and overbearing. Halt scratched his ear reflectively for a second or two, then replied.

'Well, let's just take stock of the situation, shall we? You're the one who's sitting there trussed up like a Yuletide goose. You can't move. Your head probably aches. And for the time being you have two ears.'

For the first time, a shadow of fear passed across the man's face. Not so much at the statement that he was tied hand and foot, more at the non sequitur about his ears.

'My ears?' he said. 'What have they got to do with it?'

'Just this,' Halt told him. 'If you don't stop talking as if you're in charge of things, I'll remove one of them for you.'

There was a whisper of steel on leather as Halt drew his saxe knife. The razor-sharp blade gleamed dully in the starlight as he held it up for the Outsider to see.

'Now,' he repeated, 'what's your name?'

The thin smile had disappeared from Halt's face now and there was an edge in his voice that told his prisoner the time for discussion was past. His eyes dropped from Halt's, the light of anger in them quickly fading.

'It's Colly,' he said. 'Colly Deekers. I'm an honest mill worker from Horsdale.'

Horsdale was a large town some fifteen kilometres away. Halt shook his head slowly. He slid the saxe back into its sheath but somehow the disappearance of the weapon did nothing to raise Colly's spirits.

'Ah, Colly,' he said, 'we're going to get on a lot better if you stop trying to lie to me. You may be from Horsdale but

I doubt that you're a mill worker. And I know you're not honest. So let's just leave those details out of our conversation, shall we?'

Colly said nothing. He was beginning to feel very uncomfortable. This was, after all, the man that he'd been sent to find — and to kill if the opportunity arose. And he had no doubt that the stranger was well aware of the fact. His mouth was dry all of a sudden and he swallowed several times.

'My friends will pay you if you release me,' he said. Halt regarded him, head tilted quizzically to one side.

'No they won't,' he replied scornfully. 'They'll do their best to kill me. Don't be so ridiculous — and don't take me for a fool. It annoys me and you're in no position to do that. I might change my mind about my plans for you.'

Colly's mouth was drier than ever now.

'Your plans for me?' he said. There was a slight croak in his voice. 'What are they?'

'In the morning,' Halt told him, 'just after first light, I'm going to release you.'

His tone was serious. There was no sign of sarcasm in his words and Colly felt a surge of hope.

'You'll let me go?'

Halt pursed his lips. 'Yes. But there is one condition attached.'

The surge of hope died as quickly as it had come. Colly looked at the Ranger suspiciously.

'A condition?' he prompted and Halt replied briskly.

'Yes. After all, you can't expect me to just turn you loose and say "no hard feelings", can you? You would have killed me if the opportunity had arisen. I'm willing to give you a chance to escape. Uphill.'

'Uphill? There's nothing up the hill,' Colly said, trying desperately to work out where this conversation was going.

'As a matter of fact there is. There's a bluff about twelve metres high, with a river running below it. The water's deep so it'll be quite safe for you to jump.' In his brief glimpse of the river, Halt had noticed that the fast-flowing water cut under the bluff in a sharp curve. That should mean that the bottom had been scoured out over the years. A thought struck him. 'You can swim, I assume?'

'Yes. I can swim,' Colly said. 'But I'm not going jumping off some bluff just because you say so!'

'No, no. Of course not. That'd be asking far too much of you. You'll jump off because if you don't, I'll shoot you. It'll be the same effect, really. If I have to shoot you, you'll fall off. But I thought I'd give you a chance to survive.' Halt paused, then added, 'Oh, and if you decide to run downhill, I'll also shoot you. Uphill and off is really your only chance of survival.'

'You can't be serious!' Colly said. 'Do you really . . .?'

But he got no further. Halt leaned forward, putting up a hand to stop the outburst. His face was quite close to Colly's as he spoke and his voice was very serious.

'Colly, take a good, long look into my eyes and tell me if you see anything, anything at all, that says I'm not deadly serious.'

His eyes were deep brown, almost black. They were steady and unwavering and there was no sign of anything there but utter determination. Colly looked at them and after a few seconds, his eyes dropped away. Halt nodded as the other man's gaze slid away from his.

'Good. Now we've got that settled, you should try to get some sleep. You have a big day ahead of you tomorrow.'

Ten

As they crested the last hill before the ground fell away to a flat plain, Will eased Tug to a stop.

'Hold it here, boy,' he said softly. He always enjoyed this moment, the moment when Redmont first came into view. The plain below spread away, cut by the Tarbus River, with Redmont village nestled along its banks. Then, on the far bank, the ground rose again to create the natural defensive position where Redmont stood — massive, solid and beginning to glow red in the late afternoon sun.

He remembered previous times he'd stopped here to draw breath: when he had almost finished the wild ride to alert the Baron and Sir Rodney about the Kalkara. And, more recently, in a happier time, when he had received Alyss's letter and ridden through the night to see her. His mouth moved in a slight smile at that thought. She was down there somewhere. He narrowed his eyes, peering into the distance to see if, just possibly, there was some sight of her tall, white-clad shape on the battlements or in the village or on the flat land in front of the castle. Not surprisingly, there was none. He shrugged, smiling at his fanciful expectation.

Away to one side, among the trees where the forest encroached on the open ground cleared around the castle, he caught a glimpse of the little cabin where he had spent his apprenticeship with Halt. The smile widened.

'We're home,' he said to Tug and the little horse tossed his head impatiently.

Not so long as we're standing here gawking, the action said and Will twitched the reins lightly on his horse's neck.

'All right. Let's get down there.'

Suddenly, they were both seized with the same sense of urgency to be home and Tug rocketed away from a standing start to a full gallop as only he could. Ranger horses were renowned for their amazing acceleration but there wasn't one in the Corps that could match Tug.

There were still workers in the fields and they looked up from their humdrum tasks of ploughing and sowing at the sound of the drumming hoofbeats. Several of them waved, recognising the slightly built figure on the stocky little horse as he thundered past them, crouched forward over Tug's neck, his mottled cloak streaming out behind.

For a brief moment, they wondered what news the fast-moving Ranger was bringing. Then, shrugging, they went back to their work. Whatever it was, good or bad, there were other people more qualified than they to deal with it. In the meantime, there was farming to be done.

There was always farming to be done.

Tug's hooves rattled briefly on the removable bridge across the Tarbus, then they began the final climb up to

Redmont itself. The sentries at the main gate had come to the ready position at the sound, alerted to the approach of the galloping horse. Then, recognising a Ranger, they relaxed, lowering their weapons — although they continued to watch with interest as he approached.

Will eased Tug down to a canter, then a trot, in the last twenty metres. He acknowledged the salute of the sentries as he rode across the moat and under the raised portcullis. One of the soldiers, who had grown up in the service of Redmont, called a greeting, in defiance of good discipline.

'Welcome back, Ranger Will!'

Will grinned and waved. 'Thanks, Jonathon. Good to be here.'

They trotted into the courtyard, the sound of Tug's hooves changing again as they went from wooden drawbridge to the cobbled surface of the castle forecourt. There were more people moving around here and they looked up curiously, wondering what had brought Will Treaty back to Redmont.

But Will didn't notice them because emerging from the bottom doorway of the main tower was a tall, graceful girl in an elegant white Courier's gown and he couldn't stop the ridiculous grin of pleasure that broke out across his face.

Alyss.

He dropped to the ground and she raced towards him, her usual air of dignity and reserve deserting her. She threw herself into his arms and they stood embracing, each drinking in the other's presence. Passers-by stopped to look and grin at the young couple, so unconscious to all around them.

'You're back,' she whispered, her voice muffled by the

fact that her face was pressed to the rough material of his cowl.

'I'm back,' he agreed, the light scent of the perfume she always wore filling his nostrils. Her long blonde hair was soft against his cheek. After several long moments, they were buffeted by a sudden shove and had to break the embrace to retain their balance. Tug was regarding them with slight embarrassment.

Cut it out. There are people watching.

Then he nudged Alyss's shoulder, urging her to notice him and stroke his soft muzzle.

I'm back too.

She laughed as she stroked him. 'Hullo, Tug. I'm glad to see you too.'

While she fussed over the horse, Will took her free hand and stood, simply looking at her, a huge grin pasted onto his face. Finally, they became aware of the small crowd who had gathered to watch them. Will turned and shrugged, his face reddening slightly.

'It's been a long time,' he said. A circle of smiling faces surrounded them. Nobody said anything and he indicated Alyss.

'Since we saw each other. A long time,' he elaborated. Several people nodded knowingly. One middle-aged gentleman tapped the side of his nose with that familiar gesture. Finally, since the spectators showed no sign of moving on, Will thought it was time to break up this little tableau. Like most Rangers, he had an aversion to being the centre of attention. He said to Alyss, out of the side of his mouth, 'Let's get out of here.'

Her own smile widened a little. 'Come on. We'll put Tug in the stables. Then you'd better report to the Baron.'

He nodded and they turned, hand in hand still, to lead Tug to the stables. Alyss knew that Will would see his horse cared for before anything else. That was the Ranger way. Behind them, the small crowd broke up, going about their separate endeavours. Some of them looked after the young couple, smiling approval. Alyss was a popular figure in Castle Redmont and the entire population took great pride in Will's achievements. He was a local, after all. They approved of the obvious affection between them.

'Any sign of Halt yet?' Will asked.

Alyss's smile faded a little. 'No. I think Lady Pauline is becoming a little worried. She tries not to show it but I can tell she's uneasy.'

Will considered this. It had been a long time since Halt had someone to worry about him, he thought.

'That's natural, I suppose,' he said. 'But Halt can look after himself.'

Halt was Halt, after all, and Will couldn't conceive of any person or situation that he couldn't handle. Alyss nodded. She was concerned because Pauline, her mentor, was worried. But Will knew Halt's capabilities better than anyone and if he wasn't worried, she felt there was no need for anyone else to be anxious.

'I suppose you're right,' she said. Then, changing the subject, she said: 'So you've decided to join this special group of Crowley's?'

'Yes,' he replied. 'I assume you approve?'

She looked sidelong at him. 'Let me put it this way. If you'd declined, I would have come after you and dragged you back here feet first until you came to your senses.'

'That might have been fun,' he murmured and she jerked at his arm in mock anger. He noticed that she didn't let go of his hand, however. As they approached the stable, one of the younger grooms hurried eagerly out to meet them.

'Good afternoon, Ranger Will,' he said, and made a gesture of welcome with his arms spread wide, as if inviting Will to inspect conditions in the stable. 'May I look after the famous Tug for you?'

Will hesitated for a second. He had been trained to look after Tug himself and not assume that someone else would do it for him. He felt a nudge against his shoulder. Tug, of course.

Hear that? The famous *Tug.*

At the same time, Alyss squeezed his hand. She could see that the stable hand would be bitterly disappointed if his offer were refused. For a young man like him, Will was a figure to be admired and looked up to. He was Will Treaty, with a list of accomplishments and famous deeds as long as your arm. It would be a privilege to take care of his horse. And she loved Will all the more because he didn't realise the fact.

'I'd be honoured, Ranger,' the groom added.

'Let him do it,' Alyss said softly. Will shrugged and passed the reins to him.

'Very well . . .' He hesitated. He didn't know the youth's name.

'It's Ben, Ranger. Ben Dooley.'

'Very well, Ben Dooley. I'm sure you'll take excellent care of the *famous* Tug.' He looked meaningfully at the little horse. 'And you behave yourself.'

Tug came as close as a horse could to raising one eyebrow. He looked at Will and Alyss, still hand in hand.

You're talking?

Will realised, not for the first time, that he would never get the last word with this horse. He shook his head ruefully.

'Let's go see the Baron,' he said.

So much was familiar. So many sights and sensations and memories came crowding back to him as he climbed the steps to Baron Arald's office. Again, Will felt Alyss twitch his arm.

'Remember *that* day?' she said. She didn't need to say which day. She meant the day when she and Will and Horace, along with Jenny and George, had climbed these stairs to be chosen by their eventual masters. In truth it was only a matter of years but it seemed as if decades had passed.

'Who could forget it?' he asked. 'What's George up to these days?'

'He's become one of the fief's leading defence attorneys,' she said. 'He's in great demand for legal matters.'

Will shook his head. 'He always had a brain for them, didn't he? And Jenny? Is she still working with Master Chubb?'

She smiled. 'No, much to his disappointment. He sees her as his finest creation and he'd love to have her with him. But some time back, she told him, "Master Chubb, there's not room in this kitchen for two artists such as we. I need to find my own space."'

'And did she?'

'She did indeed. She bought a share of the inn at

Redmont village and runs one of the finest dining halls for miles around. Chubb's a regular customer, too.'

'Really?'

'Really. Apparently, one night he made a suggestion, very politely, I must say, that perhaps a dish might benefit from a hint more spice. She told him, "Less is more, Master Chubb. Less is more." And then she rapped him on the head with her ladle.'

Will was incredulous. He couldn't imagine anyone with the nerve to rap Chubb on the head.

'I guess it was ladles at ten paces after that?' he said but Alyss shook her head.

'On the contrary. He very meekly apologised. Secretly, I think he loved it. He's *very* proud of her. Here we are,' she added as they arrived at the anteroom to the Baron's office. Reluctantly, she released his hand. 'I'll leave you to report in. Come and find me later.'

She leaned forward, kissed him lightly on the lips and slipped away, waving her hand in a farewell gesture behind her. She skipped down the steps. It was such an excellent day, she thought.

Will watched her go. Then he turned, gathered his thoughts and knocked on the door to the Baron's anteroom.

Eleven

The first hint of daylight was showing over the top of the bluff. Off to the right and left, it was already touching the treetops where the mass of the steep hill didn't cast a long shadow. That suited Halt's purpose ideally. When the sun finally broke clear of the top of the bluff, it would be in the eyes of the men at the bottom of the hill, adding to their uncertainty.

Colly was dozing uncomfortably as Halt released the thumb and toe cuffs, wrinkling his nose once more as he came close to the man's feet. Then he stepped back and nudged him with the toe of his boot, his hand ready on the hilt of his saxe.

As he woke, realisation dawned in the criminal's eyes that his hands and feet were free. He tried to rise quickly, but the stiff, cramped muscles in his arms and legs defeated him. He cried out in pain and rolled onto his side, making helpless little scrabbling movements.

'It'll take a few minutes for those muscles to loosen up,'

Halt told him. 'So don't try anything foolish. In the meantime, slip off your jacket.'

Colly, lying on his side, looked up at him. 'My jacket?'

Halt raised an eyebrow impatiently.

'Your ears aren't cramped,' he said. 'Take off the jacket.'

Slowly, Colly worked himself into a sitting position and unbuttoned his thigh-length over-jacket. He tossed it to one side, then looked a question at Halt. The Ranger nodded.

'So far so good. Now put on the cloak beside you.'

For the first time, Colly noticed that Halt's camouflage cloak was lying on the ground near him. Clumsily, he threw it round his shoulders and fastened it in place. He had obviously decided that there was no future in asking questions. And besides, he was beginning to understand what Halt had in mind.

'Now let's get you on your feet,' Halt said. He gripped one of Colly's forearms and hauled him upright. For a second or two, Colly stood unmoving, testing the feeling in his arms and legs. Then, rather predictably, he tried to throw a punch at Halt. Halt ducked under the wild blow, then, stepping in and pivoting his upper body, he hit Colly with a palm strike to the jaw, sending him sprawling again.

'Don't try that again,' he said. There was no anger in his voice. Just a calm certainty that he could handle anything Colly attempted. While the Outsider clambered shakily to his feet again, Halt slid on the thick woollen jacket he had discarded. His nose twitched again at the combined smells of grease, sweat and dirt.

'This is nearly as bad as your socks,' he muttered.

Then, stooping, he picked up Colly's narrow-brimmed felt hat and placed it on his own head.

'Move around a little,' he told his prisoner. 'Shake your arms and legs to get the blood flowing. I want you in top form when you start up the hill.'

Colly's jaw set in a stubborn line as he tried once more for defiance.

'I ain't running up that hill,' he said.

Halt shrugged. 'Then die here. They're the only two choices you have.'

For the second time, Colly looked into those dark eyes and saw no sign of pity or compromise there. And for the second time, his gaze dropped from the other man's. He began to shake his arms and legs, grimacing with pain as blood flowed back into his muscles. While he did so, Halt retrieved his longbow and quiver, slinging the latter around his shoulders with one easy movement.

After a few minutes, when he judged that the man's movements had become easier, Halt motioned for him to stop. He beckoned him towards the uphill side of the rock outcrop that sheltered them from sight.

'All right, here's what's going to happen. When I give you the word, you're going to start running up the hill.' He saw a momentary gleam of cunning in Colly's eyes, which the outlaw tried unsuccessfully to conceal.

'If you try anything else, I'll put an arrow through the fleshy part of your calf. Not enough to stop you running, but enough to cause a great amount of pain. Are we clear?'

Colly nodded, his brief moment of defiance fading away.

'Good. Now I'm going to stand here waving and yelling. When you hear me start, run harder.'

'They'll think I'm you,' Colly said, indicating the treeline at the bottom of the hill where his companions lay in wait. Halt nodded.

'And they'll think I'm you. That's the general idea.'

'So they'll chase me up the hill,' Colly said.

This time, Halt shook his head. 'Not if you jump off into the river. They'll go down and around the base of the hill to the river bank to go after you. Which will leave the way clear for me.'

'What if I don't jump?' Colly asked.

'But you will jump. You'll notice there's no worthwhile cover at the top of the bluff.'

Colly looked again. The grim stranger was right. There were no trees or rocks at the top of the bluff, just long grass, but not long enough to cover him. He swallowed nervously.

'If you stop at the top of the bluff, I'll put an arrow ten centimetres above your head. Just to show you I can.'

Colly frowned, a little puzzled. Then Halt continued.

'Then, five seconds after that, I'll put an arrow twenty centimetres *below* your head. Got that?'

Colly glanced down nervously. Twenty centimetres below his head would put the arrow right in the middle of his chest. He nodded his understanding.

'Got it,' he said. His throat was dry and the words came out as a hoarse whisper. He watched as Halt drew an arrow from the quiver and, in one movement, nocked it to the string of his massive longbow.

'So, let's get ready. I'm told a nice morning run is good for the health.' He paused, then added with a hard edge, 'And a nice swim is even better.'

Colly's eyes flicked from Halt to the open ground above them, then down to the treeline where his companions were still concealed.

'I meant what I said,' Halt told him. 'And just so you know I can hit what I aim at, do you see that rotten tree stump, about forty metres up the hill?'

Colly peered in the direction Halt had indicated and made out an old blackened tree stump about a metre high. It was the only standing remnant of a tree that had been struck by lightning some years ago. The rest of the tree, gradually being devoured by rot, lay angled down the hill below it. He nodded.

'I see it. What about it?'

'When you draw level with it, I'm going to put an arrow in it. See where there's the beginning of an old branch jutting out to the right?'

Again Colly nodded. The remains of the branch were only just visible at this distance.

'That's where the arrow's going to hit. If I miss the mark, you might think you have a chance to start running back downhill.'

Colly opened his mouth to say something when Halt forestalled him.

'But I won't miss. And remember, you're a lot bigger than that branch.'

Colly swallowed again. His throat was very dry. 'Can I have some water?' he asked. Anything to put off the moment when he started uphill. He knew what Halt had said he was going to do. But he couldn't help wondering if the Ranger wouldn't simply shoot him down once he reached the top of the bluff. After all, that would cause his companions to come running uphill after him, leaving the way clear for Halt to make his escape downhill.

Halt gave him that cold little smile again. 'Of course,' he said. 'All you want. Just as soon as you hit the river. Now get going.'

Still Colly hesitated. Halt flexed the bowstring experimentally. There was no practical purpose in the movement, other than to draw Colly's attention to the broad-headed arrow nocked on the string. Halt frowned as the Outsider still hesitated. The sun had lifted above the edge of the bluff now and it was at its most dazzling for the men below.

'GO!' he shouted suddenly, making a lunging motion towards Colly at the same time.

The loud noise and sudden threatening movement galvanised his prisoner into action. Colly broke from cover and began to run up the hill, his legs pumping, the camouflage cloak billowing out behind him. Halt let him get twenty metres away then stepped out of cover himself, waving and shouting to the unseen men he knew would be watching from below.

'He's getting away!' he yelled. 'He's getting away! After him!'

He heard shouting from the trees and the sudden surprised yelping of the dogs as they were roused by their handlers. A few men appeared from the shadows of the trees and hesitated uncertainly, watching the man in the Ranger's cloak as he ran. Then more of the watchers broke cover.

'He's getting away! Get after him!' Halt yelled. He turned and glanced uphill. Colly was almost at the tree stump. Halt stepped back behind a rock to conceal his actions from the men below. Casually, he brought the bow to full draw and released, in one smooth motion. At a forty-metre range, even shooting uphill, he had to allow only a minimum amount for drop. The arrow hissed away from the bow.

Almost at the tree stump, Colly heard the arrow split the air to his left, then smack into the rotten branch of the stump, which disintegrated into a shower of splinters under the impact. Even though Halt had warned him what would happen, he couldn't believe that anyone could manage the shot that he'd just seen. He shied sideways, away from the stump, in a reflex action — far too late, of course, to do him any good — and redoubled his efforts, driving his legs as hard as he could.

Now the Outsiders were moving out of the trees in greater numbers. Some of them were beginning to start up the hill after Colly. But there was no real urgency in them so far. They knew there was nowhere for the running man to go. The tracking dogs were yelping furiously, restrained on their long leashes by their handlers. Halt counted about a dozen men. At least, he thought gratefully, they hadn't loosed another of the war dogs.

He glanced back at Colly, now labouring against the steep slope of the last few metres of the hill. He knew the man would hesitate at the bluff. It was inconceivable that he wouldn't. He had another arrow on the string and his eyes narrowed as he judged speed and distance and estimated his arrow's flight time. Colly was a few paces from the edge of the bluff when Halt drew the arrow back until he felt his right forefinger touch lightly against the corner of his mouth, sighted and released.

The arrow sped uphill in a shallow arc.

Colly was staggering, his breath coming in ragged gasps, as he reached the bluff. Below him, still in shadow, the water of the river was a black sheet. There was no way he could tell if it were deep enough for him to jump and, as Halt had predicted, he hesitated, looking back down the hill to the figure by the rocks.

A second after he had stopped, he heard a hissing, whistling sound and actually felt the passage of Halt's shot as the arrow passed a few centimetres above his head. Just as the Ranger had said it would.

His sides were aching with the effort of the mad uphill run. His chest was heaving and he doubled over, trying for breath. He saw the Ranger's right arm go up as he drew another arrow from the quiver over his shoulder. Very deliberately, the Ranger nocked the arrow and raised the bow again, bringing the string back to full draw.

Colly could feel a burning sensation in his chest. The point where Halt had said the next arrow would go. He remembered the smashing impact of the first arrow on the tree stump and the sudden lurch of terror as the second arrow had passed within a hand's breadth of his head. All this flashed through his mind in a second as he watched the figure below him and he knew that he had only one chance to survive.

He jumped. He howled with fear all the way down, then smashed into the surface of the river in an enormous explosion of spray. He sank deep under the surface but there was no sign of the bottom. In fact, the river at this point was at least fifteen metres deep. Then, with an enormous sense of relief that he had survived the drop, he began to claw his way back up. His left knee had been twisted and wrenched by the impact with the water and a lance of pain shot through him as he kicked for the surface. He cried out, swallowed water and remembered too late to keep his mouth shut. Coughing and spluttering, his head broke the surface and he gasped for air, swimming sideways to ease the pain in his knee as he stroked weakly for the bank.

On the hillside, the pursuers had stopped as the cloaked figure hurled himself off the bluff. They were familiar with the territory and knew the river lay below him. Now they paused, but a voice from above directed them.

'He's in the river! Cut round the bottom of the hill and head him off!'

Several of the quicker-witted among them saw the gesticulating figure, whom they took to be the scout sent out during the night. He was waving them back and to one side and they realised the sense of what he was saying. There was no point continuing to the top unless they wanted to jump after their quarry. Back down the hill and round to the river bank was the quickest way.

'Come on!' shouted a burly dog handler. 'Get to the river bank!'

He gestured for his dogs to lead and he ran, following them. All it took was one man to start the movement and the others fell in with him. Halt watched with grim satisfaction as the knot of men plunged back downhill, angling off to the left to reach the river bank below the bluff.

As the last of them disappeared from view, he clicked his fingers twice. Abelard stepped clear of the rocks where they had sheltered through the night. Halt swung easily up onto his horse's back. Abelard twisted his head to look accusingly at his master, taking in the greasy woollen jacket that had belonged to Colly.

'I know,' Halt said resignedly. 'But his socks were even worse.'

He set Abelard to a lope and they moved quickly down the hill. As they reached the cover of the trees, Halt did a strange thing. Instead of turning east, back towards Redmont, he swung Abelard's head north-west, back to the fishing village. Again, Abelard turned his head to look inquiringly at his master. Halt patted the shaggy mane reassuringly.

'I know. But there's something I need to attend to,' he said and Abelard tossed his head. So long as his master knew what he was doing, he was content.

Farrell, the leader of the Outsiders group, was having an uncomfortable time trying to calm the villagers. They were openly suspicious that he and his people had played a hand in the unsuccessful raid on the boats. As Farrell tried to reassure them that he knew nothing about the raiders, he could sense their disbelief growing.

Might be time to move on, he thought. He could allay their suspicions for a short time, but in the long run, it would be safer to take what they had gained so far and try their luck elsewhere.

'Wilfred,' he was saying now to the village head man, 'I assure you that my people are innocent of any wrongdoing. You know us. We're just simple religious folk.'

'Funny how all these troubles have started since you "simple religious folk" have turned up, though, isn't it?' Wilfred said accusingly.

Farrell spread his hands in a gesture of innocence. 'Coincidence, my friend. My people and I will pray for you and your village to be protected from further misfortune. I assure you . . .'

There was the sound of a scuffle outside the entrance to the marquee that Farrell was using as a headquarters and main centre of worship. Then a bearded stranger burst through the entrance. At least, Farrell thought he was a stranger. Then he realised there was something familiar about him.

The newcomer was shorter than average height, dressed in simple brown leggings and boots and a dull green jacket. A massive longbow was in his hand and a quiver of arrows was slung over his shoulder. Then something in Farrell's memory clicked.

'You!' he said in surprise. 'What are you doing here?'

Halt ignored him. He addressed his remarks to Wilfred.

'You've been robbed,' he said briefly. 'This man and his band are about to run out on you. And they'll be taking the gold and jewellery you've given them.'

Wilfred's gaze, which had been drawn to Halt at his sudden entrance, now switched back to Farrell. His eyes were narrow with suspicion. Farrell forced a nervous laugh, indicating the massive golden altar that dominated the far end of the marquee.

'I told you, we used the gold to build our altar — so we could pray for your people! D'you think we're going to just walk away with that? It's solid gold! It must weigh tons!'

'Not quite,' Halt said. He strode quickly towards the altar, the villagers following him uncertainly, Wilfred making sure that Farrell came along with them.

Halt drew his saxe knife with a soft hiss and sliced its razor edge along one gleaming side of the golden altar. The thin veneer of gold leaf that had covered it peeled away, revealing the plain wood beneath it.

'Not as solid as it looks,' Halt said and he heard an angry growl from the villagers as they moved to encircle Farrell. The Outsider's eyes flicked from Halt to the circle of hostile faces around him. His mouth opened as he instinctively tried to think of some plausible explanation for the deception, then closed as he realised there was none.

'They used a small amount of gold to coat the wooden altar. The rest of it is probably in sacks underneath, ready to be taken away tonight.'

Wilfred gestured and one of the younger men moved forward, roughly tearing the altar covering away. Under the altar was a neat pile of sacks. The villager toed one and it emitted a metallic jingle. The head man glared at Farrell, who was standing white-faced with fear. He tried to move behind Halt, as if hoping that the Ranger might protect him.

'You're a dead man, Farrell,' Wilfred said in an ominously quiet voice.

But Halt shook his head. 'You've got your gold back. Be grateful for that. But you're not taking him. I need him to answer some questions.'

'And who do you think you are, telling us what to do?' said the young man who had removed the altar cloth. Halt turned his unwavering gaze on him.

'I'm the man who just saved you a fortune,' he said. 'And the other night, I saved your boats from burning.

Be grateful you still have your money and your livelihood. You can keep the others. Do what you like with them. But I'm taking this one with me.'

The young man started to reply but a curt gesture from Wilfred stopped him. The head man stepped forward to face Halt.

'I assume you have some kind of authority to make these demands,' he said.

Halt nodded. 'I'm an Araluan Ranger,' he replied.

There was a murmur of recognition around the pavilion. The villagers might not be part of any fief, but they knew the reputation of the Ranger Corps. Taking advantage of the villagers' moment of uncertainty, Halt gripped Farrell by the elbow and started towards the entrance to the marquee. After a moment's hesitation, the group parted to allow them through.

As he emerged with his prisoner into the warm morning sunlight, past the unconscious form of the Outsider guard who had tried to stop him, Halt was frowning slightly. He was remembering Farrell's words when he had pushed his way into the marquee.

You? What are you doing here? The words, and Farrell's manner, implied that the Outsider priest had recognised Halt. And that was why the Ranger frowned now.

Because he knew they had never met before.

Twelve

The dining room at the inn was crammed full of customers, almost every table filled with noisy, happy diners from the village and the castle. Will and Alyss sat at the table of honour, right in the middle of the room, underneath a wheel-shaped chandelier that held two dozen candles.

Will had grimaced at the table when they were shown to it. Typically, he would have preferred to be tucked away in a corner, out of sight. He preferred to see and not be seen. Alyss grinned at him, noticing his moment of hesitation.

'Get used to it,' she said. 'You're a celebrity. Some people actually enjoy that, you know.'

He frowned. 'How could anyone enjoy having every eye in the room on them?' he asked. He was still casting around for a table in a less prominent position.

'Nevertheless, people do. I'm surprised there aren't crowds of sketch artists outside the entrance, waiting to draw our pictures as we leave.'

'Does that really happen?' he asked, incredulously. Alyss shrugged.

'So I'm told.' She shoved him gently towards the table. 'Come on, Jenny will be disappointed if she can't show you off.'

And here was Jenny herself, threading her way through the crowded room, with a delighted smile lighting up her pretty face. A large wooden ladle, symbol of her office, dangled loosely from her right hand.

'Will!' she shrieked. 'You're here at last! Welcome to my humble dining hall!'

She threw her arms around him and he ducked instinctively, expecting the ladle in her right hand to whip round and crack the back of his head. But Jenny had it under control. She laughed at him.

'Oh, come on! I haven't hit anyone since second year! At least, not anyone I didn't mean to hit. Sit down! Sit down!'

Will hurried to hold Alyss's chair, while Jenny watched approvingly. He'd always had nice manners, she thought. Then he took his own chair and looked around the room, gesturing to the crowds of diners.

'Not so humble. There must be fifty or sixty people in here!'

Jenny appraised the room with a practised eye. 'They're not all diners, however. Some are just here for a drink.'

'The place is usually this full,' Alyss put in. But Jenny shook her head.

'There are extras here tonight. Word got out that the famous Will Treaty and his beautiful girlfriend would be dining here and the bookings just flowed in.'

Will reddened slightly but Alyss took the comment in her stride. She and Jenny had known each other since childhood, after all.

'How did that word get out, I wonder?' she said with a raised eyebrow. Jenny grinned at her and spread her hands innocently.

'I have no idea. But it's great for business.' She looked back at Will, her smile widening. 'It really is wonderful to see you again. It's been too long. And I believe you'll be staying with us from now on?'

Will's eyes widened in surprise. 'How did you know that?' He had assumed that the facts about Crowley's Special Task Group were secret.

Jenny shrugged carelessly. 'Oh, I heard about it a few weeks ago. Someone mentioned it. Not sure who.'

Will shook his head. He'd only been told within the past five days. It never ceased to amaze him how quickly people found out about so-called secrets. Jenny didn't notice his reaction.

'Will there be just the two of you?' she asked.

Alyss shook her head. 'Lady Pauline will be joining us.'

Jenny's smile widened even further. 'You people are going all out to give my little establishment a good name, aren't you?' she said.

Alyss shook her head. 'You don't need us to do it.'

Jenny rubbed her hands briskly. It was time to get down to business.

'Now, did you want to order? Or shall I do it for you?'

Will sensed her eagerness to show off her skills. He set both hands palm down on the table in a gesture of readiness.

'I think we'd be mad to refuse your offer,' he said.

Jenny clicked her fingers at a passing table boy. 'Set another place here, Rafe,' she said. The boy, a heavy-boned youth of about sixteen, looked as if he'd be more at home behind a plough or a blacksmith's furnace but he nodded eagerly.

'Yes, Mistress Jenny,' he said. Clumsily, he began to lay cutlery and another platter in the place she'd indicated. The tip of his tongue protruded slightly at the corner of his mouth with the effort of trying to remember where everything went.

'I've got a rather nice first course,' Jenny said. 'I've deboned some quail and stuffed them with a mix of cranberries and apples, lightly spiced, then poached them in a red wine sauce.'

Without breaking her flow, or even looking at the table server beside her, she flicked her wrist, swinging the ladle in a diagonal arc so that it cracked noisily on Rafe's head.

Will winced but he had to admire her accuracy and skill.

'Knife on the right, fork on the left, all right? I've *told* you that, Rafe.'

Rafe looked at the offending implements in some confusion. His lips moved as he repeated the mantra, *knife on the right, fork on the left.* Jenny sighed patiently.

'Hold up your right hand,' she said. Rafe hesitated, his eyes fixed warily on the ladle, swinging in a gentle arc like a snake about to strike. 'The hand you write with,' she prompted.

'I don't write,' he said in a dejected tone. To her credit, Jenny was a little taken aback, fearing that she'd embarrassed the boy. She was, after all, only trying to teach him so that he might have a career other than plodding along in the wake of a plough horse.

'The hand you fight with,' Will put in. 'Your sword hand.'

Rafe's face cleared and a wide smile spread across it as he raised his muscular right arm. Jenny smiled at Will.

'Thanks, Will,' she said. 'Good thinking. All right, Rafe, that's your right hand, your sword hand. And a sword is like a big knife really, so that's the side the knife goes. All right?'

'Tha's fine,' Rafe replied happily. 'Why didn't you tell it to me like that before?'

Jenny sighed. 'I suppose I never thought of it because I'm not a famous Ranger,' she said. The irony was wasted on Rafe.

'Nay, mistress. But thee's a fine cook, I'll say that for thee.'

Confidently, he switched the knife and fork to their proper places. Then he checked to make sure he was right, wielding an a imaginary sword. Satisfied, he nodded and turned to Jenny.

'Will there be any more, mistress?'

'No. Thank you, Rafe. That'll be all for now.'

He grinned and bowed slightly to her and her guests, then ambled contentedly back towards the kitchen.

'He's a nice boy,' she said. 'I'm hoping I can turn him into a good head waiter one of these days.' She hesitated, then amended the statement. 'One of these years.'

Will looked at her appraisingly. He had noticed there was something different about her when she had first approached the table. Now he realised what it was.

'You've lost weight, Jen,' he said. He wasn't the smoothest operator when it came to girls but he knew that was something that all girls liked hearing. And in Jenny's case, it was the truth. She still had what might be described as a full figure, but she had fined down somewhat. Jenny beamed, then twisted to look over her shoulder, trying to assess herself from behind.

'You think so? Maybe a little. It's funny, when you run a restaurant, you don't get so much time to eat. Tasting, yes. Eating? No.'

'It suits you,' he said. He thought that Gilan would be interested to see Jenny looking like this. The tall Ranger had been quite taken with her when they first met at Halt and Pauline's wedding. Later, on the journey to Arrida, he had asked Will about her several times.

She smiled at him, then rubbed her hands together briskly, getting back to business.

'The main course is a rack of lamb, seasoned in oil and lemon juice and rosemary. I'll be doing that with new potatoes, roasted alongside the lamb, and wilted green vegetables. Or I have a beautiful fresh turbot that I can steam and serve with ginger and a little chili. Which would you prefer?'

Alyss and Will exchanged glances. She knew what he was thinking and answered for him.

'We'll have the lamb,' she said.

Jenny nodded. 'Good choice. And then . . . hullo, here's Lady Pauline.'

She'd noticed a slight movement at the entrance and as Alyss and Will turned to follow her gaze, they saw the tall figure of Lady Pauline entering the restaurant. A few paces behind her, and somehow seeming to fade into the background, was another figure — a cloaked and cowled Ranger.

'Halt!' said Will, rising from his seat, a wide smile of welcome starting to spread over his features. Then the smile faded as the Ranger threw back his cowl and he saw the sandy hair and beard. 'Crowley!' he said in surprise. 'What's he doing here?'

Jenny frowned slightly, trying to assess whether her main dish would stretch to another diner. Then, remembering the keen appetite that most Rangers displayed, she decided it wouldn't.

'Tell me later,' she said, turning away. 'I'd better get another lamb rack in the oven.'

As she hurried to the kitchen, they heard her calling, 'Rafe! Another setting at table one!'

Alyss had risen as well and was beckoning to her mentor. Lady Pauline saw her and led the way through the crowded room to the table. She seemed to glide, Will thought. He noticed that all conversation had died away in the room as the other occupants stared expectantly at the two Rangers and their Courier companions. This gathering, they sensed, was something out of the ordinary.

The two newcomers joined Will and Alyss. Lady Pauline beamed at the young Ranger and leaned forward to kiss him lightly on the cheek. Like Halt, she had come to look upon Will as a son.

'How lovely to see you here, Will. I'm so glad you decided to come home.'

He knew she was referring to his decision to join Halt in the Task Group. He smiled at her.

'Someone has to keep Halt out of trouble, my lady.'

She nodded gravely at him. 'That's exactly what I've been thinking. He's not getting any younger, after all,' she replied. 'And Will, that's enough of the "my lady" if you don't mind. I think "Pauline" will do quite nicely.'

'Very well, Pauline.' He tried the name out and found that he quite liked it. They smiled at each other across the table.

Crowley cleared his throat noisily. 'I assume you *were* planning to greet your Corps Commandant, weren't you, Will? I know I'm just another silver-haired dodderer like Halt but you could say hello, at least. Alyss, you're looking more beautiful by the moment,' he added before Will could respond.

'You're a silver-tongued flatterer, Crowley,' Alyss replied easily. 'Welcome to Redmont.'

Will finally had an opportunity to speak. 'Yes. Welcome, Crowley. And tell me, what brings you here?'

Crowley was about to reply when Rafe appeared beside him, a bundle of knives, forks and platters in his arms. He hesitated a moment, shifted the load to his left arm and mimed a sword stroke in the air. Crowley looked over his shoulder at the serving boy with some concern.

'Planning on beheading me, are you?' he asked.

Rafe smiled at him. 'No sir, Ranger. Just getting the right side, like. Just shift yourself over while I put these down, before I forget which side is which now.'

Crowely glanced a question at Will. The younger Ranger shrugged.

'Jenny's training him as a head waiter,' he explained. Crowley glanced sideways at the server, whose lips were moving, framing the words *knives on the right, forks on the left, platter in the middle*.

'She's got a way to go then,' he said. Then, as Rafe finished and moved away, he replied to Will's question.

'What brings me here is Halt,' he said. 'He sent me a pigeon message from one of our West Coast stations two days ago. Asked me to meet him here. Asked for Horace to come as well — he'll be following in a day or so. Had a few loose ends to tie up.'

Knowing the value of speedy communications, Crowley had recently set up a network of message stations around the Kingdom. At each one, a station manager looked after a flock of homing pigeons, trained to return to Crowley's headquarters in Castle Araluen.

At the mention of Halt's name, Will leaned forward eagerly.

'Did he say what it was all about?' he asked. But Crowley shook his head.

'Said he'd tell us when he got here. I actually expected he might get here before me.'

'I was delayed. I had a prisoner to drag along,' said a familiar voice behind him.

'Halt!' Will sprang to his feet in delight. None of them had noticed the Ranger's entry into the room, nor his silent approach. Now Will hurried around the table, upsetting his chair as he went to embrace his teacher.

'So what's this all about?' he asked. Then, before Halt could answer, he continued with a barrage of further questions. 'Who's this prisoner you mentioned? Where have you been? Why did you want Horace to come here as well? Have we got our first mission? Where are we going?'

Halt broke from his bearhug and rolled his eyes to heaven.

'Questions, questions, questions!' he said. 'Now I remember what you were like, I wonder if I haven't made a terrible mistake. Would you mind terribly if I said hello to my wife before we go any further?'

But as he turned to embrace Pauline, he couldn't keep up the pretence that he was displeased. A smile was lurking at the corner of his mouth, breaking through in spite of his best efforts to stop it.

Jenny, emerging from the kitchen, saw the extra person at the table and spun on her heel.

'Frances!' she called. 'Fetch another lamb rack from the cool room. And Rafe . . .'

'I know, I know, mistress! Another setting at table one!'

Thirteen

The meal was excellent. Halt insisted that they should enjoy the food without being distracted by discussing business.

'Time enough for that when we have coffee,' he said firmly. He successfully dodged the subject of what he had been doing by asking for details of the Gathering – the first he'd missed in many years. He smiled quietly as Will described his effort with the three first-year apprentices, and nodded in satisfaction when he heard of Gilan's promotion to Whitby Fief – and the fact that he would be available to take over Redmont if Halt and Will were sent on a mission.

'I wondered how you'd manage that,' he said to Crowley. 'Good thinking.'

Crowley smiled, in a self-satisfied way. 'As I told Will, I'm a genius when it comes to organisation,' he said. Halt raised an eyebrow at that but made no further comment.

Then at Halt's prompting, Lady Pauline brought him

up to date on events at Castle Redmont since he'd been gone. His eyes widened when she related how Sir Rodney, head of the Battleschool, had recently been keeping company with Lady Margaret, a rather attractive widow.

'Rodney?' he asked, incredulously. 'But he's a dyed-in-the-wool, cranky old bachelor!'

'Just what they used to say about you,' Pauline replied calmly and he nodded, conceding the point.

'So, Rodney ready to settle down, eh? Who would have thought it? I suppose you'll be next, Crowley?'

Crowley shook his head. 'Married to the job, Halt. And never found the right woman.'

In truth, Crowley had long harboured a deeply felt admiration for Lady Pauline. But, being one of the few people in the Kingdom who knew how things stood between her and Halt, he had never let the fact be known.

Eventually, the meal was finished and Rafe set the coffee pot and cups out on the table, fortunately without having to resort to any phantom sword brandishing.

Pauline watched with a tolerant smile as Halt took a long sip of his coffee, smacking his lips in appreciation. Then he set his cup down and leaned forward, elbows on the table.

'Right!' he said. 'Let's get to it. The Outsiders are back in business and they're planning on returning to Araluen. Just as soon as they've got Hibernia under their thumbs.'

'Hibernia?' Lady Pauline said in surprise. 'What are they doing there?'

'Basically, taking control of the country,' Halt told her. 'When we chased them out of Araluen, some of them made it to Hibernia. They've been waiting there, gathering strength and numbers and gradually undermining the six kingdoms. They've almost completed that task. They've got control of five of the kingdoms. Only Clonmel is left — and that's due to go soon.'

'Clonmel?' said Crowley. 'That's where you came from, isn't it, Halt?'

Will looked up in interest as Halt nodded. He'd always had a vague idea that Halt had originally come from Hibernia but this was the first time he'd heard it confirmed.

'Yes,' he said. 'King Ferris of Clonmel is weak. And like all the Hibernian kings, he's so busy worrying that one of the other kings is about to betray him or usurp his throne, he's missed the real threat.'

'These Outsiders are getting ambitious, aren't they?' Lady Pauline said. 'They used to be thieves and criminals, which was bad enough. But now you say they're actually seizing power in Hibernia?'

Halt nodded. 'They create chaos and fear throughout the countryside. When the king is too weak or self-centred to protect his people, they step in and offer to solve the problem.'

'Easy for them to do, of course,' Crowley put in, 'since they're the ones causing it.'

'That's right,' Halt replied. 'Pretty soon, they're seen as the only people who can keep the peace. They gain power and influence. More and more converts join their band and from there it's a short step to taking control.'

Will frowned. 'But why do the Hibernian kings stand for it? Surely they can see they're being undermined?'

'The leader of the Outsiders is a man called Tennyson,' Halt told him. 'And he's been clever enough not to oppose any of the kings directly. He lets them stay on the throne — but he takes effective control of the kingdom. He assumes all the real power and influence and money.'

'While the king retains the appearance of being in charge?' Pauline asked.

'That's right. And for most of them so far, that's enough.'

'They can't be much use as kings then,' Will said in disgust.

Halt nodded, a look of sadness in his eyes. 'They're not. They're weak and self-interested. And that's created an opportunity for a strong, charismatic leader like this Tennyson to step in and provide leadership and a sense of stability. He's already managed it in five of the kingdoms. Now it looks as if Clonmel will be next.'

'Halt.' Crowley leaned forward in his turn now, his eyes seeking out those of his old friend. 'All of this is tragic for Hibernia, of course. But how does it concern Araluen? I'm sorry if I sound a little cold-blooded there, but I'm sure you take my meaning.'

Will looked quickly between the two senior Rangers. He could see what Crowley meant. Halt was affected by this because he was Hibernian by birth. But what did it have to do with his adopted homeland?

'I do indeed, Crowley,' Halt was saying. 'No need to apologise. It affects us because once Tennyson has taken control in Clonmel, the last of the six Hibernian kingdoms, he's planning to use it as a base to return to Araluen.'

'You know this for a fact?' Crowley asked.

Halt nodded. 'I have a prisoner who'll swear to it,' he said. 'His name is Farrell and he was sent to prepare a foothold in Araluen – at the port of Selsey. That's where I've been,' he added. 'It's a safe harbour and it's out of the way. Just the place Tennyson would choose to bring his damned cult back here.'

'And you're suggesting that we should stop him before he does so,' Lady Pauline said. Halt glanced at her.

'You don't wait for a snake to bite you before you kill it,' he told her. 'I'd rather stop them now before they gather any more momentum.'

'Do you think that you're up to the task? Just you and Will?' Crowley asked.

'And Horace,' Halt added.

The Commandant nodded, conceding the point.

'And Horace. You don't think you need a larger force?'

'We can hardly invade Hibernia. King Ferris hasn't asked for our help. Nor is he likely to. I think we're better suited fighting trickery and superstition with more trickery and superstition. There's an old Hibernian legend about a master swordsman from the east that I thought I could make use of.'

'Horace, naturally,' Will put in and his old teacher smiled at him.

'Exactly. I feel we can approach King Ferris of Clonmel and convince him to resist the Outsiders. If we can break their power in Clonmel, we can roll them back through the other kingdoms.'

'And keep them out of Araluen,' Alyss said.

'It's a matter of momentum. If we can stop theirs, people will have time to see that they're being tricked.

A movement like this either keeps rolling or collapses. It can't stay still.'

'What makes you think you can get this King Ferris to listen to you? Does he know you?' Crowley asked.

'Yes, he knows me all right,' Halt said. 'He's my brother.'

Fourteen

'**I** can't get over the fact that King Ferris is your brother,' Horace said.

It wasn't the first time he'd said it. Since he and the two Rangers had left Redmont and headed for the coast, he kept coming back to the fact, each time with a wondering shake of his head. Usually, it happened when there was a lull in the conversation, Will noted.

'So you keep saying,' Halt said. There was a warning tone in his voice that Will recognised. Horace, however, seemed oblivious to it.

'Well, it's a bit of a surprise, Halt. I'd never have thought of you as . . . well, being royalty, I suppose.'

Halt's baleful gaze turned to focus on the tall young knight riding beside him.

'Oh, really?' he said. 'I suppose I'm just so un-royal in my bearing, is that it? Too coarse and common altogether?'

Will turned away to hide a smile. Horace seemed to have a real knack for getting under Halt's skin with his attitude of innocence.

'No, no, not at all,' Horace said, realising that he'd annoyed the Ranger but not sure how it had happened. 'It's just you don't have the . . .' He hesitated, not quite sure what it was that Halt didn't have.

'The haircut,' Will put in.

Halt's glare swung towards him. 'The haircut.' It was not a question. It was a statement.

Will nodded easily. 'That's right. Royalty has a certain sense of fashion to it. It has to do with bearing and behaviour and . . . haircuts.'

'You don't like my haircut?' Halt said. Will spread his hands innocently.

'Halt, I love it! It's just that it's a little Rufus the Roughnut for the brother of a king. It's not what I would call . . .'

He paused, leaning across in his saddle to study Halt's pepper-and-salt hair more closely, ignoring the drawn-together brows and the dangerous look in Halt's eyes. Then he found the word he was looking for.

'. . . sleek.'

Horace had been watching this exchange with interest, grateful that Halt's ill temper had been channelled away from him for the time being. Now, however, he couldn't help buying back in.

'Sleek! That's the word. That's it. Your haircut isn't sleek enough. Royalty is sleek, above all other things.'

'Do you find King Duncan . . . sleek?' Halt asked.

Horace nodded emphatically. 'When he wishes to be. On state occasions. There's a definite sleekness to the man. Wouldn't you agree, Will?'

'Absolutely,' the young Ranger said.

Halt's gaze swivelled back and forth between the two of them. He had a sudden impression of himself as a bull between two dogs as they darted in on alternate sides to nip at his heels. He decided it was time to change the point of his attack.

'Horace, remember when we were in Gallica, when we challenged Deparnieux?'

Horace nodded. A shadow flitted across his face for a moment at the memory of the evil warlord.

'I remember.'

'Well, I said then that I was related to the royal line of Hibernia. Remember?'

'Yes. I seem to recall words to that effect,' Horace said. Now it was Halt's turn to spread his hands out in a perplexed gesture.

'Well then, did you think I was lying?'

Horace opened his mouth to reply, then shut it. There was a long and uncomfortable pause as the three horses trotted along, the only sound being the irregular clopping of their hooves on the road.

'Is that a red hawk?' Will said, pointing to the sky in an attempt to change the subject.

'No, it's not,' Halt said, without bothering to look in the direction Will was pointing. 'And to hell with it if it is. Well?' he said to Horace. 'You haven't answered me. Did you think I was lying?'

Horace cleared his throat nervously. Then in a small voice he said:

'As a matter of fact, yes.'

Halt drew rein on Abelard and the small horse stopped. Will and Horace had to conform to his action, turning their horses so that the three of them faced each other in a rough circle in the centre of the road. Halt regarded Horace with a hurt expression on his face.

'You think I was lying? You challenge my basic honesty? I am deeply, deeply hurt! Tell me, Horace, when have I *ever* lied?'

Will frowned. Halt was laying it on a little thick, he thought. The indignation, the hurt expression, just didn't ring true somehow. He sensed that his mentor was trying to get the better of Horace in this exchange, working on Horace's basic good nature to make him feel guilty.

'Well . . .' said Horace uncertainly, and Will thought he saw a small self-satisfied shift to Halt's shoulders. Then the knight continued. 'Remember those girls?'

'Girls? What girls?' Halt asked.

'When we first landed in Gallica. There were some girls at the harbour front in rather short dresses.'

'Oh, those . . . yes. I think I recall them,' Halt said. There was a wariness to his manner now.

'What girls were these?' Will put in.

'Never mind,' Halt snapped out of the corner of his mouth.

'Well, you said they were couriers. That they had short dresses because they might have to run with urgent messages.'

Will let out a snort of laughter. 'You said what?' he said to Halt. Halt ignored him.

'I might have said something along those lines. It's been a while.'

'You said exactly that,' Horace told him accusingly. 'And I believed you.'

'You didn't!' Will said incredulously. He felt like a spectator at a boxing match. Horace nodded solemnly to him.

'I did. Because Halt told me and Halt is a Ranger. And Rangers are honourable men. Rangers never lie.'

Will turned away at that. Now Horace was laying it on a bit thick, he thought. Horace turned accusing eyes on Halt.

'But you did, didn't you, Halt? It was a lie, wasn't it?'

Halt hesitated. Then, gruffly, he replied: 'It was for your own good.'

Abruptly, he touched his heels to Abelard and the little horse trotted away, leaving Will and Horace facing each other in the middle of the road. As soon as he felt Halt was out of earshot, Horace allowed a broad grin to spread over his face.

'I've waited years to get him back for that!'

He wheeled Kicker in turn and headed off at a fast trot after Halt. Will stayed where he was for a few moments, pondering. Horace had always been so guileless, so straightforward and sincere, that he'd made an easy target for practical jokes. Now, it seemed, he'd developed a cunning streak of his own.

'Probably been around us too long,' he said, and turned Tug after the other two.

Later that night, wrapped warmly in his blankets, his head pillowed on his saddle, Will looked up at the stars, clear and bright in the night sky, and smiled quietly to himself. He could feel the chill of the night air on his face, but that only served to make the rest of his body, under the blankets, feel warm and comfortable.

It was good to be back on the road, heading for another adventure. It was even better to be doing so in the company of his two closest friends.

For an hour or so after the confrontation on the road, Halt had attempted to maintain a haughty pretence of injured pride. But eventually, he couldn't keep it up any longer and, with a show of great dignity, he announced that he would forgive Horace for his transgression. Horace, for his part, had affected to be grateful to the bearded Ranger. But he spoiled the effect a little by sneaking a covert wink to Will. Once again, Will realised that Horace these days was not the innocent of old. He would bear watching, Will thought. There was a long history of practical jokes between them that Horace might be looking to redress.

As the stars wheeled in the night sky above him, he found he couldn't sleep and his thoughts turned to the morning they had left Redmont. Crowley, Sir Rodney, Baron Arald and all their friends were there to see them off, of course. But Will's memory focused mainly on two of them: Lady Pauline and Alyss.

Alyss had kissed him goodbye and then whispered a few private words in his ear. He smiled now at the memory of them.

Then Alyss had moved to farewell Horace, who had arrived to join them the previous night, and Will had found himself facing Lady Pauline. She kissed his cheek softly then leaned forward to hug him. As she did, she said quietly, 'Look after him for me, Will. He's not as young as he thinks he is.'

With a slight shock, he realised she meant Halt. Will

could think of no one who needed looking after less than Halt but he nodded, nonetheless.

'You know I will, Pauline,' he said and she looked deeply into his eyes for several seconds.

'Yes. I do know,' she said and then she moved to embrace her husband and re-tie the fastenings of his cloak, patting them into place the way wives do for husbands.

It was strange, Will thought now. He had been desperately sorry to leave Alyss and his other friends at Redmont and the moment of parting brought an uncomfortable lump to his throat. Yet now that they were on the road again, camped under the stars, enjoying the close-knit bond of true friendship that existed between the three of them, he felt remarkably happy. Life was good, he thought. In fact, life was close to perfect. And he fell asleep with that thought.

Two hours later, Horace shook him awake to take over the watch and he rolled blearily out of his warm blankets into the cold night.

Perhaps, he reflected, life wasn't quite so close to perfect at that moment.

Fifteen

It took the travellers five days to reach the Kingdom of Clonmel.

They travelled first to the coastal village of Selsey, where Halt prevailed upon the head man to provide a boat to take them and their horses across the narrow stretch of sea to Hibernia.

At first Wilfred was less than delighted with the idea. The village and its people had grown used to being independent over the years, and they had little interest in the doings of the outside world. They saw Halt's request as an infringement on this independence and an unwelcome disruption to their normal routine. Halt had to remind him that, although Selsey was not part of any fief, it was still part of Araluen and subject to King Duncan's authority — which he, as a Ranger, represented.

He further pointed out that he had saved part of their fishing fleet from destruction, then prevented the Outsiders from absconding with a considerable amount of gold, silver and jewellery belonging to the villagers. On top of that, Halt had arranged for an armed party from Redmont to hunt down and arrest the bandits who had been working with Farrell and his group, ensuring the village's continuing safety.

Wilfred eventually, although still grudgingly, conceded the point and provided a boat and crew to ferry them to Hibernia.

They landed on a deserted stretch of beach in the south-east corner of Clonmel, just before first light. The three companions quickly mounted their horses and rode into the woods fringing the beach, out of sight of any possible prying eyes. Will looked back as the trees loomed over them, cloaking them in shadows. The boat was already far offshore, the sail no more than a pale speck among the dark waves as her skipper headed back out to sea, wasting no time getting back to the fishing grounds.

Halt saw the direction of his gaze.

'Fishermen,' he said. 'All they ever think of is their next catch.'

'They were a friendly lot,' Horace said. In fact, the sailors had hardly addressed an unnecessary word to their passengers. 'I'm not sorry to be off that tub.'

Halt concurred with the thought, although not entirely for the same reason. As always, his stomach had betrayed him once the boat had left the calm waters of the harbour and begun to plunge and roll on the open sea. The all-pervading smell of stale fish guts hadn't helped matters, either. He had spent the greater part of the voyage standing in the bow of the boat, his face pale, his knuckles white where he gripped the railing. His two young companions, familiar with his problem, decided the best course was to ignore it and leave Halt to his own devices. From past experience, they knew that any show of sympathy would lead to a snarl of dismissal. And any sign of amusement would lead to far worse.

They rode into the wood, soon crossing a path. It was a narrow, winding game trail and there was no way to ride abreast. They rode in single file, following Halt's lead as he headed north-west.

'What now, Halt?' Will asked. He was riding second in line behind his teacher. The grey-bearded Ranger twisted in his saddle to reply.

'We'll head towards Ferris's castle, Dun Kilty. It's maybe a week's ride from here. That'll give us a chance to see how things are in Clonmel.'

It soon became apparent that things in Clonmel were far from good. The game trail meandered haphazardly and eventually led them to a broader, more permanent high road. As they followed it, they began to see farmlands interspersed with the woods. But the fields were untended and overgrown with weeds, and the farmhouses they saw were shuttered and silent, with the farmyard entrances barricaded by wagons and hay bales, so they resembled improvised armed camps.

'Looks like they're expecting trouble,' Will said as they passed by one such collection of farm buildings.

'Looks like they've already had it,' Halt replied, pointing to the blackened remains of one of the outbuildings, where a pile of ashes and collapsed timbers were still smouldering. They could also make out the huddled shapes of several dead animals in the fields. Ravens perched on the swollen carcasses, tearing chunks out of the rank flesh with their sharp beaks.

'You'd think they'd have buried or burnt those carcasses,' Horace said. He wrinkled his nose as the breeze brought the unpleasantly sweet smell of rotting flesh to them.

'If they're afraid to go out to plough and plant, they're hardly going to expose themselves to bury a few dead sheep,' Halt told him.

'I suppose not. But what are they afraid of?'

Halt eased his backside from the saddle, standing for a few seconds in the stirrups before resuming his seat.

'At a guess, I'd say they're hiding from this character Tennyson — or at least, from the bandits that work with him. The whole place seems like a country under siege.'

The farms and smaller hamlets that they passed all exhibited the same evidence of fear and suspicion. Wherever possible the three Araluans bypassed them, remaining unseen.

'No point in revealing our presence,' Halt said. But by midmorning of the second day, his curiosity was beginning to nag at him, and when they sighted a small hamlet of five ramshackle houses grouped together, he jerked a thumb towards it.

'Let's go and ask the price of eggs,' he said. Horace frowned at the words as Halt led the way out of the trees and along the road that led to the hamlet.

'Do we need eggs?' he asked Will.

Will grinned at him. 'Figure of speech, Horace.'

Horace nodded, assuming a knowing expression just a little too late. 'Oh . . . yes. I sort of knew that. Sort of.'

They urged their horses after Abelard, catching up when they were fifty metres short of the hamlet. This was the closest they'd been to one of these silent groups of buildings and as they grew closer they could see the rough palisade that had been thrown around it in more detail. Farm carts and ploughs were formed in a circle around the hamlet. The gaps between were piled with old furniture — benches and tables — and the remaining gaps were filled with hurriedly constructed earthworks and spare timber. Halt raised his eyebrows at the sight of one table, a family heirloom that had been lovingly polished and waxed over the years, now shoved roughly on its side into a gap in the defences.

'Must be dining *al fresco* these days,' he said softly.

Seen closer to, they also realised that the hamlet was far from deserted. They could make out movement now behind the barricade. Several figures were moving to group together at the point they were heading for. At least one of them seemed to be wearing a helmet. The midmorning sun gleamed dully off it. As they watched, the man clambered up onto a wagon that obviously served as a gate through the barricade. He was wearing a leather coat, studded with metal. It was a cheap and primitive form of armour. In his right hand, he brandished a heavy spear. There was nothing cheap or primitive about it. Like the helmet, it reflected the sun's rays.

'Someone's been sharpening his spear,' Horace observed to his friends. Before they could reply, the spearman called out to them.

'On your way!' he yelled roughly. 'You're not welcome here!'

To reinforce the statement, he brandished the spear. Several of the other occupants growled in agreement and the three travellers saw other weapons waving above the barricade. Several swords, an axe and a selection of farm implements like scythes and sickles.

'We mean you no harm, friend,' Halt called back. He leaned his elbows on the saddle pommel and smiled encouragingly at the man. They were too far away for the farmer to see the expression, but he knew the body language was non-threatening and he hoped the smile would soften his tone of voice.

'Well, we'll mean you plenty if you come any further!'

While Halt parleyed, Will was studying the barricade intently, particularly the weapons that appeared sporadically to be waved threateningly above the top. After a few seonds, he saw a small figure pass a behind a narrow gap in the defences, followed by another, heading for the left-hand end. A few seconds later, weapons were being brandished at that position. He noticed that none were now visible at the right-hand end, where a few minutes ago they had been waving energetically.

'Halt,' he said out of the corner of his mouth, 'there aren't as many of them as they'd like us to think. And some of them are either women or children.'

'I thought as much,' the Ranger replied. 'That's why they don't want us any closer, of course.' He spoke again to the spearman. 'We're simple travellers, friend. We'll pay well for a hot meal and a tankard of ale.'

'We don't want your money and you're not getting our food. Now be on your way!'

There was a note of desperation in his voice, Halt

thought, as if any moment the man expected the three armed riders to call his bluff. Halt knew then that Will was right and the majority of 'defenders' behind the barricade were women and children. There was no reason, the Ranger concluded, to cause them any further concern. Things seemed bad enough in this part of the country anyway.

'Very well. If you say so. But can you tell us if there's an inn anywhere close by? We've been on the road for some time.'

There was a slight pause, then the man answered.

'There's the Green Harper, at Craikennis. It's west of here, less than a league. Mayhap you'll find a place there. Follow the road you're on to the crossroads and you'll find a sign.'

The farmer was obviously glad to be able to direct them somewhere else, and an inn would tend to denote a larger settlement — a village or even a small town. Such a place might be less likely to turn strangers away. Halt waved in farewell.

'Thanks for the advice, friend. We'll bother you no further.'

There was no reply. The man remained standing on the cart, his spear in hand, as they turned their horses and began to trot away. After a hundred metres or so, Will twisted round in his saddle.

'Still watching us,' he said.

Halt grunted. 'I'm sure he'll keep doing so till we're out of sight. And then worry half the night that we might turn back after dark and try to surprise him.' He shook his head sadly. Horace noticed the action.

'That's one frightened man,' he said.

Halt looked at him. 'Very frightened. And fear is the Outsiders' most potent ally. I think we're starting to get an idea of what we're up against.'

They rode on and came to the road sign directing them to Craikennis. The fact that there was a road sign, and that the place actually had a name, all pointed to the possibility that it was a larger settlement. Still, Halt wanted to avoid the sort of non-welcome they had just received.

'I think we might split up,' he said. 'The sight of three armed men might be a bit daunting for people in this area, and I don't want to be unceremoniously thrown out before we get in. Will, you've got that lute of yours, haven't you?'

Will had long ago given up trying to tell Halt that his instrument was a mandola. And in any case, Halt's question was a rhetorical one. Will always carried the instrument with him and he'd played it around their camp fire the night before.

'Yes. Do you want me to become a travelling minstrel?' He'd foreseen where Halt's thinking was heading. There was something un-threatening about a travelling musician.

Halt nodded. 'Yes. For some reason, people tend to trust a minstrel.'

'And of course, this one has such a trustworthy face,' Horace put in with a grin. Halt looked at him for a few seconds in silence.

'Quite so,' he said at length. 'We'll find a place to camp, then you go in ahead of us and start up some singing. Horace and I will slip in while everyone's watching you. Book a room at the inn. That's what you'd usually do, isn't it?'

Will nodded. 'It's the normal thing for an entertainer to ask for a room — or a bed in the barn if the inn's full.'

'You do that, then. We'll have a meal and listen around to see what we can find out. Then we'll go back to the camp. See if you can get any information from the innkeeper but don't look too nosy. We'll compare notes tomorrow morning.'

Will nodded. 'Sounds simple enough.' A grin stole over his face. He knew Halt had a total lack of interest in music. 'Any requests for tonight?'

His old teacher looked at him for a long moment.

'Anything but *Greybeard Halt*,' he said.

Horace clicked his tongue in disappointment. 'That's one of my favourites.'

Halt regarded the two grinning young faces.

'Why do I have the feeling that I'm going to regret agreeing to this Task Group?' he said.

Sixteen

Halt and Horace reined in at the outskirts of Craikennis. There was a makeshift palisade here as well, obviously a recent construction. Outside the barrier, in front of the entrance, a canvas shelter was set by the roadside, with three armed men inside, sheltering from the chill of the night. There was a large iron triangle hanging from a pole, with a hammer hanging beside it. In the event of an attack, one of the men would sound the alarm by clanging the triangle with the hammer, Horace thought.

One of the sentries emerged from the shelter now, took a burning torch from a bracket and advanced on them, holding the light high to see their faces. Halt obligingly shrugged the cowl back from his head so the light could play upon his features.

'Who are you and what do you want?' the man demanded roughly. Horace grimaced. Clonmel wasn't the friendliest country he'd ever been to, he thought. Then again, there was little wonder, in the light of what they'd seen as they travelled through the countryside.

'We're travellers,' Halt told him. 'On the way to Dun Kilty to buy sheep at the markets there.'

'Do shepherds usually go armed?' the man asked, taking in Halt's longbow and the sword that hung at Horace's waist. Halt gave him a thin smile.

'They do if they plan to get their sheep home in one piece,' he said. 'Or are you not aware how things are these days?'

The man nodded morosely. 'I am that,' he replied. The stranger was right. There was little of law and order in Clonmel these past weeks. The smaller man might well be a shepherd, he thought. He was a nondescript-looking character. The taller of the two had a different feel to him. He was doubtless an armed guard, hired by the shepherd to help safeguard his flock on the return journey.

'We're looking for a meal and a fire to warm us and then we'll be on our way. We're told there's an inn here in Craikennis?'

The watchman nodded, satisfied that the two men offered no real threat to the security of the village. He glanced out into the darkness, making sure they had no companions lurking in the shadows. But there was no sign of movement on the road. He stepped back.

'Very well. But don't cause any trouble. You'll have us and a dozen others to reckon with if you do.'

'You'll see no trouble from us, friend,' Halt told him. 'Where do we find this inn of yours?'

The sentry pointed down the single main street of the village.

'The Green Harper, it's called. Just fifty metres that way.'

He stepped out of the road to let them pass and they rode on into Craikennis village.

The Green Harper stood at the midpoint of the main street. The village itself was a substantial establishment, with fifty or sixty houses grouped around the central street and a network of lanes and lesser streets that ran off it. They were all single-storey, of mud brick and thatched roof construction. They looked smaller than the houses Halt and Horace were used to — lower. Horace guessed that if he were to enter one, he would have to stoop to avoid the door lintel. The inn was the largest building in the village, as would be expected. It was also the only two-storey building, with narrow dormer windows in the upper storey suggesting that there might be three or four bedrooms provided for guests.

The Green Harper's identifying sign swung, creaking noisily in the wind that gusted down the main street of the village. It was a weathered board showing the faded remnants of a dwarf-like figure dressed all in green, plucking the strings of a small harp. As Horace studied the sign, he noted that the face was twisted in a rather unpleasant leer.

'Not a friendly type, is he?' he said.

Halt looked at the sign. 'He's a *laechonnachie*,' he replied and, sensing Horace's inquiring look, he added, 'A Little Person.'

'I can see that,' Horace said but Halt shook his head.

'The Little People are the subject of a great deal of superstition in this country. They're enchanted figures, faerie folk if you like. Good people to avoid. They have a nasty sense of humour and they tend to be spiteful.'

There was a burst of noise from the inn as a score of voices rose in song, joining in the chorus to one of Will's numbers. He had ridden into Craikennis an hour ahead of Horace and Halt. Apparently, from the noise and the burst of applause they now heard, he had been roundly welcomed by the locals.

'Sounds as if he's bringing down the house,' Horace observed.

Halt glanced up at the building, noticing the way none of the walls were true and the upper storey seemed to lean and teeter over the narrow main street of the village.

'That wouldn't take a lot of doing,' he muttered. 'Come on. Let's get inside while it's still standing.'

He led the way to the tethering rail outside the inn. There was one other animal tethered there, a disinterested pony harnessed to a small cart. Aside from the driver, there were seats for two passengers, set either side of the cart and facing outwards.

'Quaint,' Horace said, as he tethered Kicker to the rail. Halt, of course, merely dropped Abelard's rein over the rail. There was no need to tether a Ranger horse.

Horace glanced around. 'Where's Tug, do you think?'

Halt jerked a thumb at a side alley leading to the rear of the inn. 'I imagine he'll be nice and warm in a stall in the stables,' he said. 'If Will's taken a room, he wouldn't leave Tug out in the street.'

'True enough,' Horace said. 'Let's get on with it, Halt, I'm famished.'

'Are you ever not famished?' Halt asked, but Horace was already heading for the inn. He led the way to the door but before he could push it open, Halt stopped him with a hand on his arm. Horace looked at him enquiringly and the Ranger explained.

'Wait until Will's started again and we'll slip in while everyone's attention is on him. Remember, keep your ears open and your mouth shut. I'll do the talking.'

Horace nodded agreement. He'd noticed during the day that Halt's accent, which usually showed only the slightest trace of a Hibernian brogue, had been thickening and broadening whenever he spoke. Halt was obviously working to recapture the accent of his youth.

'No need to let everyone know we're foreigners,' he had said when Horace had commented on the fact.

They paused now, hearing Will's voice raised in song, and the rippling accompaniment of his mandola. Then the noise redoubled as the entire room joined in on the chorus. Halt nodded to Horace.

'Let's go,' he said.

They slipped into the room, hesitating briefly as the wave of heat from the open fire and thirty or forty bodies hit them. Will stood in a well-lit space by the fireplace, leading the company in song — not that they needed much encouragement, Halt thought wryly. Hibernians loved music and singing and Will had a good repertoire of jigs and reels. As the two Araluans paused in the doorway, two of the spectators in front of Will, a man and a woman, leapt to their feet and began dancing and heel-and-toeing in time to his driving rhythm. The rest of the room roared encouragement, clapping in time to urge the dancers on. Halt and Horace exchanged a glance, then Halt nodded his head towards a table at the rear of the room. They moved to it. Will, of course, ignored their entry. Only one or two of the people in the room seemed to notice them. The rest were totally engrossed in the music and the dancing.

But the innkeeper noticed the two new arrivals — it was his business to notice such things, after all. Before too long, a serving girl made her way through the customers to their table. Halt ordered coffee, and lamb stew for them both, and she nodded, sliding away with the skill of long practice through the packed customers.

Will crashed out the final chord of the song and the two dancers slumped, exhausted, onto their benches. At Halt's suggestion, he had discarded the distinctive mottled Ranger's cloak when he left their camp, wearing a long, thick woollen outer coat instead. By the same token, he had left his bow and quiver behind, and unclipped his throwing knife and sheath from the double scabbard arrangement at his belt, leaving the larger saxe knife in a single scabbard. The throwing knife had gone into a sheath sewn inside his jerkin, under the left arm. Some years earlier, Will had experimented with a sheath sewn into the back collar of his jerkin, with near disastrous results.

Halt, of course, wore his normal Ranger's outfit and carried his bow. There was nothing significant about that in a countryside where everyone seemed primed for trouble. The mottled appearance of the cloak might be a little unusual but, even so, he had the appearance of a woodsman or farmer. Horace wore a plain leather jacket over his leggings and boots, with his sword and dagger in a belt round his waist. He wore a cloak, of course, to keep out the biting cold of the wind. But unlike Halt's, it had no cowl. Instead, he wore a close-fitting wool cap, pulled down over his ears. He wore no armour or insignia of any kind. To outward appearances, he was a simple man at arms.

As a result of these varied costumes, there was nothing to connect the two newcomers to the foreign minstrel who had arrived earlier in the evening. And with Halt's carefully renewed Hibernian accent, they didn't even appear to be foreign.

Their food arrived, and the coffee, and they fell to eating with a will. Horace was particularly willing but, over the years he had known the young warrior, Halt had become more or less accustomed to the younger man's prodigious appetite. Horace spooned the savoury lamb and potato stew into his mouth, using the thick slice of bread that came with it to mop up the juice. Finishing his own bread, Horace noticed the half slice remaining in front of Halt and reached for it.

'You going to eat that?'

'Yes. Hands off.'

Horace was about to protest but a warning shake of Halt's head stopped him. He realised that Halt, while maintaining the appearance of eating his meal, was eavesdropping on the other diners. With the music halted temporarily while Will took a break, a babble of conversation had broken out around the room.

There were three men seated at the next table. Villagers, by the look of them. Probably tradesmen, Horace thought. He could see them while Halt, with his back to them, was much closer and in a better position to hear what they were saying. Not that it was too difficult to do that. With the level of background noise in the hot, smoky room, they had to raise their voices to be heard.

'A bad business is what I've heard tell,' a bald man was saying. From the flour that coated the front of his shirt, Horace guessed he was either the local miller or baker. He caught another warning head shake from Halt and realised that he was staring at the next table. Hastily, he looked down at his plate, just as Halt slid the crust of bread across the table towards him. Smiling, he took it and began to make a show of wiping the remains of his meal from the plate with it.

'Four killed, so I've heard. A terrible thing. My wife's brother was there just three days gone. Happen he'd been there yesterday, he could be among the dead now.'

Halt pretended to take a sip at his coffee. He was tempted to turn and ask the locals for more information. But so far, he and Horace had gone virtually unnoticed in the room. The locals might be willing to discuss this freely among their companions. With strangers it might be a different matter altogether.

'What think you about these religious folk at Mountshannon?' asked another of the men. Horace took a quick glance at him. He was a few years younger than the bald-headed miller/baker. Possibly a merchant of some kind. Not a warrior, Horace thought.

The man's two companions snorted derisively.

'Religious quacks is more like it!' said the third, the one who hadn't so far spoken. The bald man was quick to agree.

'Aye! Claiming to be able to keep Mountshannon safe. Funny how religious folks like that say their god will protect them — right up until someone hits them with a club.'

'Still,' said the merchant, seeming unconvinced by their scorn, 'the fact remains that Mountshannon has been untouched so far. While at Duffy's Ford there's four dead and the rest scattered God knows where in fear.'

'There are over a hundred people at Mountshannon,' the bald man explained to him. 'Duffy's Ford is no more than three or four houses. Barely a dozen folk to begin with. It's the bigger villages that have less to fear. Like Mountshannon.'

'And Craikennis,' put in the one who'd agreed with him about religious quacks.

'Aye,' said the bald man, ' I'll warrant we're safe enough here. Dennis and his watchmen do a good job keeping an eye on strangers to the village.'

As he said the words, he glanced up and became aware for the first time of Halt and Horace at the next table. He muttered a guarded warning to his companions and both of them turned to glance at the strangers behind them. Then they leaned forward over their own table and continued their conversation in lowered tones, inaudible against the buzz of a dozen other conversations in the room. Halt raised his eyebrows at Horace, who essayed a slight shrug. He had no doubt that they'd hear no more from them now.

A few minutes later, there was a stir of interest in the room as Will struck up the opening chords of a new song. People turned from their conversations and settled back in their seats to listen. When the serving girl came to collect their platters and see if they needed a refill on their coffee, Halt shook his head and dropped a handful of coins on the table to pay for their meal. He jerked his head at Horace.

'Time to go,' he said.

They rose and threaded their way to the door. The bald man looked up after them briefly. Then, deciding there was nothing threatening about the two strangers, he turned his attention back to the music.

Outside, the cold wind cut into them again as they retrieved their horses and mounted.

Horace shivered briefly, huddling down into the warmth of his cloak.

'We should have taken a room ourselves,' he said. 'It's damned cold out here.'

Halt shook his head. 'This way, we'll be forgotten within half an hour. If we'd stayed, more people would have noticed us. More people would be asking questions about us. You'll soon warm up back by our camp fire.'

Horace smiled at his grim-faced companion.

'Is it such a bad thing to be noticed, Halt?'

The Ranger nodded emphatically. 'It is to me.'

They rode past the sentry station, nodding to the men who were on duty. This time, none of them felt the need to come out into the wind, away from the fire they had burning in a steel grate inside the shelter. As Halt had predicted, within an hour, their presence in Craikennis had been forgotten.

Seventeen

The following morning, Halt and Horace were sitting around their camp fire when Abelard gave a snort of welcome. A few seconds later, Will and Tug rode into the clearing where they had made their camp. He glanced at the two small tents, barely a metre in height and two metres long. It had rained during the night and the canvas sides were beaded with moisture.

'Sleep nice and warm, did we?' he grinned.

Halt grunted at him. 'At least we weren't eaten to death by bedbugs.'

Will's grin faded just a little.

'Yes, I'll have to admit the Green Harper could do with a thorough spring cleaning. I do seem to have had one or two little visitors.' He scratched idly at an itchy spot on his side as he said the words. Halt looked down at the fire, hiding a satisfied smile.

Will dismounted, unsaddled Tug and set him loose to graze. He joined the others by the small fire, where a coffee pot sat in the coals to one side.

'Still,' he continued, 'they do a good breakfast at the Harper. Bacon, sausages, mushrooms and fresh bread. Just the thing to set you up on a cold morning.'

There was a low groan from the point where Horace sat, poking idly at the coals with a dead stick. Will wasn't entirely sure if the groan had come from Horace or from his stomach. Breakfast at the camp had been a frugal matter of flat, slightly stale bread, toasted over the fire and eaten with a ration of dried meat.

'Hard rations build character,' Halt said philosophically. Horace looked mournfully at him. Already the vast helping of lamb stew he'd eaten the previous evening was nothing but a dim memory.

'They also build hunger,' he said. Will waited a few seconds more, then relented and tossed a substantial bundle wrapped in a napkin down beside Horace.

'Fortunately, the kitchen girl saw fit to give me some food for my journey,' he said. 'Seems she's a music lover.'

Horace eagerly unwrapped the bundle, to reveal a pile of still-warm food inside.

He transferred a large portion to his plate, which was standing by the fire, and reached for his fork. He paused as he saw Halt moving to join him and take his own share of the bacon and sausages, ripping off a chunk of fresh, soft bread to go with it.

'I thought you said hard rations build character?' Will said, managing to stay straight-faced. Halt looked up at him with some dignity.

'I have character,' he said. 'I have character to spare. It's young people like you two who need their characters built.'

'I'll build mine tomorrow,' Horace said through a

mouthful of food. 'This is excellent, Will! When I have grandchildren, I'll name them all after you!'

Will smiled at his friend and took a seat by the fireplace, pouring himself a cup of coffee. He added honey and drank appreciatively.

'Aaah!' he said. 'They may know their way around bacon and sausage at that inn. But their coffee doesn't hold a candle to yours, Halt.'

Halt grunted, his mouth too full to answer. He finished off the plate of food that he had taken and sat back, patting his stomach. Then he couldn't resist leaning forward and taking one more piece of crisply fried bacon.

'So, did you hear anything at the inn?' he asked as he finished off the titbit.

Will nodded. 'The main talking point was an attack on a place called Duffy's Ford — a small settlement by a river some ten kilometres from here.'

'Yes. We heard about that too,' Halt said. 'Did you hear any mention of a village called Mountshannon?'

Will drained his cup and tossed the dregs into the fire before answering.

'Yes. Quite a few people were talking about it. Sounds as if our friends have set up headquarters there.'

'We heard they were claiming to be able to protect Mountshannon from the sort of thing that happened at the ford,' Horace put in. Although he hadn't heard too clearly the night before, he and Halt had discussed the matter when they reached camp.

'I heard much the same thing. Opinion seemed divided as to whether there was any value to the claim,' Will said. Halt looked at him shrewdly.

'What did most people think? Did you get any idea?'

Will shrugged. 'I'd say it was two to one against. Most people I spoke to, or heard discussing the matter, seemed to think Mountshannon could look after itself. It's a big village, apparently. They talked about it quite a lot after I'd finished singing.'

Halt chuckled briefly. 'That's the handy thing about your being able to pose as a minstrel,' he said. 'People seem to think you're one of them. They'll talk far more openly about matters in front of you. Anything else?'

Will considered. He wasn't quite sure how Halt would react to the next piece of intelligence he had learned. Then he decided there was no way to sugar coat the message.

'General opinion is that King Ferris is a broken reed. There's precious little respect for him. Nobody seemed to think that he was capable of sorting out the mess that Clonmel's in. The ones who think the Outsiders might have the answer were particularly strident about it. And if anything was going to sway the others to their point of view, it was the fact that Ferris is weak and ineffectual. They all agreed on that.' He paused, then added, 'Sorry, Halt. But that's the way people see it.'

Halt shrugged. 'I can't say I'm surprised. For years Ferris has cared so much about just being King that he's neglected to act like one. He was like that from the beginning.' There was a note of bitterness in his voice and Will regretted having to pass on the negative information about his brother.

Horace checked the spread-out napkin to make sure there were no leftovers remaining. Then he shifted to a more comfortable position.

'Halt,' he said now, in a serious voice, 'I think it might be time you told us more about you and your brother.'

There was no trace of his former light-hearted tone when he had grumbled about breakfast. This was a serious matter. But there was also no trace of apology in his words. He was prying into Halt's past, he knew, but it was time he and Will learned all the facts about King Ferris, and his relationship with his brother. Will and Horace were in a potentially dangerous situation in Clonmel and Horace had learned that it was important to understand as much as possible about a situation like this.

Reflecting on that, he realised that it was his long association with the two Rangers that had taught him that lesson. He saw that Halt was watching him now, with those calm, serious eyes of his. And he saw that Halt agreed with him.

'Yes. You're right,' the Ranger said. 'You should know all the facts behind the current situation. For a start, there's one pertinent fact you should be aware of. Ferris and I aren't just brothers. We're twins. That's why the Outsiders' leader at Selsey thought I looked familiar. He'd spent some time in Clonmel and he'd seen Ferris several times.'

'Twins?' Will sat up at that news. In all the years he had spent with Halt, he had never had the slightest inkling that his mentor had any siblings, let alone a twin brother.

'Identical twins,' Halt said. 'We were born seven minutes apart.'

'And you were the youngest?' Horace said. He shook his head. 'It's funny, isn't it? But for that seven minutes, you'd be the King of Clonmel now and Ferris would be . . .'

He paused, not sure how to continue. He had been

about to say, 'Ferris would be a Ranger', but then he realised, from what they had heard about the vacillating, ineffectual King, he would never have become a Ranger. Halt regarded him, seeing the sudden question in the young warrior's mind.

'Exactly,' he said quietly. 'What would Ferris have become? But you're not exactly right there, Horace. I was actually the one who was born first. Ferris is my younger brother.'

Horace frowned as the implications of what Halt had said sunk in. But it was Will who asked the obvious question.

'Then what happened? Surely as the elder brother, you should have become King? Or isn't that the way it works here in Hibernia?'

'Yes. That's the way it works here, just like everywhere else. But I had a problem. My brother resented those seven minutes bitterly. He felt he had been cheated out of his birthright. Cheated by me,' he added.

Horace shook his head in disbelief. 'That's crazy. It wasn't your fault you were born first.'

Halt smiled sadly at Horace. So honest. So straight-forward. So free of deceit and jealousy. If there were more men like Horace, and fewer like my brother, the world would be a better place, he thought. It saddened him but he recognised the fact that it was accurate.

'He made himself blame me,' he told them. 'That way, it was easier for him when he tried to kill me.'

'He tried to kill you?' Will's voice rose in disbelief. 'His own brother? His *twin* brother?'

'His older brother,' Halt added. He looked deep into the smoking embers of the fire as he recalled those long-ago days. 'You know, I don't really enjoy talking about this,' he began and both Will and Horace reacted immediately.

'Then don't!' Will said.

'It's none of our business anyway,' Horace agreed. 'Let it go, Halt.'

But Halt looked up at them both now, letting his gaze move from one to the other. *Both of these two I would trust with my life,* he thought. *But my own brother?* He let out a short, bitter laugh at the thought, then continued.

'No. I think you need to know this. And I certainly need to face it. I've been running away from it for too long.' He saw their reluctance to hear more and reassured them.

'You need to know this, really. It could be important to you. So let me get it out of the way as quickly and pain-lessly as possible. Ferris believed the throne was rightly his. Why he believed that I have no idea. But he did. Maybe it was because he was the more popular with our parents. And that may have been because they felt he needed their attention more than I did. After all, I was going to be King and they possibly felt that he needed something in compensation for that fact. Plus he was open and friendly and cheerful and I was . . . well, I was me, I suppose.

'When we were sixteen, he tried to poison me. But fortunately, he got the amounts wrong and only succeeded in making me violently ill.' He grinned wryly. 'I still can't face the sight of a plate of shrimp.'

'But didn't your parents . . . do something?' Will protested.

Halt shook his head. 'They didn't know. *I* didn't know. I only found out later. I just thought the food had been spoiled and I was lucky to survive.

'The next time was six months later. I was walking in the castle yard when a pile of roof tiles hit the ground half a metre behind me. They smashed and cut my legs pretty badly. But they didn't land on me, which was the intent. I saw Ferris on the battlements above me. He ducked back out of the way but not quite quickly enough.

'Worst of all, I saw the expression on his face. You'd expect someone who had just witnessed his brother miss death by a few centimetres might look concerned. Ferris looked furious.

'Bear in mind, I had no real proof that he was trying to kill me. And at that time, my mother and father were arguing nonstop — they were never what you might call a happy couple. About the only bright thing in their lives was happy young Ferris. Somehow I couldn't bring myself to spoil that for them by accusing him. The only one who believed me was my younger sister. She could see what was going on.'

Horace and Will exchanged surprised looks. They were learning more about Halt in these few minutes than they had in the past five or six years.

'You have a sister?' Will said. But Halt shook his head sadly.

'I had a sister. She died some years back. I believe she had a son.' He paused a for a few seconds, thinking about her, then he shook himself and went on with his story.

'The final time was a year after the roof incident, when my father was close to death. Ferris knew he had to act quickly. We were salmon fishing and I leaned over the side of our boat to untangle my line. Next thing I felt a shove in the back and I was in the water. When I came up, Ferris was trying to reach me with an oar. At first, I thought he

- 144 -

was trying to help. Then, when the oar hit me, I knew what he was doing.'

Subconsciously, he rubbed his right shoulder, as if he could still feel the pain of that blow, all these years later. Will and Halt were horrified. But neither said anything. Both realised, somehow, that Halt had to finish this story, to purge his soul of the blackness that he had concealed all these years.

'He tried for me again but I ducked underwater and swam for the bank. Nearly didn't make it, but I managed to drag myself ashore. Ferris followed me in the boat, insisting that it had been an accident, asking if I was all right, trying to pretend that he hadn't just tried to kill me.'

He snorted in disgust at the memory. 'I knew then that he'd never let up. If I were to be safe, I had to do one of two things. Kill him or leave the country. Even if I were to simply stand aside, to abdicate, I knew he'd never trust me. He'd expect me to try to seize the throne from him at some time in the future. I guess it was just worth more to him than it was to me. It was worth his brother's life.

'That's what I told him. Then I left.' He smiled at the two concerned young faces opposite him now and added, 'And the way things turned out, I'm rather glad I did.'

The two young men shook their heads. There were no words that could express their sympathy for the grim-faced Ranger who meant so much to both of them. Then they realised that Halt didn't need words from them. He knew how much they cared about him.

'You might have noticed,' he said, trying to lighten the mood around the camp fire, 'I've been left with a distinct aversion to royalty and inherited authority. The fact that a person's father is a king doesn't necessarily mean that he will be a good one. All too often he's not. I prefer the Skandian method, where someone like Erak can be elected.'

'But Duncan is a good king,' Horace answered quietly.

Halt looked at him and nodded. 'Yes. There are always exceptions. Duncan is a fine king. And his daughter will make an excellent queen. That's why we all serve them. As for Ferris, I confess I wouldn't be heartbroken if this Tennyson character dragged him screeching off the throne of Clonmel. But then Araluen would be in danger, so we need to prop him up.'

'Unpalatable as that may be,' Will said.

'Sometimes we act for the greater good,' Halt said. Then he stood up, dusting himself off, as if to disperse the cloud of melancholy that had settled over them as he talked. He continued in a brisker tone.

'Speaking of which, it's time we got moving. Will, I want you to go to Duffy's Ford and pick up the trail of these bandits. Track them to their camp and see what you can find out about them: numbers, weapons, that sort of thing. If you can get any inkling of their plans, that'd be good. But be careful. We don't want to have to come and rescue you. Don't underestimate these people. They may look like an untrained rabble but they've been doing this for some years now and they know what they're about.'

Will nodded his understanding. He began to gather his equipment together and whistled to Tug, who walked forward to be resaddled.

'Will I meet you back here?' he asked.

Halt shook his head. 'We'll meet at Mountshannon. Horace and I are going to take a look at this Tennyson character.'

Eighteen

Duffy's Ford crossed a long, slow curve in the river. Over hundreds of years, the action of the water running through the curve had cut away the bank, eroding it so that the river gradually became wider. As that happened, the moving water was spread over a larger area, and its speed and depth were both reduced accordingly, providing a crossing point for travellers. There was no logical reason why people on the road shouldn't break their journey at any point along the way but travellers tend to look for landmarks or significant features to sit back, relax and enjoy a meal. Duffy's Ford, with its wide, flat grassy banks, sheltered by willows, provided an ideal location.

As is often the case, the fact that travellers were drawn to a location resulted in the growth of a small settlement designed to serve their needs. The trees had been cleared and there was a small huddle of buildings to one side of the ford.

Or there had been. Will dismounted and walked forward to look around. He studied the blackened remains of what had been a group of buildings, where wisps of smoke still rose in places. The largest, which had provided food and drink to passers-by, had been a rambling, single-storey affair, gradually added to over the years. Will guessed, correctly, that it had provided overnight accommodation to those who wanted it. Now less than half the building remained. The rest was a pile of blackened ashes. The roof had gone, of course, being made of thatch. And the mud and daub walls had cracked in the heat of the fire that had swept through the building and collapsed. But some of the timber framework remained in place — a skeletal structure of blackened beams and uprights that tottered precariously over the charred remains of beds, tables, chairs and other furnishings. There were several half-burnt casks in one room. Will guessed that it must have been the tap room, where thirsty travellers could relax over a glass of ale. Remarkably, demonstrating the capricious nature of a fire like this, one corner had remained relatively untouched and there were several dark bottles still standing on a shelf behind the collapsed charred bench that had been the bar. Gingerly, Will picked his way through the ashes and debris and picked one up. He unstoppered it and sniffed the cork, wrinkling his nose in distaste at the powerful smell of cheap brandy. He re-stoppered it and went to put it back but then a thought struck him. It could come in handy at a later date. So he slipped the bottle into an inner pocket.

He made his way back onto clear ground and walked around the perimeter of the ruined central building, turning his attention to the other three destroyed structures. One had been the stables, placed behind the main building. There was nothing left there. It had burnt fiercely, the flames not even extinguished by a heavy rainstorm that had saved some of the main building.

'Probably full of straw,' he said to himself. The dried-out hay would have been perfect fuel, defying the efforts of the rain to quell the flames.

Beyond the ruined stable there were two other, smaller buildings. In front of one was a stone fireplace, where an assortment of blacksmith's tools — hammers, awls and pliers — were scattered. It made sense, he realised, for a smithy to set up shop here. There's be plenty of trade from passing travellers needing wagons repaired, horses shoed or tack mended. The other building had probably been a residence — perhaps for the smithy and his family. There was little left of it now. The small settlement had a forlorn feeling to it — deserted and lifeless.

As the last word came to his mind he became conscious of something else — the by now familiar nauseatingly sweet smell of rotting bodies. As he walked further to the back of the smithy, he made out the shapes of several carcasses in the small meadow behind it. Sheep, most of them. But there was also one huddled furry body that had been the dog that guarded them.

The survivors of the attack must have buried or carried away the bodies of the four human victims. But they had no time or inclination to dispose of the remains of the animals.

'Can't say I blame them,' he said, and moved back to the main building, where the strong smell of charred wood and ashes masked the unpleasant smell of corruption. He began to cast around the site for tracks, stopping almost immediately at the sight of a large red-brown stain on the grass on the shallow slope leading to the river.

Blood.

There were more signs in that spot. Footprints, faint now after a few days had passed, and the marks where several horses had ridden up from the river. The hoofprints were deep and easily visible in the softened ground — far deeper than a walking animal would have left. These horses had been galloping. And one of them had galloped right past the spot where the large blood stain still marked the grass.

He looked around, from the river to the main building, picturing what had happened.

The raiders had crossed the river then, led by several mounted men, had charged up the shallow slope, across the open grassy meadow. One of the men from Duffy's Ford had run forward to stop them — or perhaps delay them while the others tried to escape. And he'd been cut down here.

Will searched around the immediate area and soon found a sickle lying a few metres away, almost hidden by the long grass. He turned it over with the toe of his boot. Already, a few rust stains were showing on the curved blade. He shook his head. The makeshift weapon would have given its owner little chance against the determined raiders. He had been cut down without a second thought. Probably a sword or spear thrust, Will thought, a weapon that would have given its owner a longer reach than the short-handled sickle. The desperate and brave defender had never really had a hope of defending himself.

He followed the hoofprints back up the slope for a few metres. One horse had diverted to the right and he followed it to another drying brown blood stain. He dropped to one knee to study the ground more closely and made out the faint trace of footprints in the grass and mud. Small footprints, he saw. A child.

He closed his eyes briefly. He could see the scene in his mind's eye. A boy or girl, terrified by the galloping, screaming men, had tried to run for the shelter of the trees. One of the raiders had swung out of line to pursue the little running figure. Then he'd cut his victim down from behind. Without pity. Without mercy. He could have let the child escape. What harm could a child have done them? But he hadn't. Will's lips set in a hard line as he realised that this atrocity had been committed, at least ostensibly, in the name of religion.

'You'd better pray that your god will protect you,' he said quietly. Then he rose from the crouching position he'd assumed to view the tracks. There was no point studying further on events that had taken place here. He knew the general outline and he could picture some of the details as well.

Now it was time to track these murderers back to their lair, wherever that might be.

He remounted Tug and urged the little horse into the river. The raiders had come from the other side. Presumably they had returned there as well. The water came no higher than Tug's belly and there was little current to contend with. The small horse splashed easily across the sandy bottom to the far bank. Leaning out of the saddle, Will searched for the party's return tracks.

It didn't take him long to find them. It had been a large party, perhaps twenty or thirty men, he estimated. It was certainly the largest group to have crossed the ford in the preceding few days, so the tracks were easy to follow. Added to that, they'd made no attempt to cover the sign of their passing, although perhaps a person without a Ranger's skill at tracking wouldn't have been able to follow them.

Or perhaps the raiders simply didn't expect anybody to dare make the attempt.

That was more likely the case, Will thought. They'd been raiding and killing and burning throughout Hibernia, virtually unopposed, for months now. It was logical that they would have begun to believe that there was no one who could be a threat to them. Will smiled grimly to himself as he followed the trail of hoofprints and footprints to the south-west.

'Just keep believing that,' he said. Tug swung his head curiously at the unexpected sound of his master's voice. Will patted the coarse-maned neck reassuringly.

'Nothing,' he said. 'Just ignore me.'

Tug tossed his head briefly. *Fine. Let me know if you want to talk.*

The raiding party had moved onto a narrow trail now and there was less need to search for every heel print, every indentation in the damp ground. Time enough for that when he reached a fork in the track. For the moment, Will could simply follow the track, noting the occasional sign that a group of people had passed by – broken branches, threads of cloth caught on twigs and at one point, a dried pile of horse droppings. This sort of tracking he could do in his sleep, he thought.

Eventually, the trail forked and he saw that the band had diverged to the left, taking the smaller of the two trails. The ground began to gradually rise and the tree cover, although still substantial, was thinning out as they climbed higher. In the middle distance, Will could make out the steep cliffs of an escarpment. He had the sense that they were nearing the end of their search. He doubted that the raiders would have climbed the escarpment. Their disregard for the possibility that they might be followed dictated against it. If they hadn't taken any steps to cover their tracks, he doubted that they'd bother with the difficulty of climbing that forbidding line of black granite cliffs, although to do so would have given a virtually unassailable sanctuary.

He reined Tug in, sniffing the air experimentally. There was a trace of something on the faint breeze — something that was just a little unexpected, just a little out of place. He turned his head from side to side, still sniffing, trying to determine what it was. Then he had it.

Smoke. Or rather, ashes. The wet ashes of a dead camp fire.

They moved on, the smell becoming stronger and more pungent. A hundred metres further along the track, he found its source, in a spot where the trail widened out to form a substantial clearing. There was ample evidence that the raiders had camped here for the night. There were the blackened circles of four fires, and flattened spaces on the grass where men had rolled into their blankets and slept. More dung showed where the band's half dozen horses had been picketed.

Will sat on a tree stump and considered the scene, Tug watching him with intelligent eyes.

'They camped here, so we can't be too close to their eventual destination,' he said. That made sense when he thought about the escarpment he had seen earlier. It must still be a good half day's ride away from their current position. If darkness had been closing in when they reached this point, it would have been an ideal place for them to camp.

'At least we know we're on the right trail,' he told Tug and the little horse cocked his head to one side.

I never doubted it.

Will grinned at him. Sometimes, he wondered how accurate his interpretations of Tug's unspoken messages were. And he wondered if other Rangers talked to their horses the way he did when they were alone. He had a suspicion that Halt did, but he'd never seen proof of the fact.

He stood, looking at the sky. There were still three or four hours of daylight left. If the trail remained as easy to follow as it had been so far, there was no reason why he shouldn't reach the raiders' camp that evening.

He rode on. The path widened a little and although it was still gradually climbing uphill, it tended to wind and twist less than it had previously. There was no need to proceed slowly. He could see where the trail led and there was no chance in the next hour or two of catching up with the raiders. They were at least two days ahead of him. So he let Tug fall into an easy lope, eating the kilometres beneath them.

As the day wore on, the black cliffs came closer. Just after midafternoon, the sun dropped behind them, throwing the surrounding countryside into shadow. When he estimated that the escarpment was an hour's ride away,

Will eased Tug to a halt. He dismounted and rested the little horse for ten minutes, splashing some water from his canteen into a small folding leather bucket so the horse could drink. He took a mouthful himself and chewed on a piece of dried smoked beef. He smiled quietly as he thought of Horace's grumbling over such rations. Will quite liked the taste of smoked beef. The chewing, of course, was another matter altogether. He might like the taste but the consistency was similar to an old boot.

He remounted and walked Tug forward. From here on, it would pay to proceed cautiously. On the evidence so far, it was unlikely that the raiders would have an outer screen of sentries around their headquarters, but it never hurt to be careful. He nudged Tug in a signal and the horse walked soft-footed, picking his way carefully as he had been trained to do, his hoofs making barely a sound on the damp earth of the track.

Once again, it was his nose that gave him warning. The unmistakable, penetrating smell of fresh woodsmoke wafted through the trees to him. They were riding along the crest of a gully and the black cliffs were ahead, seeming close enough to touch. They were only one or two hundred metres high, he saw. Not the biggest cliffs he'd ever come across. But their sides were sheer, glistening black rock. They'd be unclimbable if there wasn't some tenuous winding track leading to the top. The smell of smoke was stronger now and he thought he caught the faint sound of voices. He brought Tug to a stop and slipped down from the saddle.

'Stay here,' he said and moved silently up to the next bend in the trail. He had resumed his Ranger's cloak when he left camp that morning. Now he ghosted among the trees, taking advantage of the uncertain afternoon light that made him almost impossible to discern.

At the bend, he stayed in the shadow of the trees and found himself looking across the wide gully to an open space at the foot of the cliffs. Tents were set out in uneven, ragged lines and fires gleamed among them. He could see men moving among the tents, or sitting round the fires. He estimated there must be at least one hundred and fifty men camped below him. Armed men, he saw. He thought about the way the people of Craikennis had dismissed the threat of a raid, and their confidence in their own numbers. If a band this size attacked a town like Craikennis, the defenders would have little chance of resisting.

He slid to the ground, his back against a tree, and studied the camp for the next hour, until night fell. He gradually identified the largest, central tent in the camp. Judging by the number of men coming and going there, it must be the leader's headquarters. Equally important, as dusk was falling he watched the picket line being set — a half circle of sentries who took up their positions where the open ground gave way to the treeline again. Even this group, overconfident as they might be, wouldn't settle for the night without some form of guard.

He noted one man who had moved a little further into the trees than his neighbours. From his elevated position, Will could see him easily. And he could see that the man wouldn't be visible to his fellow sentries. Perhaps he had found a more comfortable spot to spend his hours on watch. Or perhaps he preferred not to be constantly under the eye of the guard commander.

Either way, it was a mistake — and one that Will planned to take advantage of.

Nineteen

After Will had left for Duffy's Ford, Halt and Horace broke camp and took the high road that headed north-west to Mountshannon. They saw only a few other travellers along the way: a single rider on a tired-looking, elderly horse and a small group of traders walking along-side a wagon pulled by a mule.

Halt greeted the traders politely as they rode past. There was no response. Four pairs of eyes followed the two riders suspiciously. Halt's bow and the fact that Horace wore a sword and rode a battlehorse were sufficient reasons for their mistrust.

The grey-bearded Ranger sighed and Horace looked at him, a question in his eyes. It was unlike Halt, he thought, to show emotion so easily.

'What's up?' he asked.

'Oh, I was just thinking,' Halt said. 'This used to be such a friendly place. People would stop and chat on the road if they met. And a road like this would be covered in travellers, all on their way to somewhere or other, all with important things to be done. Now look at it.'

He indicated the long empty road. It ran in a straight line at that point and Horace could see for perhaps a kilometre in either direction. Ahead of them, the road was deserted. Behind, there was only the plodding cart and its four attendants, becoming smaller and smaller with each passing minute.

If they expected traffic on the road to increase as they neared Mountshannon, they were disappointed. The wide, dusty highway continued to stretch empty before them.

Gradually, the forest on either side of the road gave way to open farmland. Here, the fields were in slightly better shape than those they'd passed when they first arrived in Clonmel. And the farms themselves weren't deserted. They could see occasional figures moving in the farmyards, although the yards themselves were barricaded in the now familiar way and it was rare to see anyone moving too far from the farm buildings.

'Things don't look quite as bad here,' Horace ventured.

'There haven't been any raids in this area so far,' Halt reminded him. 'People are a little more confident this close to a large village like Mountshannon. And the farms themselves aren't so isolated.'

There was a warning shout from a farmhouse they were passing and they glanced across at it, in time to see two men running in from a field where they had been stacking hay to take shelter behind the barricaded farmyard wall. They still carried their pitchforks, Halt noticed.

'A little more confident,' he repeated. 'Not a lot.'

Mountshannon was similar to Craikennis, although considerably larger. One main street held the principal buildings of the village — an inn, and the buildings of the various traders that would be found in any sizeable centre: blacksmith, wheelwright, farrier, tool maker, harness maker and general store, where the ladies of the town could buy cloth and yarn and dried foodstuffs while their menfolk could buy seed, tools, oil and those hundred and one items that were always needed on a working farm.

The store was only a stopgap measure, of course; the main trading would take place in a weekly market.

Small lanes ran off the main street, linking to a network of back streets that ran more or less parallel to the high road. These were lined by houses, where the town's population lived. As in Craikennis, the majority of the houses were single-storey, roofed with thatch and constructed with whitewashed clay set over timber frameworks. The inn was two storeys, as was the farrier's building. There was a hay loft there, with a derrick projecting over the street to raise and lower the heavy hay bales stored inside.

Once again, the two riders had to submit to an examination when they approached the town. There was no barricade here but a small stream ran past the village, at right angles to the road, and a guard post had been established at the bridge that crossed it. As in Craikennis, it was a simple canvas pavilion with a couple of chairs and beds inside and a charcoal-burning brazier for warmth at night. It was manned by two members of the town watch, both armed with heavy clubs and with long daggers in their belts. They stepped out onto the road now, eyeing the new arrivals suspiciously. As before, Halt had tossed the cowl back from his face.

'What's your business in Mountshannon?' the taller of the two men asked. Horace eyed them critically. They were both big men, probably reasonably competent fighters, he thought. But, from the self-conscious way they handled their weapons, it was obvious to him that fighting wasn't their principal business. They weren't warriors.

'I'm looking to buy sheep,' Halt said. 'A ram and a pair of ewes. I need to replace my breeding stock. You'll have a market here, no doubt?'

The man nodded. 'Saturday,' he said. 'You're a day early.'

Halt shrugged. 'We've come from Ballygannon,' he said, naming an area that was well in the south, where the Outsiders had been active for some time. 'Better a day early than a day late.'

The watchman frowned thoughtfully at the name. He'd heard rumours of what had been going on in the south. Everyone had. But Halt was the first person he'd seen in some weeks who had actually been through the troubled area.

'How are things in Ballygannon?' he asked.

Halt eyed him bleakly. 'As I said, I need to replenish my breeding stock. They didn't all drop dead of old age at the same moment.'

The watchman nodded understanding. 'Aye, we've heard dark tales of doings in the south.' He looked now at Horace. Like the man in Craikennis, he could see the broad-shouldered young man didn't have the look of a farmer or woodsman. Besides, there was a long sword at his hip and a round buckler strapped at the back of his saddle. 'And who's this?' he asked.

'My nephew Michael. He's a good boy,' Halt told him.

The other man spoke now for the first time. 'And would you be a farmer too, Michael?' he asked.

Horace gave him a cold look. 'A soldier,' he said briefly.

'And what's a soldier going to do at the markets?' the second man asked.

Halt hurried to answer. Horace's accent was foreign and he didn't want the youth saying more than the odd word.

'I'm here to make sure I get the sheep home,' he said. 'Michael is here to make sure I get home.'

The watchman considered them for a few moments. It made sense, he thought. 'And he looks like the boyo who could do it,' he said, a faint smile thawing his features a little.

Horace said nothing. He simply met the man's gaze and nodded once. Strong, silent type, he thought.

The two watchmen seemed satisfied. They both drew back to the side of the road, waving Halt and Horace into the town.

'Ride in,' said the one who had spoken first. 'There's an inn in the main street or, if you've a mind to save a few pennies, you can pitch camp in the market ground at the far end of the village. Stay out of trouble while you're here.' He added the last statement almost as an afterthought. It was something all watchmen felt the need to say, Horace realised. He probably would have said it if they were two eighty-year-old dodderers hobbling along on walking sticks.

Halt touched a finger to his forehead in a informal salute and urged Abelard forward. Then he stopped, as if the thought had only just occurred to him, calling to the two men as they headed back to their pavilion.

'One thing,' he said and they turned back to face him. 'I've heard talk along the road of a man called Tennyson — some kind of priest?'

The watchmen exchanged sceptical glances. 'Yes,' said the leader, 'he's some kind of priest, all right.' There was a hint of sarcasm in his tone.

'Is he . . .?' Halt began but the second man answered the question before he could ask it.

'He's here. He and his followers are at the market ground too. Chances are you'll hear him preaching this afternoon if you've a mind.'

'Chances are,' his companion put in with now unmasked sarcasm, 'you'll hear him preaching *every* afternoon.'

Halt maintained a noncommittal expression, appearing to think over their words. 'Perhaps we'll listen in.' He looked at Horace. 'It'll break the monotony, Michael.'

'Break your eardrums more like,' said the second watchman. 'You'd do better to spend your time at the inn, you ask me.'

'Maybe,' Halt agreed. 'But we'll give the man a hearing at any rate.'

He nodded to them again and urged Abelard on. Horace, who had been waiting a few metres down the track, fell in beside him.

Twenty

While there was still some light left, Will returned to Tug and retraced his steps down the trail, looking for a place to set up his own camp. Two hundred metres back from the spot where they had stopped, he sighted a small glade a short distance from the side of the path. A large tree had fallen here, some years ago judging by the moss that covered its trunk. As it came down, it had taken several of its smaller neighbours with it, clearing an open space. It was an ideal spot. Not far off the path and almost unnoticeable. If Will hadn't actually been looking for a camp site, he would have ridden straight past. Most casual travellers would do the same, he reasoned.

He led Tug through the trees and waist-high under-growth that marked the edge of the trail and looked around, assessing the spot. The trail was almost invisible from here, which meant that the clearing would be the same for someone on the trail. There was an open space some five metres by four — more than enough for his camp site.

Not that it would be much of a camp, he thought. There'd be no tent and no fire. But there was thick grass for Tug to graze on and Will's real purpose was to find a spot where Tug would be out of sight.

He watered the horse again and made the 'free' hand signal, which told Tug he could graze if he wished to. The little horse moved around the clearing, nose to the ground, assessing the quality of the local fodder. Apparently finding it to his liking, he began to rip bunches of the thick green grass from the ground, chewing it with that grinding noise that horses make.

'Sorry I can't unsaddle you,' Will said. 'We may have to move out in a hurry.'

Tug glanced up at him, ears pricked, eyes alight with intelligence.

No matter.

The horse knew from long experience that Will would never neglect his comfort, unless there was a good reason to do so. Will sat, his back against the fallen tree trunk and his knees drawn up. He'd need to get back to his vantage point soon, he thought. He wanted to see when the guards were changed. He hoped that whoever relieved the man he'd selected would stay in the same spot. There was no reason why he shouldn't, he thought, but you never knew.

As the last light was fading, Will stood. Tug raised his head instantly, ears up, ready to move forward for Will to mount him. But Will shook his head.

'Stay here,' he said. Then added the one-word command: 'Silent.'

Tug understood the command; it was one of many that the little horse had been taught when he had been trained by Old Bob, the Ranger Corps' horse trainer. 'Silent' meant that if Tug were to hear any movement in his vicinity – which in this case meant along the path – he was to freeze in place and make no sound. That, coupled with the gathering darkness, would ensure that no passer-by would have the slightest idea that the little horse was just a few metres from the trail.

Gathering his cloak around him, Will moved back to the path. He paused as he reached the edge of the trees, listening both ways for the sound of anyone approaching. Then he quickly crossed the path and slid into the trees on the far side, moving parallel to the track and a few metres inside the tree cover.

An observer, had there been one, might have thought he had seen a grey shadow flit briefly across the open ground and then disappear into the trees. Once that was accomplished, he wouldn't have seen another trace of the silently moving Ranger.

Will regained his previous vantage point and settled down to watch. It had been barely three hours since he had seen the guards take their positions and he reasoned that the original men would still be at their posts. People were creatures of habit, he knew, and the most common term for sentry duty was four hours. Why that was so he had no idea. To his way of thinking, three hours would be a better term. By the end of four hours spent staring into the darkness, most sentries had sunk into lethargy. Of course, a three-hour term meant that more sentries would be needed through the course of the night and, as Will sensed, the posting of guards here was really more of a gesture than anything else. These raiders didn't expect to be attacked or infiltrated.

Which was why he had brought the half bottle of brandy from Duffy's Ford. He touched his inner pocket now to make sure the flask was still there. If he were going to make his way into the enemy camp, he would have to remove one of the guards – probably the one he had observed earlier. Of course, if necessary, he could make his way through the sentry line undetected without resorting to violence. But it would take considerably longer. Unseen movement across an open space like the one that faced him would be a slow and time-consuming business. And he would be silhouetted by the glow of the camp fires behind him.

So the quickest and safest way was to remove one of the sentries, leaving a gap in the screen that he could slip through. But that raised another problem. He didn't want the enemy to know he'd been here and an unconscious sentry was a sure sign that someone had infiltrated the camp.

Unless he was drunk. If a sentry were found reeking of brandy and sleeping peacefully under a tree, no amount of protesting on his part would convince his superiors that he had been attacked.

Will peered into the dark shadows below him now. Earlier, he had noted a few reference points to guide him to the point where the sentry was based. Now he saw a slight movement near that spot. He began moving down the slope towards the level ground, moving crabwise across the slope to bring him out at a point level with the sentry.

There was a constant murmur of conversation from the camp. Occasionally, a burst of laughter or the angry sounds of voices raised in an argument would punctuate the sound. That underlined another reason why Will didn't want to take too long getting inside the sentry line. He wanted to move around the camp while the men were still awake and talking. If he could eavesdrop on their conversations, he might pick up some idea about what they were planning. Once inside the camp, he was confident he could move freely about. Paradoxically, once he was inside, the less he tried to conceal himself the less likely he was to be stopped and questioned. But it was the first hundred metres of clear space between the sentry line and the camp that was the main danger. There was no reason why anyone should be moving towards the camp from that direction. Those inside the tent lines, their eyes dazzled by the fires, would be unlikely to spot him. A sentry, standing in the dark and looking back to the light, could easily see him silhouetted.

He felt the ground levelling under him now and he knew he must be close to the sentry's position. He slipped between the trees like a shadow, making a few more metres. Then he heard the sound of a man clearing his throat and shuffling his feet. He couldn't have been more than ten metres away. Close enough, Will thought. He slid down behind the bole of a tree, keeping its mass between himself and the sentry, wrapped himself in his cloak and settled down to wait.

He was there for the best part of an hour. Unmoving. Silent. Invisible. From time to time he heard the sentry moving about, or coughing. Once or twice, the man yawned, the sound clearly audible in the silence of the trees. The murmur of voices from the camp formed a constant background and Will was grateful for it. When the time came, it would help conceal any small noise he might make.

As he sat there in the darkness, he reflected that this had been the hardest part of his training: schooling yourself to remain unmoving, to resist the sudden urge to scratch an itch or to shift your position to ease a cramped muscle. This was why it was so important to assume a comfortable position in the first place, and to let the body relax completely. Yet there was no such thing as a completely comfortable position — not after you had been in it without moving for more than thirty minutes.

The ground beneath him had seemed soft and resilient when he sat down. He guessed it was formed of a thick mat of fallen leaves. Yet now he was conscious of a twig or a rock digging uncomfortably into his backside. He longed to lean to one side, reach under his backside and remove it but he resisted the urge. Chances are he could do it without making noise. But to do so would be to give in. Then, the next time he felt the urge to shift his position, it would be that much easier to convince himself that it was safe to do so. And the time after that, easier still. The result would be that he would be constantly shifting and, no matter how quietly he managed it, movement was the surest way to be discovered. So he sat without moving. He clenched his fist and concentrated on the pressure on his fingers and the muscles in his forearm to take his mind off the discomfort in his behind. The trick worked, at least for a while. When the twig made its presence felt once again, he bit gently on his lower lip to distract himself from it.

'There you are! Wondered where you'd got to!'

For a brief moment, he thought that the words, spoken

so close to him, were actually addressed to him. Then he realised that it was the sentry's relief, speaking to the man who'd been on duty for the past four hours.

Of course, the original sentry had taken a spot under the trees, where he was screened from the rest of the line. The relief must have had difficulty in locating him.

'About time you showed up,' said the original sentry. He sounded slightly aggrieved. Sentries usually did. They all assumed that their relief was late. Will could make out the small sounds of the man gathering his gear together, preparing to return to the camp.

The new man ignored the complaint. 'Not a bad little nook you've got here,' he said.

'Well, it's out of Tully's sight, that's the best thing. And happen it should rain, you'll be sheltered by the trees here.'

Tully, Will assumed, was the sergeant of the guard.

'I'll be off then. What's the grub tonight?' said the first sentry.

'Not too bad at all. The hunters brought in a few deer and some geese. For once the cooks didn't ruin it completely.'

The departing sentry grunted in appreciation. 'Well, I'd best get to it then. I'm famished. Enjoy yourself,' he added sardonically.

'Thanks for your kind thoughts,' his replacement said, matching the tone. The men might be comrades in arms, Will thought, but judging by their respective manners, they weren't friends.

While they had been talking, he had taken advantage of the noise they made to rise and slip closer to them. He wasn't concerned that he'd be seen by either man — his cloak and the surrounding darkness made sure of that. Now he was barely three metres from the new sentry, his face shadowed by the cowl of his cloak and a striker grasped in his right hand. In moving closer, he had gone in an arc, so that he was behind the sentry. He waited, flattened against a tree, until the departing guard's footsteps had faded away. As he had expected, the new sentry began to make himself comfortable, setting down his gear and checking his sightlines.

The time was now, Will thought, before he had a chance to settle in, while his mind was still distracted by the recent conversation. He risked a glance around the tree. The man was standing with his back to Will. He was armed with a spear and a spiked mace hung at his belt. His cloak was bundled on the ground beside him — presumably he'd don it when the night became colder — and a flask and mug were placed on the ground at the base of a flat rock that stood about a metre high. As Will slipped forward, the man leaned back, resting on the flat rock, his spear in his right hand. He sighed quietly — the sound of a man resigned to four hours of boredom and mild discomfort.

Will hit him hard behind the ear with the striker. The sigh, barely finished, turned to a strangled grunt and the man collapsed sideways off the rock, unconscious. His grasp on the spear was relaxed and it fell in the opposite direction, making barely any noise on the forest floor.

Will stood over the sprawled form for a few seconds, the striker poised, ready for another blow if needed.

But the man was well and truly out. His arms and legs lay at odd angles, indicating a total lack of tension in his muscles. He should remain this way for at least an hour, Will thought. That should be ample time for him to scout around the camp. He rolled the man over onto his back and, seizing him by the shoulders of his jacket, dragged the lifeless form to a tree. As ever, he marvelled at how heavy a human body could become when it was completely limp like this. He propped the man into a semi-reclining position against the tree, arranged his arms and legs to look as if he were sleeping, then poured the brandy over the front of his jerkin. For good measure, he pried the man's lips apart and sloshed some of the spirit inside his mouth.

He stepped back, eyeing his handiwork. Now, even if the man regained consciousness and raised the alarm, the spilt liquor would tell its own story to his superiors. Tossing the flask down beside the recumbent form, Will gathered his cloak about him and slipped out of the trees into the open space leading to the camp site.

He dropped to the ground and moved in a rapid crawl, dragging himself with his elbows, driving himself forward with his knees. Once he reached the tent lines, he continued to crawl until he was past the first few rows. Then, in the shadowed area between two tents, he rose carefully to his feet and waited for a few seconds.

There was no indication that anyone had noticed him. He slipped back the cowl from his face, stepped out of the shadows and walked casually through the camp towards the large central tent. Noticing a bucket full of water standing outside one tent, he glanced around to see if anyone were observing him. Satisfied that he had aroused no attention, he hastily grabbed the bucket and continued on his way.

A few metres on, he passed three men. Seeing the bucket, they assumed he had gone to fetch water. *Always seem to have a purpose,* Halt had taught him years ago. *If people think there's a reason you're in a place, odds are they won't bother to challenge you.*

'Right again, Halt,' he muttered to himself, and continued to make his way further into the camp.

Twenty-one

From his vantage point above the camp, Will had taken note of several of its key features. The cooking area was in the centre of the untidy cluster of tents. That was only to be expected. If the cook fires were placed to one side in a large camp like this, some of the men would have to traverse the entire area to get their food. This was the most convenient position for everyone. The luckiest, of course, would be those closest to the cooks. Being just minutes from the cook fires, they'd enjoy hot meals. So the more senior members of the band had placed their tents towards the middle. People on the fringes of the camp would find their meals lukewarm by the time they brought them back to their tents. The lower your rank, the further from the cook fires you were.

Which also dictated the position of the commander's tent. It was close enough to the cooking fires so that the leader's food would be hot and fresh, but just far enough away to be clear of the noise and the smoke.

Will headed now for the cook fires. It wasn't hard to get a bearing on them. Fires to provide for the needs of over a hundred men would need to be big and numerous. The leaping sparks whirled up into the sky above them and the glow of the flames was visible from anywhere in the camp.

He walked into the clear space around them. Men were bustling about, preparing the meal. As the sentry had stated, there were several deer carcasses turning on spits. Another smaller fire had a brace of geese turning slowly, dripping fat with each revolution so that the flames leapt and spluttered. In addition, there were large cookpots set over several smaller fires. As he watched, a sweating attendant, his face livid in the firelight, dumped a bucket full of peeled potatoes into one, leaping back hurriedly to avoid the splash of boiling water.

Will knew it was important that he keep moving. If he were to stand around gaping, sooner or later someone would challenge his presence and want to know who he was. He had the cowl on his cloak thrown back, of course, and in the uncertain firelight the cloak's camouflage pattern wasn't really noticeable. He had left his bow and quiver with Tug and was armed only with his two knives. To all intents and purposes, he looked like anyone else in the camp. Except none of them were standing still, looking at what was going on around them. He moved forward towards the man who'd just dumped the potatoes into boiling water. The cook looked up at him, a scowl on his face.

'We'll tell you when the food's ready,' he said unpleasantly. Cooks were used to being harassed by the men. Either the food wasn't ready on time or, if it were, it was too cold. Or overcooked. Or undercooked. Or just generally not good enough.

Will made a negative gesture with his free hand, indicating he wasn't trying to jump the queue. He held up the bucket of water.

'John said to bring you this water,' he said.

Two things he was sure of. In a camp this large, there would be half a dozen people named John. And cooks were always in need of water. The cook frowned now.

'Don't remember as I asked him,' he said. Will shrugged and turned away, still with the bucket in his hand.

'Suit yourself,' he said. But the cook stopped him quickly. He might not have asked for water but he'd need it sooner or later and it would save him the trouble of fetching it.

'Put it by here, then. Might as well have it if you've brought it.'

'Fine.' Will set the bucket down. The cook nodded a reluctant acknowledgment.

'Tell John thanks,' he said and Will snorted.

'Wasn't John who had to lug it here across the camp, was it?' he said archly.

'True enough.' The cook understood the implied message. 'See me when we're serving. There'll be some extra for your plate.'

Will touched his forehead. 'Grateful to you,' he said, and moved away. He glanced back after a few paces but the cook had already lost interest in him. Will moved away, his pace brisk, heading for the central command pavilion. It was less than thirty metres away and he could see it clearly. It stood a little apart from its neighbours, at the top of a slight slope, with a large fire in front of it. There were two sentries placed either side of the entrance and as he watched, three men approached, waited to be recognised, and headed inside. Shortly after, a servant appeared with a tray bearing thick glass tankards and a wine flagon. He went inside and reappeared a minute or so later.

Will walked past the large tent, staying well away from it, on the far side of the cleared area. Out of the side of his eyes, he regarded the position. Sentries at the front, of course. But he was willing to bet the back of the tent was unguarded. After all, he realised, the two sentries were more a mark of authority than a security measure. There was little chance of anyone attacking the command tent in this camp. He continued on. The open space ended and now the ragged lines of tents resumed, the individual tents placed only a few metres away from each other. He passed several where the tent flaps were open and men were sprawled inside or on the ground outside, talking among themselves. He muttered a greeting to one group who looked up at him with mild curiosity. He waited until he had passed several unoccupied and unlit tents. Then, glancing quickly around to see that nobody was watching, he dived into the shadowed space between two of them. Crouching, he moved to the rear, and so to the next avenue of tents. Now he dropped full length, pulling the cowl of his cloak over his head once more, and lay like a shadow, observing the next lane that he had to cross. There was little activity here. He waited several minutes to make sure, then rose smoothly to his feet and moved across the line into the space between two tents on the opposite side. One of them was occupied and lit from within and he could see a shadow on the canvas as the occupant moved around.

Again, he moved to the back of the tents. He estimated now that he would be behind the command pavilion if he were to head back along the next lane. Checking as before that the way was clear, he rose and walked unconcernedly back the way he had come.

He could see the command tent again. It bulked much larger than the others and stood in its own empty patch of ground. He was right. His movement back through the tent lines had brought him out level with the rear of the big tent. His original assumption also proved to be correct. There was no guard at the rear. Still, he could hardly hope to walk out of the tent lines and stroll up behind the pavilion to eavesdrop without someone noticing him, so he cut left between two more tents and moved to the next lane.

He took stock of the situation. There were men in front of some of the tents in the next line. But the two closest to the open space where the pavilion was pitched were dark and empty. Will looked around quickly. The tent to his left was occupied, but the flaps were drawn closed. There was a bundle of kindling by the small fireplace in front of it. Quickly he moved to it, stooped and swung the bundle up over his shoulder. He trudged along the tent line now, carrying his firewood, passing the men who were sitting talking. They barely gave him a glance. As he reached the final tent, he swung the pile of branches down and placed it beside the fire, then, in one quick movement, he slid out of the tent lines to the darkened area beside them and went quickly to ground, his cloak wrapped around him, his face concealed once more beneath the cowl.

He snake-crawled several metres into the open but unlit space, driving himself forward with elbows and knees. After a few moments he stopped to see if there had been any reaction to his approach. Nothing. He glanced up to get his bearings and slithered towards the back of the pavilion, sliding through the rank grass like a serpent, the mottled pattern on his cloak breaking up the outline of his body and letting him merge into the shadows and uneven hollows of the ground around him.

He moved carefully now and it took ten minutes for him to cover the thirty metres to the rear of the pavilion. At one stage, a group of men emerged from the tent lines and headed towards the larger tent. There were four of them and they came dangerously close to the spot where he lay, not daring to move a muscle. He felt his heart hammering behind his ribs, was sure they must be able to hear the sound as well. No matter how many times he had done this, there was always the fear that *this time* they must see the prone shape lying unmoving a few metres away. The men were drunk and talking loudly, staggering slightly on the uneven ground. One of the sentries stepped forward, holding up a hand to stop them. Will lay, his head to one side so that he could watch what was happening.

'That's far enough, you men,' the sentry called. A sensible man would have realised that his tone brooked no argument. But these weren't sensible men. They were drunk.

They stopped. Will could see they were swaying slightly.

'Wanna word with Padraig,' one of the men said, slurring the words badly.

The sentry shook his head. 'That's Captain Padraig to you, Murphy. And you can believe he doesn't want a word with you.'

'We've got a legitimate complaint to make,' the man called Murphy continued. 'Any man can make his case to Padraig. We're brothers in this band. We're all the equals of each other.'

His companions chorused their agreement. They all took a pace forward and the sentry lowered his spear. They stopped again. A voice from inside the pavilion caught the attention of all of them.

'We may be equal in this band, but I'm more equal than anyone, and it pays to remember that. Quinn!'

The sentry straightened, turning to look back at the pavilion. The voice obviously belonged to Padraig, the leader of the band of cutthroats, Will thought. It was a harsh, uncompromising voice — the voice of a man used to instant obedience.

'Yes, Captain!' the sentry replied.

'Tell those drunken fools that if they continue to disturb me, I'll start taking their ears off with a blunt knife.'

'Aye, Captain!' Quinn said. Then, in a lowered tone, he said urgently to the four drunks, 'You heard him, Murphy! And you know the captain is not a man to cross. Now get yourselves out of here!'

Murphy swayed belligerently, unwilling to back down in front of his friends. Yet Will could tell from his body language that he was cowed, and after a show of defiance, he would give in.

'Well then,' he said, 'we wouldn't want to disturb the great captain's rest, would we?'

With an exaggerated bow, he turned away with his companions and they lurched back down the sloping ground to the tent lines.

Realising that the sentries' eyes were on the drunk men, Will slipped forward quickly, slithering into the dark shadow at the rear of the pavilion. He pressed forward, easing the cowl back away from his ear to hear what was being said.

'. . . so at first light, Driscoll, you'll take thirty men and head for Mountshannon. Take the valley road. It's more direct.' It was Padraig speaking, the man who had threatened to separate the drunks from their ears.

'Is thirty men enough?' a second voice asked.

Another man answered impatiently. 'Twenty would be enough for what we have in mind. But with thirty I can make a better show of it.'

Obviously the one named Driscoll, Will thought. Then Padraig resumed talking.

'That's right. Now, you others, I want the rest of the band ready to move out by midday. We'll follow the ridge trail and head for Craikennis. Driscoll can rendezvous with us at the intersection with the Mountshannon road the morning after tomorrow. Then we'll put on another show for Craikennis.'

The one called Driscoll chuckled. 'More than a show, I think. There'll be no holy man to send us packing.'

There was a ripple of laughter from the others. Will frowned. He had the uncomfortable feeling that he had just missed something important. He edged a little closer to the canvas wall. He heard the clink of glasses from inside and the sound of pouring. The men were refilling their drinks.

There were one or two appreciative sighs — the sound a man makes when he has taken a deep draught of wine.

'You keep a good cellar, Padraig, and no doubt to it,' said a voice he hadn't heard so far.

'There'll be more where that came from in a few days,' Padraig said. 'Now, once we've rendezvoused with Driscoll, here's what we'll . . .'

Whatever they were going to do, Will never learned. At that moment, there was a shout of alarm from outside the camp. Then a voice was raised in anger and men started shouting and running towards the open space that led to the forest.

Will knew what had happened. The unconscious sentry had been found and the alarm had been raised. He'd hear nothing further tonight, he realised. He wriggled back a few metres from the tent, then, knowing that all attention would be turned towards the point where the shouting was going on, he rose into a crouch and melted back into the tent lines again.

He began running towards the sentry line, following scattered groups of men. As he passed one tent, he saw several spears stacked together outside it. He grabbed one, sending the others clattering to the ground like giant pick-up sticks, and ran out onto the open grassy area that separated the camp from the forest. He passed several other men as he did so. He could hear sergeants bellowing orders, trying to bring some sense into the chaos of the disturbed camp. But for now, this confusion was exactly what Will needed.

'This way!' he shouted, to nobody in particular, and angled towards a point in the trees which he knew to be some fifty metres from where he had knocked the sentry out. The more noise he made, the more conspicuous he made himself seem, the less notice anyone would take of him. If anyone actually followed him into the forest, he was confident that he could lose them within a few minutes.

He glanced over his shoulder but nobody had followed his lead. Already, as word filtered back that it was nothing but a sentry found sleeping on watch, men were beginning to slow down and stop. Some had even turned back to the camp.

None of them noticed when Will plunged into the forest. Within seconds the darkness beneath the trees seemed to have swallowed him. All that was left was the spear, lying half concealed in the long grass where, having no further use for it, he had tossed it to one side.

He smiled to himself as he ran silently through the trees. There'd be several unhappy men in the camp that evening. The owner of the spear would wonder what had become of his weapon — good spears were expensive. And the man who had gathered the bundle of kindling would be furious to discover that one of his comrades had stolen it.

As for the unconscious sentry, Will didn't envy him having to convince his superiors that he had been attacked. Particularly as he would be reeking of brandy. Chances were he'd be punished — and severely. In a band like this, sleeping on watch would attract savage punishment.

So the evening would be ruined for at least three of the outlaws, Will thought.

'All in all, a good night's work,' he said to himself.

Twenty-two

The market ground was a large meadow at the eastern end of the village. To the north and south were open farmlands – ploughed fields and fields under crops. Several small farmhouses were visible in the near distance. On the eastern side of the meadow there was a thick band of trees where the forest began again.

'Look who's here,' Halt said quietly. Horace followed his gaze. In the south-western corner of the meadow was a large white pavilion. Several figures in white robes were moving around the pavilion, tending a fire and preparing food.

'That's them?' Horace asked and Halt nodded once.

'That's them.'

They pitched their two small tents by a blackened ring of firestones some distance from the pavilion.

'What now?' Horace asked.

Halt looked up at the sun. He estimated that it was past noon.

'We'll have a bite to eat,' he said. 'Then, later on, we'll go and listen to what Tennyson has to say.'

Horace's face brightened at the mention of food. 'Sounds like a plan to me.'

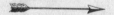

In the late afternoon, people began making their way towards the Outsiders' camp. Halt and Horace joined the rapidly growing crowd. Halt raised an eyebrow as he saw that Tennyson's followers had set up several casks of ale and wine under a large, open-sided marquee and were serving generous mugs of both to all comers.

'That's one way to get a congregation together,' he muttered to Horace. They edged their way through the throng who were jostling for position at the refreshment tables. 'Try to look diffident,' he added to Horace.

The tall warrior frowned. 'How do I do that?'

'Look as if you're not certain you should be here,' Halt said. 'As if you're uncertain of yourself.'

'Well, I'm *not* certain I should be here,' Horace said.

Halt sighed. 'Then stop striding along so confidently. Look as if you think I'm going to whack you over the head any minute. That'll do the trick.'

'Are you?' Horace asked, smiling to himself. 'Are you going to whack me over the head?'

Halt turned a baleful glance on the younger man. But before he could speak, another voice interrupted them.

'Greetings, friends! Greetings!' The voice was deep and resonant, the powerful, well-modulated voice of a trained orator. Halt and Horace turned to view the speaker, who was walking towards them. He was a tall, heavily built man in a long white robe. In his right hand, he held a staff.

Flanking him, but a few paces behind him, were two startling identical figures. They were massively built, well over two metres in height. Tall as the leader might be, he was dwarfed by these two men. Both were totally bald. Horace studied them for a few seconds, then turned his attention back to the speaker.

His face was broad, with strong features and a prominent nose. The eyes were a startling blue. They gave the impression that their owner was looking far into the distance and seeing things normal folk could not. Horace was willing to bet that this was a look the man had carefully cultivated. On a closer inspection Horace realised that the man was well built but somewhat overweight. Obviously, he wasn't a warrior. He was bare-headed and his hair was shoulder length, brushed back from his forehead, and grey all over. Not pepper and salt grey like Halt's, but a uniform shade of white-grey throughout. The man assessed Halt and Horace quickly, then addressed himself to Halt as the obvious leader.

'You're new to the town.' His tone was friendly and he smiled in greeting. 'I saw you arrive earlier today.'

Halt nodded. He made no attempt to return the other man's smile. 'And you're taking a census, are you?'

Horace stayed silent, content to let Halt take the lead. He realised that the Ranger was playing the role of a typical country person — guarded and suspicious of strangers. His manner didn't seem to bother the newcomer, however. He seemed genuinely amused by Halt's curt rejoinder.

'Not at all. I'm just always glad to greet a new friend.'

'I wasn't aware that we were friends,' Halt said.

The burly man's smile widened. 'I'm a servant of the

Golden God Alseiass. And he says all men are my friends — and I should be a friend to all men.'

Halt shrugged, still unimpressed. 'Can't say I've heard of Alseiass, either,' he said. 'He's new, is he? Just arrived from another part of heaven, perhaps?'

The man chuckled. It was a rich, deep sound. Horace found himself thinking that, if he didn't know who this man was, he would find him easy to like.

'I'll admit that Alseiass isn't well known in this part of the country,' the man said. 'But that will change. My name is Tennyson, by the way. I'm the Golden God's minister and these are my assistants Gerard and Killeen, who are also disciples of Alseiass.' He indicated the two silent giants behind him. 'We bid you a warm welcome to our camp site.'

Neither Gerard nor Killeen looked particularly warm or welcoming, Halt thought. He could read the underlying message in Tennyson's words: *Welcome to my camp site and here are my two tame bruisers in case you get out of hand.*

'Please enjoy our hospitality,' Tennyson continued smoothly. 'Alseiass tells us we should all share our bounty with our friends.' He smiled again. 'Particularly new friends.'

This time, his warm smile embraced both Halt and Horace. Then he turned to look at the crowd gathering around a dais at the far end of the marquee.

'The people are waiting,' he said. 'I should go.'

He raised a hand, describing a curve in the air in what was obviously a form of blessing. Then he turned and strode away. Flanked by his two disciples, he made his way through the crowd, stopping here and there for a quick word or a smile or to deliver a blessing.

'So that's Tennyson,' Halt said softly. 'What did you think of him?'

Horace hesitated, then, a little reluctantly, he replied: 'Actually, I found him rather impressive.'

Halt nodded. 'So did I.'

There was an buzz of interest from the crowd as Tennyson mounted the dais, smiling at those around him and holding up his hands for silence. An expectant hush fell and he began to speak, his deep, resonant voice carrying easily to all corners of the marquee so that nobody had to lean forward to hear his words.

He was a polished performer, there was no question about it. He began with a joke at his own expense — a story about a disastrous attempt at milking a cow. Such a task was second nature to a rural audience like this and the laughter swelled as he described his complete ineptitude. Then he segued neatly to the fact that all people had varying skills and the trick to life was to find ways for people to work together and make the most effective use of their abilities. From there it was a short step to the need for people to stick together in troubled times such as the ones they were going through.

'There are evil, lawless men abroad in the world. They are the servants of the black spirit Balsennis. I see his hand everywhere I go, bringing sorrow and despair and death to the people of this wonderful country,' he said. 'Where will we find the help we need to defeat them, to drive them out? To put this country back to the way it was before? Who will help us do this?'

'The King?' said a tentative voice from the side of the crowd. Halt was willing to bet that it was one of Tennyson's own followers who had said it.

The burly orator allowed himself a small, sad smile. 'The King, you say? Well, I'll agree with you that he *should* be the one to set his own country to rights. But can you see him doing so?'

An angry muttering swept through the crowd. Tennyson had hit a sore point with that thrust. But the people's dissatisfaction wasn't quite strong enough for them to come out in the open and agree with him. Privately, and to each other, they agreed. Publicly, they weren't quite ready to commit themselves. Open criticism of a king was a dangerous path to tread.

Tennyson let the dissatisfaction grow for a few seconds, then he resumed. 'I can't see him doing anything. I can't see his troops on their way to flush out these bandits and outlaws who are destroying the country. After all, he's the man with the power, isn't he? Does he allow anyone else to keep a body of trained soldiers for protection?'

The word 'No!' rang out from several points in the crowd. Tennyson's stooges again, Halt thought. Then the cry gathered strength and momentum as more and more people began yelling it. A few fists were raised and shaken in the air. Tennyson raised his hands for silence and the shouting gradually died down.

'Now a king, any king, deserves the loyalty of his subjects. We all know that . . .' he began. An angry under-current of muttering went through the crowd again as they disagreed with him, thinking he was about to make excuses for King Ferris. Again, Tennyson held up his hands for silence and, reluctantly this time, the crowd went quiet.

'But. . .' he said, then repeated it with greater emphasis, '*But!* That loyalty must pass both ways. If subjects must be loyal to their king, then kings must apply that same loyalty to their subjects. Otherwise . . .' He paused and the crowd seemed to lean forward, seeing where he was going before he actually went there. 'The king abandons any claim to loyalty from his people.'

There was a roar of agreement from the villagers. Halt leaned close to Horace and said in his ear, 'Dangerous stuff. This is sedition. He must be pretty sure of himself.'

Horace nodded and turned his own head to reply in a similar soft tone. 'From what you've told us, he's had plenty of practice.'

As the crowd settled down once more, Tennyson continued. 'King Ferris has done nothing to save the people of Clonmel from the depredations of the outlaws and bandits and killers who roam the land, doing the evil work of Balsennis. What did he do for the people of Duffy's Ford?' He paused and looked expectantly at the faces before him.

A ragged chorus rose from a dozen or so throats. 'Nothing.'

Tennyson cupped a hand behind one ear and turned his head a little, a puzzled look on his face.

'What was that?' he asked and this time the answer was a full-throated roar from the entire assembly.

'NOTHING!'

'Did he help that innocent twelve-year-old girl who was murdered at the ford? What did he do for her?'

Again: 'NOTHING!'

'It's not that Ferris can't help. The fact is, he refuses to do so!' Tennyson thundered. 'He has the power, if only he would choose to use it on your behalf. But he's content to hide behind the walls of his castle at Dun Kilty, on soft cushions, with plenty to eat and drink, and do nothing. He will not raise a finger to help his people. He has no loyalty!'

His voice rose to a crescendo on the last few words. He paused, looking out over the crowd. In twos and threes, they called their agreement. Hesitantly at first, then with growing conviction. Tennyson said nothing. And this time, he made no sign for silence. He let the resentment seethe, let the people build to a pitch of anger. Then, as they realised he was waiting for them to fall silent, they did so. This time, when he spoke, he forsook the dramatic thundering and said in a quiet, carrying voice:

'And if he shows no loyalty to you, then you owe him none at all.'

Again, the voice of the mob rose and, this time, Tennyson soared above them.

'Ferris will do nothing to help you. You must look to one who will protect you!'

Now people began calling the same plea from different points around the crowd. Funny, Halt thought, how they all used the same words and phrases.

'Tennyson!' they shouted, and the cry spread to all parts of the crowd. 'Tennyson! Protect us!'

But now Tennyson was holding up his hands to calm them and shaking his head at their cries. When they fell silent, he spoke to them again, in that clear, ringing voice.

'No! No! No! Believe me, I'm not the one, my friends. I can't protect you. Your safety lies with the power of Alseiass.'

There was a groan of disappointment from the left-hand side of the crowd.

Then a voice called, 'We don't need fairy tales and superstition! They won't stop the bandits!'

Other voices were raised in agreement. But Halt noticed that they didn't seem to be a majority. The greater part of the crowd sat uncertainly, looking round at each interjection, studying the speakers and assessing the worth of what they said. They weren't willing to commit either way, he saw.

'We want swords and soldiers! Not pie in the sky, Tennyson!'

'You lead us!' a third voice called. 'You lead and we'll follow! We'll teach these brigands a lesson without some strange god's help.'

That, Horace and Halt saw, was a popular position. The majority of the crowd, uncertain which way to go, followed this lead eagerly. They began shouting for Tennyson to lead the way. To lead them against the outlaws who were preying on the countryside. They sensed the man's strength and authority. The chant grew, becoming louder and more insistent as more people joined in.

'No god! No king! Tennyson! No god! No king! Tennyson!'

Tennyson smiled around the mass of faces, many of them red now with excitement and the passion of the moment.

'People, you do me honour. But I tell you, I'm not the one!'

'Yes you are!' a lone voice shouted and several others raised a ragged chorus of agreement. But the majority sat, quiet now, watching him.

'No. Please believe me. I'm no war leader. Any strength

I have comes from Alseiass, the Golden God. The All-Seeing One. Believe me.'

Halt leaned over to Horace again and whispered, 'My god but he's good. He could have taken the reins then and there and offered to lead them.'

'Then why didn't he?' Horace asked.

Halt chewed his lip thoughtfully. 'He needs a bigger reputation than he'll get from exciting a few hundred country villagers. He's taking on a king. He needs something big. Something supernatural. He needs them to believe in this god of his.'

But now Tennyson had stepped down from the podium he had been speaking from and approached the front row of the crowd. He spoke to them with warmth and friendliness as he walked among them.

'I promised you when I first arrived here that I wouldn't try to force my god upon you,' he said in a reasonable tone. 'Have I tried to do that?'

He spread his hands in question and looked from side to side. Halt and Horace could see heads shaking as people agreed with him.

'No. I haven't. Because that isn't Alseiass's way. He doesn't care to force himself upon you. If you have other gods you prefer, or no god at all, he doesn't condemn you. He respects your right to decide, without being harried or bullied or shouted at.'

'Interesting method,' Halt said softly. 'Most evangelists threaten fire and brimstone if you don't accept their teachings.'

'But I know Alseiass's power,' Tennyson continued. 'And I tell you this: whether you are his followers or not, he can protect you. And he will protect you. I'm simply the channel to him. Remember, Alseiass loves you. And because he does, he respects your right to disagree with me. But if you need him and I call upon him, he will arrive with power such as you've never seen.'

The meadow was silent now as he walked among the crowd. Those at the front turned to watch him as he moved past them.

'And then, if you see his power and compassion and want to turn to him and join our band, then Alseiass will make you doubly welcome.'

'Well said, Tennyson!' a woman shouted and he smiled at her.

'But let's hope that it doesn't come to that,' he said. 'Let's all hope that this lovely village of yours remains a haven of peace and Alseiass won't need to be asked to protect it.'

There was a murmur from the crowd. Horace sensed a feeling of contentment in those around him. It was an interesting proposition Tennyson had put: *You don't have to believe in my god. But if danger arrives, he'll protect you nonetheless.* It was what he'd heard described as a win-win situation. Gradually, the crowd began to break up as Tennyson stopped once more to chat with individuals and smaller groups.

Horace caught Halt's eye. 'D'you think Alseiass will be called on to maintain the peace of this beautiful village?'

Halt let one corner of his mouth turn up in a cynical smile.

'I'd bet my life on it.'

Twenty-three

Tug welcomed Will back to the little clearing with a brief toss of his head. Will moved to the horse and stroked his soft nose.

'Good boy,' he said quietly. Tug snorted softly in reply, aware that if Will were speaking, there was no need to maintain his own silence. Will considered his situation for a moment, then decided that there was time for a few hours' rest. The man called Driscoll was leading his raiding party out at dawn. But they were going by the lowland route to Mountshannon, crossing the river that ran past the camp and following a trail that led through the flatlands below the hills. He wouldn't be bothered by them.

The second group, as Padraig had ordered, would be moving out around midday, and following the ridge trail that Will was on. But he planned to be on his way before first light, so there was no chance that they'd catch up to him. That decided, he prepared to get a few hours' rest. He'd been on the move all day and well into the night, after all.

He unsaddled Tug. There was no need for the little horse to endure the discomfort of the saddle now. Tug shook himself gratefully and moved away to crop the grass. Will looked up through the tree canopy to the sky. He could see the stars quite clearly. Occasionally, a wisp of cloud would slide across the sky, blotting them out. But he could tell there was little chance of rain so he didn't bother to set up the small one-man tent that was rolled behind his saddle. He'd sleep in the open tonight, he thought.

He ate a cold meal. He wanted to leave no trace of his presence here so he couldn't light a fire. He reflected, as he chewed doggedly on the tough dried beef, that he'd be glad when this was over and he could find a good hot meal.

Potatoes would be nice, he thought. Boiled in their jackets, perhaps, and then smothered in butter, salt and pepper. His stomach growled at the thought and he glanced with disfavour at the unappetising twist of dried beef in his hand. Earlier in the day, he had reflected that he quite enjoyed the taste. In the ensuing hours, it seemed to have lost some of its appeal.

There was something still niggling in the back of his mind about the conversation he'd overheard in Padraig's tent. Something was illogical but he couldn't put his finger on it. Then it fell into place.

From all he'd heard, Mountshannon was considerably larger than Craikennis. Yet Driscoll was attacking the larger village with thirty men only. Then he was rendezvousing with another force of fifty men, led by Padraig himself, to attack Craikennis. It didn't make any sense. Surely the larger force would be needed for Mountshannon?

Perhaps he'd heard wrong?

He took a drink of cold water from his canteen, regretting the lack of a good cup of hot, sweet coffee.

No. He was sure he'd heard it correctly. Thirty men for Mountshannon. The combined force of eighty for Craikennis.

Unless they're not actually attacking Mountshannon, he thought. Maybe Driscoll is leading a reconnaissance in force? But he shook his head at that thought. If he wanted to reconnoitre, half a dozen men would be sufficient. Even fewer.

He replaced the cap on the water bottle and set it to one side, yawning hugely. Now that he had decided that he would get some rest, the efforts of the day, and the tension he'd been under, made themselves felt and he couldn't wait to turn in. Taking his blankets, he moved across the clearing and quickly made himself a bed inside the trees, where a large bush would shelter him from unfriendly eyes.

His mind kept turning over the problem that was nagging at him. Eventually, he shrugged it away and fell asleep within a few minutes.

Twenty-four

arket day in Mountshannon was well under way. There had been a few showers of rain just after dawn, when most of the stall holders had arrived to set up their shelters and lay out their goods for display. But as the morning wore on, the sun came out and set the dampened ground steaming.

Horace and Halt had watched preparations from their camp site as they breakfasted. The villagers knew that market day was a case of first in gets the best goods, so they had thronged to the market while the rain was still drifting down. Now the large meadow, formerly deserted but for their two small tents and the Outsiders' pavilion, was a throng mass of stalls, people, performers, animals, carts and food vendors.

Tennyson and his people were taking advantage of the crowd to promote their message. A small group of them, all in the usual white robes, were singing country folk songs, with the occasional hymn of praise to Alseiass.

The singing was good and they were managing a three-part harmony, according to Horace. He commented on the fact to Halt.

The Ranger shrugged. 'Three donkeys braying is much the same as one,' he said, 'save that it's louder.' Halt was not a student of music. Horace smiled at him.

'Nonetheless, they are good. I'd go and listen to them if I were just passing by,' he admitted.

Halt eyed him. 'You would?'

Horace nodded emphatically. 'Definitely. They're good entertainers, Halt.'

Halt nodded thoughtfully. 'Insidious might be a better term,' he said. 'But this is the way they work. They worm their way into people's affection. It's all very easygoing and non-confrontational. Then they spring their trap.'

'Well, they're good trappers. And their bait is very effective,' Horace told him. Again, Halt nodded.

'I know. That's what makes them so dangerous.' He stood up, dusting off the seat of his pants. They had spread a canvas square over the wet ground outside their tents but his backside still felt a little damp. 'Come on, we'd better look at livestock. Although thank God I've seen little in the way of good animals arrive so far. Otherwise I might have to buy some.'

'We could always eat 'em,' Horace suggested cheerfully. Halt turned a baleful glance on him.

'It always gets back to eating with you, doesn't it?' he asked.

'I'm a growing boy, Halt,' the young warrior said. Halt snorted and led the way towards the market.

They strolled among the stalls and the livestock pens.

There were plenty of chickens and ducks and geese for sale. And quite a good selection of pigs. There were no cattle and only a few scrubby, ill-conditioned sheep. Horace commented on the fact.

'The animals for sale here are the ones that people raise close to the farmhouse,' Halt explained. 'Chickens, ducks and pigs all stay close by, so the farmer has no call to go out into the fields to tend them.'

'And of course,' Horace replied, understanding, 'people are staying close by their houses these days.'

'Exactly.' Halt stopped by a small pen that held three sheep. Their wool was coated and matted with mud. He nodded to the owner and stepped into the pen. He caught the nearest, held it between his knees and pried its jaws apart, peering at its teeth. The sheep struggled in protest at this treatment and eventually he released it, dusted his hands together and looked at the owner again, giving a small shake of his head. He stepped out of the pen and they moved on.

'So, what was wrong with them?' Horace asked after a few moments.

Halt turned a curious gaze on him. 'Wrong with what?'

Horace jerked his thumb back towards the small sheep pen. 'The sheep's teeth. What was the problem?'

Halt made a small moue of understanding, then shrugged. 'Haven't the faintest idea. What do I know about sheep?'

'But you . . .'

'I looked at his teeth. That's what people seem to do when they look at animals. They look at their teeth. Then they usually shake their heads and walk off. So that's what

I did.' He paused, then continued. 'Did you want me to buy it?'

Horace raised both hands in a defensive gesture. 'Not at all. I just wondered.'

'Good.' Halt smiled sardonically. 'For a moment there I thought you might be feeling peckish.'

They stopped at a fruit stall and bought several apples. They were good. Crisp and juicy, with just a hint of tart flavour hiding behind their sweetness. The two of them crunched away as they inspected a stall full of camping gear and kitchen utensils.

'Good filleting knife,' Halt said. He asked the price of the stall owner, haggled for several minutes, made to walk out in mock disgust, then settled on a price and bought the thin-bladed knife. As they left the tent, he said to Horace, 'We should fish for some trout in the streams around here. Make a nice change to the menu.' He paused and looked around the nearby stalls. 'Might as well look for some almonds if we're going to catch trout.'

'Fishing for and catching are two different matters,' Horace said and Halt eyed him sidelong.

'Are you casting aspersions on my fishing ability?'

Horace met his gaze. 'You don't strike me as the fishing type. It's a genteel sort of sport and I can't picture you sitting sedately with a fishing rod in your hands.'

'Why use a rod when you can use a bow?' Halt replied and Horace frowned at him.

'You *shoot* the fish?' he said. And when Halt nodded, he went on, 'That's not very sporting, is it?'

There was a good deal of hunting and fishing done around Castle Araluen, usually involving the royal family.

It was all done according to strict rules and conventions. A gentleman, Horace had been taught, only fished for trout with a rod and with a man-made lure — never live bait. He certainly didn't skewer them on the end of an arrow. At least, he thought ruefully, Halt didn't use live bait.

'I never said I was sporting,' Halt said. 'I said I catch fish. I doubt they care whether they're killed by a hook or an arrow. And they taste pretty much the same.'

Horace was about to reply when they heard a cry of alarm. Both of them stopped. Halt's hand went instinctively to the saxe knife at his belt. Horace's left hand closed over the top of his scabbard, ready to steady it if he needed to draw his sword quickly.

There was a buzz of fear from the people around them. The shout was repeated and this time they could make out where it came from — the line of trees that marked the eastern side of the market ground. Without needing to confer, they started in that direction. Already a few families were hurrying the opposite way, back to the shelter of the village.

'Sounds like it's started,' Halt said. 'Whatever "it" may be.'

They threaded their way through the stalls towards the trees. For a moment, Halt considered returning to their camp to fetch his bow. He hadn't brought it as it didn't quite match the picture of a shepherd looking for new stock in the market. Then he decided against it. He had an instinctive feeling that he wouldn't need the bow. He didn't know why he had that feeling. He just did.

They emerged from the cluster of market stalls into clear ground.

'Over there,' said Horace, pointing.

An armed man stood a few metres clear of the trees. Behind him, half hidden by the uncertain shadows among the trees, more armed men were visible. Standing between Halt and Horace's position at the edge of the market ground were three of the village's watchmen. They too were armed, but their weapons — clubs, a sickle blade mounted on a spear handle and one slightly rusty sword — seemed inadequate when viewed against the chain mail, swords, shields and maces wielded by the newcomers.

As the two Araluans watched, one of the village guards called a challenge to the man standing clear of the trees.

'That's far enough! You have no business here. Turn around and be on your way!'

The stranger laughed. It was a harsh sound and totally devoid of any humour.

'Don't tell me where my business lies, farmer! I'll come and go as I please. My men and I serve Balsennis, the mighty god of destruction and chaos. And he's decided that it's time your village paid him tribute.'

A buzz of recognition went round the marketplace as he spoke the name Balsennis. They had heard Tennyson warn of this dark and evil spirit, heard him blame the god for the reign of lawlessness and terror that was sweeping Clonmel.

Several more of the town watchmen had thrust their way through the crowd. They had obviously armed themselves in haste and most of them carried makeshift weapons. They formed up in an uneven line behind the first two. There were ten of them. If their intent was to discourage the stranger with their numbers, they were doomed to failure. He laughed again.

'That's what you have to oppose me? A dozen of you, armed with sharp sticks and sickles? Get out of my way, farmer! I've got eighty armed fighting men in the trees here. If you choose to resist, we'll kill every man, woman and child in the village, and then take what we want. Drop your weapons and we might spare some of you! I'll give you ten seconds to think it over.'

Halt leaned closer to Horace and said in a low tone: 'If you wanted to frighten people with your overwhelming numbers, would you keep them hidden in the forest?'

Horace frowned. He had been thinking much the same thing. 'If I had eighty men, I think I'd show them. A show of force like that would be more frightening than simply talking about them.'

'So the odds are,' Halt said, 'that he's bluffing about having eighty men.'

'Probably. But he's still got the watchmen outnumbered. I can count at least twenty men in the trees. Of course,' he added, 'the village can probably muster more men given time. Those dozen out there are just the ones on duty at the moment.'

'Exactly. So why give them time, as he's doing now?'

'Time's nearly up, farmer! Make up your mind. Stand aside or die!'

There was a bustle of movement within the crowd and Halt looked in the direction it was coming from. He nodded slowly.

'Ah. I thought something like this might happen.'

Horace followed his gaze and saw the burly, white-robed figure of Tennyson pushing through to the front of the crowd. He was followed by half a dozen of his acolytes.

Horace recognised them as the group who had been singing earlier in the day, two women and four men.

Strangely, for such a threatening situation, there was no sign of Tennyson's usual giant retainers.

The white-robed priest strode purposefully out to stand between the watchmen and the bandit chief. He carried his staff, with the unusual double circle emblem of the Outsiders at its head. His voice, deep and sonorous, carried clearly to all in the market ground.

'Be warned, stranger! This village is under the protection of Alseiass, the Golden God of friendship.'

The bandit laughed once more. But this time there was genuine amusement in his voice.

'What do we have here? A fat man with another stick? Pardon me while I tremble in fear!'

As he spoke, some of his men emerged from the trees and moved to form a line behind him. There were perhaps fifteen of them in all. They joined in his laughter and called insults and curses at Tennyson. The burly priest stood unflinching, his arms spread out wide. When he spoke again, his voice drowned out the catcalls and insults.

'I give you warning. You and your false god cannot stand against the power of Alseiass! Leave now or suffer the consequences! If I call on Alseiass you will know pain such as you have never felt.'

'Well, priest, if I take my sword to your fat hide, you'll know some pain yourself!'

The bandit drew his sword. His followers did likewise, the rasp of steel sounding across the field. The dozen watchmen, who were slightly behind Tennyson, began to move forward, but the priest signalled for them to stay back. At the same time, the outlaws began to advance towards him. More of them emerged from the trees, swords drawn.

Tennyson stood firm. He turned and said a quiet word to his six followers. Instantly, they dropped to their knees in a semicircle around him, facing the outlaws, and began to sing. The words of their song were in some foreign tongue. Tennyson raised his long staff and pointed it at the line of advancing bandits.

The intruders continued to advance. Then the singers hit a strange and discordant harmony — a strident sound that rang in the air, the overtones setting up a harmonic vibration that seemed to pulse and throb eerily. Tennyson now raised his staff high in the air and his singers held the note, swelling the volume.

The effect was instantaneous. The leading bandit stopped and staggered backwards, as if struck by some invisible force. His men also seemed to lose the use of their limbs, staggering and blundering in wild circles. Some threw up their free hands as if to ward off a physical blow. They cried out in pain and fear.

The choir paused for breath, then sang the same chord once more, even louder this time, as Tennyson gestured for them to rise to their feet. With the invisible barrier of the chord preceding them, they began to advance towards the staggering, disorganised bandits.

It was too much. The intruders, their spirit broken, turned and fled in terror and confusion, staggering and blundering into one another as they ran back into the trees. As the last of them disappeared into the shadows, Tennyson called a halt and his choir fell silent.

Now the priest turned back to the people of Mountshannon, who had watched open-mouthed with awe as he drove the intruders off. He smiled at them, holding both his arms wide as if to embrace them.

'People of Mountshannon, give praise to the god Alseiass who has saved us this day!' he boomed.

And the spell was broken as the villagers streamed forward to surround him, calling out his name and the name of his god. He stood among them, smiling and blessing them as they swarmed around him, seeking to kneel before him, to touch him, to shout his name and to thank him.

Halt and Horace stood back and exchanged a glance. Horace scratched his chin thoughtfully.

'Funny,' he said, 'those bandits were completely disabled. That strange chord hit them like a ton of bricks, didn't it?'

'It certainly seemed to,' Halt agreed.

'Yet I couldn't help noticing . . .' Horace went on. 'They were staggering and suffering and terrified and completely disoriented by the whole thing. But not one of them dropped his sword.'

Twenty-five

Will kept Tug moving at a steady lope throughout the day. It wasn't the Rangers' forced march pace, but it ate up the distance on the road to Mountshannon and he knew Tug would keep up the pace as long as he was asked.

He also knew that he would probably reach the village after Driscoll had put on what he had referred to as his 'show'. Even though he was mounted, the ridge road was long and circuitous and the thirty-man raiding party had far less distance to cover on the lower road they were following.

He was becoming convinced that there would be no attack as such. The bandits were planning a thrust at Mountshannon, but for what purpose he wasn't yet sure. Driscoll had referred to a 'holy man' and Will assumed that was Tennyson. He wasn't sure where the preacher fitted into the overall plan, nor what role he would play. But it was becoming increasingly obvious that the real attack would be on Craikennis the following day.

He reached Mountshannon in the middle of the after-noon. As he passed the guard post by the bridge, Will raised his eyebrows when he saw it was deserted. So were the streets of Mountshannon. For a moment, he feared the worst. But as he rode in, he heard a good deal of noise coming from the other end of the village. Singing, shouting, laughing.

'Someone's having a good time,' he said to Tug. 'Wonder if it's Halt?'

Halt's no singer, the horse replied.

He followed the noise to the end of the village. It seemed that the entire population was gathered on a large meadow outside the protective barricade, where a market-place had been set up. But the stalls and livestock pens were deserted now and a sizeable crowd was gathered in front of a large white pavilion set in the south-west corner of the meadow.

He reined Tug in, staying in the shadow of a house while he surveyed the scene before him. In the adjacent corner, he made out the two low tents that Horace and Halt had pitched. But he could see no sign of his friends there.

He turned his attention back to the large pavilion. It was surrounded by a noisy mass of celebrating villagers. Food was roasting over several open fires and a cask of ale had been perched on a table and broached. By the looks of things, most of the villagers had taken their share.

In the centre of the throng he could see a smaller group of white-robed figures. The large, heavily built man with shoulder-length grey hair must be Tennyson, he thought. He was the centre of attention, with a constant stream of villagers coming up to him, touching his arm, patting him on the back and offering him choice cuts from the roasting meat.

'Something's happened,' Will said to himself. Then he made out Halt and Horace standing at the back of the crowd. As he saw them, the bearded Ranger glanced round and made eye contact. Will saw him nudge Horace, then point unobtrusively to the two small tents some fifty metres away. Will nodded and urged Tug forward in a walk. He headed around the far side of the market stalls to lessen the probability that he'd be noticed. But he sensed nobody was looking his way in any event. Tennyson and his people were the focus of all attention.

He reached the camp site, unsaddled Tug and rubbed him down thoroughly. The little horse had put in a hard day and he deserved some attention. Then he foraged in his pack and found an apple. Tug crunched it blissfully, his eyes closed as he concentrated on the flavour and the spurting juice of the apple. Will slapped his neck affectionately. Tug was nosing round his pockets, searching for a second apple, when Halt and Horace made their way back to the camp site. In response to the persistent nudging from the little horse's blunt nose, Will unstrapped his pack and found another apple for him.

'You spoil that horse,' Halt said.

Will glanced round at him. 'You spoil yours.'

Halt considered the thought, then nodded. 'That's true,' he admitted.

'Welcome back,' Horace said, deciding not to join this discussion of how a horse should be treated. He knew that when Rangers started talking about their horses, it could take a lot to shut them up.

Will stretched himself, imagining he could hear the tendons cracking and groaning in his stiff arms and legs. It had been a long ride and he was thirsty. He grunted in satisfaction as he relaxed his muscles and looked meaningfully at the coffee pot, upside down beside the fire.

'I'll make it,' Horace said. He filled the pot from a canteen hanging in a nearby tree, then blew on the embers of the fire to get the flames going again. He added a handful of kindling until the fire was burning brightly, then shoved the pot into the hot coals beside the flames.

Will settled himself onto the soft ground by the fireplace. There was a convenient log for him to rest his back against and he sighed in contentment. He nodded towards the noisy gathering some hundred metres away.

'I take it that's our friend Tennyson?'

Halt nodded. 'He's quite a local hero.'

Will raised an eyebrow. 'A hero, you say?' He sensed the irony in Halt's tone.

Horace, readying a handful of ground coffee beans from a small linen sack, glanced up from his work. 'Saved the village of Mountshannon from a terrible fate, did Tennyson,' he put in.

Will looked from Horace to Halt, a question in his eyes.

'Bandits tried to attack the village a few hours ago,' the Ranger explained. 'A force of armed men came out of those woods there, threatening all sorts of dire consequences if the villagers put up any resistance. And our friend Tennyson just calmly strolled up and told them to be off. And off they went.'

'Not before his followers sang at them,' Horace reminded him.

Halt nodded. 'That's true. A couple of verses and the bandits were staggering around, hands over their ears.'

'The singing was that bad?' Will asked, straight-faced. He had a pretty good idea what had happened earlier in the day. Now Driscoll's cryptic comment about a holy man began to make sense.

'The singing was very good, so Horace tells me. But the sheer force of Tennyson's personality, and the power of his god Alseiass, was enough to see off a force of eighty men.'

'Thirty,' Will said and his friends looked at him inquisitively. 'There were only thirty. They were led by a man called Driscoll.'

'Well, we only *saw* about thirty,' Horace said. 'But he claimed to have another fifty men hidden in the woods. After all, why would you attack a large village like this with only thirty men?'

'He was never going to attack,' Will said. Halt leaned forward curiously.

'You know this?' he said. 'Or are you assuming it?'

'I know it. I eavesdropped outside their leader's tent last night. The plan wasn't to attack Mountshannon. They referred to "putting on a show" here. But then one of them said they'd do more than that at Craikennis, because "there'd be no holy man to send them packing".'

'Which Tennyson did here,' Halt said, seeing the connection.

'Exactly. But tomorrow at Craikennis, there will be eighty of them. They're joining up with a further fifty men and this time they won't be pretending. They'll tear the place apart.'

His expression darkened as his mind went back to the

scene at Duffy's Ford. He knew how pitiless these raiders could be.

Halt scratched his beard thoughtfully. 'So the fake attack here was simply an opportunity for Tennyson to demonstrate his power.'

'And his ability to protect the village,' Horace put in. 'Remember what he was saying yesterday? "Who can protect you?" This was obviously intended to make his point — only Alseiass, by virtue of Tennyson.'

'Exactly,' Halt said, his eyes narrowing. 'Craikennis will demonstrate what happens if Tennyson isn't around. Bandits attack Mountshannon and Tennyson chases them off. A day later, bandits attack Craikennis and there's no sign of Tennyson. It's obvious what the result will be.'

'The villagers will be massacred,' Will said quietly. 'Craikennis will be Duffy's Ford all over again, but ten times worse.'

'That's the way I read it,' Halt said. 'It'll be an object lesson for the people of Clonmel. With Tennyson on your side, you're safe. Without him, you're dead.' He turned to Horace. 'It's the big event I said he needed.'

Horace studied his friends' grim faces.

'We're going to have to do something,' he said. He felt his anger rising at the thought of the helpless villagers attacked by vicious bandits. When he had been knighted, Horace had sworn an oath to protect the weak and the helpless.

Halt nodded agreement. 'Saddle up. We'll leave the tents here so it'll look as if we're coming back. I don't want Tennyson wondering why we've suddenly left. We have to get to Craikennis tonight and warn them. That way, they can organise their defences.'

'What about us?' Will asked. 'Are we going to take a hand in this?'

Halt looked at his two young friends. Will's face was grim and determined. Horace was flushed with anger and indignation. The grey-bearded Ranger nodded.

'Yes,' he said. 'I rather think we are.'

Twenty-six

They took a circuitous route out of Mountshannon. Halt wasn't sure if Tennyson was watching their movements but if he were, the Outsider would have seen them depart to the south-west. Once clear of the village, however, they followed a series of back roads and smaller trails that took them in a giant circle until they were headed due east, to Craikennis.

'What was the name of the fellow who led the false attack?' Halt asked Will at one stage.

'Driscoll,' Will told him.

'Well, we need to make sure that we don't run into him and his scruffy band. Keep your eye on the ground for any sign of tracks.'

Will nodded. They were all aware that Driscoll and his thirty men were heading in the same general direction they were, to rendezvous with Padraig and the main party a few kilometres from Craikennis. But as the afternoon wore on into evening, they saw no sign of them. Halt assumed they had taken a different route.

There was an early moon and they continued riding after dark. To make up for the time they'd lost taking their original detour to the south-west, Halt led them off the road and they cut across country, directly for Craikennis. Around nine in the evening, they saw the lights of the little village across the fields. The three travellers eased their horses to a stop and took stock of the situation. They were on a slightly elevated position and could see the main road leading out of Craikennis — the road down which Padraig and his men were expected to come the next day. There was no traffic on the road now, no sign of the outlaw band.

Halt grunted in satisfaction.

'Looks quiet enough,' he said. 'But keep your eyes and ears open.' He touched Abelard with his heel and the little horse trotted forward.

They crossed two more fields then rode out onto the high road. As on their previous visit, the guard post was manned by two watchmen. Halt had hoped that they'd encounter the guards from their previous visit. It would save time identifying themselves. But unfortunately, these were two new men. They stepped out into the road, one of them holding his hand aloft in a signal for the three riders to stop.

'Idiots,' Halt muttered to his companions. 'If we were here to cause trouble, we could simply ride them both down.'

The sentry who had signalled them to stop stepped forward and peered suspiciously at them. These were not run-of-the-mill travellers, he thought. Two of them wore mottled, hooded cloaks, rode small shaggy horses and carried massive longbows. The other rider was taller, and rode a heavyset battlehorse. A long sword hung at his side and there was a round buckler strapped to the saddle ties behind him.

These were fighting men and the sentry was suddenly conscious of the fact that he was outnumbered.

'What do you want?' he called. His uncertainty made him abrupt and more strident than he'd intended.

The leader of the three riders, the bearded one, leaned forward and crossed his forearms over his saddle pommel. 'We mean you no harm,' he said. The voice was quiet and reassuring. But that was no guarantee that the words were the truth.

'Don't come any closer!' the sentry called. He wished he'd brought his spear out of the guard shelter. His companion had a spear, but he was armed only with a heavy, long-handled mace.

'We won't,' Halt told him, in a reasonable tone. 'We're content to stay here. But we need to speak to your commander.'

'Our . . . what?' the sentry asked.

He wasn't a military man, Horace thought.

Halt revised his request. 'Your village head man. Or the senior member of the watch. We need to speak to someone in authority.'

The sentry eyed him suspiciously. If he sent Finneas, the other guard, to fetch the head man, he'd be left here facing these three alone. He didn't like the idea of that. But at least if he called the head man he could hand this problem over to someone else, he thought. He hesitated, then decided.

'The head man's asleep,' he said eventually, not knowing whether he was or not. 'Come back tomorrow.'

'Dismount, boys,' Halt said and the three of them swung down from the saddle, in spite of the guard's shrill orders.

'No! You stay as you are! Turn around and ride away, d'you hear me?'

The sentry's voice trailed off as he realised that the three strangers were taking no notice of him. Their leader spoke again.

'We're setting our weapons down.' He led the way, moving to the side of the road, unstringing his longbow and laying it on the grass verge. The younger bowman followed suit. The tall youth unclipped the scabbard from his belt and the long cavalry sword joined the two longbows on the grass. That done, the three strangers stepped back onto the road, away from their weapons.

'There,' said Halt. 'Now fetch your head man or watch commander.' He paused a few seconds and added emphatically, '*Please*.'

The two watchmen exchanged a glance. Finneas raised one shoulder in a shrug. The strangers seemed trustworthy, he thought. He sensed what was troubling his friend.

'You fetch Conal. I'll keep an eye on them.'

The senior man let go an involuntary sigh of relief. Anything to get this problem off his hands. He came to a decision. Then he thought he'd better make it seem as if this was his idea and he was giving the orders.

'All right. You keep them here. I'll get Conal.'

Finneas looked at him and raised an eyebrow. He wasn't fooled by the mock-decisive manner of his companion.

'Yes, we could do it that way instead,' he said sarcastically.

'Could we do it some time before dawn?' Halt asked in an exasperated tone. The watchman took a pace towards him, his hand on the handle of his mace.

'I'll go when I'm good and ready!' he snarled.

'Which is now, right?' Finneas cut across him.

The senior watchman drew himself up, trying to reclaim his dignity. 'Err . . . yes. Which is now.' He turned about and hurried towards the village. He looked back several times but the three strangers hadn't moved, and Finneas stood at ease, facing them, leaning casually on his spear. He turned and increased his pace a little, until he was half running.

Fifteen minutes later, he returned with Conal. Halt was quietly pleased to see that Conal, who turned out to be the head watchman, was the same man he and Horace had spoken to several nights previously. The man had struck him as sensible and reasonable. He was certainly going to be easier to deal with than the panicky guard who had gone to fetch him.

That wasn't to say that Conal didn't view the three travellers with suspicion. Halt noticed that he had taken the precaution of arming himself. He wore a sword and a long dirk in his belt. As he approached, the nervous senior guardsman darted into the shelter to fetch his spear.

Conal glanced at Finneas, then at the three figures standing by their horses in the road.

'Well, Finneas, what do we have here?' he asked. Finneas was standing facing them, his spear grounded beside his feet. He touched the spear head lightly to his forehead in salute.

'Three travellers, your honour,' he said, grinning. 'They've given me no trouble.'

Conal looked more closely at Halt and Horace. 'I know you two,' he said and Halt nodded. Then the watch commander shifted his gaze to Will, his brow furrowing. 'And you? Weren't you here the other night as well?' The young man looked familiar, he thought, but he couldn't quite place him.

'He's the singer, Conal,' Finneas put in and Conal nodded slowly as recognition dawned.

'Of course,' he said slowly. 'But you weren't wearing that cloak. Or carrying that bow. What are you up to?'

The question was asked of all three as his gaze shifted from one to the other. There was something suspicious here and in these times, suspicions were not to be disregarded. His hand dropped to the hilt of his sword. Then he noticed the trio's weapons were laid by the side of the road and he relaxed a little. Just a little. He glared at Halt.

'I take it you're not a shepherd looking for stock?' he said and the bearded man nodded.

'No. You're right about that.'

'Then you lied to me the other night. Why?' The challenge was gruff and uncompromising. Halt seemed to take no offence at being called a liar. He replied in a calm, reasonable tone.

'We weren't sure what we were walking into,' he said. 'These are troubled times, as you may well know.'

'Aye, and they're not helped by people skulking around claiming to be what they're not,' Conal replied with a little heat. He could hear a rustle of movement from behind him. He glanced quickly over his shoulder and relaxed slightly as another dozen members of the guard came shuffling at a half run down the high street. When he was first alerted to the presence of three strangers at the guard post, Conal had sent his son to rouse a platoon of the town guard, telling them to arm themselves and join him. Now they had arrived and he felt a little more in control of the situation. The numbers were comfortably on his side.

Horace sighed to himself. He was a direct sort of person and this verbal sparring was beginning to annoy him. He and his friends were here to help the people of Craikennis, not to bandy words in the street in the middle of the night. Conal heard the slight exclamation and turned to him.

'Something to say, boy?' he demanded.

Halt's eyebrow went up. 'I wouldn't be so free and easy with the word "boy" if I were you,' he said warningly. But Conal ignored him and Horace was already replying.

'Yes. I've got something to say. My friends and I are here to help you. If you keep us standing here much longer while you throw accusations and insults, we'll just ride on and leave you to the bandits.'

He was remarkably self-assured for one so young, Conal thought, his brow puckering at the last word.

'Bandits? What bandits would they be?'

'There are eighty of them heading this way. They're planning to attack you tomorrow and wipe your village out. We came to warn you and to offer you our help. But if you prefer, you can go back to bed and we'll just ride on. It's really no skin on our nose.'

Halt glanced sidelong at Horace. The young man's face was flushed with annoyance.

'I think that's "*off* our nose",' he pointed out. Horace glanced briefly at him.

'Whatever. He gets my meaning.'

And Conal did. So far, Craikennis had remained undisturbed. But there had been bandits and outlaws running amok in the south of Clonmel, and the trouble had been gradually spreading north, like a dark stain of spilled ink advancing over a map.

'How do I know you're not with them?' he asked and instantly regretted the question. If they were, they would never admit it and asking had only shown his own indecision. 'Who are you anyway?' he added angrily, trying to cover the mistake.

'We're King's Rangers from Araluen,' Halt told him, indicating himself and Will. 'And this tall, rather aggravated young man beside me is a knight of the Araluen court.'

Conal frowned. He had no idea what Rangers might be. He guessed they must be woodsmen or scouts. But he knew what a knight was and the tall stranger, in spite of his youth, had the look of a warrior about him.

'Your Araluan king has no authority here. King Ferris rules — in a manner of speaking,' Conal told them.

Interesting, Will thought. There had been a hint of distaste in Conal's voice as he spoke of the King. He glanced at Halt to see if his mentor had noted it. But Halt's face was a blank mask.

'Nevertheless, we're all trained fighters and we might be useful to you,' Halt said.

Conal scratched his ear, inspected his fingernails and then replied. 'Exactly. And I'm thinking if there's an attack coming, it might not be the wisest move to let three armed fighting men into the village.'

'Then don't,' Halt said immediately. 'We'll camp in the trees there. If there's no attack tomorrow, we'll go on our way. If there is, you might be glad of a bit of support.'

'And how much use will three men be against eighty?' Conal asked. He did it more to gain time than anything else. He could see no real danger if these three were content to wait outside the village's hastily constructed defensive barricade.

'That depends on the three,' said the third member of the group, the one who had posed as a minstrel a few nights ago.

The bearded one turned to smile at him. 'Well said, Will,' he said quietly. Then, to Conal: 'However much help we can provide, it'll be more than nothing. My main aim is to make sure you have your defences ready, your men armed and warned. The outlaws will be looking to surprise you. If they find you ready and waiting, it might take a little starch out of them.'

Conal considered the point and nodded slowly. 'Aye, that makes sense,' he said. 'I'll have the men stand to at dawn. We do that every day.'

Halt smiled grimly. 'Then do it tomorrow. But the odds are, they won't attack then.' He smiled. 'The enemy will expect you to be ready at dawn. Most places "stand to at dawn", as you put it. My guess is, they'll wait for you to lower your guard when nothing happens. If I were them, I'd hit you at noon, when people are relaxing, tired from the morning's work and looking forward to their midday meal.'

Conal regarded the bearded man. He was small for a warrior, the Hibernian thought. But he carried an air of confidence and authority. He suddenly thought that if there were to be a fight, he'd prefer to fight with this man than against him.

'Good advice,' he said. 'I'll make sure everyone stays ready. Where will you be?'

Halt gestured to the forest north of Craikennis. 'We'll bed down inside the trees. Then we'll take a position on that low hill outside the treeline.'

Conal stepped forward and offered his hand to Halt. He was a little awkward, realising that this man had come to warn the village and, so far, had been treated with suspicion and distrust.

'I owe you thanks,' he said.

Halt took his hand. 'Thank me tomorrow, if we're all still here,' he said. Then he and his two companions retrieved their weapons from the grassy verge, mounted their horses and rode away across the fields to the north.

They'd gone a hundred metres or so when Horace urged Kicker alongside Abelard.

'Halt?' he said and the Ranger looked at him.

'Something troubling you?'

'Yes. I just realised, we've left all our camping gear at Mountshannon,' Horace said.

Halt let out a deep sigh. 'Yes. I remembered that too — just after I told him we'd camp out in the trees.'

Horace glanced at the sky above them. There were dark clouds scudding across it, blanking out the stars as they passed.

'Do you think it's going to rain tonight?' he said.

'Probably,' Halt replied gloomily.

Twenty-seven

It did rain during the night, a light shower that fell for about fifteen minutes just after midnight. But the camp site wasn't quite as uncomfortable as Halt and Horace had envisaged. They had overlooked the fact that Will still had his tent and camping equipment with him.

Even though the tents were designed for one man, it was possible to squeeze two people into one. And of course, at any time, one of the group was on watch.

Will had the final shift and, as dawn was slowly spreading over the countryside and birds were waking up in the trees and bushes, he saw Halt crawling out of the low tent.

The older Ranger looked with annoyance at the damp patches on his knees. It was impossible to emerge from a low tent like that on wet ground without getting your trousers wet, he reflected. He stretched and walked to where Will was watching the road, wrapped in his cloak.

'Any sign of them?' he asked.

Will shook his head. 'Not so far,' he said. Then he

added, 'I thought you said a dawn attack would be too obvious and they probably wouldn't attack until midday?'

Halt picked up Will's canteen and took a swig of cold water, rinsing it round his mouth, then spitting it out.

'I did. But then they might decide to do the obvious thing after all,' he said.

'Oh, it's a case of *they think I'll think that they'll do A, so they'll do B because I wouldn't think they'd think of that but then because I might think I know what they're thinking they'll do A after all because I wouldn't think they'd think that way*,' Will said.

Halt looked at him for a long moment in silence. 'You know, I'm almost tempted to ask you to repeat that.'

Will grinned ruefully. 'I'm not sure I could.'

Halt moved away to rummage in Will's pack for the coffee pot.

'Might as well light a small fire,' he said. 'They won't see it among the trees and if they smell the smoke they'll think it's from Craikennis.'

Will cheered up at the words. He'd assumed they'd have a cold camp. The idea of hot coffee was a pleasant surprise. A few minutes later, Horace crawled out of the tent. He made sure he emerged on hands and toes, not letting his knees touch the wet ground. Halt scowled at him as he saw him spring athletically to his feet.

'I hate young people,' he said to himself.

Horace wandered over and took a cup of coffee to Will, then went back for one for himself. The three stood, sipping the hot, restoring drink, easing the cramps of a night spent on the hard, damp ground out of their muscles. It took a little longer for Halt to manage this.

He muttered darkly about young people again. Horace and Will, wisely, chose to ignore him.

After a few minutes, Horace asked: 'So what's the drill for today, Halt?'

Halt pointed to a small knoll a few metres from the treeline.

'That's our position there. Will and I will see if we can't thin out Padraig's numbers a little.' He looked at his former student. 'Don't take any chances, but whenever you can, shoot to wound or disable.' He saw the unspoken question in Will's eyes and continued, 'I know, these men are killers and murderers and I have no compunction about shooting to kill. But a wounded man takes another man out of the battle — he has to tend to him.'

Horace smiled. 'I thought you were getting sentimental in your old age there, Halt.'

The Ranger said nothing. He glared at Horace for a long moment and the big warrior wished he could take back the phrase 'old age'. Over the past weeks, he'd noticed that Halt was a little prickly about the fact that he wasn't getting any younger.

'Sorry,' he mumbled eventually. Halt said nothing. He snorted angrily and Horace suddenly found it necessary to take a great interest in adjusting his belt buckle until it was just right. Halt let him suffer for a few moments, then beckoned him to follow.

'I want you mounted and ready, Horace. But stay back out of sight till I call you. And I want you to put this over your shield.'

He searched in his saddlebags and brought out a folded piece of heavy linen, handing it to the younger man.

Horace spread it out and found it to be a circular piece, a little larger than his shield, with a drawstring around the edge. It would slip over the shield and the drawstring would pull tight to hold it in position. Sometimes, he knew, knights used these covers in tournaments, when they wanted to cover their insignia and fight incognito.

But this wasn't blank. It had a strange and rather striking design in the centre. It was a reddish-orange circle, with the bottom third of its arc cut off by a straight black line that protruded a few centimetres either side. It reminded Horace of something, but he couldn't quite place it.

'It's the insignia of the Sunrise Warrior,' Halt told him. Horace cocked his head to one side interrogatively and the Ranger continued. 'He's a figure of Hibernian myth. The story goes that when the kingdoms are in peril, the Sunrise Warrior will rise up from the east and restore order within the kingdoms.'

'And you want me to be him?' Horace said. Now that Halt had mentioned the word 'sunrise', he realised that was what the design had reminded him of.

Halt nodded. 'Your legend begins today, when you save the village of Craikennis from two hundred men.'

'Eighty,' Will said. He had strolled over to watch as Horace fastened the cover over his shield. For this trip, Horace's normal green oakleaf insignia had been painted over and his shield was blank.

Halt looked up at the interjection.

'There'll be two hundred by the time I finish telling it,' he told Will. 'We might even get you to compose a ballad of praise to the Sunrise Warrior.'

Horace grinned. 'I think I'd like that,' he said. Will gave him a pained look but he pretended not to notice it and went on, 'But really, Halt, what's all this legend and myth got to do with anything?'

'We'll fight fire with fire. Tennyson is claiming the support of Alseiass, the almighty Golden God. Says Alseiass is the only hope for the Kingdom, the only hope of protection from these outlaws. And people are buying his message. So we'll enlist the Sunrise Warrior and offer him as an alternative. Sooner or later, Tennyson will have to challenge us. When he does, we'll see him off.'

'Couldn't we just capture him and get rid of him without all this rigmarole?' Will asked.

'We could. But we have to break his power, his hold over the people. We have to destroy the myth of the Outsiders. And we have to be seen to do it. Otherwise, he'll be seen as a martyr and one of his followers will simply rise up and continue this damned business.

'The whole Outsiders plan works because there's a power vacuum. The King is weak and incapable so Tennyson can step into the gap to provide strong leadership and a symbol to rally round. We have to discredit both Tennyson and Alseiass, and provide a viable, visible alternative — and that's the Sunrise Warrior.'

'You mean I'm going to have my own cult?' Horace asked and Halt nodded reluctantly.

'In a way. Yes.'

Horace beamed. 'Then perhaps you two might start showing a little more respect.'

'That's unlikely,' Will told him.

But Horace ignored him as before, beaming even more

widely. 'I rather like the idea of having you two as my acolytes,' he said.

Halt and Will exchanged a glance.

'Don't push it,' they both said at the same time.

The morning wore on. After the sun had dried out his tent, Will packed it away, along with most of his camping equipment. He left out only their basic needs for cooking and, of course, the ever-present coffee pot.

While his friend attended to these details, Horace cleaned and sharpened his weapons, running a stone down the already razor-sharp edges of his sword with a pleasing zzzz-ing sound. He laid out his mail shirt and helmet, ready to put them on at short notice, and saddled Kicker. He checked every inch of his harness but left the girth straps loose for the time being. There was no point in subjecting his horse to the discomfort of a tightly cinched saddle while they waited.

During the next few hours, they were conscious of considerable movement inside the nearby village. The sentry post outside the barricade was left unmanned, but they could see men moving behind the barricade itself, in greater numbers than they'd seen on previous occasions, and the low buzz of voices carried across the field to them. From time to time, the bright morning sun reflected off weapon blades or the occasional helmet as the defenders moved from one place to another.

'Looks as if Conal is taking your warning seriously,' Will said.

Halt, who had spent the morning watching the road,

hunkered down with his back against a tree, glanced at the village and nodded.

'He struck me as a reasonable man,' he said. 'I hope he doesn't tip his hand too soon. It'd be better if Padraig wasn't aware that the entire garrison is expecting him.'

'That might be too much to hope for,' Will said. 'It's more likely Conal will be hoping that a show of force will avoid a fight.'

'It won't,' Halt said grimly.

'You know it and I know it,' Will said. 'But does Conal?'

But in spite of his cynicism, it appeared that Conal did understand the value of surprise, and the inevitability of an attack. As the sun rose closer to the overhead position of noon, they saw a distinct decrease in the amount of visible activity at the barricade. The men on duty no longer craned over the top of the makeshift wall to see if the enemy were coming. And the babble of voices died away. The village appeared to be sleepy and peaceful. There was no sign of any defenders, no indication that Craikennis was expecting an attack. An observer would think that the villagers were relaxing over their midday meal, with perhaps a little nap to follow afterwards. The sun was hot and insects buzzed drowsily. There was even a slight shimmer of heat haze along the high road. It was a peaceful, restful, normal day in the country – up to the point where Halt spoke.

'Here they come,' he said.

Twenty-eight

Will and Horace had been dozing close by the tree Halt was leaning against. They were seasoned campaigners and they knew there was nothing to gain by remaining tensed up, waiting for the action to start. Far better, they knew, to conserve energy and rest while they could. As Halt spoke, they both snapped awake, their hands instinctively reaching for their weapons.

'Relax,' Halt told them. 'It's only the advance scouts.'

He indicated a point several hundred metres away, where the road passed over a crest. Three armed men had suddenly come into view, moving furtively, as if they could avoid being seen by stooping. They stopped, peering at the peaceful-looking village. One of them shaded his eyes with his hands. Nothing stirred in Craikennis and the leader of the three scouts, apparently deciding that the village was unaware of their approach, faced back down the road and waved his so far unseen companions forward.

Gradually, the raiders came into view over the crest.

They moved in two files, either side of the road. The watchers in the treeline could hear the faint jingle of weapons and equipment as they moved. Most of them were on foot, although Padraig and four of his senior commanders rode horses. They were small animals, however, not bred for fighting like Horace's massive battlehorse.

Horace moved quickly back into the trees and tightened Kicker's girth straps. The big horse, sensing imminent combat, shifted expectantly from one foot to the other, tossing his head and snorting softly while Horace soothed him and patted him, keeping a firm hold on his bridle. Kicker was bred and trained for battle, as was his master. Horace felt a familiar tightening in his stomach now. Not fear. More expectation and nervous energy as adrenaline flooded his system. He knew that once he mounted Kicker and charged at the enemy, he would relax. It was the waiting that got him tensed up. He wondered if Will and Halt felt the same way as the older Ranger led his apprentice towards their vantage point on the knoll. Horace smiled to himself. Even though Will was a fully fledged Ranger in his own right, Horace always thought of him as Halt's apprentice. Will thought the same way, he knew.

'We'll stay below the crest of the knoll,' Halt was saying. 'With just our heads and shoulders visible, chances are they'll never see where we're shooting from, or how many of us there are.'

'Or how few,' Will suggested and Halt considered for a few seconds before agreeing.

'Or how few,' he said. He glanced back at Horace,

standing calmly beside Kicker, talking in a low, soothing voice to the horse. 'Horace looks calm enough,' he said.

Will glanced back at his friend. 'He always does. I don't know how he manages it. This is the time when I've got butterflies in my stomach the size of fruit bats.' He had no compunction about admitting his own nervousness. Halt had taught him long ago that a man who doesn't feel nervous before a battle wasn't brave, he was foolish or overconfident — and either condition could prove to be fatal.

'He's a good man to have at your back,' Halt agreed. Then he nodded his head towards the enemy. 'Hullo. They're getting ready.'

The outlaws had stopped their advance fifty metres from the village. The two files now began to spread out in two extended lines. Padraig and his companions remained behind the formation. From the village, a shout of alarm was heard, then someone began ringing a bell. A man appeared on the barricade. Even from this distance, Will and Halt could recognise him as Conal.

'Stop there!' he called. 'Come no further!'

Now there were growing sounds of panic and alarm within the village. The bell continued to toll and men were taking up positions on the barricade. But they were piti-fully few and they appeared alarmed and surprised. Padraig obviously knew his business and understood that nothing would be gained by parleying. That would only give the villagers more time to organise their defences. He drew his sword and held it above his head.

'Forward!' he called, his voice ringing clearly across the field. His men responded, moving forward at a steady walk. There was no point in running at this stage. They'd only arrive out of breath and exhausted at the barricade that way.

From their position, Halt and Will had a side-frontal view of the battle line as the outlaws advanced. It was a perfect position for enfilade shooting. The two ranks began to increase their pace, jogging now as they approached the barricade.

'Three arrows,' Halt said quickly. 'Shoot for the centre of the front rank.'

From his position behind them, Horace watched with some awe as the two Rangers released six arrows in rapid succession. All six were in the air within the space of a few seconds. And within a few seconds, six men in the centre of the advancing line went down. Two of them made no sound. The others cried out in pain, dropping their weapons. One blundered into the men around him as he reeled in a circle, trying to pull the arrow from his shoulder. Then he sank to his knees, groaning in agony.

Those beside and behind the stricken men stopped in confusion. The even line of advance broke up as the centre stopped and the two wings continued forward, unaware of what had happened.

'Left flank,' Halt said and the two longbows sang their dreadful song once more. Another five men went down. Will frowned angrily. His second shot had been ineffective. His target, seeing a man close by sink to the ground, had involuntarily thrown his shield up and Will's arrow had glanced off it. Angrily, Will snapped off another shot and the man went down, the arrow arcing down above the rim of his shield.

But in spite of Will's initial miss, the overall effect of the second volley was successful. The left-hand end of the line stopped and the men faced outwards, trying to see where this new threat had come from. This meant the right wing was advancing on its own, and they covered the last few metres to the barricade at a run, letting out a roar as they went.

Only to be answered by a matching roar of anger and defiance as an unexpectedly large mass of defenders appeared above the barricade, thrusting down at the attackers as they tried to scale the improvised barrier of carts, trunks, tables, hay bales and odd items of furniture and timber.

Some of the defenders' weapons were improvised too — scythes and sickle blades mounted on long shafts were scattered among the spears and swords being wielded by the defenders. Will saw several pitchforks being used as well. But improvised or not, they were effective against the attackers, who were at a disadvantage as they tried to climb up the barricade.

The right wing, isolated from the rest of the attacking force, were savaged as they tried to breach the defences. They fell back, leaving a number of their companions sprawled lifeless on the ground and on the barricade itself. Instead of being part of a co-ordinated attack along the entire line, they had paid the penalty for assaulting a well-defended position on their own.

Padraig raged at his men, urging his horse forward and yelling at the rest of the line to move up and close the gap. He sensed that the arrows were coming from his left but could see no sign of archers out there. From the number of his men who had gone down before the hail of arrows, he estimated there must be at least half a dozen archers, firing from the shelter of the trees. Through narrowed eyes, he saw a vague flicker of movement from a small knoll. Ten seconds later, three more men in the centre of the line were struck down by arrows.

He yelled at a squad of a dozen men in the rear rank. They were all armed with swords or maces, and most of them had shields. The squad commander looked at him, a question on his face, and Padraig pointed with his sword towards the knoll.

'Archers. Behind that knoll! Clean 'em out!'

Archers were always lightly armed, he knew. And they were cowards who'd slink away at the first sign of a real threat. They'd never stand against an attack by a force of armed men protected by shields. The dozen men dropped out of the line and bunched up behind their squad leader. He motioned them forward and they started towards the knoll with a yell of fury.

Halt saw Padraig stop and look. Saw him send the squad towards their position. No need to panic yet, he thought.

'The command group,' he told Will. 'Put them down.'

And while the younger Ranger sent a rapid volley soaring off at Padraig and his subordinates, Halt took the time to thin out the dozen men running towards them. A shield could only cover so much of a man's body and the outlaws had no idea of the accuracy that their opponents could achieve. An arrow through the calf, thigh or shoulder of a running man would stop him just as effectively as a killing shot, Halt knew. One after another, the running men began to fall or falter.

Will's first arrow was aimed at Padraig. But Will's luck was out that day. As he released, one of the outlaw's lieutenants urged his horse forward to speak to his leader and the arrow struck him from the saddle. Will swore as he realised Padraig was unscathed. He'd already sent another three shots off, aimed at the men around him.

In the space of a few seconds, Padraig found himself alone, surrounded by riderless horses, while his commanders lay writhing on the grass. Sizing up the situation, he slid from the saddle, placing his horse between himself and the knoll.

Will was nocking another arrow but Halt stopped him. 'Save it,' he said. He had a better idea as to how Padraig should be dealt with. Besides, they had a more immediate problem. The remaining seven outlaws were getting closer now and he turned and waved to Horace, pointing at the running men.

'Horace! They're yours!' Then to Will, he said, 'Cover Horace if he needs it.'

Horace needed no further invitation. He clapped his heels against Kicker's sides and the mighty horse lumbered forward, gathering speed like a thundering juggernaut. He burst out of the treeline and the approaching outlaws saw him for the first time. They stopped in panic, eyes riveted on the bared teeth of the horse and the long, glittering sword in its rider's hand.

They began to back away but they were too late. Kicker smashed into two of them, hurling one to the side and trampling the other. Horace struck down at a man to his right, then, sensing danger on his disengaged side, he pressed his right knee into Kicker's ribs.

Kicker responded instantly, rearing onto his hind legs and spinning in a half circle. His shoulder slammed into an outlaw who had been about to thrust up at Horace. The impact hurled the man several metres away.

As the horse came back to all fours, another outlaw was already moving forward, a long-handled mace in both hands, drawn back for a killing blow. But Horace's reactions were lightning fast and his thrusting sword took the man in the shoulder, outside his chain mail vest. The outlaw staggered back, the mace dropping as he tried to stem the gush of blood from the wound.

Horace wheeled Kicker again to clear his back, the flashing forehooves ready to decapitate any potential attacker. But there was no need. A sixth outlaw was already sinking to his knees, staring with disbelief at the black arrow buried in his chest. His head drooped forward on his chest. The one survivor looked at his companions, scattered and broken, some of them lying still, others trying desperately to crawl away from the terrible horse and rider. Then he turned and ran, throwing away his sword as he went.

Horace wheeled his horse again, not sure what to do next. He looked back at the knoll and saw Halt pointing towards Padraig, still dismounted and sheltering behind his horse.

'Get the leader!' Halt shouted. He looked quickly towards the village. The bandits had recovered after the initial disruption of their attack. It had cost them a lot of lives but now they were pressing hard at the defenders. The key to the situation was Padraig, Halt realised. If the outlaws saw him defeated, if they found themselves leaderless, they'd melt away.

Horace waved his sword in acknowledgement and spun Kicker again. He could see the outlaw leader sheltering from the arrows behind his horse. Horace's lips curled in scorn as he realised that Padraig was also staying well back from the battle at the barricade. He tapped Kicker with his heels and began to canter towards the outlaw.

Padraig heard the drumming of approaching hooves. He had watched in fear as Horace scattered seven of his men with absolute ease. Now the warrior with the sunrise insignia was coming after him. He decided he'd risk the arrows and scrambled up into the saddle, wheeling his horse and setting it to a gallop towards the south.

But Kicker, in spite of his slow initial acceleration, was faster than the outlaw's horse and he gradually began to make up the distance between them. Padraig heard the hoof beats growing closer. He looked back fearfully and saw that the young warrior was almost on him. He realised, with a shock of surprise, that his pursuer was merely a youth. The face was young and unbearded. Perhaps it had been a fluke that he'd scattered those seven men, Padraig thought. After all, his band were cutthroats and bandits, not trained fighting men, whereas Padraig himself had been trained as a soldier. He wheeled his horse to face his pursuer, drawing his own sword and settling his shield on his left arm.

Horace reined in Kicker a few metres short of his quarry. He saw the hatred glowing in the man's eyes, took in the set of shield and sword. Padraig knew what he was doing, Horace thought.

'Throw the sword down and surrender. I'll say it once and once only,' he told the bandit leader. In answer,

Padraig snarled and drove his horse forward, swinging an overhead cut at Horace. Kicker danced easily to the side and Horace deflected the sword with his shield. His answering stroke slammed into Padraig's shield and staggered the other man with the force behind it, nearly unseating him. But Padraig recovered, wheeled his horse clumsily and rode in for another attack. He flailed blindly at Horace and the young warrior took the blows easily on his shield and sword, content to let Padraig tire himself out.

Finally, Padraig drew back, chest heaving with exertion, perspiration streaming down his face. He stared in disbelief at his adversary. Horace was breathing easily, sitting relaxed in the saddle.

'We don't have to do this,' Horace said calmly. 'Throw down your sword.'

It was the calm, unflustered attitude that caused something to snap inside Padraig. He launched himself forward again, sword swinging down in a vicious arc. This time, as Horace deflected it with his own blade, he remembered the words of Sir Rodney, his own mentor at Castle Redmont years ago.

Give any opponent a chance to surrender, but don't take risks with him. Something can always go wrong in a duel. A snapped girth, a cut rein, a lucky blow that gets through your guard. Don't take chances.

He sighed. He'd given Padraig two opportunities. Rodney was right. To do more would be foolish. As he deflected the Hibernian's sword, he quickly brought his own blade up and hammered four rapid overhand cuts at the man. His sword slammed down repeatedly on the outlaw's shield, denting and bending it out of shape as

Padraig held it high, cowering under it. Then, as the sound of the fourth stroke was still ringing across the field, Horace spun Kicker fast to the left, using the momentum of the spin to bring the long blade in a scything forehand across Padraig's exposed ribs.

The wet, crunching sensation as the stroke went home told him it was a fatal blow. Padraig stayed upright for a few seconds, a puzzled expression on his face. Then all expression left him and he toppled sideways from the saddle.

As the battle still raged at the barricades, several of those in the attackers' rear ranks had turned to watch the encounter. Now they saw their leader fall to the ground as the mounted warrior dealt him one final crushing blow. They looked for his lieutenants for orders. But they were either dead or wounded by Will's volley of arrows.

Gradually, a few of those in the rear began to melt away, running to the south. Within a few minutes, the trickle became a flood and the outlaws streamed, without leaders or direction, away from the barricades, leaving half their number dead or wounded on the field, or draped over the barricade.

The battle for Craikennis was over.

Twenty-nine

The aftermath of a battle was always a sobering sight, Horace thought. The dead lay in awkward, unnatural poses, draped on the barricade or sprawled on the ground before it, looking as if they'd been carelessly scattered by some giant hand. The wounded sobbed or cried pitifully for help or relief. Some tried unsuccessfully to hobble or crawl away, fearing retaliation from the people they had so recently been attacking.

The people of Craikennis moved among the defeated men, rounding up those with less serious injuries and holding them under the hostile gaze of a squad of village watchmen. The women tended to the more seriously wounded, bandaging and cleaning wounds, bringing water to those who cried out for it. Funny how a battle left your mouth and throat parched, the young warrior thought.

Will supervised a group of villagers as they collected weapons and armour from the outlaws. One of the villagers asked him if he wanted to retrieve his and Halt's arrows but he shook his head hastily. Half of them would be broken anyway and the idea of cleaning and reusing a blood-stained arrow was distasteful in the extreme. Besides, they had plenty of spares in the arrow cases they both carried tied behind their saddles. He watched while one of the village women cradled a wounded outlaw's head and let him take small sips of water from a cup as she held it to his lips. The man groaned pitifully, his hand weakly searching for hers to try to keep the cup to his mouth. But the effort was beyond his strength and his hand fell limply back to his side.

Strange, Will thought, how the most evil, murderous outlaw can be reduced to a sobbing little boy by his wounds.

Halt was talking with Conal and the village head man, Terrence.

'We owe you our thanks, Ranger,' the watch commander said. Halt shrugged and gestured towards Horace. The young warrior, as Halt had told him to, was sitting mounted on Kicker, on the raised knoll where Halt and Will had based themselves. The early afternoon sun shone off the white shield cover, accentuating the rising sun emblem.

'Your thanks should go to the Sunrise Warrior,' he said and saw the instant flicker of recognition in Terrence's eyes. He'd guessed correctly that the older head man would be familiar with the ancient myths and legends of Hibernia.

'That's the . . .?' He stopped, not quite daring to pronounce the fabled name.

'Who else would it be?' Halt asked him. 'You see the

rising sun emblem on his shield. And you saw him cut down nine of the enemy to reach their leader — who now lies dead out there.' There had been seven men in the group Horace attacked but Halt knew it was never too early to start exaggerating numbers.

Terrence shaded his eyes with his hand and peered at the tall figure on the bay battlehorse. He certainly looked imposing, he thought.

Horace, for his part, was puzzled. He'd been willing to take part in the clean-up after the battle. But Halt had told him to mount Kicker, ride to the knoll and sit there.

'Look enigmatic,' he had instructed.

Horace had nodded, then frowned.

'How do I do that?' he asked. Halt's eyebrow went up and Horace hastily added, 'Well, if I get enigmatic wrong, you'll be angry with me. So it's better I ask.'

'All right. Look as if you have plenty to say but you're not going to say it,' Halt told him. He saw the doubt in Horace's eyes and quickly altered his instructions. 'Forget that. Look as if someone has shoved a week-old fish under your nose.'

'I can do that,' Horace said, and cantered away. He practised curling his lip in distaste as he went.

Now, as he sat there, he saw Halt gesture towards him and saw the unmistakable start of interest from the older man, Terrence. He wondered briefly what the conversation was about and then he sighed. Halt was a devious character when he chose to be, he thought. He was confident it would be something that he, Horace, would probably disapprove of. He was also confident that, whatever Halt was saying, it had little to do with the truth.

At the barricade, Halt continued to elaborate on the theme of Horace's identity.

'You know the old legend,' he said to Terrence. He was sure the head man did, but he thought he'd spell it out anyway. 'The Sunrise Warrior will come from the east when the six kingdoms are in dire peril.'

Terrence nodded as he spoke. Halt glanced quickly at Conal and saw the cynicism in the younger man's eyes. He shrugged mentally. No matter. He hadn't expected a practical man like Conal to subscribe to old myths and legends. But at least Conal had seen Horace's undoubted weapons skill. He'd been impressed by those, all right.

'So, what thanks does your . . . Sunrise Warrior ask?' Conal said now. 'Is there some tangible reward that he's looking for?' The slight pause before he spoke the title was clear evidence that he set no store by the legend. He obviously expected Halt to demand some kind of cash tribute in the Warrior's name.

Halt faced him, his gaze level and unblinking.

'No thanks are necessary. Just spread the word that the Sunrise Warrior has returned to bring order to Clonmel,' Halt told him.

He saw a slightly puzzled frown crease Conal's forehead and smiled quietly to himself, although his face showed no trace of it. It didn't matter that Conal didn't believe. Halt had noticed that several of the villagers working nearby had heard his words and were looking with interest at the tall warrior mounted on his battlehorse. He heard the phrase 'Sunrise Warrior' repeated several times in lowered tones. Gossip and hearsay would spread the word of the Warrior's appearance here within a few days. Halt always wondered how such things could spread so quickly through a fief or shire. But he knew they could and that was what he needed. He also knew that the farther the word spread, the more exaggerated the facts would become. By the end of the week, he was willing to bet, the story would be that the Sunrise Warrior had faced Padraig's band all alone, in an open field, and cut down all of them with three mighty sweeps of a flaming sword.

'We'll do that,' Terrence said fervently.

Conal studied Halt's face. Instinctively, he had trusted this grey-bearded stranger when they had met the previous night, and his trust had been borne out. Now he sensed that Halt wanted this rumour spread and Conal saw no harm in that. He was no fool and he'd heard rumours about a religious band that was moving through Clonmel, with a prophet claiming to offer safety and protection under the wing of his god. He suspected that Halt was working to undermine this group. Why, he didn't know. But he trusted and liked the small man in the mottled cloak. And if Conal had little time for myth or legend, he had even less for hysterical religious cults.

'Aye, we will,' he agreed. His eyes met Halt's and a message of understanding passed between them. The Ranger nodded his thanks and Conal continued. 'Will you stay the night? You'll be welcome inside the barrier this time,' he added, with a smile.

Halt shook his head. 'I appreciate the offer. But we have business in Mountshannon.'

Of course, no word had reached Craikennis of events in the neighbouring village. But now that the outlaw band was broken and scattered, it would only be a few days before traffic on the roads was more or less back to normal. Halt was curious to know what Tennyson had been up to in the time they'd been gone — and whether word had reached him of today's events.

He shook hands with the two men and turned away to where Abelard and Tug were quietly grazing, side by side. Will was a few metres away and he caught Halt's eye. The older Ranger gave an imperceptible nod and Will hurried to join him. They mounted together and rode towards the knoll, where Horace sat waiting for them.

'What's Horace looking so enigmatic about?' Will asked. A faint trace of a smile touched Halt's lips.

'Someone gave him a stale fish,' he said and was gratified by Will's puzzled reaction. Sometimes, he thought, you had to keep these youngsters guessing.

Mountshannon was deserted. No more than half a dozen older residents remained in the village — people too old or infirm to travel — and they seemed anxious to stay out of sight. The three Araluans rode down the silent high street of the village, where shuttered windows and locked doors greeted them on either side. Occasionally, they caught a glimpse of a face at a window, hurriedly withdrawn as its owner stepped back to avoid being seen. But such sightings were few and far between. It was late afternoon and the long shadows thrown by the lowering sun seemed to accentuate the air of desertion that hung over the village. Halt nudged Abelard into a trot and the others matched his pace. They made their way to the market ground, only to find it empty.

The market stalls were gone. The large white pavilion that Tennyson used as a headquarters was gone as well. The only sign of recent habitation was the two small green tents pitched in the far corner of the big empty field. There was a huge charred patch in the centre of the field, evidence of a massive bonfire. The grass all around it was flattened, trampled that way by several hundred feet.

'What do you think happened here?' Will asked, indicating the blackened circle. Halt regarded it for a few seconds.

'I'd say the villagers were giving thanks to Alseiass for saving them.'

'You mean I could have had a bonfire and a party at Craikennis if I'd wanted?' Horace asked and they both looked at him. He shrugged apologetically. 'Well, you said you told them that I'd saved their village.'

'Yes,' Halt replied. 'And?'

'And . . . you know, I could have done with a little adulation for my trouble. Maybe a bonfire, a feast perhaps. I would have made sure that a reasonable share went to my faithful servants,' he finished, indicating the two of them with a lordly sweep of his hand. Then he spoiled the effect by allowing a grin to break through.

Halt muttered something inaudible and set Abelard to a canter, heading for the tents.

'I was just being enigmatic!' Horace called after him.

That evening, they packed up their camp and rode back into the village, where they hammered at the door of the darkened inn. There was no reply to their repeated attempts to raise someone inside. Horace stepped back into the street and bellowed at the top of his voice.

'Hullo the inn! Is there anyone there? Hullo!'

Both Will and Halt winced at the sudden noise.

'Warn us if you're going to do that, will you?' Will said sourly.

Horace gave him an injured look. 'I was only trying to help.'

But there was no reply from the inn. As they stood uncertainly, contemplating breaking in so they could spend a night in comfort, they heard shuffling footsteps behind them. An old woman, wrapped in a shawl, hunched with age, had emerged from the cottage next to the inn, wondering who could be causing the disturbance. She gazed at them now through watery, faded eyes, sensing instinctively that these three strangers offered no danger to her.

'They've gone. All gone,' she told them.

'Gone where?' Halt asked her. She made a vague gesture towards the north.

'Gone to follow the prophet to Dun Kilty, so they said.'

'Dun Kilty?' Halt asked. 'That's the castle of King Ferris?' The old woman regarded him with tired, knowing eyes and nodded.

'That it is. The prophet —'

'You mean Tennyson?' Will interrupted.

She frowned at him, not appreciating the interruption. 'Aye. The prophet Tennyson. He says that's where this god of his will bring peace to the Kingdom once more. He called on the people of Mountshannon to follow him and bring that peace and they all went, like the simpletons that they are.'

'But you didn't,' Halt said.

There was a long silence as she regarded them.

'No,' she said finally. 'Some of us here worship the old gods. We know the gods send us good times and bad to try us. I don't trust a god that promises only good times.'

'Why not?' Horace urged her gently, when she seemed unwilling to say more. Now, as she looked at him, there was a definite knowing look in her eyes.

'A god who brings you good and bad in equal amounts doesn't ask for much,' she said. 'Maybe a prayer or two. Maybe the odd sacrifice of a beast. But a god who promises only good times?' She shook her head and made the warding sign against evil. 'A god like that will always want something of you.'

Halt smiled at her, nodding his head in acknowledgement of the wisdom that comes with years, and the cynicism that comes with wisdom.

'I fear you're right, Mother,' he told her.

She shrugged. She had little use for his words of praise.

'I know I'm right,' she said. Then she added, 'There's a small door at the side that's never locked. You can get in there. It might stop you knocking and bellowing to raise the dead.' She gestured down the narrow alley beside the inn. Then she turned slowly away and hobbled back to her cottage and the warmth of her fireplace. The late afternoon air brought no comfort to her old bones. At this time of life, she reflected, a person needed to stay close to the fire.

They found the door and let themselves into the inn. While Halt lit a fire and a few candles, Horace searched the pantry for food and Will took care of stabling their horses in the barn behind the main building.

A short while later, the three sat comfortably around the fire, eating slightly stale bread and cheese, with some slices off a good country ham and tart local apples, washed down with the inevitable coffee. Halt looked around the deserted room. Normally, he knew, it would be packed with customers.

'So it's started,' he said. When his two young companions looked questioningly at him, he elaborated. 'It's the final phase of Tennyson's plan – the classic Outsiders' pattern. He's got a solid group of converts now, ready to attest to his ability to make bandits fall down in fear and run away. He's probably arranged for some of his acolytes to bring in other groups from villages that he's already *saved* in the south. They'll move from village to village and his band will grow larger with each passing day. The hysteria will grow as more people join him.'

'And eventually,' Will said, 'they'll arrive at Dun Kilty and challenge the King's power.'

Halt nodded. 'Not directly, of course. They're too clever for that. Tennyson will pretend at first to be working on the King's behalf. But gradually, as people come to depend more on him, the King will become increasingly irrelevant and Tennyson will assume power.'

'Judging by the way people talk about the King, that shouldn't take long,' Horace said. 'Seems like he's well on the way to being irrelevant.' He hesitated, realising that he was talking about Halt's brother, and added awkwardly, 'Sorry, Halt. I didn't mean . . .'

His voice trailed off but Halt made a small gesture dismissing the need for apology.

'It's all right, Horace. I don't have much regard for my brother. And it's obvious that his subjects share my feelings.'

Will stared thoughtfully into the fire, thinking over what Halt had described.

'Won't the fact that we beat off the attack at Craikennis stop him?' he asked.

Halt shook his head. 'It'll be a setback. But in itself, it's not enough to cause him major trouble. It's only one instance in a chain of attacks and massacres. He can still use the hysteria and adulation of the Mountshannon villagers. Of course, it would have been better for him if Craikennis had been overrun, but it's not an insurmountable obstacle.'

'Unless we make it one,' Horace said thoughtfully. Halt smiled at him. The young warrior had a way of seeing through to the core of a situation, he thought.

'Exactly. Chances are he doesn't even know what's happened at Craikennis. If I were one of the men who ran away when Horace finished off Padraig, I wouldn't be in any hurry to go telling him. People like Tennyson have a nasty habit of punishing those who bring them bad news. So as he moves on, gathering more followers, he'll be expecting rumours of a massacre to follow him. If they don't, he won't be too concerned. But if we spread the word about the Sunrise Warrior's victory, it'll be a different matter. If we arrive at Dun Kilty with the story of how the Sunrise Warrior defeated two hundred bloodthirsty bandits, single-handed, he'll have to see it as a challenge to his position. He won't be able to ignore us.'

'And that's a good thing?' Will said, frowning. Halt looked at him for a few moments in silence.

'It's a very good thing,' he said. 'I'm rather looking forward to a confrontation with Tennyson.'

He leaned back in his chair and stretched. It had been a long day, he thought. And there were more long days to come.

'Let's get some sleep,' he said. 'Will, tomorrow I want you to go after Tennyson and keep an eye on him. He's seen Horace and me but he doesn't know you. You can do your minstrel act again.'

Will nodded agreement. It would be relatively simple to join a large unorganised group like the one that would be following Tennyson. As a minstrel, he'd be able to move easily among them.

'If he follows the usual Outsider pattern, he'll take a long swing through the countryside gathering followers and reach Dun Kilty in a week or so. But once you get an idea what he's up to, come and let us know.'

'Where will I find you?' Will asked, although he sensed that he already knew the answer. Halt's reply confirmed his suspicions.

'We'll be at Dun Kilty. It's time I had a family reunion with my brother.'

Thirty

Dun Kilty was an impressive castle, Horace thought. Built inside a walled town, and set on a craggy outcrop that gave it its name, it loomed high over the lesser buildings of the town that surrounded it, its massive grey walls standing ten metres high in places.

'This wasn't thrown up in a hurry,' he said to Halt as they made their way up a street crowded with merchants, food stalls, artisans at work and people pushing carts full of everything from building materials to vegetables, from sides of meat to piles of fresh manure. Horace noted with some misgivings that the last two tended to brush together, leaving some of the manure smeared over the carcasses. He decided he'd have fish for dinner that night.

'It's an ancient fortress,' Halt told him. 'It's several hundred years older than Castle Araluen. And it was here long before the town grew up around it.'

Horace pursed his lips, suitably impressed. Then Halt ruined the effect by adding, 'Draughty as all hell in winter, too.'

They'd parted company with Will two days before, electing to ride directly for Dun Kilty. As Halt had predicted, vague rumours of the result of the battle at Craikennis had already gone ahead of them. Once again, he marvelled at the way it happened without any apparent human agency.

Rumours were also spreading of the way Tennyson had repulsed the attack on Mountshannon and Halt sensed an air of uncertainty among the people they spoke to. People weren't quite sure which banner they should flock to. Rumours about the Outsiders, and their ability to protect villages and settlements from the lawlessness that was rife throughout the country, had been circulating for some time now. Word had even come from the other kingdoms. The Sunrise Warrior was a new phenomenon. But the legend was well known and people weren't sure which way to turn. There was a sense of 'let's wait and see', which was exactly the result Halt had hoped for.

The previous night, camped by the side of the highway, he had been busy. Horace watched him unwrapping his pens, inks, parchments and sealing wax tablets and sighed. Halt was about to indulge in what he called 'creative documentation'. Horace called it forgery. He remembered a time when Halt's skill as a forger had horrified his honest, straightforward soul. I'm more devious now, he thought. It doesn't bother me so much. Not for the first time, he decided that his declining moral standards were a result of his spending too much time in the company of Rangers.

Halt glanced up, seeing the expression on the younger man's face and guessing the reason for it.

'It's just a *Laissez Passer* from Duncan. A request that

you be allowed entry to the royal throne room,' he said. 'It'll give us access to Ferris.'

'Couldn't you just tell Ferris you're back?' Horace said. 'Surely he'd agree to see you?'

Halt stuck his bottom lip out while he considered the statement. 'Maybe,' he said. 'Or maybe he'd find it simpler to have me killed. This is better. Besides, I want to pick the right moment to let him know that I am back.'

'I suppose so,' Horace agreed. He still wasn't completely happy about the idea of carrying forged credentials. He watched as Halt applied a perfect copy of the Araluan royal seal to a splodge of soft wax at the base of the document.

Halt glanced up. 'Duncan would have given us one himself if we'd had the time to ask. I don't know why you're so worried,' he said.

Horace pointed to the seal as Halt returned it to the small leather sack where he kept it.

'Maybe. But does he know you have that?'

Halt didn't answer immediately. 'Not really,' he said, 'but what he doesn't know won't hurt him. Or me, more importantly.'

It was a capital crime in Araluen to even possess a replica of the King's seal, let alone use it. Duncan, of course, was only too aware that Halt had forged his seal and signature on numerous occasions. He thought it better overall to pretend that he knew nothing about it.

Halt shook the sheet of paper to dry the ink and allow the wax to harden. Then he laid it down carefully.

'Now for your shield,' he said.

The linen shield cover had been badly torn during

Horace's encounter with Padraig. He needed something more permanent. During the afternoon, they had passed a village and Halt had procured paint and several brushes. Now he busied himself painting the sunrise insignia onto Horace's shield. Horace noted that the tip of Halt's tongue tended to protrude as he concentrated. It made the grizzled Ranger look surprisingly youthful.

'There!' he said, as he concluded drawing the horizontal black line along the bottom of the three-quarter circle depicting the sun. 'Not bad at all.'

He held the shield up for Horace's comment and the warrior nodded.

'Nice work,' he said. 'A bit more stylish than the old oakleaf you painted on my shield in Gallica.'

Halt grinned. 'Yes. That was a rush job. Bit rough, wasn't it? This is much better. Mind you, circles and straight lines are a bit easier to paint than an oakleaf.'

He leaned the shield against a tree stump to dry. By morning, the paint had hardened and they rode on, Horace once more bearing the insignia of the Sunrise Warrior.

Occasionally, as they rode through Dun Kilty, there were murmurings and fingers pointed at the insignia. Comments were made behind hands. People had noticed, he thought. And they recognised the design.

Something had been troubling Horace and he decided it was time to raise it.

'Halt,' he said, 'I've been wondering . . .'

Instantly, he regretted beginning that way as Halt assumed the long-suffering look he always adopted when either of his young companions gave him an opportunity. Instead of waiting for Halt to reply, he forged on.

'Aren't you concerned that people might . . . recognise you at the castle?'

'Recognise me?' Halt said. 'Nobody there has seen me since I was a boy.'

'Well, perhaps not you. But you and . . .' He hesitated, then decided that it might not be wise to mention Halt's relationship to Ferris in the street. '. . . you know who . . . are twins, right? So presumably you look alike. Aren't you worried that people might go, "Oh look, there goes . . . you know who . . . in a grey cloak."'

'Aaah, I see what you mean. I doubt it'll happen. After all, the cowl of my cloak hides most of my face. And people will be looking at you, not me.'

'I suppose so,' Horace admitted. He hadn't considered that.

Halt continued. 'In any event, there are substantial differences these days between you know who and myself. I have a full beard, whereas he trims his as a goatee, a ridiculous tuft on the chin only. And his moustache is smaller.' He saw the question in Horace's eyes and explained, 'I have been back here occasionally. I just never let anyone know.'

Horace nodded, understanding.

'In addition,' Halt continued, 'he wears his hair drawn back from his face while mine is sort of . . .' He hesitated, looking for the right word.

'Shaggy and unkempt?' Horace stopped himself just too late. Halt's haircut was a sore point. People were always criticising it. The Ranger eyed him grimly.

'Thank you for that,' he said. There was a pause and he concluded stiffly, 'I don't think it will be a problem.

Nobody expects a king to be "shaggy and unkempt", as you so kindly put it.'

Horace considered replying, but decided it might be wiser not to. They rode on, up a steep, winding path that led to the castle gates. They rode slowly, passing traffic travelling on foot. They were the only mounted men to approach the castle and they drew interested glances from the locals.

'Look haughty,' Halt said out of the side of his mouth. 'You're on an official mission for the King of Araluen.'

'I'm on a forged mission, as a matter of fact,' Horace replied in the same lowered tone. 'That's not something to look haughty about.'

'They'll never know. I'm an expert forger.' He sounded pleased with the fact and Horace glanced at him.

'That's not really something to be proud of, you know,' he said.

Halt grinned cheerfully at him. 'Aaah, I enjoy being around you, Horace,' he said. 'You remind me of how decadent I've become. Now look haughty.'

'I'd rather look enigmatic. I think I've got that down pretty well by now,' Horace told him. Halt glanced up in mild surprise. Horace was growing up and gaining in confidence, he realised. It wasn't as easy to confuse him these days as it used to be. Sometimes, Halt even had the suspicion that Horace was indulging in the sort of leg-pulling that Halt used to do to him. He couldn't think of a suitably crushing reply so he simply grunted.

The castle gates were open. There was, after all, no immediate threat to the town and there was a constant stream of traffic moving in and out of the castle forecourt.

Wagons, carts, people on foot carrying bundles on their backs, all streamed back and forth. A royal castle, of course, had a constant need for foodstuffs and other comforts such as wine and ale. And in an ancient castle like this, there was always repair work to be done. Providores mingled with workmen and tradespeople in a mass of seething humanity. Horace was reminded of a disturbed anthill as he looked around him.

Yet, even though the gates were unlocked, there were still guards either side of the entry. Seeing the two mounted strangers, they stepped forward, holding their spears crossed to bar them access until they were identified. A few pedestrians in front of Halt and Horace shoved and sidled past the crossed spear shafts, anxious to get inside and get on with their work.

'And who might you be when you're at home?' the taller of the two guards asked.

Horace hid a smile. Things had a certain raffish informality here in Clonmel. At Castle Araluen, a guard would have pronounced the formulaic demand: *Stand and be recognised*.

'Sir Horace, knight of the Kingdom of Araluen, the Sunrise Warrior from the east, with messages from Great King Duncan for King Ferris,' Halt replied. Horace stared straight ahead, his face a mask. So, King Duncan was *Great King Duncan* whereas Ferris was just *King Ferris*. Halt seemed to be indulging in a little verbal one-upmanship, he thought.

Horace kept his face impassive but his eyes were alert, darting around the crowd, and he saw a few people stop and take notice as Halt said the words *Sunrise Warrior*.

The guard, however, didn't seem to be impressed by the title. Guards were seldom impressed by anything, Horace thought. The guard held out a hand to Halt.

'Documents now? Would you be having any of 'em to say you are who you say you are?'

Hibernians had a lilting way of talking, Horace thought. But he reached into his gauntlet and produced the *Laissez Passer* that Halt had prepared the previous night. He passed it to Halt, who passed it to the sentry. Horace looked away and yawned. He thought that was a nice touch — the sort of thing he might do if he were haughty. Or enigmatic.

The sentry scrutinised the pass. Of course, he couldn't read it but the royal crest and seal of Araluen looked official and impressive. He looked at his companion.

'They're all right,' he said. He handed the document back to Halt, who passed it to Horace. Then the sentries uncrossed their spear shafts and stood back, allowing Halt and Horace to pass into the courtyard of the castle.

They rode towards the central keep, where the administration section of the castle would be situated. They went through the rigmarole of having their documents examined once more, this time by a sergeant of the guard. Horace reflected that Halt had been right. Few people looked at the Ranger. Instead, they tended to concentrate their attention on Horace, who, in full armour and riding a high-stepping battlehorse, appeared to be the more impressive of the two visitors. If any of the guards were asked later to describe Halt, he doubted that they'd be able to.

They left their horses outside the keep and were directed inside by another guard, to the third floor, where

Ferris's audience room was situated. Here they were stopped yet again – this time by his steward, a young, pleasant-faced man. Horace studied him keenly. The steward had the look of a warrior about him. He wore a long sword and looked as if he might know how to use it. He was nearly as tall as Horace, although not so broad in the shoulders. Dark, curly hair framed a thin, intelligent face and he had a ready, if slightly tired, smile for them.

'You're welcome here,' he said. 'We're always glad to see our Araluan cousins. My name is Sean Carrick.'

From the shadows of his cowl, Halt looked at the young man with interest. Carrick was the royal family name. This young man was some relative of Ferris's. That made sense, he thought. Kings often appointed their family members to positions of trust. It also meant he was a relative of Halt's.

Horace reached out a hand. 'Horace,' he said. 'Knight of the court of Araluen. Company commander of the Royal Guard, champion to the Royal Princess Cassandra.'

Sean Carrick glanced down at the document that Halt had tendered yet again, a small smile on his lips. 'So I noticed,' he said. Then he added, his head cocked sideways, 'But I've heard rumours about someone called the Sunrise Warrior?' He let the question hang between them, looking pointedly at the insignia on Horace's surcoat. In addition to the shield art, Halt had provided Horace with a new linen surcoat bearing the sunrise coat of arms.

'I have been called that,' Horace told him, neither confirming nor denying the identity. Sean nodded, satisfied with the answer. He glanced at the woodsman standing slightly behind the tall warrior facing him. He frowned. Was there something vaguely familiar about the man? He had the feeling that he had seen him somewhere before.

Before he could frame the obvious question, Horace said casually, 'This is my man. Michael.' He recalled that he had been Michael earlier in the week. It was a name that got about, he thought, grinning to himself.

Sean Carrick nodded, instantly dismissing Halt from his mind. 'Of course.' He glanced at a massive pair of doors behind his desk. 'The King has no visitors with him at the moment. Let me see if he's prepared to receive you.'

He smiled apologetically, then slipped through the doors, closing them behind him. He was gone for several minutes. Then he returned, beckoning them forward.

'King Ferris will receive you now,' he said. 'I'll ask you to leave your weapons here.'

The request made sense. Horace and Halt left their various weapons on his massive desk. Horace noted, with slight misgivings, that although Halt's throwing knife scabbard was empty, the weapon was nowhere to be seen on the desk. He pushed the moment of doubt aside. Halt knew what he was doing, he thought, as they moved towards the big double doors.

Carrick ushered them into the throne room. It was small as throne rooms went, Horace thought, although he really only had experience of Duncan's throne room. That was an elongated affair with high, soaring ceilings. This was square in shape, with the sides of the square no more than ten metres in length. At the far end, on a dais and seated on a plain wooden throne, sat King Ferris.

Sean Carrick introduced them and then backed away. Ferris looked up at them curiously, wondering why there was a delegation from Araluen and why he hadn't heard of it any sooner. He beckoned them towards him. Horace led the way, Halt shadowing him a few steps behind.

As they came closer, Horace studied the King of Clonmel. The relationship to Halt was plain, he thought. But there were differences. The face was fuller and the extra flesh meant that the features were not so well defined. Ferris was obviously a man who enjoyed the comforts of his table. And his body showed signs of it as well. Whereas Halt was lean and tough as whipcord, his twin was slightly overweight and looked soft.

Then there were the differences of style. As Halt had said, Ferris wore his beard in a goatee and the moustache above it was trimmed neatly. His hair was pulled back tightly from his forehead and held in place by a worked leather band that went round his temples. And Ferris's hair and beard were jet black, making him look at least ten years younger than his grizzled, grey-bearded twin. Horace looked more closely. The hair colour was artificial, he decided. It was too glossy and too even. He came to the conclusion that Ferris dyed his hair.

The eyes were different as well. Where Halt's were steady and unwavering, Ferris seemed to find it difficult to hold eye contact for a long period. His eyes slid away from those who faced him, searching the back of the room, as if ever fearful of trouble.

They heard the door click softly shut behind them as Carrick left the room. They were alone with King Ferris, although Horace was willing to bet there were a dozen men within easy reach of the throne room, all peering through spyholes to make sure no threat was offered to the King.

Ferris spoke now, indicating the cloaked, cowled figure beside Horace.

'Sir Horace,' he said. Horace started slightly. The voice was almost identical to Halt's. He doubted that he'd be able to tell the difference between the two if his eyes were closed. Although Ferris's Hibernian accent was more marked, he realised. 'Does your man have no manners? It's not fitting that he keeps his head covered before the King.'

Horace glanced uncertainly at Halt. But the Ranger was already reaching up to push the cowl back from his face. As he did so, Horace glanced at the King once more. He was frowning. Something was familiar about the roughly dressed figure before him but he couldn't quite . . .

'Hello, brother,' Halt said quietly.

Thirty-one

Tennyson, prophet of Alseiass the Golden God, leader of the Outsiders, was in a black fury. He glared at the man who grovelled before him, head bowed, unwilling to meet the leader's gaze.

'What do you mean, they were *defeated*?' He spat the last word out as if it were poison.

The huddled figure before him crouched lower, wishing he hadn't obeyed the instinct to report the defeat at Craikennis. He had been one of Padraig's men and he had a vague idea that Tennyson might reward him for the information. Now he realised, too late, that bearers of good news were rewarded. Bearers of bad news were reviled.

'Your honour,' he said, his voice shaking, 'they were waiting for us. They knew we were coming.'

'How?' demanded Tennyson. He stalked back and forth across the inner room of the white pavilion, site of the altar of Alseiass. A low footstool was in his way and he kicked at it in fury, sending it spinning towards the cowering messenger. 'How could they know? Who could have possibly told them? Who betrayed me?'

His voice rose in fury and he considered the question himself. Padraig had not been the most intelligent of men. But he knew his business and he knew better than to allow advance warning of an attack to reach his enemies. And indeed, there had been little opportunity for it to do so. But somehow, word had got out and now he was without the support of the eighty men he had committed to the attack. Those who hadn't died before the barricades or been captured were now scattered hopelessly.

Not that that was an insurmountable problem. He had numbers enough now, and the outlaws had served their purpose, creating fear and uncertainty and giving him the opportunity to rise up as the uncontested saviour of the Kingdom. But the planned massacre at Craikennis had been an important part of his end game. Now that had been taken away. The unfortunate man before him looked up, saw his leader's face twisted with fury.

'Your honour,' he said, 'perhaps it was the Sunrise Warrior who told —'

He got no further. Tennyson was upon him. His face was dark and flushed now as he heard that ridiculous phrase. The messenger had mentioned it before. Now Tennyson let his rage loose as he beat back and forth at the wretched man with his closed fists. Blood flowed from the crouching man's nose and he huddled lower, trying to protect himself from the savage fists.

'There is no Sunrise Warrior! I tell you he does not exist! If you use that name before me again I'll . . .'

He stopped suddenly, the blinding rage gone almost as

soon as it had formed. This stupid Hibernian superstition could be a problem, he thought. If people started believing in the Sunrise Warrior, it would undermine his position. His mind was working rapidly. So far as he knew, he was the only one who was aware that there had been no massacre at Craikennis. At least, he thought sourly, no massacre of the villagers. If he moved quickly, he could spread the rumour that the village had been razed to the ground, all its inhabitants killed. By the time the truth was known, he would be in an unassailable position. He had four hundred followers with him now, all prepared to swear that he had the power to defeat the marauding bandits who were scourging the Kingdom.

So, he reasoned, any mention of this Sunrise Warrior must be quashed.

He became aware that the man was watching him fearfully. The blood still streamed from his nose and one eye was swelling shut where Tennyson's fists had struck him. He smiled now and stepped forward, offering his hand. His voice was silken and low, conciliatory.

'My friend, I'm sorry. Forgive me, please. It's just that I become enraged when Alseiass's will is denied. I should never have struck you. Say you forgive me? Please?'

He gripped both the man's hands in his own and looked deep into his eyes. Warily, the former bandit began to relax a little. There was still a shadow of fear behind his eyes but it was receding. Tennyson released his hands and turned to the altar, where a small pile of offerings to Alseiass was assembled. He selected one, a chain of heavy golden discs linked together. It caught the light and gleamed as it twisted in his hand.

'Here, take this as a sign of my repentance. And as thanks for bringing me this news. I know it must have been a difficult choice for you.'

The man's eyes were locked on the chain now. The linked discs turned slowly, rich and gleaming and heavy. It was a fortune to a man like himself. He could live comfortably for years if he were to sell that chain. He seized it, marvelling at the weight of it as Tennyson released it to him. What were a few bruises and a bleeding nose compared to this, he thought.

'Thank you, your honour. I thought I should . . .'

'You did your duty, friend. Your duty to me and to Alseiass. Now tell me. What is your name?'

'It's Kelly, your honour. Kelly the Squint, they call me.'

Tennyson looked at him, careful to keep the distaste he felt off his face. He could see why the man had been given such a name. His two eyes wandered in different directions.

'Well, Kelly, I'll rename you Friend of Alseiass. I'll wager you didn't have much to eat on your way here?'

'No, your honour. I did not.'

Tennyson nodded, smiling beneficently at the man. 'Then Kelly, Friend of Alseiass, take yourself to my tent and tell my man there to serve you food and wine. The finest I have.'

'Why thank you, your honour. I must say, I . . .'

Tennyson held up a hand to silence him. 'It's the least I can do. And tell them I said they are to tend your bruises as well.' Tennyson took a fine silk cloth from his sleeve and dabbed gently at the blood on Kelly's face, tut-tutting as he did so, the very picture of concern. Satisfied that he had cleared most of it, he stepped back and smiled reassuringly at the man. 'Now be off with you.'

He waved a hand in blessing and dismissal and Kelly the Squinting Friend of Alseiass hurried from the pavilion. When he was gone, Tennyson began pacing again. After a few minutes, he called to one of his massive bodyguards, stationed outside the curtain that separated the inner tent from the main part of the pavilion.

'Gerard!'

The curtain parted and the enormous creature entered. He and his twin were from the western isles. Massive brutes, they were. And killers.

'Lord?' he said.

'Find me the leader of the new men. Bring him here.'

Gerard frowned, puzzled. 'New men, my lord?'

Tennyson repressed the instinct to shout at the giant oaf. He remained patient, his voice silken.

'The three new men who joined us two days ago. The Genovesans.'

Gerard's face cleared in understanding. He knuckled his brow in salute and hurried from the tent to look for the leader of the three Genovesans Tennyson had hired. Originally from a land far to the east, on the northern shore of the Constant Sea, the Genovesans could now be found in all the major kingdoms of the main continent. They were a race of mercenaries, each man armed with a crossbow and a selection of daggers. They were also very efficient assassins, with a comprehensive knowledge of poisons, and Tennyson had decided that it might be useful to have people with such skills working for him. They didn't come cheaply, but chances were there'd be more than one occasion over the coming days when he'd need to get rid of a troublesome critic. Or someone who simply knew too much — for example, someone who knew about the defeat at Craikennis. Of course, the massive twins could handle that sort of thing with ease, but he felt there were occasions like this one when more subtlety and discretion was needed. And they were not qualities that the hulking islanders possessed in any quantity.

Tennyson waited outside the pavilion for Gerard to return with the Genovesan. He watched a small group of recently joined followers listening to the songs of a young minstrel. He frowned. The singer was a new addition, he thought. He hadn't seen him around before and he'd bear watching. Tennyson wasn't sure that he wanted anyone else commanding an audience among his followers, no matter how small that audience might be. He decided that he'd issue an edict from Alseiass the following morning, banning any music that wasn't a hymn of praise to the Golden God.

His attention was distracted by the arrival of Gerard with the Genovesan.

'Thank you, Gerard. You may go,' he said. The giant hesitated. Usually he and his brother dogged the leader's footsteps, their presence adding to his aura of authority. But now, as he hesitated, Tennyson's brow darkened in anger.

'Go,' he repeated, a little more forcefully. The huge man touched his forehead in obedience and entered the pavilion, leaving Tennyson with the newcomer.

He was slim and swarthy, wearing a wide-brimmed hat with a long feather in it. It was the Genovesan national headwear, Tennyson knew. The man was dressed completely in tight, body-fitting leather and he had a superior smile on his face. Tennyson was sure that he wore perfume.

'Signor?' the Genovesan asked now.

Tennyson smiled at him and moved towards him, putting an arm around his shoulder. The leader of the Outsiders set great store by touching and laying hands on his followers.

'Luciano, that's your name, isn't it?'

'Si. That is what people call me, signor. Luciano.'

'Let's walk a while then, Luciano.' He kept his arm on the smaller man's shoulder and led him away from the tent. Behind him, he was aware of the minstrel finishing a song and the hearty burst of applause from his audience. He scowled momentarily. He would definitely issue that edict tonight at prayers. Then he brought his mind back to the matter at hand and assumed the smile again.

'Well now, my friend, there's something you can do for me.' He paused but the other man said nothing so he continued. 'There's a man called Kelly in my tent right now. An ugly little person with a terrible squint. My servants are feeding him and tending him. He's been a little bruised around the face, poor man.'

'Yes, signor?' Luciano was an experienced mercenary and assassin. He could see through the false concern in Tennyson's voice. There was usually only one reason for an employer to point out a third party to a Genovesan, he knew.

'When he leaves my tent, follow him and wait for a moment when there's no one around.'

'And then what should I do, signor?' But Luciano already knew what Tennyson wanted and a wolfish smile was creasing his face in anticipation.

'Then you should kill him, Luciano. Then you should kill him.'

Luciano's smile broadened, matched by an answering smile on Tennyson's face. The two men looked into each other's eyes and understood each other perfectly.

'Oh, one other thing, Luciano,' Tennyson added as an afterthought. The Genovesan said nothing but arched an eyebrow questioningly.

'You'll find a gold chain on his person. He stole it from me. Bring it back to me when the job's done.'

'It shall be as you say, signor,' Luciano said. And Tennyson, still smiling, nodded in satisfaction.

'I know,' he replied.

Thirty-two

Ferris went white. Horace saw the colour literally drain from his face and his hand went up to his throat in an involuntary gesture of shock. After initially recoiling, the King took control of himself and stepped forward a pace, peering into the face of the grim, grey-bearded man who stood before him.

'Brother?' he said. 'But you can't . . .' He stopped, then tried to take possession of himself once more, tried to assume an air of dignified mystification. 'My brother is dead. He died many years ago,' he said, the conviction in his voice growing as he spoke. He made a small sign with his right hand and Horace heard the large doors behind them open, heard several sets of hurried footsteps on the stone flooring and knew that Sean Carrick and a small group of men at arms had entered the throne room.

He'd been right about the unseen observers, he thought grimly.

'Your majesty, is everything all right?' Sean Carrick asked.

Halt glanced over his shoulder at the group of armed men. He stepped a little closer to Ferris. Instinctively, the King began to back off a corresponding pace. Then he seemed to realise that, by doing so, he was giving Halt the upper hand. He stopped, watching Halt warily. Halt spoke softly so that only his brother and Horace could hear his words.

'If you're frightened, brother, then let Sean stay. He has a right to hear me. But unless you want your men to hear what we're about to discuss — and I don't think you do — send them outside again, where they can see but not listen.'

Ferris looked at him, then at the armed men standing ready by the door. Halt and Horace were both unarmed, he realised, while he was wearing his sword. Sean Carrick was similarly armed and Ferris knew his steward was a more than capable swordsman. That was one of the reasons Sean held the position that he did. Years of guilt and fear, long suppressed, now swam to the surface of his mind. He realised instinctively that he didn't want his soldiers to hear whatever it was that Halt planned to say. He knew it would not show himself in any favourable light. Abruptly, he decided.

'Sean!' he called. 'Dismiss the men to their posts and come stand by me.'

Carrick hesitated and Ferris turned to look directly at him.

'Do it,' he ordered.

Carrick still hesitated another second or two, then nodded to the men. As they turned and trooped out of the room, Sean waited till the doors closed behind them, then strode forward to stand beside the King.

'Uncle,' he said, confirming Halt's earlier suspicion, 'what's the trouble? Who is this man?'

He was looking at Halt, frowning. From the relative positions of the three men, Halt and Ferris facing each other, Horace standing a pace or two back, it was obvious now that the Araluan knight was not the leader here, but the follower. And now Sean had that same sense that he'd felt before, that there was something very familiar about the smaller man.

Halt turned to face him.

'Uncle?' he said. 'You'd be Caitlyn's son then?'

Sean nodded. 'What do you know of my mother?' he asked, his tone defensive and a little belligerent. Ferris let out a deep sigh of anguish and turned away, moving to sit on a low bench beside the throne, his head in his hands.

'She was my sister,' Halt told him. 'I'm your uncle too. My name is Halt.'

'No!' Sean rejected the statement vehemently. 'My uncle Halt is dead. He died over twenty years ago!' He looked to the King for confirmation. But Ferris's face remained in his hands and he refused to look up and meet Sean's gaze. He shook his head repeatedly from side to side, as if trying to deny the scene before him. Sean's conviction began to waver and he looked more closely at the small, rather stocky man in the mottled cloak.

The beard was full and covered the face. And the moustache was heavy as well. But if that shaggy mop of hair were drawn back as Ferris's was . . .

Sean shook his head now. The features were the same. They were more defined in the stranger's face. In Ferris's, they were blurred somewhat by the extra flesh he carried.

A person's features become altered by their actions over their lifetime, he knew. A face is a canvas where the years paint their marks. But if you could strip away the effect of the years from these two faces, remove the excesses, the joys, the pains, the triumphs and disappointments of twenty years or more, then he sensed that they would be identical.

And if you looked beyond the faces to the eyes . . .

The eyes! They were the same. Yet in one important way, they were different. Ferris, he knew, could never meet your gaze for more than a few seconds at a time. His eyes would slide away from yours uncertainly. That was why Ferris set great store by the fact that people should not gaze directly into the face of a king. But this man's eyes were steady and unwavering. And as Sean Carrick looked into them now, he saw something else, a faint hint of sardonic humour deep behind them.

'Finished looking?' Halt asked him.

Sean stepped back. He wasn't totally convinced, but his mind couldn't ignore the evidence that his eyes were seeing. He turned to Ferris.

'Your majesty?' he said. 'Tell me.'

But the only response from Ferris was a deep groaning sound, and an ineffectual wave of the hand. And in that moment, Sean Carrick knew. A second later, Ferris confirmed it with one word.

'Halt . . .' he began uncertainly, raising his eyes at last to look at his brother. 'I never meant you any harm. You must believe that.'

'Ferris, you're a lying sack of manure. You meant me a great deal of harm. You meant to kill me.'

'No! When you left I sent men after you to find you!' Ferris protested. Halt laughed, a short, barking sound that had no humour in it.

'I'll bet you did! With orders to finish what you'd started!'

It was too much for Sean. Nobody had ever taken such a tone to the King and the habit of years now made him intervene. He stepped forward, interposing himself between Ferris and Halt, his eyes locked on Halt's, each of them unwilling to drop his gaze.

'You can't talk to the King like that,' Sean said with some force. Halt held his gaze for several seconds before he replied quietly.

'I'm not talking to the King.' He jerked a contemptuous thumb at his brother. 'He is.'

The thought was so outrageous, so directly opposed to everything that Sean had lived by for his entire adult life, that it checked him like a physical blow. Yet he realised it was true. If this was Halt, then he was the rightful King of Clonmel, and Ferris was a usurper. No ceremony of coronation and consecration could change that basic fact. And as he looked into Halt's eyes again, then tried to look at Ferris, only to have the so-called King avert his gaze, the last doubt disappeared from Sean's mind. This was Halt. This was the rightful King of Clonmel.

'Your majesty . . .' he said and began to sink to his knees before Halt. The Ranger quickly stopped him, stepping closer to seize his forearm and draw him back to his feet. Ferris made a choking sound in his throat. Significantly, Sean thought, he made no protest about Sean's demonstration of fealty to Halt.

'Very kind of you,' Halt said, 'but we don't have time for that nonsense. I'm really not interested in being King. I prefer to work for a living. Now, Ferris, we need to talk.'

Ferris looked wildly about the room, as if seeking some form of escape. He knew that he was about to face retribution for his crimes. So he was quite startled when Halt continued, in a bad-tempered tone.

'Oh, for God's sake, man! I'm not here to steal your throne! I'm here to help you keep it!'

'Keep it?' Ferris, said, bewildered. Events were moving too fast for him. 'Keep it from whom?'

'Let's sit down, shall we?' Halt saw several low benches to one side and he picked one up and brought it close to the throne, gesturing for Horace and Sean to do likewise. Ferris stood watching them, uncertain what to do next, plucking nervously at the hem of his satin sleeve.

'You hop up on your throne,' Halt told him. 'I'm sure you'll enjoy that.' He glanced at Sean. 'I don't suppose there's any chance we could get some coffee sent in, is there?' he asked.

Sean looked doubtful. 'We don't drink coffee here. The King —' he corrected himself '— Uncle Ferris doesn't like it.'

'Might have known,' Halt said, scowling. He looked at Horace and curled his lip in distaste. Horace couldn't help grinning. Halt seemed more antagonised by the fact that his brother didn't like coffee than by the fact that he had stolen the throne from him. Typical, the young warrior thought.

'Well, never mind,' Halt continued. 'We'll just get this over as quickly as we can. Now, Ferris, you've heard of a group called the Outsiders, I take it?'

'Yes . . .' Ferris was taken aback. He hadn't expected this turn in the conversation. 'They're some kind of religion. Harmless, I would have said.'

'Harmless my eye. They're a cult, not a religion. And you're going to have to take a stand against them. They're on their way here and they plan to seize power in Clonmel.'

'Seize power? That's ridiculous! What makes you say that?' Ferris was openly sceptical of the idea. Halt gazed steadily at him. Sean noted that the King averted his eyes after a few seconds, as ever.

'I've heard their leader speak. And I've heard him whipping people up — inciting them to rebellion.'

'Nonsense!' Ferris seemed sure of himself now, back on secure ground. 'Tennyson is a simple preacher, that's all. He wishes me no harm.'

'Tennyson?' Halt said, seizing on the name, and the familiarity in Ferris's voice when he mentioned it. 'You know him?' A light of understanding dawned in his eyes. 'You've been in contact with him, haven't you?'

Ferris was about to answer, then hesitated. Halt pressed him further.

'Haven't you?'

'We have . . . communicated. He sent a delegate to see me, to reassure me.'

'When?' The question burst from Sean's lips before he could stop it. As the King's steward, he was aware of any and all delegations who came to see Ferris. This was the first time he had heard of any approach from this Tennyson. Ferris looked at him, trying to retain his dignity and authority.

'It didn't concern you, Sean. It was a confidential visit.'

He realised how flimsy the excuse sounded as it hung in the air of the throne room. A long and ugly silence stretched out.

'Have you come to some arrangement with him?' Halt asked. But Ferris didn't answer the question directly.

'Halt, the man has done wonders. There have been outlaws and brigands terrorising the countryside and I've been powerless to stop them.'

'You tend to be powerless when you refuse to do anything,' Halt said contemptuously. 'The truth is, you've sat here and twiddled your thumbs while outlaws have been killing and robbing your people, haven't you?' He didn't wait for an answer but turned quickly to Sean. 'Has he done anything? Sent troops out to hunt these outlaws down? Garrisoned any of the larger towns and villages? Has he even made a statement promising to act and denouncing the outlaws' actions?'

Sean looked at the King, then back at Halt.

'No,' he said. 'I offered to take a patrol out and . . .' He stopped, feeling awkward. Somehow it seemed disloyal to say that he had wanted to do something but the King had refused his request. But the truth was that the King had done nothing, tried nothing. Slowly, Sean shook his head. Halt sighed and his shoulders slumped. He looked at Ferris with contempt. The King tried to explain himself.

'Don't you see? That's why I agreed to see Tennyson's messenger. He can stop the outlaws. He can bring an end to the lawlessness!'

'Because he controls them!' Halt came to his feet so violently that the bench he was seated on crashed over behind him. 'Surely you can grasp that, you almighty fool?'

'He . . . controls them?' Ferris's face creased in a puzzled frown.

'Of course! They do his bidding. Then he pretends to chase them off and claims to be the only person in the country with the power to do so. I've heard him preaching sedition against you, Ferris! "Can the King protect you?" he asks. And the answer is a resounding "No!" from those he speaks to. "Can anyone protect you?" he asks, and they fall over themselves to tell him that he is their only hope. Not you. Not the rule of law in this country. Him! Ferris, he is planning to seize power in Clonmel. Just as he has done in the other five kingdoms.'

'No! He said I'd be safe. I'd remain as King! He said . . .' Ferris stopped, rèalising he'd said too much. He was used to the contempt in Halt's eyes. Now he saw it in the eyes of the two younger men as well.

'You'd remain as King,' Horace said. 'You'd be his puppet on the throne. And all the while, he'd bleed your people dry.'

'They're not his people,' Halt corrected him. 'He doesn't deserve them. And they certainly don't deserve him. Get up, Ferris. Get up and face me.'

Reluctantly, the King stood so that he was facing his brother.

'There's one way to stop Tennyson and put an end to his depraved cult. A figure of authority has to stand up against him and denounce him. He's successful because nobody is ever willing to act or speak against him. Or if they do, they're quickly removed and murdered. But he couldn't do that to you.'

'Me?' Ferris was horrified at the concept. 'What do you expect me to do?'

'Speak out! Take control of your Kingdom and offer the people an alternative to this charlatan! Break this cult of his. Roll it back and destroy his power! It's built on an illusion anyway. Offer them another illusion.'

'What?' Ferris asked. 'What illusion do I have?'

'The illusion of your own authority,' Halt said sarcastically. 'That won't go far. But fortunately for you, we've provided an additional one.' He pointed to Horace. 'The Sunrise Warrior.'

'But that's a myth!' Ferris cried and Halt laughed bitterly.

'Of course it is! Just as Alseiass, the all-loving Golden God of the Outsiders, is a myth. Make the Sunrise Warrior your counter-myth. Make him your champion, summoned by you to bring the rule of law back to Clonmel.

'We've already prepared the ground for you. The warrior was seen at a village called Craikennis just a few days ago. He wiped out a band of three hundred outlaws.'

'Three hundred?' Horace, said, surprised. 'You're coming it a bit strong, aren't you, Halt?'

The Ranger shrugged. 'The bigger the rumour, the easier it is to make people believe,' he said. But Sean had reacted instantly to the mention of Craikennis.

'It's true, your majesty. I heard rumours of the Warrior in the marketplace yesterday. And I heard mention of a battle at Craikennis as well.'

Ferris looked from one to the other. He made an ineffectual, undecided gesture, one hand flapping in the air.

'I don't know. I . . . I just don't know.'

Halt stepped close to him so that their faces were only centimetres apart.

'Do this, brother. Speak out and denounce Tennyson and his cult. Offer the people the protection of the Sunrise Warrior at the head of your soldiers and I promise we'll give you every support.'

He saw that Ferris was wavering and added his final inducement.

'Do it and I swear I will make no claim against you for the throne. I'll return to Araluen as soon as we've destroyed the Outsiders, and Tennyson with them.'

That struck home, he saw. For a second or two, Ferris was on the brink of agreeing. But decisiveness had never been his long suit and still he vacillated.

'I need time to think about this. I need a few days. You can't just walk in here and expect me to . . .' He hesitated and Halt finished the sentence for him.

'Make a decision? No, I suppose that's a pretty foreign idea for you. All right. We'll give you a day.'

'Two days,' Ferris replied instantly. Then, in a pleading tone, 'Please, Halt, there's a lot for me to take in here.'

Halt shook his head. The longer Ferris had to think about this, the more likely he would find a way to weasel out of his predicament. It was not impossible that he wouldn't try to contact Tennyson again.

'One day,' he said firmly. His tone told Ferris that there would be no further discussion of the matter and the King's shoulders slumped in resignation.

'Very well,' he muttered.

Halt studied the submissive figure for a few seconds. Ferris seemed cowed, but he still didn't trust him. He turned to Sean.

'Do I have your word that you'll prevent any trickery?'

Sean nodded instantly. 'Of course. I'll make sure he keeps his side of the bargain,' he said, then added, 'Uncle.'

A grim smile touched Halt's face at the word. He studied Sean for a few seconds. The eyes were clear and honest. The face was a trustworthy one. He felt a surge of warmth for this young man. Halt had lived his life without any knowledge of his family. At least one of them had turned out well, he thought. Pity about the other one in the room with them.

'That's good enough for me.' He looked back to Ferris. 'We'll be back at noon tomorrow for your answer. Let's go, Horace.'

They turned and walked towards the big double doors, their boot heels ringing on the flagstones. They were almost there when Ferris's cry stopped them.

'Wait!' he called, and they turned to face him again. 'What if my answer is . . . no?'

Halt smiled at him. At least, it might have been called a smile. Horace thought it was closer to the way a wolf shows its fangs to an enemy.

'It won't be,' he said.

Thirty-three

Will was seated under a tree, his back comfortably against the trunk, repairing a part of Tug's harness. He worked the point of an awl through the tough leather strap, wincing as the sharp end caught the ball of his thumb.

'I'm going to have to stop doing that,' he told himself. Perhaps the key to doing so would be to keep his eyes on the job in hand. But the broken strap was merely a ruse to occupy him while he studied the sprawling camp of Tennyson's followers.

He had joined the band two nights previously, riding in after dark and being challenged by a sentry from the picket line thrown around the camp. He identified himself as a travelling minstrel and said he was anxious to join the followers of Alseiass. The sentry grunted, seeming to be satisfied, and waved him inside the camp.

There were nearly four hundred people massed under Tennyson's banner. Most of them were people from villages along the way, who had joined after hearing the enthusiastic testimony of the residents of Mountshannon. Some had been summoned from other villages further south, where Tennyson had already driven off parties of outlaws. The prophet had left some of his henchmen in each of these villages and, once the march on Dun Kilty began in earnest, they had been summoned, along with their converts, to join the band.

But there was also a solid core of Tennyson's acolytes, recognisable by their white robes. Most obvious of all were the two massively proportioned bodyguards who always stood close to the leader. They were surly brutes, Will thought. The Golden God Alseiass hadn't imbued them with his much-professed love for their fellow man.

As the numbers grew, Tennyson continued to preach, stressing the King's lack of decision and action, and laying the blame for Clonmel's troubled situation squarely on his shoulders. And at each of these sessions, his subordinates moved among the crowd, collecting gold and jewellery in tribute to Alseiass.

As an outsider — Will smiled at the inadvertent use of the word — he could see the sharp division in the camp. There were the fervent, hopeful new converts, the large mass of people who had chosen to follow Tennyson and who looked to him and his god as the new hope for peace and prosperity. That group grew larger each day as new converts flocked into the camp.

And there was the hard-edged core of existing followers, who collected the gold, protected Tennyson and, Will was sure, dealt with anyone who chose to speak out against Alseiass's prophet.

The previous day, the latter group had been reinforced by three remarkable newcomers. Dressed in tight black leather, they wore dull purple cloaks and wide-brimmed, feathered hats of the same colour. They were olive skinned and dark haired and obviously foreigners. And they weren't simple pilgrims come to join the throng. They carried crossbows slung on their backs and, from Will's careful observation, each of them had at least three daggers on his person — in belt sheaths, in their boots and under the left arm. They were dangerous men. They carried themselves with an air of assurance that said they had confidence in their weapon skills.

He wondered who they were and where they had come from. He was less curious as to their purpose. They were Tennyson's hired killers. Earlier, Will had been singing close to the white pavilion and had watched as one of them followed a shabbily dressed man out of the camp and into the forest. Fifteen minutes later, the foreigner returned alone, going straight to Tennyson's pavilion to report. Will, who had discreetly followed them part of the way, waited by the edge of the forest until sundown. But there had been no sign of the other man returning.

He heard a raised voice a few metres away and glanced up. One of the white-robed inner circle was walking among the haphazardly pitched tents and shelters, issuing orders to the people there. Will rose and moved closer to hear what was being said.

'Pack up your camp tonight after prayers. Get your goods loaded on your carts and horses and be ready to strike camp tomorrow. Tennyson wants everyone ready to move out by ten o'clock! So get busy! Don't leave it till tomorrow! Get it done tonight and sleep in the open if you must!'

One of the pilgrims stepped forward and addressed the white-robed figure deferentially.

'Where are we going, your honour?' he said and half a dozen voices echoed the question. For a moment, the messenger looked as if he wasn't going to answer, out of simple contrariness. Then he shrugged. There was no need to keep it a secret.

'We're marching directly to Dun Kilty. It's time King Ferris was told his hour has come!' he said and there was a swelling buzz of approval from those who heard him.

Interesting, Will thought. He threaded his way through the tents to the edge of the settlement, where his own small tent was pitched and Tug stood grazing close by. He quickly lowered the tent and packed it away. Tug looked at him curiously as he did so.

'We're moving out tomorrow,' Will told him. He checked that everything was tightly rolled and secured. He'd be content to sleep in the open tonight. He glanced at the sky. There were clouds scudding overhead, obscuring the stars from time to time. It might rain but his cloak was waterproof and he'd be comfortable enough.

'You!'

The voice startled him. It was rough and overloud and as he turned he felt a twinge of uneasiness as he saw who had spoken. It was one of the giants who attended to Tennyson — Gerard or Killeen. He had no idea which was which and there seemed to be no way to tell them apart.

The huge man pointed a finger at him.

'You're the singer, is that right?' he said, a challenging tone in his voice. Will nodded uncertainly.

'I am a jongleur, that's true,' he said, wondering where this was leading. The word seemed unfamiliar to the man and Will explained further. 'I'm a minstrel. A musician and singer.'

The man's face cleared as he heard a description he understood. 'Not any more you're not,' he said. 'Tennyson has barred all singing — except hymns to Alseiass. You know any of them?'

Will shook his head. 'Sadly, no.'

The big man smiled evilly at him. 'Sad for you, because you're out of business. Tennyson says you're to bring your lute to him after the evening prayer session.'

Will contemplated whether there was any point in telling this oaf that he played a mandola, not a lute. He decided against it.

'Tennyson wants my . . . instrument?'

The man scowled at him. 'Isn't that what I said? No more music and hand in your lute! Clear?'

Will hesitated, thinking about the order and what it meant, and the man spoke, this time even louder and more abruptly.

'Clear?'

'Yes, of course. No more music. Hand in my . . . lute. I understand.'

Gerard or Killeen nodded in a satisfied manner. 'Good. Make sure you do.'

He turned on his heel and swaggered away, his huge frame visible over the tents for some distance. Will sat on his rolled pack and looked at the mandola in its boiled-leather, shaped case. It was a beautiful instrument, made by Araluen's master luthier, Gilet, and given to him as a present by a grateful Lord Orman of Castle Macindaw. If he handed it in to Tennyson, he had no doubt that he'd never see it again.

Besides, he thought, he'd learned as much as he could about Tennyson's plans. The prophet was heading directly for Dun Kilty, cutting short his original scheme to gather an increasing number of followers in a triumphal progression through the countryside. Not that he needed any more. He had hundreds of them already.

Then there was the matter of the three new arrivals — the crossbowmen. It might be timely for Halt to hear about them. Will was sure that his old mentor would know who they were — or at least, where they came from and what their purpose would be.

All in all, Will decided, it was time for him to leave the followers of Alseiass.

He clicked his tongue and Tug trotted briskly to him, all thoughts of grazing forgotten. Quickly, Will saddled the horse, strapping his pack, mandola case and camping gear to the ties provided for them. Then he took a long oilskin-wrapped bundle that remained on the ground and opened it to reveal his longbow and quiver. He strung the longbow, slipped the strap of the quiver over his shoulder and mounted Tug.

He rode quickly through the outskirts of the camp, not making any attempt at concealment. That would only attract suspicion, he knew. As the tent lines began to thin out, he increased the pace to a trot, stopping briefly when one of the outer ring of pickets stepped into his path, his hand raised.

'Just a moment! Where do you think you're going?'

'I'm leaving,' Will said. The man was standing on his right side and Will slipped his right boot out of the stirrup.

'Nobody leaves,' the sentry said. 'Get back into camp now.'

He had a spear. So far, he had kept the haft grounded but now he began to raise it, to bar Will's way.

'No. I have to go,' Will said in a pleasant tone. 'You see my poor old aunty on my mother's side sent me a letter and said . . .'

A little pressure from his left knee had told Tug to shuffle closer to the man as he was talking. He could remember Halt's teaching: *If you're planning to surprise someone, keep talking to him right up until you do it.* He could see the annoyance on the sentry's face as he rambled on about his aunty on his mother's side. The man was drawing breath to cut him off and order him back into camp when Will shot his booted right foot forward, straightening his knee and slamming the sole of the boot hard into the man's face.

In the same instant the man stumbled and went down, Will urged Tug into a gallop. By the time the dazed sentry had regained his feet and found the spear that had gone spinning out of his hand, Will and Tug had been swallowed by the early evening gloom. There was only the sound of fast-receding hoof beats to mark the fact that they had been there.

Thirty-four

Halt and Horace returned to the courtyard, where Kicker and Abelard waited patiently.

Halt was silent as they mounted and rode out of the castle, deep in thought. Horace was hardly surprised. Halt at the best of times was taciturn and today he had a lot to occupy his mind. Horace tried to imagine what it must have been like for his unofficial mentor — for he too had learned a great deal from Halt and continued to do so — to face his treacherous brother after his long absence. A wry grin touched his mouth as he considered the other side of the coin. Presumably it had been a disturbing experience for Halt. But it must have been ten times worse for Ferris, he thought, and the King's behaviour had borne that out. The thought of the King brought a question to his lips and he asked it abruptly, without any preamble.

'Do you trust him, Halt?'

The Ranger looked up at him and his answer told Horace that he had been thinking along the same lines.

'Ferris? Not as far as I could kick him. And I'd enjoy seeing how far that might be,' he added, with a hint of bitterness in his voice. 'But I trust Sean. He'll keep Ferris in line. And he'll make sure he keeps his word.'

'He's a good man,' Horace agreed. 'But can he really do that? After all, Ferris is the King. Surely he can do as he likes?'

But Halt shook his head. 'It's not that easy, even for a king. Especially for this one,' he added. 'Ferris knows he needs Sean. He relies on him. You don't think any of those castle guards care a fig about what Ferris wants, do you? Didn't you notice that when Ferris dismissed them, none of them moved until Sean gave them the nod? If Ferris tries to cheat us or trick us, he'll alienate Sean. And right now, he needs him.'

'I suppose so,' Horace agreed. Halt invariably knew more about this sort of thing than he did. Horace, like most soldiers, hated politics, and avoided it as much as he could. Rangers, as he'd noted on more than one occasion, seemed at home with the secret dealing, scheming and subterfuge that seemed to go with ruling a country. If Halt was satisfied, Horace thought, that was good enough for him. He had more pressing matters to engage his attention.

Like lunch.

'What do we do now?' he asked after a few more minutes of silence. Halt looked up, snapped out of his reverie by the question.

'I suppose we find a comfortable inn,' he said. Horace nodded, then a thought struck him.

'What about Will? How will he know where to find us?'

'He'll manage,' Halt said confidently. Then he

stretched his stiff back and shoulder muscles. 'Let's find that inn. I don't know about you but I could do with a few hours' sleep.'

Horace nodded agreement. 'Yes, a good meal and then a few hours in a soft bed would do wonders.'

'I think I'll skip the meal,' said Halt.

Horace looked at him, horrified. How anyone could contemplate such a thing was beyond him.

They found a suitable inn at the base of the hill that led up to Dun Kilty castle. The inn was a two-storey building — as most inns were — but this was more substantial than most. The tap room and bar were large and the ceilings a little higher than normal, avoiding the cramped feeling that Horace had experienced in the Mountshannon and Craikennis inns. He could stand erect under the ceiling beams in this building and he gave a small sigh of relief when he realised the fact. More than once since they'd been travelling in Hibernia, he'd managed to crack his head on low ceiling beams.

The guest rooms were on the second floor. They were large and airy, with glass-paned windows that opened wide to let the breeze in and allowed a view of the high street in either direction. If you craned out, as Horace did, you could even catch a glimpse of the castle, high on the hill above them.

The sheets on the beds were clean and the blankets had been well aired. Too often in his long career, Halt had been forced to stay in establishments where the sheets bore ample evidence of those who had gone before him. He looked around the room with approval, tested the mattress with his hands and the approval grew.

'We'll take it,' he told the landlady who had showed them the room. She nodded. She had expected no less.

'How many nights?' she asked. Halt considered the question.

'Tonight and tomorrow night,' he told her. 'We may stay longer but that'll do for the moment.' He reached into the wallet hanging at his belt and paid her in advance for the two nights. The landlady curtseyed with surprising grace for one with such a large girth and squirrelled the money away into a pocket in her apron.

'Thank you, your honour,' she said and Halt nodded.

She stood expectantly. 'Will there be anything else?'

'No. We'll be fine,' Halt said. But Horace interrupted him.

'Are you still serving food in the tap room?' he asked and her face was wreathed in a huge smile.

'God's love but of course we are, young man! And you with the look on you that you could eat a horse!'

Halt never ceased to be fascinated by the way women, young or old, big or small, could never resist the temptation to feed Horace.

'I'd prefer a steak,' the young warrior said, grinning.

The landlady chuckled, her multiple chins wobbling with the effort. 'And you'll have it, young sir! I'll tell Eva to put one on for you.'

'I could be a bit peckish myself,' Halt said peevishly. He wasn't. He merely said it to see what would happen. As he guessed, his comment was completely ignored. The landlady continued to beam at Horace.

'Just come on down whenever you're ready, young sir,' she told Horace effusively.

Halt shrugged and gave up. He slumped back on the bed, hands behind his head, and heaved a sigh of satisfaction. The landlady regarded him icily.

'Boots off the bed cover!' she said archly and Halt complied quickly.

She sniffed and was turning away as he mumbled, 'Bet you wouldn't have said that to Horace.'

She swung back instantly, suspicion written large on her face. 'What was that?'

In his life, Halt had faced Wargals, the terrible Kalkara, blood-mad Skandians and charging Temujai hordes without a quaver. But a bad-tempered landlady was a different matter altogether.

'Nothing,' he told her meekly.

When Horace returned an hour later, his belt satisfyingly tight around his middle, Halt was stretched out on one of the beds. Horace locked and bolted the door, then smiled as he saw that the Ranger's boots were standing together beside the bed and the cover had been turned back.

Halt was snoring softly, a fact that interested Horace. He had never known Halt to snore when they were camped out in hostile territory. The Ranger always slept as light as a cat, woken by the slightest sound. Perhaps when they were in such situations, Halt never reached the realm of deep sleep that led to the gentle whiffling sound that he heard now.

Horace yawned. The sight of the Ranger stretched out and relaxed made him realise how tired he was himself. It had been a hectic few days and the only good night's sleep they had enjoyed had been at Mountshannon, in the deserted inn. Since then, there had been a lot of hard riding. He sat on the other bed, removed his boots and lay back. The pillow was soft and the mattress, after weeks of sleeping on cold, unyielding earth, was heavenly. He was still marvelling at how comfortable he felt when he fell asleep.

Someone coughed.

Instantly, Horace shot upright in the bed, confused and disoriented, wondering where he was for a few seconds before he remembered. The light outside the window was dying as dusk crept over Dun Kilty. He glanced at Halt. The Ranger was still prone on the bed, hands behind his head. In the dimming light, Horace could see that Halt's eyes were closed, but the Ranger spoke now without opening them.

'That's a nasty cough you've got there,' he said.

'I thought I'd stumbled on Sleeping Beauty and her ugly sister,' said another voice, 'waiting for the kiss of true love to wake them from their slumbers. Forgive me if I didn't oblige.'

Horace spun round at the voice. A cloaked, cowled figure was sitting in the darkest corner of the room — Will, he realised.

Halt's voice was scornful when he replied. 'Sleeping? I've been wide awake since you stumbled up the stairs and crashed through the door like a one-legged kick-dancer. Who could sleep through that racket?'

I could, obviously, Horace thought. Then he remembered that he had locked the door behind him and wondered how Will had managed to bypass that little problem. He shrugged. Will was a Ranger. They could do such things. His friend laughed as he replied to Halt's statement.

'That's a strange noise you make when you're wide awake,' he said, the smile evident in his voice. 'What is it they call it? Oh yes, snoring. Quite a talent. Most people can only do it when they're asleep.'

Halt sat up now, swung his legs off the bed, stretched his arms above his head and shook himself.

'Well, of course I continued with the pretence of snoring,' he said. ' I wanted to see how long you'd continue to sit there.'

'And how long did I?' Will challenged.

Halt shook his head sadly and turned to Horace. 'Horace, when you get older, try to avoid being saddled with an apprentice. Not only are they a damned nuisance but apparently they constantly feel the need to get the better of their masters. They're bad enough when they're learning. But when they graduate, they become unbearable.'

'I'll bear it in mind,' Horace said gravely. But he noticed that Halt had contrived to avoid answering Will's question. The younger Ranger had noticed it too but he decided to let his mentor off the hook.

Halt busied himself lighting the small lantern on the table between the two beds. As the flame flared up and the lens of the lamp spread its soft light into the corners of the room, he turned to Will curiously.

'I didn't expect you so soon,' he said. 'Did something go wrong?'

Will shrugged. 'Not really. Tennyson decided that minstrels weren't welcome in his camp and wanted to confiscate my mandola, so —'

'Your what?' Halt asked, frowning.

Will sighed in frustration. 'My lute.'

Halt nodded, understanding now. 'Oh. Right. Carry on.'

Will raised his eyebrows at Horace and the warrior smiled in sympathy.

'So,' Will continued, 'I decided to get out. They're breaking camp anyway and they're heading directly here.'

Halt rubbed his beard reflectively. 'I didn't expect that,' he said. 'I thought he'd spend a few more days gathering supporters.'

'He doesn't need them. He must have four hundred with him now. Plus I think the news of Craikennis has spooked him. A messenger arrived the other day and his news had Tennyson very upset indeed. I think he had the messenger killed, as a matter of fact.'

'Makes sense,' Horace put in. 'He wouldn't want news of the Sunrise Warrior's victory getting out.'

'No. He wouldn't,' said Halt. 'And you say he has four hundred people with him now?'

'At least,' Will said. 'Of course, the bulk of them are country folk, not trained fighters. But he's got an inner circle of supporters, including those two giant bruisers, Killeen and Gerard.'

'Still, a force of four hundred isn't to be sneezed at. I doubt if Ferris could raise more than a hundred, maybe a hundred and fifty troops. That's if they chose to obey him.'

'How did it go with Ferris?' Will asked. 'Was he pleased to see you after all this time?'

'Hardly,' Halt said dryly. 'He'd already been in contact with Tennyson. He was thinking of selling out.'

'Was?' Will prompted.

'I think Halt persuaded him otherwise,' Horace said, with a grim smile. 'We're going back for his decision tomorrow.'

Will shook his head doubtfully. 'You're cutting it fine then. The Outsiders could be here by tomorrow.'

'That could make things awkward,' Halt said. 'But there's nothing we can do about it. If I try to rush him and see him tonight, he'll dig his heels in. Particularly if he thinks we're panicking.' He considered the matter in silence for a few seconds, then continued. 'No. We'll stick to the original schedule. Will, for the moment, we'll keep you out of sight. You stay here.'

Will shrugged. 'If you say so. Any particular reason? You're not ashamed of me, are you?' he added in a bantering tone.

A faint smile touched Halt's face, the equivalent of a guffaw in anyone else. 'No more than normally,' he said. 'No. But Ferris is used to the two of us. If we turn up with an extra person, it'll make him suspicious.' He sighed. 'Anything makes that man suspicious. And besides, it might be useful if we keep you in reserve. It never hurts to have a potential ace up your sleeve.'

'So I'm an ace?' Will grinned. 'I'm flattered, Halt, flattered. I had no idea you regarded me so highly.'

Halt gave him a long-suffering look. 'I might have been more accurate to say a joker.'

'Whatever you say.' A thought struck Will. 'Oh, I meant to say: Tennyson has three new recruits. Foreigners, dressed in leather, with dull purple cloaks and large, feathered hats. They carry crossbows and a whole array of nasty-looking daggers — and they look as if they know how to use them.'

Halt's expression grew serious as he listened to the description. At the mention of the weapons, he nodded.

'Genovesans,' he said softly.

Horace frowned at the word. 'Who-novesans?' he asked. He'd never heard the word before.

Halt shook his head. 'You warriors don't do much geography in Battleschool, do you?'

Horace shrugged. 'We're not big on that sort of thing. We wait for our leader to point to an enemy and say, "Go whack him." We leave geography and such to Rangers. We like you to feel superior.'

'Go whack him, indeed,' Halt said. 'It must be comforting to lead such an uncomplicated life. They're from the city of Genovesa, in Toscana. They're mercenaries and professional assassins — that's pretty much the main industry in the city. In addition to their weapons, they usually know a dozen ways to poison their victims. If Tennyson has hired three of them, he's upping the stakes. They don't come cheap and they're trouble.'

Will was nodding knowledgeably. 'Genovesans. I thought as much,' he said. Horace shot a pained look in his direction.

'You had no idea,' he said and Will couldn't manage to keep a straight face.

'Maybe not. But I knew they were trouble,' he said. His smile faded as Halt replied.

'Oh, they're trouble, all right. They're big trouble. Be very careful if you come up against them, both of you.'

Thirty-five

'I can't do it,' said Ferris.

Halt's eyes darkened in anger as he looked at his brother. Ferris quailed before the look, shrinking back onto his throne as if the oversized wooden seat gave him strength.

'I won't,' he repeated petulantly. 'I can't. And you can't force me to do it.'

'Don't be too sure of that,' Halt told him. He glanced at Horace and Sean, saw the contempt on one face and the bitter disappointment on the other. But he knew Ferris was right. He couldn't force him to stand up to Tennyson.

'Why should I, Halt? Why should I do what you say? What's in it for you, after all?' His eyes narrowed in suspicion as he said the words. In Ferris's world, people only did things out of self-interest. Now he wondered what Halt stood to gain if he, Ferris, denounced Tennyson as a charlatan. And as he had the thought, the obvious answer rose up before him. He slid off the throne and stepped forward to face Halt, emboldened now that he could see his brother's ulterior motive.

'Suddenly, I see. You want me to stand against Tennyson in the hope that he and his followers will kill me. That's it, isn't it? You'll let them do your dirty work for you, and then you'll magically reappear and take my place on the throne. And I wager you'll simply accept Tennyson's conditions when you do.'

Halt studied his brother's face for a few seconds, saw the devious mind working behind the ever-shifting eyes. He shook his head in utter contempt.

'I might think that way, Ferris. If I were you. But my real concern is for the people out there.' He gestured in the direction of the town below them. 'The ones who call you their King — who look to you for leadership and protection. And God help them for they'll get little of either from you.'

'Please, your majesty,' Sean said, stepping forward. 'Please reconsider. Halt is right. The people do need you. They need someone to lead them. To take charge.'

Ferris laughed scornfully at his nephew. 'Oh, it's "please, your majesty" now, is it, Sean? Yesterday, you were all too ready to call *him* your majesty, weren't you? Don't think I don't see through your treacherous ways. You're in it with them.'

Sean stepped back now, as if being too close to his uncle made him feel unclean. His voice was low and angry as he spoke.

'I have never been disloyal to you, your majesty. Never!'

The anger was so palpable that Ferris eyed his nephew nervously. Perhaps he had gone too far. He knew how much he relied on Sean. But he still refused to budge on the main question.

'Perhaps I spoke too hastily,' he said in a conciliatory tone. Then his voice hardened and he turned to Halt. 'But I will not do as you ask. If you want to oppose Tennyson, you take the risk. You go out and rally the people behind this ridiculous Sunrise Warrior of yours.'

'If it comes to it, I will,' Halt told him. 'But I'm a stranger here and you're the King. It will seem . . .'

Before he could continue, Ferris seized on his words and interrupted. 'That's right. I am the King. I'm glad someone here remembers that small fact. I am the King and I will decide for myself.'

He drew himself up, trying to look haughty and decisive. But the eyes, as ever, gave him away as they constantly shifted and slid away from any contact with the other three.

Halt silently cursed Ferris. He had hoped to browbeat him into defying Tennyson. But the King's abject and cowardly refusal meant his plan was in ruins. Without the King's authority, any resistance to the Outsiders would be ineffectual. The people would not follow an unknown stranger and a young warrior against Tennyson, the saviour of Mountshannon and half a dozen other villages, a skilled orator and an expert at whipping a crowd into a frenzy.

And a man with hundreds of fanatical followers at his back.

In spite of his inner turmoil, Halt allowed no sign to show on his face. He drew breath for one last attempt to convince Ferris. He wasn't sure what he was going to say, for it had all been said already. He stopped when he heard a commotion outside the throne room doors. Then one of the doors opened and a guard entered, hurrying towards the small group at the far end of the room. Halt noticed that he reported to Sean, not Ferris. That might be simply protocol. Or it might indicate where the man's real loyalty lay.

'Sir Sean, there's a messenger outside. Claims it's urgent. He wants to see this one.' He indicated Halt.

Sean turned to him. 'Are you expecting a message?'

Halt hesitated. It could only be one person. He addressed the guard. 'Is he dressed like me?' he said, indicating the mottled cloak and empty double scabbard — as before, they had left their weapons outside.

The guard nodded. 'He is indeed. Exactly so, your honour.'

'Yes,' Halt told Sean. 'I was expecting him. He has important news bearing on this problem.' He had no idea why Will had come after them. But he reasoned that it must be important.

Sean nodded to the guard. 'Let him in.'

The guard withdrew and a few seconds later Will entered the room. Ferris let out a snort as he took in the cowled cloak, the drab brown and green tunic and leggings.

'Brought your own follower, have you, Halt?' he sneered. 'I'd say that Tennyson has a few more than you.'

Will glanced curiously at the King, seeing the same similarities, and dissimilarities, that Horace had noted the day before. Then he dismissed him and looked to Halt.

'He's here,' he said simply. For a moment, the significance didn't register with Horace, but Halt saw it immediately.

'Tennyson?' he said and Will nodded.

'They're setting up their camp. He's announced that he'll be addressing the people at three o'clock.'

There was a twelve-hour water clock in the throne room and Halt looked quickly at it. It was just before one o'clock. Inwardly, he was seething but, as before, he controlled his emotions so there was no trace of them on his face or in his manner.

'Very well,' he said. 'Thanks, Will. Go and keep an eye on them. Let me know if anything else develops.'

Will nodded. He glanced inquisitively at Ferris, then back at Halt, his eyes asking a question: *How is it going here?* But Halt's quick headshake told him not to ask it aloud. Will gathered all was not well.

'Right, Halt. I'll be at the market ground. That's where they're setting up the pavilion.'

He turned and left the room quickly. Halt studied his brother's set features and he felt a very unfamiliar sensation — that of failure. But he had to try once more.

'Ferris . . .' he began.

Ferris raised an eyebrow. 'That's your majesty, I think.' He sensed that Halt was going to try appealing to his better nature. Perhaps even to plead with him. And now, as he knew he had the upper hand, his confidence flowed back. Halt glared but before he could say anything, the young warrior who had accompanied him cut him off.

'Your majesty,' Horace said and his tone was conciliatory, even respectful, 'I think I might see a way to resolve this problem — and it's one that we might all profit from, if you take my meaning?'

He rubbed finger and thumb together in the universal

gesture of greed — a gesture that Ferris understood only too well. The King turned to him, interested to hear what he might say.

But Halt interrupted before Horace could go further.

'Leave it Horace. It's useless,' he said, his voice tired.

Horace pushed his bottom lip out, assumed a thoughtful expression and replied, in a slightly disparaging tone, 'Oh, Halt, let's skip your claptrap about honour and duty to the people. You've tried. You've failed. Face up to it and move on. Now I can see a definite opportunity with this Sunrise Warrior nonsense. Why shouldn't we make a little cash for ourselves here?' He looked back to the King. 'And a lot for you, your majesty.'

Ferris nodded. Horace was talking the language he understood best. Self-interest. Halt's angry reply convinced him.

'Horace, shut up! You've forgotten your place! You've got no right to —'

'Oh, come off it, Halt! Admit for once that your way isn't going to work,' Horace told him, cutting him off. Halt stopped, but the fury was still evident on his face as he glared at his young companion.

He's speechless, Ferris thought delightedly. Then Horace turned to the King again.

'Well, your majesty? Interested?'

Ferris smiled and nodded. It wasn't just the promise of money that attracted him. It was seeing his brother bested, and seeing his impotent rage when one of his followers turned against him.

'Go on,' he said. He barely heard Halt's bitter exclamation as his brother turned away. He could see the disappointment in Sean's face at Horace's unexpected interruption. Serve him right. Sean was an idealist, and it was time he learned a little about the realities of life. Horace looked around the big, echoing throne room, saw a small curtained doorway to one side.

'Perhaps if I could have a few words in private, your majesty. Could we . . .?' He indicated the side room.

'My robing room,' Ferris said and led the way towards it. 'We can talk in there, undisturbed.' He looked meaningfully at Sean and Halt as he said the last word.

Horace followed him, shouldering his way past Sean as he did so, a smirk on his face. Sean shook his head and turned despairingly to Halt. The Ranger had his eyes lowered but as the King and Horace went through the curtain, he looked up to meet Sean's gaze. The young Hibernian was startled to see that Halt was grinning.

He went to speak but Halt held up a hand. A second or so later, they heard the sound of a fist striking against flesh and a sudden cry of pain, cut off by the clatter of furniture being knocked over. Then Horace's voice came from behind the curtain.

'Can you come in here, Halt?'

Sean followed as the Ranger crossed the room and stepped behind the curtain. The chamber was a small annexe where the King's official robes for state occasions were kept. It contained a large wardrobe for the purpose, along with several chairs, a dressing table and a mirror. There was a small fireplace in the corner. The King was stretched unconscious on the floor, an overturned chair beside him. Horace was shaking his right hand, nursing his obviously bruised knuckles.

'Horace Altman,' Halt said, 'what on earth have you done?'

Horace gestured to the wardrobe full of official garments. 'I've just elected you King,' he said. 'Start getting dressed.'

Thirty-six

'Are you mad?' Halt asked. But Horace said nothing so he went on. 'Take a look at the two of us. There's a certain similarity, even a strong one. But we do not look the same.'

Sean had moved quickly to kneel beside the unconscious figure on the floor of the robing room. He felt for a pulse, was relieved to find there was one, then looked up at the two Araluans, now facing each other — Halt angry and perplexed, Horace calm and unflustered.

'He's out cold,' he said.

Horace glanced at him. 'Do you have a problem with that?'

Sean considered the question for a few seconds. 'Not really. But you might have when he wakes up. He'll bring the guards down on you like a ton of bricks. And I doubt I'll be able to protect you.'

Horace shrugged. 'It won't be a problem. I'll be walking out of here with the alternative King.' He indicated

Halt and again the Ranger showed his frustration. Horace seemed incapable of facing facts.

'Horace, take a good look at Ferris. Then take a good look at me.'

'I have,' Horace said calmly. 'All we need to do is pull your hair back off your face and fasten it with that leather headband he wears . . .'

'That's the royal crown of Clonmel,' Sean felt he had to interject.

Horace glanced at him. 'All the better. Adds to the illusion.'

'You've noticed that our beards are completely different?' Halt said sarcastically and Horace nodded.

'Luckily, yours is fuller than his. I noticed you've been letting it grow since we've been on the road.'

Halt shrugged. 'That was intentional. I didn't want people to notice my similarity to Ferris.'

'Well, now we do want them to. So we have to remove some of it. Be a bit difficult if the situation were reversed. Hard to put more beard on.'

'You're planning to shave me?' Halt said. For the first time in many years, he was taken aback by the turn of events.

'Halt, don't you see? This is an ideal opportunity! We need the King to appear in public and denounce Tennyson and the Outsiders . . . and to invoke the myth of the Sunrise Warrior. You know that it has to be the King. You know that he's refused to do it. Well, with a bit of work, we can make you look like him. Put on one of those robes and that leather thingy . . .' He looked at Sean, who had opened his mouth to protest. 'All right, the royal crown thingy . . . and I'll bet nobody will see the difference. They'll see what they expect to see. Isn't that what you always say?'

It was true. Halt knew that an impersonation was already halfway to success if people were expecting to see the real subject. And of course, few in Clonmel would have seen the King at close quarters. But Halt was stuck at one thought.

'You're planning to shave me?' he repeated.

Horace nodded, turning to Sean. 'I'll need my dagger. Can you get it for me without making too much fuss about it?'

Sean met his gaze coolly. 'You expect me to go along with this?'

Horace answered without hesitation. 'Yes. Because you know it's the only way. And you know that he,' he jerked his thumb at the unconscious Ferris, 'is willing to sell this country out to Tennyson and his thugs.'

His confidence was a mask. As he said the words, he found himself hoping that he'd been right in his judgement of the young Hibernian. Halt, disguised as Ferris, and in the company of the King's steward, would most likely be accepted as the King. If Sean wasn't with them, they'd never get past the guards outside the throne room doors.

Sean hesitated a moment longer. Yet he realised that, when he failed to call the guards the moment he had seen Ferris sprawled on the floor, he had already decided to throw in his lot with the two Araluans.

'You're right,' he said. 'I'll get the knives. I suppose it'd be too obvious if I asked for a razor?'

'My dagger will do. It's sharp enough,' Horace said. But Halt demurred as Sean began to turn away.

'Not the dagger. Get my saxe. It's good enough to cut my hair. It'll shave me.'

Horace was looking at him, fascinated by the revelation.

'So it's true,' he said. 'You really do cut your hair with your saxe knife.' It had long been a subject of discussion in Araluen; now Halt was confirming it. The Ranger didn't bother to reply.

'And get a bowl of hot water,' Halt continued to Sean. Then he glanced at Horace. 'You're not shaving me dry.'

'Make it tea,' Horace corrected him. 'A pot of hot tea. People might wonder why we'd want a bowl of hot water. But a pot of tea won't make them curious.'

Sean hesitated. 'You're going to shave him in tea?'

'You're certainly not going to shave me in tea,' Halt added. But Horace made a conciliatory gesture.

'It's still essentially hot water. And we can use it to darken the parts of your face where the beard has been.'

Sean looked from one to the other. Then he nodded agreement. Horace was right. Shaving Halt would expose an area of his face that had been protected from sun and wind for years. It would show like a beacon unless they disguised it somehow.

'Saxe knife and tea,' he muttered, as if it were some bizarre kind of shopping list. Then he hurried from the robing room.

'Have you considered,' Halt asked Horace, 'that Ferris's hair is dark, while mine is a dignified shade of grey?'

'He dyes it,' Horace said and Halt exploded irritably.

'Well, of course he dyes it! But somehow I don't think tea will do the trick for me. Any thoughts?'

'Soot,' Horace told him. 'The fireplace and chimney will be full of it. We'll rub it through your hair. We might mix a bit into the tea for your face as well.'

Halt reached down and righted the chair that had been knocked over when Ferris went down. He slumped on it, resigned to his fate.

'It just gets better by the minute,' he said gloomily.

An hour later, the doors of the throne room crashed open. The six guards in the outer room all came to attention as Sean emerged.

'The King has decided to visit the market ground,' he announced. 'Form up to escort him.'

The guards hurried to obey as the King, dressed in a heavy green satin cloak, decorated with intricate brocade work and trimmed with pure ermine, swept out of the throne room. The cloak reached to the ground and had a high collar, which the King had turned up. One of the foreign visitors accompanied him. There was no sign of the second foreigner but the guards, if they registered his absence, didn't have time to dwell on it. They formed up rapidly, two in front of the royal party and four behind, maintaining a respectful distance so that they were close enough to protect the King if required, without being able to eavesdrop on the royal conversation.

Sean led the way, with the King and Horace side by side behind him. Sean had to agree that Horace's handi-work had been effective. Halt's hair, darkened with chimney soot, was parted in the middle, slicked down with tea and drawn back beneath the royal crown. A close inspection of the King's face would have revealed a rather patchwork effect on the lower areas, where an uneven paste of soot, dirt and tea dregs had been smeared on the pink flesh left bare by Horace's inexpert efforts with the saxe knife. The paste also went some way towards concealing half a dozen small nicks and cuts on his face, where the saxe had not been quite up to the task of dealing with Halt's wiry beard. Horace had quickly found that a thick slurry of soot and tea served to staunch the bleeding quite effectively.

'I'll get you for this,' Halt had told him as he dabbed the disgusting mixture on the worst of the cuts. 'That soot is filthy. I'll probably come down with half a dozen infections.'

'Probably,' Horace had replied, distracted by his task. 'But we only need you for today.'

Which was not a comforting thought for Halt.

Also aiding their deception was the fact that Ferris, over the years, had made it clear that he did not want his subjects looking directly into his face. Most people, even many of those in the castle, had never had a chance to study the King's features in detail. They had an overall impression of him and that impression was matched by the way Halt looked, talked and moved.

Preceded by two of the throne room guards, the party marched out of the keep tower into the courtyard. Abelard and Kicker were standing close by the doorway. Kicker's reins were fastened to a tethering ring. Abelard, of course, simply stood where he was until he was wanted.

He looked up as the party emerged and nickered a soft *hello* to his master, who was dressed in an unfamiliar green cloak and had dirt plastered on his face. Halt glanced at him, brow furrowed, and silently mouthed the words 'shut up'. Abelard shook his mane, which was as close as a horse could come to shrugging, and turned away.

'My horse recognised me,' Halt said accusingly out of the side of his mouth to Horace.

Horace glanced at the small shaggy horse, standing beside his own massive battlehorse.

'Mine didn't,' he replied. 'So that's a fifty—fifty result.'

'I think I'd like better odds than that,' Halt replied.

Horace suppressed a grin. 'Don't worry. He can probably smell you.'

'I can smell myself,' Halt replied acerbically. 'I smell of tea and soot.'

Horace thought it was wiser not to reply to that.

The small group marched down the ramp to the town itself. As they approached, Halt was conscious of the fact that, while people drew back from their path and lowered their heads or curtseyed as their King passed, there was no sign of cheering or waving. Ferris, now unconscious and bound and gagged in the wardrobe of the robing room, had done little to endear himself to his subjects.

They made their way into the town proper and the way continued to clear for them — whether out of respect or because of the armed men who flanked them, Halt couldn't tell. He suspected it was a combination of the two. They turned down a side street and at the end of it he could make out an open space. The buzz of hundreds of voices carried to them. They were approaching the market ground, where Tennyson was already addressing a large crowd.

'They've started without us,' he said.

'They may have started,' Horace replied, 'but we'll finish it.'

Thirty-seven

Will stood towards the back of the crowd in the marketplace. Tennyson's followers had been hard at work for some hours, preparing for the time when he would address the assembled crowd. A raised platform had been constructed and, to one side, there was a cooking fire surmounted by a large spit. Two of the Outsiders, stripped to the waist and glistening with sweat, were turning the spit, which suspended a sheep's carcass above the fire. As the spit turned, fat from the beast dripped down onto the glowing coals of the fire, causing flames to leap and splutter and fragrant smoke to drift around the market ground.

Will hadn't eaten and the smell of the roasting meat set his stomach growling. From time to time, the Outsider in charge carved choice pieces from the outside of the meat. Another tore pieces of flat country bread to use as plates and the meat and bread were distributed to the waiting crowd. A cask of wine and another of ale had been broached and the townsfolk were invited to bring their mugs and tankards forward to be filled up. The atmosphere was a jovial one, almost like a holiday. The food and wine were good and it was a pleasant break in the day-to-day humdrum life of the town. The market ground buzzed with conversation and goodwill.

Then Tennyson began to speak. At first he was cheerful and welcoming, beginning with a series of amusing anecdotes — often at his own expense — that set the crowd chuckling. He was a good performer, Will thought. He spoke of the happy times he and his followers spent as they moved through the countryside, caring for each other and worshipping their god. A choir of a dozen Outsiders filed onto the platform with him and, at his signal, they launched into song.

They sang popular country songs that had their audience tapping their feet and swaying in time until, at Tennyson's urging, the townsfolk joined in the chorus. Then the choir sang a simple hymn of joy to Alseiass. It had an easy and catchy chorus that the crowd could join in — and did. Then the choir moved off stage and, as more wine circulated, Tennyson's mood became less cheerful.

He was a skilful orator. He did it by degrees, first becoming wistful as he described the evil that had seemed to spread over Clonmel in recent months — a dark cloud that was so diametrically opposed to the simple, cheerful life espoused by Alseiass and his followers. His tone darkened into indignation, then anger as he described horrors like the massacre at Duffy's Ford, and others that had gone before. The details were unfamiliar to most in the crowd, but there had been rumours of evil-doing at half a dozen towns and villages through the south of the

Kingdom. The place names were familiar and since rumour is by nature imprecise, Tennyson was able to embellish and exaggerate events, painting a picture of bleak horror while he assumed an air of righteous indignation at the suffering of the people of Clonmel.

Will sensed the change in the crowd's mood. There was fear stalking among them, unseen and as yet unrecognised, as Tennyson pointed out how the killings, the attacks, the burnings, were gradually tracing a path north, towards Dun Kilty itself. The uneasiness grew as the level in the wine mugs fell. And as Tennyson detailed atrocity after atrocity, his white-robed followers began to echo his words. Then members of his newly converted group would step forward and attest to the truth of what he spoke.

'The prophet Tennyson has the right of it!' a new convert would cry. 'I was at Carramoss,' (or Dell or Clunkilly or Rorkes Creek or whatever the site he had mentioned might be) 'and I saw these things for myself!'

'There's evil stalking this land,' Tennyson said, reaching the heart of his address. 'Evil in the form of the dark spirit Balsennis! He's a depraved spirit who preys on the simple folk of this land and brings his dark hordes to plague and murder them! We've seen his hand before, haven't we, my people?'

He addressed this last question to the solid cadre of followers behind him and their voices chorused confirmation of the fact. Then Tennyson continued, his voice rising in intensity and volume.

'He must be stopped! His evil followers must be crushed and defeated! And who will do that for you? Who will protect you from his attacks? Who will face the bandits, criminals, murderers and outlaws who flock to his banner? Who will turn them back in confusion and defeat?'

The crowd muttered restlessly. There was no answer that they knew to his question.

'Who has the power to stand against Balsennis and protect you from his dark and evil ways?'

Once more, Tennyson allowed the muttering and uncertainty to work its way through the crowd. Then he stepped forward and his deep, sonorous voice went up yet again in volume.

'Will your King do it?'

Silence. An awkward, nervous silence as the crowd looked at each other, then looked hurriedly away. This close to Castle Dun Kilty, no one was willing to make the first step towards denouncing the King. Yet, in their hearts, they all knew that the answer to the question was no. Tennyson's voice rose out of the silence again.

'Has your King –' the contempt in his voice was all too obvious as he said the word 'king' '– done anything to alleviate the suffering of his people? *Has he?*'

The intensity of his voice, the passion that showed in his face, demanded an answer. From the rear of crowd, a few hesitant voices rose.

'No!'

And once the lead had been given, more voices joined in, until the cries denouncing King Ferris were coming from all sides, and the volume was growing.

'No! No! The King does nothing while the people suffer!'

'He's safe in his mighty castle! What about the rest of us?'

The first few voices were probably plants, Will realised. They were Tennyson's cronies, scattered through the crowd and dressed in simple country clothes, without their tell-tale white robes. But the voices that swelled the chorus condemning the King were coming now from the people of Dun Kilty.

Tennyson raised his hands for silence and, as the yelling gradually died away, he spoke again.

'Who was it who turned back the attack on Mountshannon? Was it the King?'

Again, the chorus of 'No!' boomed around the market square. As it subsided, Tennyson asked another question.

'Then who? Who saved the people of Mountshannon?'

And behind him, a group of villagers from Mountshannon shouted their enthusiastic response, practised over the past week in half a dozen villages and settlements along their way.

'Alseiass!' they shouted. 'Alseiass and Tennyson!'

And the people of Dun Kilty took up the cry until it echoed back from the buildings around the market square, redoubling itself as it did so, becoming one long, rolling cry: 'Alseiass-and-Tennyson-yson-Alseiass-seiass-Tennyson-yson-Alseiass.' And it seemed to Will that the people were hypnotised by the rolling, echoing roar until they had to join in and reinforce the sound, the echo and the hysteria that was sweeping over the square.

This is getting very dangerous, he thought. He had never experienced mob hysteria before. Standing in the middle of it, he felt the full, ugly, unreasoning force of it.

Tennyson's hands went up again and the rolling thunder of voices gradually stilled.

'Who stood against evil at the gate to Craikennis?' he demanded. And this time, before his planted followers in the crowd could answer, Will decided to take a hand.

'The Sunrise Warrior!' he yelled at the top of his voice.

Instantly, a hush fell over square. People around him turned to stare and Tennyson, taken by surprise, was silenced for a few seconds. Will seized the opportunity.

'I was there! He destroyed his enemies with a flaming sword! He drove them back! Hundreds of them defeated by one man — the mighty Sunrise Warrior!'

He heard voices echoing the phrase 'Sunrise Warrior' around the square. For rumours had reached Dun Kilty of events at Craikennis and there was confusion now as to who had actually saved the town. But Tennyson shouted him down, pointing a finger at him.

'There is no Sunrise Warrior! He's a myth!'

'I saw him!' Will insisted but Tennyson had the advantage of a raised platform and a trained orator's voice.

'Lies!' he thundered. 'It was the Golden God Alseiass!'

Again, a chorus of 'Alseaiss! Praise Alseiass!' arose from the white robes around him. Tennyson's finger continued to point at Will and the young Ranger realised that Tennyson was pointing him out to his followers in the crowd. Any moment now, a knife would slip between his ribs, he thought.

'He lies!' Tennsyon continued. 'And Alseiass strikes down those who bear false witness!'

Will glanced around quickly. He saw a glimpse of dull purple in the crowd, off to his right side and slipping through the crowd towards him. He watched from the corner of his eye as the figure drew nearer. Even without the wide-brimmed hat, he recognised him for one of the Genovesans. And he saw the gleam of a dagger held close against the man's leg.

'The Sunrise Warrior!' he shouted again. 'He can save us! Praise the Sunrise Warrior!'

A few people took up the cry and it began to spread. Will, watching Tennyson, saw him nod towards someone close to him in the crowd. He looked to his right. The Genovesan was almost upon him. Will saw surprise, then annoyance, in the foreigner's eyes as he realised that he had been spotted by his quarry. A fraction of a second later, Will brought his right elbow up to face height and pivoted on his right heel, slamming the point of his elbow into the man's face, breaking his nose and sending him reeling back against the people around them. Blood sprang from his nose and the dagger clattered to the ground. Seeing it, those closest to him drew back, shoving each other and calling out warnings.

Will decided enough was enough. Dropping into a crouch so that Tennyson could no longer see him, he shoved through the crowd, running to a new position some fifteen metres away. Once there, he stood erect again and yelled: 'Praise the Sunrise Warrior!'

Then he dropped to a crouch again and burrowed through the crowd before Tennyson could pinpoint him.

Tennyson had seen the flurry of violent movement that resulted in his assassin being sent reeling. But then he lost sight of the infuriating heckler who was destroying his momentum. Now, as the voice rang out from another part of the crowd, he went on the attack.

'The Sunrise Warrior?' he sneered. 'Where is he? Let's

see him if he's so powerful. Produce him here and now. There is no Sunrise Warrior!'

His sycophants echoed the scornful words, demanding that the Sunrise Warrior step forward and be seen. But now a deep voice answered them, and a scuffle of movement could be seen at the front of the crowd, below the platform where Tennyson stood.

'You demand the Sunrise Warrior, you charlatan? Then here he is! And here I am with him!'

At least a hundred surprised voices all exclaimed at once. 'The King!'

And a stocky figure in a green brocade cloak shoved his way onto the stage, flanked by a broad-shouldered warrior with a sunrise insignia on his surcoat, and a slimmer, dark-haired warrior who many recognised as the King's steward, Sean Carrick.

There was a collective gasp of surprise from the people assembled in the marketplace. It was Ferris, they all realised. And confirming it was the fact he was escorted by half a dozen members of the palace guard, who now took up positions screening him.

Will's eyes narrowed. He saw the drawn-back, dark hair, the shaved face and the royal robes. But somehow, he knew this wasn't Ferris. It was Halt. And just in time, he thought. Then, as the robed figure revealed the full force of his personality, he knew he was right.

'Who will protect you?' he thundered. 'I will! And not this mountebank, this sideshow performer from a county fair! He talks about some unseen god. I have the real power of ancient legend with me! The Sunrise Warrior!'

He indicated Horace, who drew his sword with a

ringing sound of steel on leather and raised it high above his head, exposing, as he did so, the bright orange sunrise insignia he wore on his chest.

'The Sunrise Warrior!' The words ran around the square. Horace stepped back, re-sheathing his sword, leaving the focus on Halt once more.

'This man,' Halt continued, indicating Tennyson, whose face was twisted in rage, 'is a liar and a thief. He'll draw you in with words of honey then he'll take all you own. And he'll do it in the name of a false god!'

'There's nothing false about Alseiass,' Tennyson began.

'Then produce him for us!' Halt bellowed, cutting Tennyson off. Unpopular the King might be, but he was still the King. And with Halt playing the role he projected a powerful aura of authority. 'Produce him as I have produced the legendary warrior who'll defend us! You asked to see the Warrior and here he is! Now I demand to see this false god you prattle about! Produce him – if you can!'

The crowd began to drift his way, echoing the demand. Seizing the opportunity this gave him, Halt turned to challenge them.

'How many of you had ever heard of this "Golden God" before this huckster told you about him?' he demanded. There was no answer and he followed up with a roar. '*Well?* How many?'

Feet shuffled awkwardly in the crowd. Then he spoke again.

'And how many have heard of the Sunrise Warrior?'

This time, there were a few mumbled 'yeses' from the

crowd, then the trickle became a torrent. Alseiass was new and unfamiliar. They all knew the legend of the Sunrise Warrior.

Tennyson, lips compressed in an angry line, stepped forward, hands up to silence them.

'Proof!' he shouted. 'Let's see proof! Anyone can put on a shirt with a picture of the sun on it and claim to be this mythical warrior! We want proof!'

A few voices agreed, then more and more. A mob was a fickle animal, Will thought. Operating on blind instinct, it could be swayed first one way, then the other.

'Give us proof!' they shouted.

Now it was Halt's turn to raise his hands for silence.

'What proof do you want?' he shouted. 'The Warrior saved the village of Craikennis! He defeated two hundred and fifty men with his flaming sword!'

'And who saw this?' Tennyson demanded quickly. 'No one here! If he's the mighty warrior you claim, let him prove it in the surest manner of all! In combat!'

Now the crowd were really aroused. They might not know which of the two men they believed, but they were all eager at the thought of seeing a duel to the death. This was turning out to be a most diverting day.

'Trial by combat!' they chorused, and the demand swelled until Halt again raised his hands. The shouts died away and he faced Tennyson.

'And who is your champion?' he demanded.

Tennyson smiled. 'Not one but two. Let him face my twin retainers, Gerard and Killeen!'

He threw an arm back in a dramatic flourish to indicate the two islander giants. They stepped up onto the platform and the crowd howled in delight at the size of them.

Again, Halt had to wait for the shouting to die down. 'You expect him to fight two men?' he asked.

Tennyson smiled again, appealing to the crowd.

'What's two men to a warrior who defeated two hundred and fifty?' he asked and the crowd yelled their support.

Halt hesitated. He'd expected a challenge to combat but he didn't believe Horace, with all his skill, could fight these two giants at the same time.

As he searched for a way out of the predicament, Horace stepped forward again. He moved close to Tennyson, invasively close, and the look in his eye caused the self-proclaimed prophet to take a small pace back. But even a small pace was enough to establish Horace's dominance.

'You talk of trial by combat, you cowardly fake!' He didn't seem to be shouting but his voice carried to all sides of the crowd. 'Trial by combat is single combat!'

Will decided it was time to join in again and make sure the crowd supported Horace. At the moment, he realised, they were ready to agree to anything.

'He's right!' he shouted. 'Single combat!'

And he felt a huge surge of relief when those around him took up the cry.

'Single combat! Single combat!' As he'd hoped, they didn't care about what was fair, but they wanted a show and they knew single combat would last longer than a one-sided competition of one on two.

Again, Horace's voice rang out over the square. His eyes were locked on Tennyson's.

'I'll fight both your mountains of blubber!' he said. 'One at a time. One after the other. I'll defeat them and then I'll fight you, if you've the courage!'

And he shoved Tennyson hard in the chest, sending the white-robed man staggering back a pace. Behind Horace, the two islander giants started forward to their leader's defence. But they'd barely moved when Horace spun to face them. His sword seemed to leap into his hand of its own volition, and stopped with its gleaming point at the throat of the nearest of the two, stopping them both in their tracks.

There was a gasp of admiration at his blinding speed. Most of those present didn't even see him move. One moment he was facing Tennyson. The next his sword was threatening the two immense islanders. Instantly, Will saw there was another way to enlist the crowd's support.

'Two fights!' he yelled. 'Two fights instead of one!'

And they took up the cry. Now they had a chance of seeing twice as much bloodshed. And to this baying, half-drunk rabble, that meant twice the entertainment.

Tennyson, his face red with anger, glared at the crowd. He seemed about to demur but the shouting intensified, drowning him out.

'Two fights! Let's see two fights! Two fights! Two fights! Two fights!'

It became a rhythmic, insistent chant, one that brooked no argument. Tennyson understood mobs and as he listened to that repetitive, mindless chant, he knew he had no way of changing their mind.

He raised his hands and the chant died away. The mob watched him expectantly.

'Very well!' he agreed. 'Two fights!'

And the mob roared in exultation, taking up the chant again. Halt looked at Horace, a question in his eyes. Horace nodded confidently.

'Not a problem . . . your majesty.' He grinned as he added the last two words.

Thirty-eight

The crowd continued to yell its approval and Tennyson stepped closer to Halt. As he did so, Horace went to move to the side of the counterfeit King, with Sean half a second behind him. But Halt, unperturbed, held up a hand to stop them.

'Something on your mind, priest?' he asked.

For a moment, a frown touched Tennyson's face. There was something vaguely familiar about the King, he thought. But he couldn't place it. He discarded the momentary distraction and his cold anger returned.

'We had an agreement, Ferris,' he said in a low tone.

Halt raised an eyebrow. 'Ferris?' he said. 'Is that the way you address a king? I think you mean "your majesty".'

'You won't be King when I'm finished with you. People do not break agreements with me. I'll destroy your Sunrise Warrior and then I'll have you dragged from the throne, screaming like a frightened girl.'

Tennyson was confused and furious. All his intelligence, gathered by spies in the months preceding his march on Dun Kilty, had led him to expect a vacillating, uncertain, weak character. This hard-eyed King came as a surprise; he faced Tennyson's threats with no sign of fear or weakness.

'Brave talk, Tennyson, especially from a man who will be doing none of the fighting. And, I assume, none of the dragging. Now let me tell you something: scum like you don't make agreements with kings. You do their bidding. And you don't make threats to them, either. I'll ruin your plan and I'll destroy your filthy cult as well. And then I'll take a horsewhip to your fat, quivering hide and drive you out of this country. And unlike you, my friend, I will do it personally!'

In the past two years, since he had begun his campaign to destabilise the island of Hibernia, nobody had dared to threaten Tennyson. Nobody had spoken to him with such an air of confident contempt. Now, looking into those dark eyes before him, he felt a slight tremor of fear. He saw no sign of doubt there. No sign that this was a man who could be cowed. Rather, he saw a promise that the King would carry out the threat he had just made. In a flickering moment of uncertainty, Tennyson wondered if he might not be wiser to withdraw from Clonmel and settle for his position of dominance in the other five kingdoms. But he sensed that the man before him wouldn't be content with that. They were both committed now and the situation would be resolved in trial by combat. He looked at his two massively built retainers, then at the muscular young warrior standing a pace behind the King. Surely no man could stand against both Killeen and Gerard, he thought.

But the young man looked supremely unworried by the prospect.

Horace, meeting Tennyson's eyes, smiled at him. Tennyson was struck by a feeling that he had seen him before as well. But at their previous encounter, he had paid little attention to Horace, who had been dusty, travel stained and roughly dressed as a hired guard. Now, resplendent in chain mail and the surcoat of the Sunrise Warrior, he was an entirely different character.

'The combat will take place in three days' time,' Halt announced, speaking so that the entire assembly could hear him. He had no need to ask Horace if that timing suited him. Horace was always ready, he knew.

Tennyson tore his glance away from Horace and regarded Halt once more.

'Agreed,' he said.

The crowd broke out in cheers once more. A public trial by combat would mean a holiday — with the added attraction of the opportunity to see at least one man killed.

Halt glanced at Sean, who gestured to the escort to form around him. Then they marched off the platform and, shoving through the cheering, jostling crowd, they headed up the hill back to the castle. As they made their way, they became aware of a chant spreading through the town.

'Hail Ferris! Long live the King! Hail Ferris! Long live the King!'

Horace grinned sidelong at Sean.

'So that's the way to win the crowd's loyalty. Throw them a few violent deaths.'

'At least,' Sean replied, 'there's no way Ferris can go back on it now. The mob would tear him to pieces if he did.'

They made their way back to the castle and into the throne room. As their escort took up positions outside the throne room, Sean ordered one of them to fetch hot water, soap and towels. Then he followed Halt and Horace into the large inner room.

Halt crossed quickly to the small robing annexe. Gesturing for Sean and Horace to remain outside, he pulled the heavy curtain aside and entered. As he did, he could hear faint, muffled thuds coming from the large wardrobe where Ferris was concealed. Opening the door, he dragged his bound and gagged brother out of the wardrobe by his collar, leaving him sprawled on the floor. Ferris, red faced and with eyes bulging, was trying to shout abuse at his brother. But the gag was a good one and the only sound was a series of muffled, unintelligible grunts. Halt, who had worn the saxe knife under his brocade cloak, produced the heavy, gleaming blade now and held it before Ferris's nose.

'Two choices, brother. I either cut your gag and ropes, or I cut your throat. You choose.'

Ferris's grunting became more impassioned than before and he strained against the restraints fastening his hands and feet. He stopped abruptly as Halt moved the blade closer to his face.

'That's better,' Halt told him. 'Now just keep it quiet or you're a dead man. Understand?'

Eyes wide with fright, Ferris nodded frantically.

'You're learning,' Halt told him. 'Now I'm going to cut you free. And you will keep quiet. If you even begin to yell out, I'll kill you. Understood?'

Halt watched him for a few seconds, making sure that the King had grasped the position. Ferris was only too willing to agree. After all, in Halt's position, he would have had no hesitation in killing his own brother.

Carefully, Halt cut him free and waited while Ferris rubbed his wrists to relieve the discomfort caused by the tight binding. The King looked up at his brother. There was nothing but malice in his eyes.

'How long do you think you can keep this up? You won't get away with this, Halt!' he said.

But Halt noted that, in spite of the animosity, Ferris was careful to keep his voice down. He smiled grimly at him.

'I've already got away with it, Ferris. You're committed now. I've made sure of it.'

'Committed? How? Committed to what?'

'You're committed to supporting the Sunrise Warrior in trial by combat against two of Tennyson's henchmen. I made the announcement on your behalf in front of the entire town. You're quite the popular figure as a result,' he added mildly.

'I won't go through with it!' Ferris said. His voice started to rise but a quick frown from Halt made him lower his tone. 'I'll call it off!'

'You do and the mob will tear you to pieces,' Halt warned him. 'They're very keen on the idea. You should have heard them shouting "Long live the King". It was very touching, really. I imagine they've never said that before.'

'I'll contact Tennyson! I'll tell him . . .' He stopped. Halt was shaking his head.

'I doubt he'll talk to you. You defied him in public. You challenged him. You belittled him. You called him a charlatan and a mountebank, if memory serves me. Worst of all, you went back on your agreement with him. No, your majesty, you're committed to defeating Tennyson because if you don't, he will surely kill you.'

Realisation was slowly dawning in Ferris's eyes as he saw how Halt had closed the trap around him. His only course now was to go along with his brother and hope that the young warrior who accompanied him could defeat not one but two men in personal combat. Halt decided it was time to force the point well and truly home.

'You're caught, Ferris. Call off the combat and the mob will kick you off the throne. If they don't, Tennyson will kill you. And if he doesn't, I will. Understand?'

Ferris's eyes dropped from Halt's and he shook his head from side to side. Eventually, he said in a low voice, 'I understand.'

Halt nodded. 'Good. Look on the bright side. If we succeed, you'll have your throne back, and your people will love you — at least until you start behaving like yourself again.'

But Ferris had nothing more to say.

'Sean! Is that hot water here?' Halt called through the curtain.

Sean and Horace hurried into the robing room, bearing a bowl of hot water, several towels and soap. They glanced at the despondent figure of the King and Halt explained what had gone between them.

'I think it might be safer if the King is kept out of sight for the next few days,' he said. 'Perhaps confined to his chambers with a nasty fit of the ague. Can you organise that, Sean? It'd be better if Ferris and I weren't seen together too often, now that Horace has savaged my poor beard.'

Sean nodded. 'I have people I trust who'll help,' he said. 'There's more than one has wanted to see the King do something about the situation we're in. They'll lend a hand.'

'Good. Just keep him quiet until the day of the combat. I take it you can organise the details for that?'

'We'll need stands for the crowd and an arena,' Sean said, his brow furrowed. 'Pavilions for the combatants and so on. I'll take care of it.'

'I'll leave that to you. Horace and I will go into smoke for the next few days. How can we contact you if we need to?'

Sean thought for a few seconds. 'There's a sergeant of the garrison called Patrick Murrell. He's a former retainer of mine. Contact him and he'll get a message to me.'

'That's it then.' Halt looked at his brother, still sitting hunched on a low stool. 'Ferris, look up and listen to me. I want you to understand something.'

Reluctantly, Ferris dragged his eyes up to his brother's. Then he stared into them, like a bird watching a snake as it slowly draws closer.

'This is your only chance of remaining King. I've told you I have no wish to take the throne and I mean it. If things work out, you'll be safe. But if you try to sabotage us, if you betray us, if you try to contact Tennyson and make some last-minute deal, I will find you. And the first you'll know I'm around is just before you drop dead, when you see my arrow standing out from your heart. Is that clear?'

'Yes.' Ferris's voice was barely a croak.

Halt drew a deep breath and let it out again. Dismissing the King from his thoughts, he turned to Horace.

'Good. Now let's get this damned soot and dirt out of my hair.'

Some time later, the guards outside the throne room saw the two visitors leave. Halt's hair had been restored to its normal shade of pepper-and-salt grey and Horace had used another mixture of soot and dirt to re-create his original beard line. Seen close to, it wouldn't stand muster. But from a few paces away, and in the shadow of Halt's cowl, it served reasonably well. With a few days' growth of stubble to enhance it, it would look even more realistic. For the moment, at least it masked Halt's similarity to his twin brother.

The two Araluans rode back down the ramp into the village, returning to the inn where they had paid for another night's accommodation.

'We'll spend a night here and give Will a chance to catch up with us,' Halt said. 'Then I think we'd better get out of town and become invisible.'

'Fine by me,' Horace replied.

Halt looked long and hard at his young friend. 'Horace, I've sort of thrown you in at the deep end with all this. I just assumed you'd be willing to go along with the trial by combat challenge. But if you want to back away from it, just say the word and we'll leave Ferris to his own devices.'

Horace was frowning at him before he finished speaking. 'Back away, Halt? Why would I do that?'

Halt shrugged uncomfortably. 'As I said, I committed you to this without asking you. It's not your fight. It's mine, really. And those two islanders could be a handful.'

Horace smiled and held out his hand, fingers spread. 'Lucky I've got big hands, then, isn't it? Halt, we've known it might come to this from the beginning. That was the reason for evoking the Sunrise Warrior legend, after all.'

He paused and Halt nodded reluctant agreement. It had been unspoken, but understood and accepted, in all their minds. Then he went on.

'I can handle Tennyson's two little playmates. That's what I'm trained for, after all. They're big but I doubt they're too skilful. As for this being your fight and not mine . . . well, you're my friend. And that makes it my fight.'

Halt looked up at the earnest young face before him and shook his head slowly.

'What did I do to deserve such loyalty?' he asked.

Horace pretended to consider the question seriously, then replied, 'Well, nothing much. But we promised Lady Pauline we'd look after you.'

To which Halt replied with a few words Horace had heard before — and several that were new to him.

Thirty-nine

The market square had been transformed into an arena. Down two sides, tiers of wooden bleachers had been constructed to provide seating for the spectators. In the centre of the tiers on the western side, which would be more sheltered from the afternoon sun, an enclosed seating area, set at the height of the third and highest tier of benches, had been built to accommodate the King and his entourage. A canvas roof had been placed over the royal enclosure and there were comfortable, cushioned seats for half a dozen people. At the rear of the box, a high-backed, well-upholstered wooden seat was placed for the King's use.

The long grass of the square had been scythed short by a group of a dozen workmen, to provide a true footing for the combatants. At either end of the square, there was a pavilion — one for Horace and one for Killeen and Gerard. A suitable open space was left around these pavilions to give their occupants a semblance of privacy as they prepared for the coming bouts. The rest of the open space was taken up by vendors, selling pies, sweetmeats, ale and wine. Although the first bout was over an hour away, they were doing a roaring trade.

The bleachers were already almost full. By some tacit agreement, Tennyson's followers had taken up their positions in the eastern stands. A central section, facing the King's box, had been left clear for Tennyson and his closest supporters. His followers had rigged a canvas screen to shield their leader from the sun and scattered deep cushions along the benches. Originally, they had approached Sean, requesting that a seating area similar to the King's be constructed. The young Hibernian had curtly refused. Ferris was King. Tennyson was an itinerant preacher. He could sit on a bench with his followers.

Of course, there wasn't enough room for everyone to find seats. The overflow gravitated to the open ground at the ends of the field, where marshals kept the crowd well away from the two pavilions.

The townspeople, who were for the most part supporting Horace as the Sunrise Warrior, had filled the western stands. There was a nonstop buzz of conversation. Excited and expectant, it hung over the arena, creating a constant backdrop of sound, reminiscent of a huge beehive at noon on a hot day.

Horace, Will and Halt, who had spent the past couple of days camped in the forest a few kilometres outside the town limits, had slipped into Dun Kilty just after first light. Even at that early hour, there had been plenty of people stirring and Horace kept his identity concealed beneath a long cloak. The two Rangers, of course, were virtually unknown in Dun Kilty and the sight of three cloaked strangers evoked little interest. Those who did see them assumed they had simply come into the town to see the combats.

They found an early-opening inn and breakfasted there. Halt was less concerned with eating than on eaves-dropping on conversations around them. From what he overheard, it was obvious that the trial by combat was going ahead and that Ferris hadn't managed to renege on his – or rather Halt's – word. Townsfolk were interested and excited about the upcoming spectacle. There was even a general feeling of goodwill towards the King, partly because he had engineered this spectacle for them and partly because, finally, he was doing something about improving the situation in the Kingdom. Halt smiled grimly to himself as he realised that he had been respons-ible for boosting the King's popularity. Hardly typical behaviour for the usurped heir to a throne, he thought.

Will managed to cram down a buttered bread roll with hot bacon layered on top of it. But his stomach felt tight and he was on edge, worrying about his friend. For his part, Horace seemed supremely unconcerned, eating large amounts of the delicious pink bacon accompanied by several fried eggs. Will found it difficult to sit still. He wanted to be up and prowling about to release the tension that he felt throughout his entire body. But, out of defer-ence to Horace, he sat quietly. He reflected on that as they sat, not speaking. There had been plenty of occasions in times past where he and Horace had been waiting for a battle and Will's Ranger training had made him seem calm and unconcerned. Horace had even remarked on his ability to sit unmoving for hours waiting for the enemy. So why did Will find it so difficult to remain calm and unconcerned today?

He realised that, on other occasions, he had been sharing the danger with Horace. When they waited for the Temujai army outside Hallasholm, for example. Or when they had crouched for several hours, conversing in whispers, under the upturned cart by the walls of Castle Macindaw, waiting for darkness. But this was different. This time, Horace would be facing the danger alone, with no help from Will. And that was almost unbearable for the young Ranger. He would have to watch his friend risk his life – twice. He would be unable to take a hand to help him – all the while knowing that it was in his power to dispatch both of Horace's opponents in the space of two heartbeats. The feeling of impotence was overwhelming.

'Time to go,' Halt said, returning to their table after one of his circuits of the room.

With a sigh of relief, Will leapt to his feet and made for the door. Horace, grinning at him, followed.

'Why are you on edge?' he asked. 'You're not fighting the Grumpy Twins.'

Will turned an anxious glance on him. 'That's why I'm on edge. I'm not used to sitting by and watching.'

They made their way to the market square and took in the preparations that had been made under Sean's supervision. A group of Tennyson's white robes, who were erecting the shelter where their leader would sit, glared at them. Horace smiled back and they turned away, muttering.

'Nice to know who your friends are,' he said. He looked at the two pavilions and saw another group of white robes outside the southern one. He turned and looked at the tent at the northern end of the field. Aside from the two marshals posted to keep sightseers away, there was nobody close to the tent.

'I guess that's us,' he said and started towards it. Will followed a few paces behind him, having to hurry to match Horace's long-legged stride. Halt walked beside him for a few minutes, then said:

'You keep an eye on Horace. I'm going to find Sean.'

Will nodded. He knew that Halt had been working on the text of Sean's announcement — an announcement that would set the combats in train. Halt wanted to be sure that Horace's victory would signal an unmistakable refutation of Alseiass's power and a total acceptance of the Sunrise Warrior. This was to be the definitive fight — or fights, he corrected himself. Sean would make that plain before the combat began, and he would require Tennyson to agree without equivocation or qualification to the conditions. If the Outsider leader hesitated or refused to agree in full, then his lack of conviction would be exposed to the crowd — and his own recently recruited followers. Support for the Outsiders would begin to crumble.

As Halt hurried away towards the royal enclosure, Will and Horace made their way to the pavilion.

It was a high tent, easily three metres tall at its middle point, so there was no need to stoop as they entered. Inside, the white canvas sides filtered the early morning sun.

There was a small screened-off space in one corner. Will poked his nose into it and saw a bucket.

'What's this for?' he asked.

Horace smiled. 'It's a privy,' he said. 'In case I need a nervous wee.'

Will hastily withdrew. Now that Horace had raised the subject, he realised that his own bladder seemed a little tight. He put it down to nerves and tried to ignore it while he examined the very basic furnishing in the pavilion.

The main part of the tent held a couch, a table, a canvas chair and a rack where Horace could store his arms and armour. His mail shirt, helmet with chain mail neck guard, and light metal greaves to protect his shins and lower legs had been delivered to the castle for scrutiny the day before. In addition, two round bucklers embellished with the sunrise insignia had been supplied at Halt's request. Now the shields and armour were neatly placed on the rack for him. He checked over each piece carefully, ensuring that nothing had been tampered with and that all straps and fittings were secure.

Sensing Will's continuing restlessness, he glanced around the interior of the tent to try to find something to keep his friend busy. His eye fell on a water jug and two mugs on the table. A quick glance told him the jug was empty.

'Would you mind filling this with cold water?' he asked. 'I know I'll have a raging thirst after the first fight. I always do.'

Glad to be able to help, Will seized the jug and started out the door. He paused, uncertainly.

'You're sure you'll be all right?'

Horace smiled at him. 'I'll be fine. See if you can find some linen or muslin to wet and drape over the jug. It'll keep it cool.'

'I'll do that. You're sure you're . . .'

'Go!' said Horace, making a mock swipe at his friend. When he was alone, Horace sat on the chair, leaning forward with his elbows on his knees, breathing deeply. He felt his pulse. It was racing a little, just as he expected. In spite of his outward appearance of calm, Horace was beginning to feel a familiar tautness in his stomach, as if a hard lump had settled there. It didn't bother him. He felt it before every battle or combat. If he hadn't felt a little nervous, he'd have been worried. A little nervousness was a good thing. It gave you an edge. Maybe, he smiled to himself, that's why they called it edginess.

But he was glad to have a few minutes to himself, without the constant, concerned scrutiny from Will. He knew Will was tensed up because he felt useless in the coming battle. Sometimes, Horace thought, standing by and watching a friend in danger could be worse than being in danger yourself. Even so, it didn't help to have Will so keyed up and tense. He'd have to find another errand for him when he came back with the water, he thought.

It took longer than he expected, but when the young Ranger returned, he had the jug full of water and Horace could hear the unexpected clinking of ice as well.

'Where did you get that?' he asked, surprised by his friend's initiative. Will grinned.

'One of the drinks vendors had a supply. He didn't want to part with any but he agreed once I mentioned my friend.'

'Me?' said Horace, raising his eyebrows. Will shook his head.

'My saxe knife,' he said, grinning. 'Plus I paid a little extra.' He set the jug down on the table, carefully draping a piece of wet muslin over it as Horace had suggested. Then, with nothing to do, he began to pace back and forth.

'So . . . are you all right?' he asked. 'Need anything?'

Horace eyed him for a moment, then had an idea.

'Will you take my sword to the steward's table?' he said. 'Weapons need to be inspected before the combat. And find out what my opponent is using if you can.'

Will was out of the pavilion before he had finished the sentence. Horace smiled and began deep breathing again, clearing his mind, emptying it of any stray distractions so he could concentrate on the task ahead of him. It wouldn't be easy, he knew. But he was confident that he could defeat the two huge twins. Just so long as he could concentrate and bring his fighting instincts up to their highest pitch. So much of a battle like this depended on aligning his instinctive reactions to the movements he'd been trained to perform, so that he could execute a sword stroke or a lunge or a shield block without having to think about it. So he could anticipate, from his opponent's eyes and body position, where the next attack was intended.

He closed his eyes, concentrating on hearing the faintest noises: the burr of conversation from the stands. The sound of a songbird in a tree. The cries of the vendors. He heard them all and dismissed them all.

He didn't hear Halt re-enter the tent, take one look at the young warrior sitting, eyes closed and preparing himself, and leave again.

When Will returned a few minutes later, Halt intercepted him and led him to a bench under a tree a few metres away, where they could sit and watch the tent without disturbing its occupant. Time passed and they heard movement and the clinking of metal from inside the pavilion. Halt led the way to the entrance once more. Horace was pulling the mail shirt over his head. He nodded a greeting to them.

'What's he using?' he asked Will.

Will glanced around the tent nervously. 'A mace and chain,' he answered and heard Halt's sharp intake of breath. 'That's bad, isn't it?'

Horace shrugged. 'I don't know. I've never faced one before. Any thoughts, Halt?'

Halt rubbed his vestigial beard thoughtfully. The mace and chain wasn't a common weapon in Araluen but he had known men who had fought against it.

'It's awkward,' he said. 'It'll give him extra reach — and he's got plenty already. And it develops massive force in its strokes. You'll feel like you've been hit by a battering ram.'

'That's encouraging,' Horace said. 'Any more good news?'

'For God's sake, don't try to parry it with your sword. It'll wrap around the blade and it could even snap it off. Most people use a battleaxe to counter a mace and chain. You could change to one,' he suggested.

Horace shook his head. 'I'm used to my sword. This is no time to try out an unfamiliar weapon.'

'True. Well, try to keep your distance. If the chain catches the rim of your shield, the spiked ball will whip over and hit your shield arm or your head. One thing in your favour, it's an unwieldy weapon and it's slow. It takes a very strong man to use one effectively.'

'And unfortunately, that's exactly what Grumble One is,' Horace said, then shrugged. 'So I just have to keep my distance, don't let him hit my shield with the chain, get hit by a battering ram and not parry with my sword. All in all, it sounds like money for jam. Now give me a hand with these greaves, Will, and I'll go out and finish him off.'

Forty

'Now listen all people! Give silence for Sir Sean of Carrick, chief steward to the King and master at arms for these combats! Silence for Sir Sean!'

The herald's voice thundered the formally worded, rather stiff announcement across the market square, dominating the loud buzz of conversation in the stands. The herald was a thickset man, with a barrel-shaped chest and massive lung capacity. He had been specially selected and trained for his role.

Gradually, the chatter in the stands died away as people realised that it was almost time for the first combat to begin. They edged forward expectantly on their seats, those at the extreme ends of the bleachers craning to see Sean as he moved to the front of the royal enclosure. He held a rolled parchment in his hand. He unrolled it and began to read. His voice lacked the stentorian qualities of the herald's but it was strong and clear and it carried easily in the sudden silence.

'People of Dun Kilty! At issue today is the legitimacy or otherwise of the so-called god Alseiass, also known as the Golden God of Good Fortune.'

There was a moment of subdued muttering from the eastern stands as he said the words 'so-called god'. It stopped as he raised his eyes and directed a hard look across the combat ground.

'Ferris, High King of Clonmel, contends that Alseiass is a false god and that his prophet Tennyson is a false prophet.'

He paused, turned and looked at Ferris, who was sitting huddled in the throne-like chair at the back of the royal enclosure. A wave of cheers rang around the arena, mingled with cries of 'Hail Ferris!' and 'Long live the King!'. Sean waited till they died away and continued.

'His majesty also contends that the one true hope of deliverance for the Kingdom is the warrior known as the Sunrise Warrior. That under his guidance and protection, we shall restore the rule of law and order in the Kingdom.'

More cheers. And stony silence from the eastern stands.

'The prophet Tennyson, for his part, contends that Alseiass is a true god.'

Now cheering rose in the eastern stands. Tennyson leaned back in his chair, looked around him at his supporters, and smiled. Halt, watching from the opposite side of the field, thought the smile was a smug one. He frowned as he noticed three figures sitting behind Tennyson, all cloaked in dull purple. The Genovesans, he realised.

Sean was continuing. 'Tennyson has guaranteed the protection of his god to those who will follow him, and vows that Alseiass and Alseiass alone can restore order to the Kingdom.

'These matters having been under contention, and with no resolution attained, the parties have agreed to the ultimate resolution of differences: trial by combat.'

The thunderous cheering that rose now was all-embracing. Both townsfolk and Outsiders alike roared their approval. After some thirty seconds, Sean glanced at the herald behind him. The heavyset man stepped forward and his voice rang out above the crowd.

'Silence! Silence for Sean o' Carrick!'

Gradually, the cheering died away, like a mighty wave that crashes in upon a beach, then recedes until there is nothing of it left behind.

'Trial by combat is the sacred, unarguable method of judgement, the ultimate court against which there may be no appeal. It is the direct appeal to all gods to decide these matters. On behalf of King Ferris, I swear the crown's willingness to abide by the final judgement, absolutely and without further argument.

'Should the followers of Alseiass prove victorious, King Ferris will withdraw all claim of the powers of the Sunrise Warrior and submit utterly to the will of Alseiass.'

There were a few scattered cheers and catcalls from the bleachers opposite the King's enclosure. For the most part, however, there was silence as the true gravity of this contest and its result sank in. And the followers of Tennyson realised that a similar binding vow would be required of their prophet — and a similar pledge to deny the god Alseiass if Killeen and Gerard were to lose. For the first time, many began to examine their own impetuous actions in joining Tennyson's band. Swept along by a mixture of excitement, fear and blind hope, they had followed Tennyson's lead without giving the matter too much rational thought. Now Sean showed them the other side of the coin — the risk Tennyson was running.

'Should the Sunrise Warrior prevail, Tennyson and his followers must give the same undertaking. The sacred trial by combat to take place here will determine whether or not Alseiass is truly a god — and whether Tennyson is a true prophet or a false pretender.'

Sean paused, staring across the open ground at the white-robed figure seated opposite him. Tennyson showed no sign of responding.

'Tennyson! So-called prophet of Alseiass! Do you swear to be bound by these proceedings? Do you swear to agree to the result of trial by combat, whatever that result may be?'

Tennyson, remaining seated, glanced around at his followers. Their eyes were on him. He nodded curtly. But that wasn't enough for Sean.

'Stand, Tennyson!' he demanded, 'And swear to it in the presence and hearing of all here!'

Still Tennyson remained seated. He was unwilling to commit to such a definite course of action. Who knew what could go wrong in a trial by combat? But as he remained seated, he began to hear muttering from his own followers. Not the hard-core fifty or so who were his inner circle. They, after all, were under no delusions that there was a god Alseiass. But his new converts, the crowds of people swept up from Mountshannon and half a dozen other villages along the way, were beginning to look at him suspiciously and doubt the level of his conviction and the truth of his teaching. In another few seconds, he realised, he could lose them. Reluctantly, he stood.

'I swear it,' he said.

Sean, opposite him, allowed himself a small, grim smile. 'Then let all here witness that fact. These matters will be settled this day by combat. All parties have agreed. All parties will be bound by the result.'

Slowly, Sean began to roll up the parchment from which he had read the ritualistic formulas setting out the parameters of the day. He glanced to the pavilions, one at either end of the field.

'Let the combatants come forward! Horace of Araluen, known as the Sunrise Warrior. Killeen of the Isles, disciple of Alseiass! Step forward and receive your weapons for this sacred trial.'

And the cheering began to build again as Horace and Killeen emerged from their respective pavilions. Somewhere, a drumbeat began, giving them a cadence by which to march. Each warrior was fully armoured. Killeen wore a shirt of scale armour — brass plates shaped like fish scales that were fastened onto an inner leather garment. Like fish scales, the brass leaves overlapped each other. Horace had small links of closely knit chainmail under his white surcoat and covering his arms. Killeen wore a full helmet that concealed his face, with only his eyes glittering through the vision slit. Horace wore his familiar conical helmet with its dependent fringe of mail hanging to his shoulders as a neck guard.

Both carried their shields on their left arms. Horace's was circular, made of steel fastened over toughened wood, painted white with the emblem of the sunrise depicted on it. Killeen's was kite shaped, with a rounded top. It bore the double circle emblem of Alseiass. Beside each strode an attendant. A white-robed acolyte flanked Killeen, and Will strode beside Horace, desperately trying to keep up. Compared to Horace and the huge figure of Killeen, he looked almost child-like.

The drumbeat came to a stop with one final ruffle as Killeen and Horace, flanked by their attendants, stopped in front of the royal enclosure, where Sean stood waiting for them. Below him, at ground level, a simple table held their chosen weapons. Horace's long-bladed, unadorned cavalry sword. Brass hilted and with a matching crosspiece, it was an unremarkable weapon. But it was perfectly balanced and razor sharp.

Beside it, massive and ugly, was Killeen's mace and chain. A thick oak handle some half a metre long, bound every ten centimetres with iron strips to reinforce it. Then the long iron chain, heavy and thick, attached to the fearsome spiked ball at its end.

It was a brutal weapon, lacking in all grace and finesse. But deadly. Horace pursed his lips thoughtfully as he studied it.

Halt's right. I'll need to stay away from that, he thought.

'Take your weapons,' Sean told them.

Horace took hold of his sword, spun it experimentally to make sure there had been no tampering with it. But its balance and weight were true. Killeen sneered at the graceful blade and took his own weapon, the chain clanking on the table as he picked it up. He hefted it, setting the cruel spiked ball swinging back and forth.

'Attendants, leave the arena,' Sean said quietly. Will ducked under the railing that marked the fighting area and joined Halt on the first row of benches. The two exchanged nervous looks. Killeen's attendant hurried across the field and took his place among Tennyson's group.

'Take your positions. Combat will begin upon the signal trumpet,' Sean told them. He glanced sideways at the trumpeter below him, making sure the man was ready. The trumpeter nodded, moistening his lips nervously. It was difficult not to get caught up in the drama of the moment.

Horace and Killeen marched to the centre of the field, where a lime-washed circle marked out their starting point. Instantly, Killeen tried to sidle to the western edge of the circle, so that the early afternoon sun would be in Horace's eyes. Sean, however, was awake to that trick. The combat would start with no advantage to either.

'Killeen!' his voice rang out. 'Move to the south side! Now!'

The massive helmet swung towards him and he imagined he could see the eyes through that slit, glaring maliciously at him. But the giant obeyed. Horace took up a position facing him.

Seeing the islander's ploy, Halt had come to his feet, his hand reaching to the quiver at his back. But as Killeen complied with Sean's command, he sat, a little reluctantly.

'Just let him breach the rules once,' he muttered to Will. 'Let him *look* like breaching them, and I'll put an arrow in him.'

'That'll make two of us,' Will replied. He was half hoping that the islander would try some underhand trick. That would give him and Halt clearance to shoot him down.

Anyone who broke the rules of trial by combat automatically forfeited the bout and his right to life.

Horace and Killeen faced each other now. Killeen crouched, knees bent. Horace stood upright, balanced lightly on the balls of his feet. The mace and chain swung heavily and ponderously between them. Horace's sword moved as well, the point describing small circles in the air.

Suddenly, shatteringly in the stillness, the signal trumpet brayed its single note.

Killeen was big and clumsy. But he was fast, faster than Horace had anticipated. And his thick wrist had the huge strength necessary to flick the mace and chain up and over, so the spiked ball came arcing down in an overhead blow. As he did so, he stepped into Horace, forcing the young warrior to spring backwards, as he brought his shield up to ward off the blow.

Halt had suggested that the mace and chain would hit like a battering ram. To Horace, it felt as if a house had fallen on his shield. Never before had he felt such massive, crushing force behind a blow. Not even when he had faced Morgarath's huge broadsword, many years ago.

He grunted in surprise and was nearly caught by Killeen's follow-up, a flailing sideways attack that slammed into his shield again, as he managed to lower it just in time. Again, Horace backed away. Only his speed had saved him from those first two strokes and as he sought the eyes behind the vision slit in the helmet, he sensed that Killeen had hoped that his unexpected lightning attack would finish matters before they really got started. Killeen shuffled after him, wary himself now that he had seen the speed of his opponent's reactions. He swung again, this time another overhead blow. But now Horace was ready and he stepped lightly to the side so that the iron ball slammed into the turf.

He cut quickly at Killeen's forearm. The mace and chain had one disadvantage. Unlike a sword, there was no crosspiece to catch blows aimed at the hand and lower arm. But Killeen wore heavy brass-plated gauntlets and solid brass cuffs. The sword cut bruised him and made him jerk back hurriedly. But his armour held and it was far from a telling blow.

Horace began circling now, moving to Killeen's right to cut off the arc of the mace and chain. He frowned to himself. He could avoid Killeen's blows, or block them with his shield. But he could see no way at the moment that he could strike back. He had to keep away from the giant, to avoid having the chain hit the rim of his shield and whip over. Had he been facing a swordsman or an axeman, he could have moved in, crowding him and cramping his weapon. But the mace and chain was a different prospect and he had to avoid that whiplash effect at all costs.

Killeen stepped in with another overhead blow. Horace took it on the shield again, feeling the shock of the blow up to his shoulder. Before he could retaliate, Killeen whipped the heavy weapon back and in again, slamming into the shield a second time.

Horace heard something crack in his shield. He danced back to give himself room and looked down at the shield. It was rapidly becoming bent out of recognisable shape. The edges were crumpled and ragged and in the centre there was a crack where the steel had fractured, exposing the wood lining underneath. Much more of this and the shield would be destroyed, he realised. His mouth went dry at the thought of facing that horrific mace with only his sword. For the first time, he considered the possibility of defeat.

Then Killeen was attacking again and Horace had no choice but to block with his shield. This time, the rent in the steel split further under the assault and the spiked ball bit deeply into the wood. For several seconds, it stuck there and there was a desperate tug of war between the two warriors. Then Killeen jerked it free and swung again.

This time, Horace ducked low and the iron ball whistled close over his head. But an idea was forming in his mind now. It was a last-ditch, desperate idea but it was the only one he could come up with. He laughed grimly to himself as he realised it was similar to the moment when he had faced Morgarath and hurled himself under the hooves of the warlord's charging horse.

Why do I always come up with low percentage ideas? he asked himself.

Killeen swung overhead again and Horace skipped lightly backwards, watching the mace head thud deeply into the turf. The Outsiders' supporters were beginning to jeer as he danced and ducked away from their champion. So far, he had been totally ineffectual in attack.

I'd jeer myself if I were with them, he thought. The other side of the field had gone noticeably silent, apart from anguished groans or gasps as the thunderous mace and chain strokes found their target.

He danced lightly to his left again, backing away a few more metres to give himself a few seconds' respite. As Killeen began to shuffle slowly after him, he glanced down at the leather strap that held his shield to his upper arm.

He had a few seconds. He slammed the sword point down into the turf and hurriedly adjusted the retaining strap, loosening it a few notches. Then he just had time to recover his sword and dance away again. This time, however, he moved to his right, surprising Killeen, who had expected him to continue to circle left.

That gave him a few more metres but now he stood and waited for Killeen. As the islander came at him, he swayed to one side to avoid the mace, then stepped quickly in and lunged the point of his sword at the vision slit in the helmet. Killeen, by now used to attacking without retaliation, was caught by surprise and only just brought his own shield up in time. The moment he was blinded by the raised shield, Horace darted to his left and hacked again at Killeen's weapon hand, then leapt back again.

Neither the thrust nor the hand strike were telling blows. But they served the purpose he had set. They infuriated the huge man facing him. Killeen stepped forward with a snarl of rage. The mace and chain whirred in giant circles over his head as he gathered momentum for one crushing, final stroke.

Eyes narrowed, Horace watched for him to release his wrist and unleash the blow. He knew he would have to judge timing and distance perfectly if his plan were to succeed.

Here it came!

Judging centimetres with the uncanny natural skill that set him apart from the normal run of warriors, Horace took a half pace forward and brought his shield up to take the blow. He grunted as the mace slammed into the weakened metal and the spiked ball bit deep into the shattered steel and wood. Bit and held.

In that same instant, he released his hold on the handgrip and slipped his arm out of the loosened restraining strap. A fraction of a second later, when Killeen jerked the mace and chain back to free it, the battered, crumpled shield went with it, firmly attached to the end of the chain. It soared high and wide in an arc behind the islander, the unexpected extra weight on the end of his weapon jerking him momentarily off balance.

It was only natural that he would turn his head in surprise to see what had happened, exposing his neck below the full face helmet for just a second or two.

Which was all Horace ever needed. Holding his sword two-handed, he stepped in and swung a lightning side stroke at the exposed two centimetres of neck.

There was a roar of surprise from both sides of the arena as Killeen's helmet went spinning away to land on the turf with a dull thud. The roar dropped to silence as the spectators realised that his head had gone with it. Killeen's giant torso slowly buckled at the knees and seemed to fold into itself as it collapsed to the ground.

Then the western stands began to cheer as they realised Horace, who had essayed only one serious attacking stroke in the entire conflict, had won.

Will and Halt were under the railing in a flash. They ran to the centre of the field, where Horace stood, his sword hanging loosely at his side. He looked at them and smiled tiredly.

'I think I'm going to need another shield,' he said.

Forty-one

Halt shook his head at Horace, a delighted grin on his face.

'Horace, you continue to amaze me! How did you ever think of that stunt with the shield?'

Horace looked at his two friends. To be truthful, he was a little surprised that he was still here and able to talk to them. There had been an ugly few minutes during the combat when he thought he'd bitten off more than he could chew.

'It seemed like a good idea at the time,' he said mildly. 'I just hope Gerard isn't using one of those damned maces. I don't think I could pull it off twice.'

'He's using a sword,' Will said, smiling up at him. He felt a great sense of relief. Like Horace, as he had watched Killeen battering his friend from pillar to post, he had begun to fear that there was no way he could survive, let alone win.

Halt clapped the tall warrior on the shoulder.

'Well done, anyway!' he said heartily. He was fond of Horace, nearly as fond of him as he was of Will. He had decided that, rules of combat notwithstanding, if Killeen had looked like winning, he was going to shoot him down.

Horace winced at the impact.

'Thanks, Halt. But I'd appreciate it if you didn't hit me just there. I'm a little tender. I've just had a giant walloping me with a large iron ball.'

'Sorry,' said Halt, but the grin was still on his face. He glanced now at the eastern stands, to see how Tennyson was reacting to the totally unexpected result. The smile faded as he did so.

The priest looked surprisingly unperturbed by the death of his bodyguard. Or by the implications of the loss. He was talking calmly to one of his white robes, smiling at the man's reply. Yet he must have been surprised by Horace's sudden reversal of fortune. During the fight, Halt had looked across several times and seen Tennyson, flanked by his three Genovesans, leaning forward, shouting encouragement as Killeen had rained blow after blow down on his seemingly helpless opponent.

A small frown creased Halt's forehead. There had been three Genovesans behind Tennyson. Now he could see only two. He turned to Will.

'Get back to the tent quickly and keep an eye on things. We'll be along shortly.'

Will took one look at his teacher's face, saw the sudden concern there and needed no further urging. He ran lightly through the milling crowd of people who had invaded the arena, making his way to the imposing white tent at the northern end of the ground. When he was a few metres short, he stopped. The crowd was thick here as the vendors had recommenced selling their wares and people were queuing for refreshments before the next bout. But, slipping through the mass of jostling people, he thought he had seen of a glimpse of dull purple, heading away from the pavilion. He shoved his way for a few more metres in pursuit and caught one more brief glimpse before the crowd swallowed the figure.

It could have been one of the Genovesans, he thought, and, if so, he had been very close to Horace's pavilion. He was torn by the temptation to follow and catch up with whoever it was. But Halt had told him to keep watch at the tent. Reluctantly, he turned back to the pavilion. As he approached the canvas flap that screened the entrance, he surreptitiously slipped the saxe knife out of its sheath, holding it low, against his leg, so that people wouldn't notice it.

The leather thongs securing the canvas door seemed to be as he'd left them, but he couldn't be sure. Quietly, he untied them and, jerking the screen back, darted quickly inside, the saxe held ready now at waist height.

Nothing.

The tent was empty. Somewhere he could hear a blue-bottle fly, trapped inside and buzzing frantically as it butted against the canvas, seeking to escape. He scanned the interior. Table, water jug and two tumblers, still draped with damp muslin. Chair, lounge, arms rack — empty now but with the spare shield standing beside it. Nothing else in sight.

It was hot inside the tent. The sun had been beating down on it and the flap had been closed, trapping the hot, stuffy air inside. He turned, meaning to tie back the canvas door flap and let some fresh air in, when he realised that he hadn't checked the screened-off privy. He crossed the tent now and jerked the screen back, saxe knife ready to lunge.

Empty.

He let out a long pent-up breath and re-sheathed the saxe. Then he busied himself tying back the door flap and opening a ventilation panel at the rear of the tent. A breeze of cooler air swept in and the interior temperature quickly began to fall. The stuffiness was dispelled as well.

Halt and Horace arrived, the former carrying Horace's sword, helmet and the battered, crumpled shield. He tossed it into a corner.

'You won't be needing that again,' he said. He looked a question at Will and the young Ranger shook his head. Nothing suspicious to report. Although Halt's remark about the shield reminded him that he should check the straps and fittings on Horace's reserve shield before the next combat.

Horace sank back on the lounge, sighing as his bruised muscles came in contact with the cushions, and glanced longingly at the jug on the table.

'Pour me a drink, would you, Will?' he said. 'I'm parched.'

His dry mouth and throat were caused by nervous tension and fear as much as exertion, he knew. And Horace wasn't ashamed to admit that he had felt fear while he was fighting Killeen. He leaned back, his eyes closed, and heard the soft tinkle of ice as Will poured.

'That sounds good,' he said. 'Make it a big one.'

He drank the tumbler in one long draught, then nodded as Will offered the jug for a refill. This time, he sipped at the cold water more slowly, enjoying the sensation of the cold liquid sliding down his dry throat. Gradually, he began to relax.

'How long till I face Gerard?' he asked Halt.

'You've got over an hour,' the Ranger told him. 'Why don't you get out of that armour and lie back and relax for a while?'

Horace went to rise, groaning softly as he did so. 'Good idea. But I should check my sword's edge first,' he said.

Halt gently stopped him. 'Will can do that.'

Horace smiled gratefully as Will moved to take the sword and check it. Normally, Horace would have insisted on doing the task himself. Will or Halt were the only people he would have trusted to do it for him.

'Thanks, Will.'

'Let's get that mail shirt off you,' Halt said and helped pull the long, heavy garment over his head. The mail shirt had a light chamois leather liner, now stained and damp with sweat. Halt turned it inside out and draped it across the arms rack, moving the latter so that it was just inside the doorway, catching the cross breeze.

'Now rest. We'll take care of things. I'll wake you in plenty of time for a massage to get the kinks out,' Halt said. Horace nodded, and lay back with a contented sigh. It was nice, he thought, to have attendants to fuss over him.

'I think I could get used to this Sunrise Warrior thing,' he said, smiling.

He could hear the gentle rasping sound as Will put an extra-sharp edge on his sword. There had been one slight nick in the blade, where it had caught against Killeen's shield, and the young Ranger set himself to remove it. The sound was oddly relaxing, Horace thought. Then he drifted off to sleep.

Halt woke him after half an hour. Horace's muscles were stiff and aching, so at Halt's bidding, he rolled over onto his stomach and let Halt work on them. The Ranger's strong fingers dug and probed expertly into the muscle and tissue, loosening knots and easing the tension, stimulating blood flow back to the bruised, strained parts of his body. It was painful, but strangely enjoyable, he thought.

The short nap had left him feeling drowsy and sluggish. He shrugged to himself. That often happened if you slept during the day. Once he started moving and got some fresh air in his lungs, he'd be fine.

He swung his legs off the lounge and sat, head down for a few seconds. Then he shook himself. Will looked at him curiously.

'Are you all right?' he asked. He'd watched over Horace while he slept, his saxe knife drawn and lying ready across his knees.

Horace looked at the weapon and grinned sleepily. 'Planning on chopping vegetables?' he asked, then answering his friend's question, 'I'm just a bit foggy, that's all.'

Halt looked at him, a small light of concern in his eyes. 'You're sure?' he said and Horace smiled, shaking off the torpor that seemed to have claimed him.

'I'll be fine. Shouldn't sleep during the day, really. Pass me that mail shirt, will you?'

The chamois lining had dried in the breeze and he pulled it on over his head as he sat on the edge of the lounge. Then he stood to let it fall to its full length, just above his knees. As he did so, he swayed and had to grasp the back of the lounge to steady himself.

Both the Rangers watched him with growing concern. He smiled at them.

'I'm fine, I tell you. I'll walk it off.'

He took the clean surcoat that Will offered and pulled it on over the mail shirt.

Halt glanced outside. The area around the food and drink stalls was becoming less crowded as the spectators made their way back to their seats. Horace and Gerard would be called to the arena in the next ten minutes. He decided that Horace was probably right. A bit of fresh air and exercise would see him right.

'Let's head up there now. The stewards will have to examine your sword again anyway,' he said, coming to a decision. In fact, the entire preamble to the combat would be repeated, as Sean made sure that neither party was ready to resile from their position. It was a bore, he thought, but it was part of the formal ceremonial ritual attached to trial by combat.

Halt and Will gathered Horace's helmet, his spare shield and his sword. Will refastened the tent flaps and they walked alongside Horace, flanking him as he made his way back to the combat ground. The dwindling crowd at the stalls made way for them, showing deference to the Sunrise Warrior. He had already become a popular figure among the people of Dun Kilty. The spectacular way he had dispatched Killeen had caught their collective imagination.

Halt watched the young warrior carefully as they approached the weapons table set in front of the King's enclosure. He let go a small sigh of relief as he saw Horace's stride was firm and unfaltering. Then his heart missed a beat as the young man leaned down to him and said, in a conversational tone and without any outward sign of concern:

'Halt, we have a problem. I can't focus my eyes.'

The three of them stopped. Halt's mind raced and he glanced instantly to where Tennyson was sitting, surrounded by his cronies. There were three purple-clad figures with him now but as he watched, Tennyson leaned over and spoke to one of them. The Genovesan nodded and slipped away into the crowd.

In that moment, Halt knew what had happened. He spoke urgently to Will.

'Will! Get that water jug in the pavilion! It's drugged! Don't let anyone interfere with it!'

He saw a moment of confusion in Will's eyes, then dawning comprehension as the younger Ranger came to the same conclusion he had just reached. If the water had been drugged, they'd need to keep it safe to prove the fact.

Will spun on his heel and darted away.

Horace jogged Halt's arm. 'Let's keep moving,' he said.

Halt turned to him. In spite of the urgency in Horace's tone, an observer would have thought they were simply discussing unimportant matters.

'We'll call for a postponement,' he said. 'You can't fight if you can't see.'

But Horace shook his head. 'Tennyson will never accept that. If we withdraw, he'll claim victory. Unless we can prove that they've broken the rules.'

'Well, of course they've broken the rules! They've drugged you!'

'But can we prove it? Even if we prove that the water's drugged, can we prove they did it? I'll have to keep going for now, Halt.'

'Horace, you can't fight if you can't see!' Halt repeated. His voice was strained now, showing the depth of concern he felt for his young friend. *I should never have got him into this,* he told himself bitterly.

'I can see, Halt. I just can't focus,' Horace told him, with the ghost of a smile. 'Now let's go. The scrutineers are waiting.'

Forty-two

The purple-cloaked figure slid easily through the last-minute customers round the food and drink vending stalls. As he approached the tall white pavilion he slowed his pace a little, glancing left and right to see if there was anybody watching him, or standing guard over the pavilion.

But he saw no sign of surveillance and walked directly to the entrance to the pavilion. As before, the tent flaps were fastened on the outside, which meant there could be nobody in the tent. Quickly, his strong fingers undid the knots. As the last one fell loose, he resisted the temptation to look around. Such an action would only appear furtive, he knew. Far better to simply walk in as if he had every right to be here.

He slipped the dagger from the scabbard under his left arm — it never hurt to take precautions — and stepped quickly into the tent, allowing the flap to fall back into place.

He let out a pent-up breath, relaxing. There was

nobody in the tent, but the water jug stood on the table where he had last seen it. Quickly, he crossed to the table, picked up the jug and poured its contents onto the ground, watching in satisfaction as the drugged water soaked into the dirt.

'And that's the end of the evidence,' he said softly, in a satisfied voice, a second before something heavy and hard crashed into his head, behind the ear, and everything went black.

'So you say,' Will said. He re-sheathed his saxe knife, satisfied that the Genovesan was unconscious. He rolled the man over on his back and searched him quickly, disarming him as he did so. He glanced curiously at the crossbow that had been slung over the man's shoulder. It was a graceless weapon, he thought, heavy and utilitarian. He tossed it to one side and resumed searching the unconscious man. There was a dagger in his belt, another in each of his boots and one strapped to his right calf. He also found the empty scabbard under the man's left arm. He whistled softly.

'Planning on starting a war?' he asked. The Genovesan, naturally, made no reply.

Will dug into his belt pouch and produced thumb and ankle cuffs. He quickly secured the man's hands in front of him and trussed his ankles, leaving enough slack so he would be able to hobble awkwardly, but not run.

Will sat back on his heels, thinking quickly. They needed proof, he knew. He'd arrived a few seconds before the Genovesan, approaching from the opposite side and entering by cutting through the canvas at the rear corner, where the privy was positioned. That way, the outer knots on the door were left undisturbed. Unseen by the assassin, he had watched as he poured away the remaining water. A second too late, he had emerged from the privy and slammed the brass pommel of his saxe just behind the man's ear.

There was something in the back of his mind — something that would help him connect the Genovesan with the drugged water. Then he had it. When he had poured the glass for Horace, he had heard the tinkle of ice. Yet the ice he'd placed in the water should have melted long ago. The Genovesan must have replenished it and there was only one place he could have done so.

He looked at the man, saw that he was still unconscious and hurried outside the tent. One of Sean's marshals, tasked with keeping an eye on the pavilion — as well as watching for the inevitable pickpockets who'd be working the crowd — was strolling nearby. He turned and approached quickly as Will hailed him.

'Keep an eye on him,' Will said, jerking his thumb at the unconscious Genovesan inside the pavilion. The marshal's eyes widened at the sight but he recognised Will as one of the Sunrise Warrior's retainers and nodded agreement.

'I'll be back,' Will told him and hurried towards the drink stalls.

There was one stall selling ice. It was where Will had bought his supply previously and, presumably, where the Genovesan had done the same. Ice was a rare commodity. It would have been cut in large blocks, high in the mountains during winter, then packed in straw and brought down, to be stored deep in a cool cellar somewhere. The vendor looked up as Will approached. Initially, he'd been reluctant to sell some of his ice without selling a drink as well, but the young man had paid well. He nodded a greeting.

'Will it be more ice for you, your honour?' he asked. But Will cut him off abruptly.

'Come with me,' he said. 'Right away.'

He was young and fresh faced, but there was an unmistakable air of authority about him and it never occurred to the ice vendor to argue. He called to his wife to mind the stall and hurried to follow the fast-moving figure in the grey-green cloak. As they entered the pavilion, his eyes also goggled at the sight of the unconscious man lying bound on the grass.

'Did he buy ice from you?' he demanded and the man nodded, instantly.

'He did, your honour. Said it was for the mighty Sunrise Warrior.' He glanced around the tent and his eye fell on the water jug. 'Fetched it in that jug, as I recall,' he added, wondering what this was all about. Then, making sure that he couldn't be blamed for anything, he volunteered more information.

'He was watching earlier when you bought the ice. I assumed he was with you.'

So that was it. Will guessed that the Genovesan, when he had drugged the water, had added ice so that the chill would mask the taste. Or simply make the water more appealing. Yet he would hardly have done so if he hadn't known there was already ice in the jug. He looked at the marshal and the vendor. In the background, he could hear cheering welling up from the arena and realised that too much time had passed while he had been occupied with this problem. The formalities must be over and Horace would be preparing to face the giant islander.

He looked at the two men.

'Come with me!' he ordered. He recovered his bow from behind the privy screen and gestured at the Genovesan, now stirring groggily. 'And give me a hand with that!'

As he and the marshal dragged the bleary-eyed assassin to his feet, he heard the single note of a trumpet. The combat had started.

'You can't do this,' Halt said out of the side of his mouth as he accompanied Horace to the centre of the field. He was carrying Horace's shield and sword, using the shield to keep a surreptitious pressure on the young man's arm so he could guide his footsteps.

'That man! What is that man doing?' Tennyson's voice rang out across the arena, rising above the cheers that rang out from both sides of the field. Halt looked and saw the white-robed figure had come out of his chair and was standing, pointing at him, shouting his protest.

'Just get me to the starting point, Halt. I'll be fine,' Horace said, equally quietly. He could hear Sean Carrick replying to the priest's protest, stating that Halt was acting as Horace's shield bearer, which was allowed within the rules. Horace allowed himself a bitter smile. Arguing over such fine points of procedure was unimportant to him. He was wondering how he was going to fight when all he could see of Gerard was a massive, blurred shape.

'His presence is a breach of the rules! He must remove himself from the field!' Tennyson shouted.

Sean drew breath to reply but stopped as he felt a hand on his shoulder. Surprised, he turned to see the King had left his throne and was standing behind him.

'Be silent, you posturing fake!' Ferris shouted. For a moment, the people of Dun Kilty were shocked to see their King taking such a positive stance. Then they roared their wholehearted approval. 'Don't quote rules unless you know them and understand them! The shield bearer is legitimate! Now sit and be silent!'

Again, his subjects yelled their approval. Ferris looked around, mildly surprised and pleased. He'd never heard that sound before. He drew strength from it and held himself a little taller. Opposite him, Tennyson pointed a threatening finger.

'You've crossed me once too often, Ferris. I'll see you pay for this!'

But he retreated to his seat, contenting himself with glaring at the King. Ferris, after enjoying the plaudits of the crowd for a few more moments, also went back to his seat.

On the field, Halt pulled the arm strap tight on Horace's shield.

'How's that?' he said and Horace nodded.

'Fine,' he said. The blurred figure of Gerard stood in front of him and he concentrated on it, squinting as he tried to see more clearly and force his eyes to focus. With the distraction of his diminished vision, he had forgotten the sense of weariness that had settled over him after he had woken up. Now he was aware of it once more. His limbs felt leaden and clumsy as he tested the balance of his sword. He realised what poor condition he was in.

He decided that his best chance lay in a sudden attack as soon as the trumpet sounded, lunging with the point for the mass of the body before him. Most combatants circled briefly at the start of a fight, looking to test their opponents' reactions. He hoped Gerard would be expecting him to do that. He sensed Halt was still close by but he didn't want to take his attention away from his mighty opponent.

'Thanks, Halt,' he said. 'You'd better go now.'

'I'll fight in your place,' Halt said, in one last desperate attempt. Horace smiled, without humour, his attention still on Gerard.

'Can't be done. Against the rules. I have to finish it. Now go away.'

Reluctantly, Halt withdrew, backing away, watching his young friend in an agony of doubt and fear. He reached the single rail fence, ducked under it and took his seat in the front row.

'Ready, combatants!' Sean called. Neither answered and he took that for a positive reply. He nodded to the trumpeter.

'Sound,' he said quietly. The braying note rang over the field.

Horace didn't wait for the sound to die away. The instant he heard it begin, he lunged forward, his right foot stamping out towards Gerard, the blade of his sword thrusting at the fuzzily seen mass before him.

It might have worked, had he not been slowed down by the effect of the drug. Gerard was expecting his smaller opponent to circle and weave, testing his own defences and speed. He was surprised by the sudden attack. The sword point struck him in the centre of his body but he managed to twist so that his hard leather breast plate deflected it, sending it skating across his ribs.

It hurt him and winded him. And it may well have cracked a rib. But it wasn't the killing stroke Horace needed so desperately. He continued the forward rush, a little more clumsily than his normal sure-footed movement, spinning to his left so that he brought his shield up to ward off the counterstroke he expected from Gerard.

He was just in time; the backhand cut clanged heavily against his shield. It was a solid blow, but nowhere near as bad as the hammering mace strokes he had taken from Killeen.

He shuffled backwards, straining to see. His eyes watered and Gerard was a shapeless mass moving towards him. He saw the vague outline of a sword arm rising and threw up his shield again. Gerard's sword slammed into it again and Horace, acting purely on instinct, cut back at the giant with his own sword.

Gerard was big and strong. But he was no combat master. In addition, knowing that Horace had been drugged, he was expecting no opposition at all and he was overconfident. His shield was poorly positioned and a fraction too low to take Horace's counter. The long blade caught the top of the shield, deflected and clanged solidly off Gerard's helmet, leaving a severe dent on the curved metal.

Horace felt the satisfying shock of solid contact up his right arm. The crowd on the western bleachers roared their approval. He saw the fuzzy lumbering shape that was Gerard move back, becoming more difficult to see as he merged into the background.

Gerard, for his part, shook his head to clear it, and stood like a huge, angry bull, glaring at the young warrior before him. The padded lining to his helmet had absorbed some of the blow he had just taken, but even so it had shaken him. He was furious now. He had been told he would face minimal resistance while he avenged his brother's death. But to his way of thinking, he had only just avoided suffering a similar fate. He roared with fury and charged at Horace.

Horace heard the roar but, virtually blinded as he was, he was slow registering the fact that Gerard was coming at him. Too late, he realised what was happening and tried to retreat. At that moment, Gerard rammed his shield into Horace's, with all the force of his charging body behind it. Horace, already beginning to move backwards, was hurled off his feet, and crashed onto his back on the grass, his sword flying from his hand.

There was a concerted gasp of horror from the western stands, a simultaneous shout of triumph from Tennyson's followers. Horace, winded and almost blind, saw the out-of-focus figure towering over him. He sensed rather than saw that Gerard was raising his sword, point down, holding it in both hands to drive it into Horace's body.

So this is how it's going to happen, he thought. He felt a vague sense of disappointment that he had let Halt down. He heard Tennyson's section of the crowd shouting encouragement to Gerard and resolved to keep his eyes open as he died, in spite of the fact that he could see almost nothing of his killer. That was annoying, somehow. He wanted to see.

He wished he wasn't going to die while he was annoyed. It seemed such a petty emotion.

Forty-three

Will heard the first clash of sword on shield as he and the marshal dragged the staggering Genovesan towards the field of combat. Curious spectators separated before the small group. The ice vendor followed behind him, puzzled, but curious to see what was about to unfold.

The crowd roared and he realised the sound was coming from the western stands, where Horace's supporters were seated. For a wild moment his hopes rose that Horace had somehow managed to win. Then he pushed through to the barrier that marked the southern end of the combat area and his heart sank. Both combatants were still standing but he could see Horace was in trouble. His friend's natural grace and speed had deserted him and he stumbled about the field, desperately warding off Gerard's attacks, and striking back with ineffectual counters.

Will saw the one useful blow that Horace struck and for a moment, as Gerard swayed, he thought the huge man might be about to fall. But then he stepped back, recovered and charged into Horace, sending him flying, to crash awkwardly on his back.

The huge sword in Gerard's hand was being held like a dagger as he prepared to drive it down, plunging it into Horace's helpless body. Acting entirely by instinct, Will shrugged his bow off his shoulder and into his left hand. As he raised it, an arrow seemed to nock itself to the string and he drew and fired in a heartbeat.

Gerard's snarl of triumph turned abruptly into a screech of agony as the arrow transfixed the muscle of his upper right arm.

He wheeled away from the prone body before him, the sword falling harmlessly from his nerveless hand, clasping with his left hand at the throbbing pain that had burst out in his arm, sending shooting blasts of agony down to his hand and fingers. The crowd, after an initial gasp of surprise, was shocked to silence.

Tennyson came to his feet, drawing breath to shout for the marshals. But another voice beat him to it. A young voice.

'Treachery!' Will yelled at the top of his lungs. 'Treachery! The Sunrise Warrior has been poisoned by Tennyson! Treachery!'

Tennyson's eyes swung towards the voice. His heart sank as he heard the accusation of poisoning and saw the bound, hobbling figure of the Genovesan. Somehow, his plot had been discovered.

Halt, on his feet now in the crowd, realised the need to maintain the momentum. He began echoing Will's cry.

'Treachery! Treachery!' And, as he had hoped, those around him took it up, not knowing the how or the why of it but caught up in the mass hysteria. The word rang round the arena.

Will, dragging the Genovesan with him, turned to the ice vendor and whispered a quick instruction to him. The man hesitated, a puzzled look on his face. Then as Will urged him, he turned and ran back towards the pavilion.

Will was almost up to the central point of the arena now, where Horace had slowly regained his feet and where Gerard crouched, hunched over and still clasping his wounded arm. He shoved the Genovesan forward, sending him stumbling to his knees.

'I caught this man in the Sunrise Warrior's pavilion, trying to destroy the evidence. Look beside Tennyson and you'll see his cohorts!'

An angry murmur swept through the crowd. Will noted that it wasn't confined to the King's side of the arena. Some of Tennyson's recent 'converts' looked questioningly at the priest, flanked by two of the Genovesans. The foreigners were unpopular. Since joining Tennyson's band, their arrogant manner had done little to endear them to their colleagues.

In the silence now, Will spoke up: 'The Warrior's drinking water was drugged by this man.' He pointed to the Genovesan, who was on the ground before him. 'And he was working for Tennyson! They've betrayed the sacred rules of trial by combat.'

Tennyson searched for a reply, knowing every eye was on him. He was close to panic. He was used to using the dynamics of mob opinion for his own benefit, not to having them turned against him. Then a lifeline was thrown to him, as Will's Genovesan prisoner struggled to rise to his feet.

'Proof!' the Genovesan shouted, his voice thickly accented. 'Where's your proof? Where is this drugged water? Produce it now!'

He looked up at Tennyson and gave him a discreet nod. The priest's spirits soared. His man had got to the tent in time to destroy the evidence. So now the situation could be reversed.

He echoed the man's challenge.

'Proof! Show us proof if you accuse us! Bring the proof here now!'

He switched his gaze from Will to the King, seated opposite. His voice rose, thundering now with all the power of a trained orator, sure of his ground once more.

'This man has violated the sacred rules of trial by combat! He has attacked my champion. Now his life must be forfeit and Gerard must be proclaimed the winner! He makes charges against me but he does so without proof. If there is proof, let him show it now!'

He frowned as he realised that eyes in the royal enclosure were looking to his right, where Will stood. He followed their gaze and saw the young man smiling triumphantly as he held up a tumbler. Beside him, the ice vendor, who had run all the way to do his bidding, stood hunched over, recovering his breath.

Will looked at the Genovesan. 'You thought you'd destroyed the evidence, didn't you? You poured the water out of the jug onto the ground so nobody would ever know.'

Tennyson saw the doubt suddenly flicker in his henchman's eyes as they fastened on the tumbler. Will raised his voice now so that more people could hear him.

'But I got to the tent first. And I poured some of the water into this mug. I thought Tennyson might try something like that. I was curious to see what this poisoner would do when he got there.'

He looked to Ferris, who had risen from his throne and moved forward to the front of the enclosure.

'You majesty, this is a sample of the poisoned water they used to drug the Sunrise Warrior. It's Tennyson and his cult who have broken the rules of fair combat. They've tried to subvert a fair trial by combat and they stand condemned.'

Ferris rubbed his jaw thoughtfully. He might have been weak and vacillating but even a weak man will resist if he's given enough provocation. And Tennyson's contemptuous threats had finally gone too far.

'Can you prove this?' he asked Will. Will smiled and gripped the Genovesan by the scruff of his collar, dragging him to his feet and shoving the tumbler against his tightly closed lips.

'Easily,' he said. 'Let's see what happens when our friend here drinks it.'

The Genovesan began to thrash frantically against Will's iron grip. But Will held him fast and again thrust the tumbler to his mouth.

'Go ahead,' he said. He turned to the marshal. 'Marshal, would you pinch his nose for me so his mouth will have to open?'

The marshal obliged and the Genovesan's lips finally parted as he had to breathe. But as Will raised the tumbler to his open lips, the assassin, with a supreme effort, tore one hand free from his restraints and dashed the tumbler out of Will's hands, sending it spinning and spilling the water onto the grass.

Will released him and stood back. He spread his hands in appeal to the King.

'I think his actions speak for themselves, your majesty,' he said. But Tennyson instantly screamed his dissent.

'They prove nothing! Nothing! This is all circumstantial! There is no real proof. It's a web of lies and tricks.'

But the crowd was against him. And now, a large proportion of those who had come here with him were also turning away. Voices were raised against him, angry voices of people who were beginning to realise they had been tricked.

'There's one certain way to find out who's lying,' Will shouted, and the arena went silent. 'Let's test it in the highest court of all.'

Ferris was taken aback. The suggestion was unexpected. 'Trial by combat?' he said.

Will nodded, jerking a contemptuous thumb at the Genovesan.

'Him and me. Here and now. One arrow each, from opposite ends of the ground,' he said.

'No! I tell you it's . . .' Tennyson began to shout but the crowd drowned him out. They were eager for another duel and they believed in the divine, unarguable power of trial by combat as a way of finding the truth.

Ferris looked around the arena. The idea had popular support, he could see. The alternative was to spend weeks in his court arguing the toss, with no prospect of a clear-cut answer. Tennyson was glaring his hatred at him and suddenly Ferris was heartily tired of the overweight, overblown charlatan in a white robe.

'Go ahead,' he said.

The crowd roared again. And now, a good proportion of those sitting on Tennyson's side joined in the chorus of approval.

Forty-four

The rules were simple. A marshal fetched the Genovesan's crossbow from the pavilion and returned it to him. He was allowed one quarrel from his quiver and positioned beside the southern pavilion.

Will took up a similar position at the northern end of the field, also with one arrow. The two opponents were just over one hundred metres apart. The area around each pavilion, where people had been visiting the vending stalls, emptied rapidly. They took up positions along the long sides of the arena, in front of the railing that had formerly kept spectators from straying onto the field of combat. A broad corridor was left down the middle, with the two antagonists at either end.

Sean Carrick was setting the rules of engagement.

'Neither party shall make an attempt to evade the other's shot. You will both stand fast and, on the sound of the trumpet, you may shoot in your own time. In the event that both miss, you will each be issued another arrow and we will repeat the sequence.'

He looked to his left and right, studying the two figures to see if there might be any sign of misunderstanding. But both Will and the Genovesan nodded their agreement.

Will was calm and collected. His breathing was easy and even. The crossbow was a fearsome weapon and it was relatively easy to achieve a degree of accuracy with it. Far easier than with the longbow. The shooter had sights, consisting of a notched V at the back and blade at the front of the crossbow. And there was no need to hold the weight of the drawstring while the bow was aimed. That was done mechanically, and the quarrel, or bolt, released by means of a trigger.

So the average person could quickly learn to become a good shot with a crossbow. That was why, years ago, the Genovesan hierarchy had selected the weapon for their forces. Because almost anybody could shoot one with reasonable success. There was no need to search for particularly talented recruits. The crossbow was an everyman's weapon.

And that was where Will believed his advantage lay. The crossbow did not require the hours and hours of practice that went into becoming a proficient shot with the longbow. You raised the bow, centred the sights on the target and pulled the trigger lever. So after some practice, it was easy for the shooter to settle for being a good shot — rather than an excellent one. And most people did settle for that.

On the other hand, the longbow was an instinctive weapon and an archer had to practise over and over again to achieve any level of proficiency and consistency. For the Rangers, there was an almost mystic union with the bow.

A Ranger never stopped practising. 'Good' wasn't good enough. Excellence was the standard they sought. To shoot a longbow well, the archer had to be dedicated and determined. And once you shot it well, it was merely a matter of application before you became an excellent shot.

A good shot versus an expert shot. That was what it boiled down to. Had they been fighting over a range of fifty metres or less, he would have called the odds even. At a little over one hundred metres, with the resulting smaller margin for error, he felt he had the edge.

There was another factor. Genovesans were, by trade, assassins, not warriors. They were not used to a target that was shooting back at them. They were more accustomed to shooting at an unsuspecting victim from a well-hidden position. Will knew from experience that nothing could affect accuracy or the need to remain calm like the prospect of being shot oneself.

So he stood now, with a half smile on his face, confident in his own ability, staring down the field at the figure in purple facing him.

He saw the trumpeter raise his instrument and laid the single arrow on his bowstring. Then he focused totally on the dull purple shape a hundred metres away. The trumpet sound split the air and Will raised his bow, drawing back on the string as he did so.

There was no need to hurry. He saw the bow coming up in the foreground of his sighting picture, with the purple figure that was his target behind it. He didn't sight down the arrow or concentrate on any one aspect of the picture. He needed to see it all to estimate elevation, windage and release.

His rhythm was set, his breathing smooth and even. He took a breath, then, fractionally before he felt his right fore-finger touch the corner of his mouth, he released half of it. It was an automatic co-ordination of the two separate actions and he wasn't aware that it had happened. But he saw the sight picture and it was good. Every element was in its correct correlation. Bow, arrow head and target all formed one complete entity.

And as he saw it and sensed that it was right he realised, without knowing how, that at the last moment, the Genovesan would try to avoid his arrow. It would only be a small movement — a half step or a sway of the body. But he would do it. Will swung his aim to a point half a metre to his right.

And released — smoothly and without jerking.

He made sure that he held the sighting picture steady after he released, not succumbing to the temptation to drop the bow, but following through with it still in position.

Something flashed by his head, a metre or so to his left. He heard a wicked hiss as it passed and he registered the fact that the Genovesan had shot before he did. And now, as he finally lowered the bow, he saw the fractional movement from the other man as he took a half-step to the left — directly into the path of Will's speeding arrow.

The purple figure jerked suddenly, stumbled a few paces and then fell face up on the grass.

The crowd erupted. Some of them had seen the slight movement the Genovesan had made. They wondered if the Araluan had allowed for it or if it was a lucky mistake. Whichever way it was, the result was a popular one. As Will walked slowly back down the field, the crowd cheered themselves hoarse, on both sides.

He glanced to his left and saw the thickset white-robed figure slumped back against his cushions, obviously in the depths of defeat.

So much for you, he thought. Then, at ground level on the opposite side, his attention focused on Halt and Horace and he grinned tiredly at them.

'What happened? What happened? Is he all right?' Horace, still unable to see clearly, was in a frenzy of worry. Halt patted his arm.

'He's fine. He's just fine.' He shook his head and sank down onto the bench. The tension of watching his two young friends risk their lives in one afternoon was almost too much.

'I am definitely getting too old for this,' he said softly. But at the same time, he felt a deep swelling of pride at the way Horace and Will had conducted themselves. He rose as Will reached them and, without a word, stepped forward to embrace his former apprentice. Horace was busy pumping Will's hand and slapping his back and they were soon surrounded by well-wishers trying to do the same. Finally, Halt released him and stepped back.

'Just as well you got to the tent in time to save that glass of drugged water,' he said. Will grinned, a little shame-faced.

'Actually, I didn't. I only just made it before he did. I had no time to get to the jug. I sent the ice vendor to fill the tumbler with any water he could find. I figured our Genovesan friend wouldn't take the chance on drinking it.'

A delighted smile began to spread over Halt's face as he realised the bluff Will had pulled off. But it faded as they heard an urgent shout from the royal enclosure.

'The King! The King is dead!'

Leading Horace, they fought their way through the surging crowd as people tried to move closer to get a better view. Sean saw them coming and signalled for them to move to the front of the stand, where he leaned down and helped haul them up onto the raised platform.

'What happened?' asked Halt.

Wordlessly, Sean gestured for them to take a closer look. Ferris was in his throne, a surprised expression on his face, his eyes wide open. Finally, the royal steward found his voice.

'I don't know. Nobody saw it in all the excitement of the duel. When I looked back, there he was, dead. Perhaps it's a stroke or a heart attack.'

But Halt was shaking his head. Gently, he tried to move the King forward and felt resistance. Peering behind the throne, he saw the flights of the crossbow quarrel protruding from the thin wood. The missile had gone through the back of the chair and into Ferris's back, killing him instantly, pinning him to the chair.

'Tennyson!' he said and dashed to the front of the enclosure, where he could see the opposite stands.

There was a heavyset figure still in the main seat. But it wasn't Tennyson. It was one of his followers, who bore a passing resemblance to the fake priest of Alseiass.

Tennyson, along with the two remaining Genovesans and half a dozen of his closest followers, was nowhere to be seen.

Forty-five

Nobody had seen him go. As Sean had said, everyone's eyes were riveted on the drama being played out on the combat arena.

'Chances are, he left before the duel even took place,' Halt said. 'He's not the type to take chances. If his man had won, it would have been easy to return and claim victory. So he sent one of the assassins to murder Ferris, then got clean away. Now he has a head start on us. And we have no way of knowing which way he went.'

They had ridden immediately to the Outsiders' camp but there was no sign of Tennyson or his party. There were a few sullen acolytes remaining there but the vast majority had been at the market ground. Those remaining in camp denied seeing their leader depart.

Halt was torn by frustration. There was so much to attend to here. Tennyson's remaining followers had to be rounded up and secured. He set Sean and the castle garrison to that task. The vast majority would be turned loose, he knew. They were simple dupes and Tennyson's behaviour had alienated most of them, revealing his true colours to them. But there were perhaps eighty white robes who had been part of his inner circle and willing accomplices to his crimes. They would have to be arrested, tried and imprisoned.

At the same time, all his instincts told him he should be out hunting Tennyson and his small party, finding which way they had gone. But he was needed in Dun Kilty. Ferris's death had left a power vacuum. Someone had to take control and, as the rightful heir, he was the logical choice. It would only be temporary. As he had told Ferris, he had no wish to be King — but every moment he delayed meant that Tennyson would be slipping further away.

Finally, he came to the logical, the only, solution.

'Go after them for me, Will,' he said. 'Find out where they're headed and send word. Don't try to stop them yourself. There are too many of them and those Genovesans will be doubly dangerous now they've seen you kill their comrade. Stay out of sight and wait for us to catch up.'

Will nodded and started towards the stable where they had left their horses that morning. Then he hesitated and turned back.

'What about Horace? His eyes . . .' He paused uncertainly, not wanting to continue. Halt patted his shoulder reassuringly.

'Sean had the royal surgeon check him over. He's pretty sure he knows what the drug was and it's a temporary condition. His vision seems to be improving already. In a day or so, he'll be back to normal.'

Will let go a small sigh of relief. 'At least that's good news.'

Halt nodded agreement. 'I think we deserved some.' Then he thought about that and realised that they had enjoyed more than their share in the past day or so.

'I haven't had a chance to say it, but you did well,' he told the young Ranger. 'Very well indeed. The bluff with the water was inspired. We needed to reveal Tennyson's treachery and that tipped the scales. A simple defeat in combat might not have convinced all his followers that he was a charlatan.'

Will shrugged awkwardly. He was embarrassed by the praise. Yet at the same time, it meant so much to him. There was only one person in the world whose approval he sought and that was his grey-haired former teacher.

'One question,' Halt said. 'How did you know the Genovesan was going to duck?'

He'd seen the flight of Will's arrow, seen the assassin step into its path. And he knew Will's standard of accuracy with the longbow. The arrow had gone where he had intended it to.

Will scratched his head. 'I don't know. I just . . . knew it somehow. It seemed so much in keeping with everything else they'd done so far. And he was right-handed, so I thought the odds were good that he'd step off his right foot, the master side. So I aimed to compensate. Call it instinct, I suppose. Or dumb luck.'

'I prefer to think that it was instinct,' Halt told him. 'Sometimes I feel we should pay more attention to it. In any event, well done. Now go and find Tennyson for me.'

Will grinned and slipped away, hurrying through the crowds who were still thronging the market square, talking excitedly about the events of the day. Within ten minutes, he was riding out the gates of the town, looking for someone who might have seen which direction Tennyson and his group had taken. This close to Dun Kilty, where hundreds of hooves and feet had trampled over the main road all day, there was little chance that he'd find tracks to follow. But once he was clear of the town, he knew he'd find country people – the sort of folk who noticed strangers riding past. It was only a matter of time. He came to a T junction in the road and stopped. Which way? North or south?

'You choose,' he told Tug and released the reins. The little horse tossed his head impatiently and turned right – to the north. It was as good a way of deciding as any, Will thought. He touched the barrel sides with his heels and set Tug to a slow, easy canter north.

Three days later, Halt had Sean call an assembly of the senior nobles in Dun Kilty. They would be the people who would have to ratify the succession of the new King, whoever he might be.

They assembled in the throne room, eyeing each other uncertainly. By now they all knew Halt's identity and knew he was the rightful King. They wondered how he would deal with the people who had accepted Ferris, a usurper, all these years. All too often, people who had been cheated had a tendency to pay back those who had cheated them – and those who had accepted the situation, even unknowingly.

Several of them were discussing this in low tones as they waited for Halt to arrive – until they realised that he was already among them. They weren't used to this. Kings were supposed to sweep into a room majestically — not suddenly appear without anyone seeing their arrival. They shifted uncertainly, waiting for the green-and-grey-cloaked stranger to state his terms — and determine their fates.

Sean of Carrick stood at Halt's side. Halt motioned for the nobles to seat themselves. A half circle of benches had been placed in front of the throne. They were surprised when he sat with them. They had expected him to take the dominant position, assuming the throne on its raised dais.

'My lords, I'll be brief,' Halt said. 'You know who I am. You know how my brother cheated me. You know I have an undeniable claim to the throne of Clonmel.'

He paused and let his eyes roam around the half circle. He saw heads nodding, and eyes dropping from his. He understood their nervousness and decided not to prolong their uncertainty any further.

'What you don't know is that I have no intention of claiming it.'

That got their attention, he thought. Heads came up round the half circle, curiosity mingled with disbelief in their looks. Nobody in his right mind refused the throne, they all thought. He allowed himself a grim smile.

'I know what you're thinking. Well, let me tell you, I have no wish to be a king, here or anywhere else. I've been gone too long to consider this my home any more. I have a home in Araluen. And I have a king I respect. I think you should have the same. Sean, who is next in line to the throne?'

He fired the question at the younger man without warning. Sean rose to his feet, a little taken aback.

'Um . . . oh . . . well, in fact, that would be . . . me,' he said. Halt nodded. He had known as much.

'Then you appear to be the most suitable candidate for the position,' he said. He looked around the room. 'Anybody disagree?'

In truth, there had been more than one who had heard Halt's disavowal of the throne and had felt a quick surge of ambition — a hope that they might be able to assume the crown for themselves. But the speed of events, and the gleam in Halt's eye, told them that it might be a bad idea to continue to nourish such ambitions. There was a hasty mumble of assent from the circle of nobles.

Halt nodded. 'I didn't think you would.'

'Just a moment! I certainly disagree!' Sean said.

The Ranger turned to him. 'You have a clear and unchallenged claim to the throne. Do you not want it?'

He saw Sean hesitate and knew that he was an intelligent young man. There were many good reasons *not* to take the crown, Halt knew. A king's hold on the throne in this country could be tenuous. Sean would need to be a strong and alert ruler at all times. And he would be surrounded by a group of venal self-seeking nobles who would take any opportunity to undermine him if it advanced their own interests. All good reasons to refuse the crown.

But before Sean could answer, he rephrased his question.

'Let me put that another way. Is there anyone here you would prefer to see on the throne?' He indicated the half circle of nobles, who were watching the byplay between Sean and Halt with growing fascination.

And that was the crux of it. The same reasons why Sean might refuse the crown were also the ones that made it imperative that he accept it.

To a man, the group assembled here was self-seeking and self-centred. If one of them took the crown, it wouldn't be long before others contested the choice and the Kingdom was thrown into disarray. Sean was the only one among them with a rightful claim to the throne and the strength of character and purpose to command their loyalty. And at heart, Sean knew it. Reluctantly, he took a step forward, towards Halt.

'Very well. I accept,' he said. It might not be what he wanted, but it was what the country needed and he was enough of a patriot to recognise that fact. Halt waited a few seconds, then turned to the others.

'Anyone object?' he asked — and it may have been a coincidence that his left hand dropped casually to the hilt of his saxe knife as he did so. The nobles hastily agreed that no, nobody objected, fine choice and congratulations King Sean.

Halt turned to his nephew. 'Now, Sean, I have one condition, before I formally renounce any claim I might have to the throne. We've broken the back of the Outsiders' movement in Clonmel. But they're still entrenched in the other five kingdoms. I want them rolled up, disbanded and their leaders imprisoned. With Tennyson out of the way and discredited, it shouldn't be too much of a problem. A bit of firm action and they'll collapse like a house of cards. And I'm sure the other five kings won't object.'

But Sean was shaking his head. 'That'll take a strong

military force,' he said. 'I don't have the men for it, unless I leave Clonmel unprotected. And I'm not prepared to do that.'

Halt nodded approvingly. The young man's answer told him that he'd been right in selecting him as the new King.

'Which is why I'm willing to write to King Duncan in Araluen and request that he send an armed force of, say, one hundred and fifty men to serve under you: knights, men at arms and a company of archers. If you agree.'

Sean considered the offer. 'And when we've got rid of the Outsiders, this force would return to Araluen?' No ruler would be eager to see a powerful foreign force on his own land without such an assurance.

'You have my word on it,' Halt said.

'Agreed,' Sean said and they shook hands. He glanced at the group of nobles and they hastened to mumble their agreement. 'I'll be needing levies of troops from all of your estates as well,' he said, and again heads nodded round the half circle.

'We can iron out the details later,' Halt said. 'Right now, Horace is waiting for me and, unless I miss my guess, he'll be hungry. Gentlemen, I'll leave you to discuss matters such as the coronation.' He smiled at Sean, one of his rare genuine smiles. 'With your permission, your majesty?'

For a moment, Sean didn't react. Then he realised he was being addressed.

'Eh? Oh, yes. Of course, Halt . . . Uncle. Carry on . . . please.'

Halt stepped a little closer so that only Sean could hear him.

'You'd better work on your regal manner,' he said.

Horace was waiting for him in the anteroom. The young warrior's eyesight was nearly fully recovered as the drug worked its way out of his bloodstream. On the surgeon's advice, he was bathing his eyes several times a day in warm salted water. They were a little red-rimmed but he was moving more certainly now.

He rose as Halt exited the throne room and the Ranger studied him briefly, glad to see he was nearly back to normal.

'So, how did it go?' Horace asked cheerfully. 'Should I curtsey to you, Good King Halt?'

'You do and I'll give you a clip over the ear,' Halt growled, suppressing a smile. 'Sean is to be King.'

Horace nodded. 'Good choice,' he said. 'By the way, a rider came in a little while ago, with a message from Will.'

Halt's head snapped up at that. It was the first word they had had from Will since he had ridden out in pursuit of Tennyson.

'He said "Fingle Bay",' Horace continued.

The Ranger pursed his lips thoughtfully. 'It's in the north. A fishing port and a small harbour. Let's collect our gear and get on the road.'

Horace gave him a pained look.

'What about lunch?' he asked. His hopes of a meal sank as he saw that familiar lift of Halt's eyebrow.

'What about lunch?' Halt replied. Horace shook his head despondently.

'I knew I should have told you *after* we'd eaten,' he said.

Epilogue

In spite of Halt's desire to cover ground as quickly as possible, they made one detour, riding to the crest of a small hill to the west of Dun Kilty.

It was a windswept area, where the trees had been cleared to leave an open meadow. In the place of the trees there was a collection of stone cairns — perhaps fifty of them in all. Some were ancient and crumbling. Others were more recent. One had been constructed only days before and the stones that formed it were bright and fresh from the quarry.

This was Cairnhill. This was the ancient burial ground where the kings of Clonmel were laid to rest.

As they reached the entrance in the low stone wall that encircled the burial ground, Horace checked Kicker, leaving Halt to ride on alone until Abelard stopped before the cairn of freshly quarried stone. For some time, the Ranger sat, not saying a word, looking at the burial cairn of his brother. After several minutes, he wheeled Abelard away from the cairn and rode slowly back to where Horace waited for him. Without a word, Horace fell in beside him and they trotted their horses down the hill and back to the main road. They planned to spend the night at Derryton, a coastal village on the road to Fingle Bay.

Horace looked at the sky. It was midafternoon but dark clouds were scudding in from the west and there'd be rain before too long, he thought.

The silence grew between them until Horace finally spoke.

'He wasn't much of a king,' he said, 'but I suppose he was the only one they had.'

It wasn't quite the way he had intended to put it and he realised that he'd phrased the thought clumsily. He glanced anxiously at his companion, hoping that he hadn't offended him.

'Sorry, Halt,' he said awkwardly. Halt looked up at him and gave him a sad smile. He knew there was no malice intended in the young warrior's words.

'That's all right, Horace,' he said. 'He wasn't much of a brother, either. But he was the only one I had.'

The first big drops of rain hit them and Halt pulled the cowl of his cloak further over his head.

'We should try to make Derryton before dark,' he said.

BOOK
NINE

Halt's Peril

Halt, Horace and Will follow Tennyson's trail to Picta. They're determined to stop the Outsider prophet and his remaining followers before the outlaws make their way across the border into Araluen. Will has defeated one of Tennyson's Genovesan assassins in Clonmel — but there are two left alive. Are the extraordinary archery skills of Will and Halt enough to save them during a duel with the assassins . . . or is Will's mentor facing his last battle?

Coming soon!

About the author

John Flanagan's bestselling *Ranger's Apprentice* adventure series originally comprised twenty short stories, which John wrote to encourage his twelve-year-old son, Michael, to enjoy reading. Now sold to twenty countries, the series has sold over one million copies worldwide, has appeared on the *New York Times* Bestseller List and is regularly shortlisted for children's book awards in Australia and overseas.

John, a former television and advertising writer, lives with his wife, Leonie, in the Sydney beachside suburb of Manly. He is currently writing further titles in the *Ranger's Apprentice* series. Visit John Flanagan's website, **www.rangersapprentice.com**, to find out more about John.

The adventures of Will and his friends aren't over yet! Visit the official Australian *Ranger's Apprentice* website for news about upcoming books, plus competitions, quizzes, games and more.

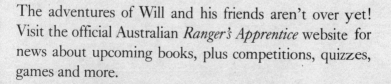

www.rangersapprentice.com.au